Knight of Flame

Scott Eder

Twilight Times Books
Kingsport Tennessee

Knight of Flame

Paladin Timeless Books, an imprint of
Twilight Times Books
P O Box 3340
Kingsport, TN 37664
www.twilighttimesbooks.com/

First Edition: December 2013

Library of Congress Control Number: 2013920912

ISBN: 978-1-60619-293-1

Cover art by Brad Fraunfelter

Printed in the United States of America

Knight of Flame is dedicated to Barb, Nathan, and Kaitlyn.
I love you guys.
Thank you for all your love, support, and tolerance.

Also, though she's not here to see it, to my mother.
Thanks for everything, Mom. I know you'd be proud.

Acknowledgments

Just as a writer enables and encourages the whims his characters, so does a dedicated group of people support the idiosyncrasies of that writer. Thank you for all that you've done to help shape *Knight of Flame*.

To my early Readers, Peter Coles, Rich Hall, Bill Walker, and Bob Backlinie, your input was invaluable.

To my Muncle Generals, East coast – Linda Letcher, West Coast – Lissa Woodury Jensen, your energetic, eager, and boisterous support of this book humbles me. Remain vigilant, our work is just beginning. The Muncle Army needs recruits.

To my Mentors, David Farland, and James A. Owen, without your guidance, wisdom and belief in me, the Knights Elementalis would not be able to step into the Light.

To my Critique Partners, Meg LaLonde, and Kelly Lagisquet, you challenged, poked and prodded my writing, making it better, stronger, and faster.

To my Editors, Joshua Essoe, and Jan Kafka, your attention to detail and dedication to storytelling led me down some unexpected and interesting paths. This book is far better for your efforts.

To my Accountability Maven, Jen Greyson, you watched and inspired, making sure the word count and progress bar moved forward.

To my Publishing Enabler, Maria DeVivo, you opened the door for *Knight of Flame* to step into the spotlight.

To my Publisher, Lida Quillen, you believed in my Knights and their story.

And to my Family. Barb, your unwavering love, support and confidence in me provided the foundation upon which all was built. Nathan and Kaitlyn, you kept me honest. Walt and Fran, your burning curiosity and glowing enthusiasm fired me up, and peaked my excitement.

Chapter 1

K NIGHTS DON'T DANCE. DEVELOR QUINTEELE WRUNG THE LEATHER-WRAPPED steering wheel and swallowed hard. The muted roar of the rented Jag's high-performance engine and smooth-as-silk ride did nothing to dispel his apprehension. Wren could have picked anything, but she chose dancing. He jammed a finger under the rigid collar of his first modern suit and yanked it away from his skin.

Great. Just great.

Dev stretched to adjust the rear-view mirror and ripped the seam of his jacket. *Armani stretch wool, my ass.* A growl rumbled in his chest and he glared at Wren, but she seemed oblivious to his distress.

"How much farther?" Wren's excitement tumbled out with each word. The sun's last rays reflected off the silver sequins of her micro-dress and sparkled across the car's dark chocolate interior. She shifted position, adjusted her dress, and crossed her legs. Despite her fidgeting, her head remained still, focused on the distant horizon, straining to get her first look at Club Mastodon.

Dev smiled through his growing unease. Though somewhere in her early twenties, Wren reminded him of a small child driving up to the gates of Disney World for the first time. Her usually tense and critical Japanese features were soft, eager and innocent. Seeing her excitement helped steady his nerves...a little.

"Just a few more minutes. You know I'm missing a *Three Stooges* marathon for this, don't you?"

"Whatevs." Wren brushed him off.

Dev checked his mirrors, vision in constant motion, and raked the hair out of his eyes. The thin, wavy strands felt foreign to his calloused fingers. He couldn't remember the last time he had more than a dark prickly shadow on top of his head, let alone mussed brown locks.

With a careless wave of his hand, he grazed the new bruise over his left eye. *Damn, forgot about that.* He prodded the tender skin, trying to gauge the size of the purpling evidence. So far, he'd managed to keep his fights at work from Wren. If she found out, he'd never hear the end of it. The last time, she went on and on about him being reckless, and jeopardizing the mission. Thankfully, she hadn't reported the incident to Stillman, his commander. It had been close, though. Cost Dev a night on the town. But it wasn't that big of a sacrifice. He loved her like a little sister, and enjoyed seeing her smile.

Brushing his hair forward, Dev tried to cover the injured area, and hoped for the best.

"This place won't be crowded, will it?" he asked. "You know crowds and I don't mix."

"Mmhm." Wren's arm shot out, pointed ahead and to the right. "There it is." The rest of her words blurred together, "I can't believe you got us on *the list*. I mean, like, I've never been to a place like this." She turned her sparkling green eyes on Dev. "Do you think a lot of movie stars will be here?"

"Breathe, Wren." Dev took the exit off I-275 south, just in sight of the Sunshine Skyway Bridge, and stopped at the traffic light across from the club. When Club Mastodon first opened he'd read about the local business leaders raising an uproar over how quickly the permits, zoning and associated building minutia were pushed through. But, when the club was bank-rolled by Alexander Gray, one of the head honchos at Daegon Gray, the normal red tape-covered bullshit disappeared.

Dev tilted his head as he caught his first glimpse of their destination through a ring of palm trees lining the property.

"Really? That's it?"

Wren didn't respond. Instead, she leaned forward, hands pressed tight against the dash, mouth open wide.

"It's just a big ass tent," Dev said. "I paid 10-K in advance to go to a circus?" His stomach rolled. "Wonderful."

The light changed and he pulled onto the gravel drive. Tires crunched on loose stones as they passed through the trees and drove the half-mile to the front of the club.

"I hate clowns," he murmured, "And elephants. I hate when they make those big bastards do stupid tricks."

Dev queued for the valet behind a sleek Mercedes SLR and waited his turn. The wait gave him a chance to assess the place without being obvious.

People. Damn. So many people, so many potential ways to piss me off.

A large number of the area celebrities milled about in front of the club's huge entrance. Beyond a set of giant wooden doors rose the three tall peaks of the monstrous Club Mastodon tent. Spotlights spaced evenly around the perimeter beamed on the white walls, causing them to glow. A smaller tent hung off the rear of the main, connected via covered walkway.

He couldn't see any exits other than the big main door, not even a window. *They really weren't kidding about the whole privacy thing.* The club was touted as the place to relax, a soothing oasis where the local aristocracy and visiting celebs could let their guard down and be themselves. In essence, society's elite could make fools of themselves without it showing up on the internet the next day. Absolutely no cameras were allowed, not even cell phones.

"It's not too late." Dev shook his head. "We could always go somewhere else." *Please...anywhere else.*

"Nope, we're good." Wren sounded distracted. Her gaze darted from one car window to the next. "Hey, isn't that Marcus Albright from the Bucs?"

"Who?"

"You know, the cornerback for the Buccaneers. Ooh, and that's the guy from that new show on AB—."

"Dennis Carlisle." The name rolled off Dev's tongue before she finished the station's call letters.

Wren oohed and aahed over a few other names he'd never heard of. Probably famous athletes or politicians or something, but he played along for her sake.

Movement. Out the window to his left. Dev tracked it out of the corner of his eye. A pair of security guards in black blazers and slacks marched down a row of exotic cars parked in tight lanes. Their heads swiveled every few feet so as not to miss anything.

More movement. Further out this time and a couple rows over. Another pair on patrol. Rent-a-cops didn't move like that. They had to be ex-military.

I bet the bulges in their jackets are compact automatic weapons.

"Geez, they take their security seriously around here." Dev spied more guards near the back tent. "Can you say overkill?"

"What are you babbling about?" Wren asked, flipping him an annoyed glance.

"Nothing...nothing." Dev moved up in line. Rhythmic burps of deep bass rattled the windows and thrummed through the steering wheel. Within seconds, the vein at his temple throbbed in time.

A valet approached the driver's side while another opened the door for Wren. Dev got out and shrugged at the tear in his jacket then met her on the curb.

"I feel naked in this." He whispered, running his hand over his chest and the expensive suit. "Out of my element."

"I feel like a princess." Wren, five-foot three, a smidgen under five-eight in her knee-high boots, twirled. Even with the added height, she only came up to Dev's chin. "Like the boots?" She modeled the right one—slick black leather that laced to the top—turning it enough to flash a red sole. "Louboutin. Got them yesterday."

Dev shrugged. "Nice, I guess. Not very practical."

She slapped his arm. "Dork. Not everything in this world is meant to be practical. I think they're gorgeous. Now, hold still." She straightened his tie and fussed with his hair, exposing his little secret.

Her eyes narrowed. "You've been fighting again." She spun on her spiked-heels, her expression blocked by the swish of her shoulder-length, ebony bob, and wound her way through the throng of socialites and celebrities.

Dev tried to keep pace, but she melted through the crowd toward the entrance. Impressed, he admired her agile dips and whirls as she put years of his hard-core physical training to unconscious use.

On her trail, he moved left and jostled the guy on his right, "Sorry," then bumped the woman on his left. "Excuse me." Anger flared, but he forced a tight smile. The shoulder-to-shoulder press of humanity reminded him of the battlefield. He slid between a pair of athletic-looking young men, but clipped one's shoulder. "Sorry, sorry."

High on alpha-male bravado, the kid tried to shove back, but Dev caught his hand before it made contact. With a deft twist, he bent the young man's wrist back and lifted him onto his toes. Dev leaned in close and bared his teeth. Anger boiled into rage, heating his body and fueling his need to fight.

"I said, pardon me." He spoke so only the impromptu ballerina could hear. Muscles tense, he wanted to yank this punk's arm off and beat him and the rest of the crowd with it, lay waste to everything around him until nothing stood between him and the entrance except Wren.

He straightened, took a loud breath through his nose, and found her off to the side near the entrance. Safe. Arms crossed. Hip cocked. Frown in place.

Crap. He'd lost control in front of her again.

"Today's your lucky day, skippy." After a last, painful wrench on his captive's arm, Dev released him and slogged his way through the crowd to Wren's side. People reacted to his rough passage, cast annoyed glances at his broad back then quickly went back to their own lives.

Every nerve, cell and fiber of Dev's being surged inside him. It didn't take much to get him going anymore. And sitting idle in Tampa for the last two years, due to a nebulous prediction of the Gray Lord's return, was not how an elemental warrior should live.

Daily skirmishes in the shipyard got him by, but he craved more. Primed for combat, he wanted a release. He wanted, no, needed, to fight. But this wasn't the time or the place. He needed to be strong, for Wren. This was her night.

"You promised the fighting would stop." Wren said between clenched teeth. "*You* stationed yourself at the shipyard to watch for signs of the Gray Lord, not play around. You don't see me getting in fights at the airport, do you?"

"It was just a minor disagreement," he said. "There were eight of them, jumped me behind the scrap metal piles."

"Eight!"

A nearby couple turned to stare at Wren. Dev took her arm and pulled her further away from the crowd.

"Look, I screwed up. They usually attack in threes. I didn't see Little Mike hiding in the garbage can. He whacked me with a crowbar." Dev looked away from her accusing stare. "It's no big deal. Won't happen again." *That you'll know of.*

"But you—"

"Let it go. Please."

Wren opened her mouth as if to say more when her eyes opened wide. "You're hot," she whispered, "Smoking."

Dev wiggled his eyebrows. "Why, thank you, thank you very much. You're looking pretty good yourself."

"That's *not* what I mean."

Dev caught a whiff of burned hair. His hand shot to the top of his head and found it still covered. As his body cooled, he found the singed stalks of the little hairs on the back of his hands. The shirt cuffs were scorched as well. *That was close.*

"Maybe this was a mistake." Wren's tentative, quiet voice touched him. "We should go."

"No." Dev stared at his shoes. Black. Leather. Uncomfortable. "No. I'm okay. You deserve this."

Wren's face scrunched as she assessed his attitude. She nodded. "Yeah, I do. Don't screw it up."

Dev blinked….

She laughed, wrapped her arm around his, "Come on, come on," and pulled him to the entrance.

Up close, the imposing entry reminded Dev of a smaller version of the village gates on Skull Island built to keep out King Kong. A dense collection of palm fronds and exotic, big-leaf plants, surrounded a pair of giant double doors unevenly framed by thick, rough-hewn timbers. The presence of security cameras positioned within the plants did little to deter from the primordial setting.

Dev smiled and waved at the camera tracking his movements.

Another pair of guards, much bigger than those patrolling the parking lot, flanked the entrance. Clad in nothing but loincloths, with long, black hair draped over heavily muscled shoulders and square pecks, they looked like stand-ins from *Conan the Barbarian*. Both stared straight ahead, boulder-crushing arms rigid at their sides. If it weren't for the slight motion of their immense chests, they could be statues. A low mist crawled around their feet and billowed in front of and under the big doors. Capping off the primitive atmosphere, flames swirled and popped above their heads in a long trench dug out of the lintel.

Blessed fire. Dev focused on the flames. He felt their lure, their potential, and the fire's raw power. A taste. That's all he needed. A quick fix to steady his nerves and help him through the night. With a thought he called to his element, drew it into him. His body tingled. Invisible tendrils of heat trickled into his chest and coalesced into a fireball behind his ribcage. It churned and roiled and intensified.

"Dev." Wren's harsh whisper seemed to come from far away.

That's nice. With another thought, he capped the flow and dispersed the warmth throughout his body. It calmed his spirit, dispelled his rage.

"Dev." An elbow to the ribs punctuated her call.

Awareness rushed in as his wind rushed out. *Damn, that girl knows right where to hit a guy.* He wheezed, tried to refill his lungs, and ignored the curious stares of the other patrons.

℡℣

Alexander Gray stood in front of the floor-to-ceiling penthouse windows and scowled at the world far below. Streetlights bathed the Tampa Bay Times Forum and Channelside shops in a sickly yellow glow. People, ants from this height, scurried through the darkness from one light post to another while a few late drivers braved the downtown Tampa streets.

His dark power surged, burrowing beneath his skin like angry wasps. With a thought he could make the shadows rise up and lay waste to those insignificant specks of life beneath him, but he reluctantly held back.

Not yet.

Out of the flat screen mounted in the corner, a local news anchor droned on about the rash of unexplained disappearances that baffled police.

Alexander smiled.

A small brown bird thumped into the window and fell dazed to the ledge. *Stupid birds.* Alexander crouched and tapped on the window. He knew neither the sound nor the vibration would penetrate the hurricane-proof glass, but he did it anyway.

"Hey there," he cooed, "Are you okay, little one?"

The bird got to its feet, shook his feathery head and leaned against the glass out of the wind.

"I have something for you." Alexander pressed his index finger against the thick pane and exerted a sliver of his will. A dark ribbon of inky-black energy oozed through the window and wriggled on the outside.

Startled, the bird hopped down the ledge.

"Take it." Alexander's face twitched. "Take it."

It hopped closer, its curious little head bobbing from side to side.

A little peck to taste the darkness.

The bird struck, tore off a hunk of black flesh, and bounced backward.

Alexander stopped the flow, folded his hands between his knees and studied his prey.

Its beak opened once, an unheard chirp of distress lost in the wind, and its chest expanded until hollow bone and skin could no longer contain the pressure. It exploded in a puff of brown-feathered clumps that floated away on the breeze.

Alexander stood, smoothing the imagined wrinkles from his pants, and stared at the human infestation below. *If only the rest of you were so easy.* A picture came to mind, one in which thousands of people writhed on the ground while their life force drained into the soil, and their skin turned the color of ash. *A pleasant notion indeed.*

A lightly spoken, "Sir?" accompanied a soft knock at the door. Alexander Gray, Master of Shadow, son of the last Gray Lord Bestok Molan, transformed into Alexander Gray, Regional President of Daegon Gray, philanthropist. Tight features relaxed and he coerced a false smile from his lips.

"Come."

The intern from the mayor's office minced through the room reeking of Chanel and french fries.

"Yes, Miss White?" Smooth, confident, and charismatic, that's what all the local papers wrote about him. His warm, deep voice put people at ease. "How can I help you, my dear?"

"M-m-m…Mr. Gray, the reporters are st-still waiting, sir." Straight blond hair framed an attractive face. She regarded him with bright-eyed innocence tinged with a delicious helping of fear. "Are you r-r-ready to start the press conference?"

Alexander savored the uncomfortable silence when he did not answer immediately. *Fresh. Young. Barely out of college. Dressed in a grown-up's business suit and conservative heels.* Even in the dim lighting, he noted the slight tremble in her limbs and her delightful habit of nibbling her lower lip. *Mmmm. Her life would taste sweet.*

A slight buzz tickled the back of his neck, but he ignored it. *Not now.*

"Yes, yes. We can start." Alexander walked over, placed his hand on her lower back and escorted her to the door.

The buzz increased to a sustained tingle, urgent, insistent. *I do not have time for this.*

At the doorway Alexander grabbed the back of his neck as it started to burn. "I am sorry, sweetheart, but I need to make a call first. I will only be a few minutes." He pushed her out and shut the door.

Snarling, he strode to his antique mahogany desk, threw himself into the high-backed leather chair and spun to the portraits on the wall. The largest, an older gentleman in a high-collared black waistcoat and black cravat, hung in the center. Dark brown eyes, small and deep-set, stared out from narrow, emaciated features under a thin fringe of white stringy hair. Brown spots littered his pallid face like dead leaves over old snow.

Alexander took a deep breath, closed his eyes, and tried to calm his murderous thoughts, but the intensity of the pain made it more difficult than usual. He had been told his impatience would get the better of him and he didn't want to let on just how frayed he was. Frustration, anger, anticipation—feelings of any kind were considered flaws, and it would not do to show weakness in front of Bestok Molan.

Emotions masked. Breathing and heartbeat normal. Body still and relaxed. He opened his eyes and met the stare in the portrait.

"Yes, Father?"

A gnarled head pushed out from the painting, stretching the canvas into three dimensions while the background colors drained away. Bestok Molan's likeness blinked its black eyes rapidly then jerked from side to side, searching. "You are alone?" A breathy voice, like a harsh and well-articulated hiss, issued from the gaunt visage. "I hear someone."

With the contact established, Alexander's pain dissipated and he stifled a relieved moan. "That is only the television, Father." Calm, flat and deferential. No hint of emotion.

"Television." The Gray Lord spat the word out as if it were a rat hair in his porridge. "The harvest is progressing, no?"

"Yes, Father."

"Good. Good." Thin, dry lips over-enunciated every word. "Tell me."

"The club has been operational for four months and produces two hundred shadow orbs per week."

Bestok Molan's dead eyes flickered, and his upper lip twitched. "That few?"

"If we drain any more of the people's energy, they will feel it. It would not take them long, even as simple-minded as they are, to trace it back to us. With the current harvest setting, they go home feeling weak and tired, which they attribute to a hard night of revelry." He gripped the arms of his chair. "As it is, the stupid sheep have no idea we are sucking out their very life essence."

The head behind the canvas tilted. "So be it."

"Father? I wish to test the orbs on something small."

"No."

"But are we sure the death magic works? That the orbs can kill?" It galled Alexander, this asking for permission to do what should be a natural act for any Shadow Lord.

Bestok Molan pushed his bulbous head further into the room, testing the strength of the canvas, and the temperature dropped thirty degrees in less than a heartbeat.

"Do not question me again, boy." An evil grin split the Gray Lord's face. "Or have you forgotten the last time?"

"No, Father." Alexander's words puffed out in a white mist as he flexed the fingers on both hands. The painful memories of that first and only time haunted the dark recesses of his mind. Changing the subject and, hopefully, the homicidal atmosphere, he steered back to the plan. "The orbs will be ready when you need them."

"They had better be." Bestok Molan melded into the painting.

"And when is that?" Alexander knew he was pushing his luck, but could not help himself. The lack of inactivity made him reckless.

"When I am ready." Bestok Molan's head flattened out and the background colors reappeared, but the distant hiss carried one more message before fading, "Wait."

I hate that word.

The portrait was solid again, ugly.

Alexander also hated that picture, and those of his three brothers to either side.

"I am tired of waiting." Alexander got to his feet, strolled back to the window, and clasped his hands behind his back.

Another light knock sounded. His hand rose out of reflex, enwrapped in rippling gray shadow, but he stopped before he blasted the door with a bolt of dark energy. It was a close call. He needed an outlet for his frustration, or he would explode and take out Tampa in a shadowy swirl of death and destruction.

That's what he should be doing, bending the world around him to his will and that of Bestok Molan's.

But the old Gray Lord says, 'Wait.' I have waited centuries for his grand plan to take shape, bounced from one menial post to another. I had hoped this time would be different, but it does not look promising. He preaches that the world must not know of our existence until we are ready to strike. That there is no need to alert the sheep that greater powers exist, for it would give them time to prepare. It is tough enough evading the Knights' constant vigil, let alone the billions of mortals on this world.

Billions. Their numbers are too vast. Time to cull the flock.

The knock sounded again and he turned toward the door with a broad, friendly smile plastered across his face.

"Come in, Miss White."

As the door opened, he swooped to her side and took her hand. "After the press conference, how about we get a drink? I know a little pla—"

Alexander's cell phone rang.

"Excuse me, my dear. I have to take this."

Chapter 2

With Club Mastadon's back door closed behind her, Maven Triessa Gray dropped her veil. Disgust at having to put up with these lesser things, these mewling beasts, curled her lip. She was sick of hiding behind a mask of humanity.

And for what? To skim some small measure of life from these creatures?

Flawless alabaster skin tightened around her cold black eyes. *We are no more than dirty beggars scratching in the filth for a copper.* Maven Triessa Gray, granddaughter to the Gray Lord himself, had never felt so useless.

Tonight, that will change.

She stormed to the security alcove in the adjacent tent. A flick of her wrist and the door slammed open on a blast of frigid air. She blew in after it and stalled before the bank of monitors. The largest one in the center, the only one with a color screen, displayed a stationary view of the storage bank below the main tent's grated floor. It was the same scene every night—a growing mass of black globes lit by erratic green and blue streaks. The live feed was hazy, distorted by the life force sucked from the unsuspecting patrons on the dance floor above.

Triessa scrutinized each screen. She spared a quick glance at the shadow orbs before searching for her opportunity. At the farthest end of the small room, the head of security shivered from the intense cold that radiated out from her dead body.

"Where?" Her voice was hard and brittle.

The security officer pointed a trembling finger to the monitor on the far right. "There, Maven Triessa." A large, muscular man waved to the camera.

"Confirmation?"

"Yes, Maven Triessa. The report from the Yukon outpost names him Develor Quinteele, the sixth Knight of Flame of the Knights Elementalis."

Triessa's face cracked into a jagged smile, shadow-fueled eyes riveted on Dev.

The officer continued. "Headquarters has been notified and Alexander Gray is on his way. ETA twenty minutes. Orders are not to move on the Knight until the Master arrives."

She turned her head. Long, fine white hair fell over half her face. She captured his attention with one eye and noted his sharp spike of wonderful fear. She could smell it, almost taste it, and felt his temperature rise as blood zoomed through his veins. In the cold silence of the room, she heard the desperate beating of his heart.

Slowly, deliberately, she reached out and placed her fingers on the naked skin of his neck. He flinched at her subzero touch, icy fingertips searing into unprotected flesh.

"You shouldn't have made that call. The Knight is mine."

The terrified officer's life throbbed beneath her fingers. She wanted it. She stole it. With less effort than it took to blink her eyes, she drew out his life force and bolstered her already formidable power.

The head of security slumped to the floor, skin gray and lifeless.

Triessa Gray, Maven of Shadow, granddaughter to the Gray Lord Bestok Molan, gazed back at the oaf grinning at her through the camera.

I'm coming for you, elemental warrior.

৪০৫৪

Club Mastodon's wooden doors burst open and a gaggle of Tampa's young elite, decked out in their silk suits, barely-there dresses and killer heels, staggered out to the techno barrage of Rammstein. Dev watched them lurch toward the valet podium. Exotic, citrusy scents trailed in their wake. The girls' short skirts flipped up with each awkward step. He tried to look away, but stood mesmerized by the brief glimpses of bare, tanned flesh and alluring curves until they disappeared into the back of a limo.

"You finished drooling now?" Wren asked.

"Hold on." Dev watched them drive away. "Now I'm done."

Wren sighed.

Two couples waited in line ahead of them to get in. A short, wiry man with greasy blond hair bounced around the first couple. He waved a security wand in his right hand and passed it over the gentleman first. When he ran it over the woman's purse, it buzzed. With a triumphant smile, the little man yanked the bag off her arm and tossed it into the bin behind him.

"No phones. You pick up later, lady."

The next couple stepped forward.

"Dev," Wren spoke out of the side of her mouth. "They have metal detectors."

"Yep. Hey, doesn't that little guy look like a monkey holding a banana?"

"You didn't bring the…" Wren flicked a glance toward his back, "…you know."

"Yep. Never leave home without it."

"What the—are you crazy?" Her eyes bulged.

"Relax. It's diamond. No worries." He hoped his nonchalance would calm her down, but she looked jumpier than ever.

The next couple passed without incident and the monkey man called Dev forward. Up close, the man with the wand scanner smelled like old cheese and freshly turned dirt.

"Name?" he asked.

"Rock. Party of two," Dev said.

The man nodded once and ran the wand over Dev first. No reaction. He scanned Wren, traced the wand slowly over her breasts in an electronic caress that clearly violated her personal space and broke several ethical codes.

"Watch it, monkey boy." Dev loomed over the little man. The dirt-ball backed off and waved them through with a last slimy leer at Wren. She took it all in stride, too focused on the imposing doors ahead.

"Almost there." Wren bobbed up and down and clasped Dev's hand in both of hers.

The huge doors opened to a wall of sound, smoke and light. No sooner had they cleared the entrance than the doors slammed shut behind them.

"Annnd, we're in. Great," Dev said.

"Hush." Wren dragged a reluctant Dev up the metal stairs and into the club proper. "This place is amazing." She twirled in place, taking everything in. "Look at that bar."

Dev had to admit the interior impressed him. Far bigger than he expected, the vast open space belied the tent's external dimensions. Lit only by fire light, the back end was lost in shadows. An enormous bonfire roared in the center, encircled by a black granite shelf that served as the bar. Smoke drifted up and escaped through a hole cut into the roof.

This is my kind of place.

More Conan extras, at least twenty of them, mixed and served drinks poured from assorted neon-colored bottles.

"Is that real?" Wren gaped at the mastodon skeleton. "What's holding him up, do you think?" Hind legs mounted on the bar, it reared up to the top of the tent some twenty five feet high. She stared straight up through the massive ribcage to the back of the beast's skull. "I don't see any wires."

Dev examined the skull. Just the head of the beast seemed larger than his whole body. Two long curved tusks stretched to the ceiling, forming one of the tent's three peaks. He spied two other skeletons mounted in similar positions cutting the bar into three equal sections.

"Maybe, but I didn't think mastodons grew much bigger than an elephant. This thing must be at least three times that size. Still, it's impressive. Must weigh a ton. They probably laced rods or wires through the bones to keep it up." He gave her an I-told-you-so grin.

"What?"

"I knew there would be elephants."

She punched him in the arm.

"Time for a drink." Dev waved the bartender over.

"I don't think that's a good idea." Wren said.

"Just one, to toast the evening."

"Dev...."

"Have you ever even had a drink?"

"Of cour—, oh alright, just one."

"Thatta girl. What'll you have?"

The bartender waited patiently, his long Conan wig brushing the top of the bar. The left side of his mouth twitched, and his eyes sparkled at their exchange.

Wren leaned over and raised her voice to be heard above the pulsing beat of the house music. "What's the specialty of the house?"

"We call it, Primal Fire." The bartender said.

Dev perked up at the name.

"Ooh. Sounds exotic." Wren said. "What's in it?"

"I'm not allowed to tell you the exact ingredients, but it's a complex recipe combining the perfect blend of ten top-shelf liquors. I serve it on fire. When mixed correctly, the flame burns a pure white."

Dev scoffed. "A pure flame is a myth. It's impossible."

"Sir, I can—"

"Sounds too strong for me." Wren interrupted. "I'll have a lemon drop."

"A lemon drop? Isn't that some kind of candy?" Dev asked. "Order a real drink, something that'll put hair on your chest."

Wren crinkled her nose. "No, thanks. I'll stick with the lemon drop."

The bartender looked expectantly at Dev.

"Scotch."

"Any specific brand, sir?"

"Dalmore. Selene."

The bartender punched a few keys on the wait station to his left. "Fine, sir, but I'll have to get it from the back."

Dev nodded and turned his back on the retreating bartender, leaned against the bar and watched the tide of people surge with the music. Club Mastodon was an odd place. He'd expected a cheesy disco ball, lasers, colored lights, a cordoned off dance floor and an obnoxious DJ, but there were none of those circa-nineteen eighties trappings here.

Open. Effective. Mysterious. The central pyre and large torches placed atop columns set around the perimeter walls and throughout the open spaces provided the only light. Shadows danced at the edges of the flickering fire-light and distorted the patron's faces, adding to the atmosphere of anonymity.

Nice. Dev recognized the lure of a place like this for those in the public eye. *It's the perfect escape.*

He shielded a yawn.

While loud and driving, the music didn't come off as strident or painful. He expected to have a splitting headache within the first two minutes, but found himself tapping his foot and nodding to the beat.

With a half embarrassed grin, Wren excused herself, dancing her way through the throng in the direction of the ladies' room.

Dev heard the footsteps behind him and turned as the waiter delivered their drinks. Closing his eyes, he swirled the glass and savored the unique scent of fine scotch. It jumped up and tickled the hair in his nose.

"*A votre santé!*" He inclined his head to the server and sipped. The first taste of the amber liquid burned, but tasted so good. He took another swallow to chase the napalm trail down his throat.

"Another, sir?"

"Hit me."

The bartender produced the bottle from under the table and poured a double. Dev nodded and started in.

He felt warm. No, hot. He felt hot, delightfully so, and fuzzy. Yeah, hot and fuzzy. The liquid heat seeped into his bones. *Hey, where's, um, where's... Wren? Yeah, Wren.*

The second glass went down quicker than the first. Within seconds he found it full again, but a single gulp solved that problem.

I feel good.

He hadn't had more than one drink in years and knew he should stop, but by some strange alcoholic magic, his octagonal glass never emptied.

A sign. He sucked back another. People and objects around him fuzzed into blobs of muted, swirling color. The music distorted, attacked his equilibrium until the room spun, and he grabbed hold of the bar to keep from falling over.

Where is that girl?

He was alone, as usual. *Has to be that way. She's not safe with me. No one is.* Had he known the price of becoming an elemental warrior, he might have chosen differently. Perhaps death would have been better than living through the centuries without....

He took another drink, but the miracle glass had run dry. Rage erupted. At the empty glass, at the bartender, at the club, at the world.

That's when the flame called to him.

He heard a pop followed by a long drawn out hiss. He jerked his head up, away from his baleful stare at the offending glass, to the central fire. It crackled and whispered in his ears, singing its siren song to his troubled spirit.

Yes, my old friend, I hear you.

Fire. To combat the memories and the infernal beast deep inside him, he needed warmth. He called to the flames. They flickered in response, leaned toward him. Nothing else existed for Dev, only he and the element that was as much a part of him as his own flesh.

He drew it into him, pulled a trickle from the inferno and absorbed it into his chest.

More.

The trickle grew to a steady flow.

More.

The heat intensified and roiled inside him. He had gone too long without the intimate kiss of the flame and he yearned for more. There was no pain, never any pain within his element, only...completion, fulfillment, but he still wanted more.

With a simple act of will, he opened himself fully to the conflagration. An invisible torrent of molten fire bored into him, melded his spirit with the pure essence of the flame and ignited his blood. It raged and screamed through his system.

I AM FIRE.

Dev held something in his hand. The glass. Oh, yes, the empty glass. He dipped his head, lips parted in a grimace. He channeled the heat and energy into his hands, to his fingertips. At first, the hard surface maintained its shape, but soon wavered under the blistering onslaught. The double-thick walls folded in on themselves in a smoking heap.

"You're going to pay for that." An icy voice blew apart his fiery solitude.

Chapter 3

Rush hour ended hours ago, but the traffic on I-275 crawled. Cassidy Sinclair drove home on autopilot while her brain rehashed the last few wasted hours of her life. After a big yawn, she blew an errant strand of auburn hair out of her face and noticed a new billboard on the side of the road that announced the grand opening of the Daegon Gray wing at St. Matthew's hospital. The date posted on the sign fell exactly one week from today.

Are you kidding me?

Four hours. She'd stood for four hours on a marble tile floor in three inch heels with those damn pointy toes. And for what? To hear the President of Daegon Gray announce the opening of the new hospital wing.

I could have saved my poor feet and read the sign. She scrunched her toes against the floor mat and winced as they cracked and throbbed.

Four hours of listening to a lobby full of overpaid, surgically enhanced, bimbette news anchors cluck about Alexander Gray. *Oh, he was so dreamy. Oh, he was so rich. Oh, he was so...give me a break.*

The worst part about the evening was that the press conference never happened. Every thirty minutes that blond chippy from the Mayor's office popped her head out of Gray's butt long enough to announce that the meeting would start in a few minutes. Then, at around nine o'clock, she came out to say that Mr. Gray received an urgent call and had to leave.

Asshole.

Cassidy took a deep breath. And then another. Ran slender fingers through shoulder-length hair. A nice long soak in the pool, that's what she needed. That, and a glass of red wine.

Yeah. And my imaginary pool boy Carlos, with the washboard abs, wide shoulders and magical hands, will start at my feet and rub his way to the top.

She rolled her head. Tight muscles stretched, joints popped.

St. Matthew's. She'd blocked that place out of her mind, but this assignment dragged it back. An older hospital, it prided itself on the care of its patients. The doctors rallied around the belief that they didn't treat patients, they treated people. During her previous life as an EMT, Cassidy saw many of the St. Matthew's doctors and nurses go far beyond what the insurance companies would approve of in order to treat a person. They didn't have the latest technology or whiz-bang medical gadgets, but they had years of experience and a truck load of compassion.

If it were up to her, she would have traded that compassion for an up-to-date burn unit.

Don't go there.

She laid on the horn. "Come on, move it."

Let it go.

Now an entry-level reporter for a local rag, she wrote fluff pieces for minimum wage. The money wasn't important. Her parents had left her a few million and a nice house on Anna Maria Island that backed up to Tampa Bay. While being a reporter had never been part of her life's plan, it got her out of bed in the morning and forced her to mingle with the living again.

Cassidy slammed on the brakes and missed the car in front of her by inches. A long line of brake lights snaked out ahead of her.

Really? Tonight this happens to me? She wanted to cry. *God, I just want to get home.*

She smacked the steering wheel. Tears built up behind the dam of her closed eyelids.

NO.

Cassidy jumped as the first notes of ACDC's Hells Bells burst from her cell and scared away the traitorous leakage.

Saved by the bells.

The adrenaline surge sent her arm scrabbling for the phone hiding near her bag and briefcase on the passenger seat. By the second bong she flipped the top and snapped at the caller.

"Yeah, yeah. Hello?"

"Sinclair." Eric Rancor, Cassidy's editor, had a high-pitched, edgy voice that colored every conversation with a sense of impending doom. "I heard about the press conference; or, should I say, lack thereof."

Great. "And?"

"We've got nothing to run and I need a Daegon Gray story. Club Mastodon is on your way home."

"Yeah, but I'm not feeling very we—"

"Good. Head on over and see what's doin'." Eric paused, probably trying to figure out how to grease her up. "I need your take on the club atmosphere."

"They won't let me in. You know, no press."

"Talk to some of the people outside. See what they have to say. Maybe we'll get lucky. You got this." *Click.*

When Eric was done, he was done. No, "Goodbye." No, "See you later." He was all click-you-very-much, now do what I told you to do.

I just want to go home.

Like a good reporter, she sucked it up and checked the exits to see how far she was from the club.

Chapter 4

W REN LEANED HER FISTS ON THE SINK AND STARED AT HER REFLECTION IN A REST-
room mirror shaped like a banana leaf. The owners had carried the primordial motif into the bathroom with bamboo stalls, large ferns and more
flickering torches.

*Coming here was a mistake. I'm supposed to keep him out of trouble, not drag
him into it.*

"Great," she said to herself, "Now I have another incident to report. That
makes like, what, a hundred in as many days. Stillman must be getting tired
of hearing about Dev's extracurricular activities."

Wren thought it weird that, when it came to official Knights Elementalis
concerns, her brain referred to him as Stillman, Precept of the Knights
Elementalis. For the personal stuff, though, or when they were alone, he went
by the more exalted title of Father.

She frowned at her reflection.

Ugh. I never could get this make-up thing right.

She snatched a linen towel from the stack on the counter and dabbed at her
blotchy mascara. The little black blobs smeared into dark smudges under her
eyes. It made her look tired and old.

Oh, what was I thinking? She wet the towel and scrubbed her eyes. *That
he's finally going to notice me because I get all dolled up for one night? Silly, girl.*

Fresh and clean, Wren tossed the towel in the bin and paused for one last
inspection.

"Much better."

A big man slammed into the restroom door, knocking it off its hinges. He
caromed off the wall-mounted vending machine and crashed into the open
stall.

Wren crouched and reached for the knife she kept strapped to her hip, but
came up empty. She'd left it back in the condo. *Duh.*

Her heart thumped, shaking her ribcage. It filled the silence left by the
missing beat of the music that had died at some point in the past few minutes.
Grunts, groans and curses sounded outside the bathroom door.

What in the world?

"Hey, man…," she looked into the stall, "You okay?"

Eyes wild, skin pale, he pulled himself up and rushed out the door without
a word.

When the screams started, Wren bolted from the restroom and dove into
a stampede of terrified revelers surging toward the main doors.

Can't leave that man alone for five minutes. The human tide swept her away from Dev until she ducked low and found a seam. Fighting against the press, she rolled off chests, bounced off hips, and shoved her way through. The pungent air, a fruity perfume mixed with sweat and desperation, made it hard to breathe.

Above the immediate roar, she heard Dev's bellow, urging everyone out.

She spun around a mountain of a man wearing a wrestler's luchador mask. *Hey, that was El Jefe. I saw him on TV las—.* A random punch to the gut set her back and she lost precious ground. *Stupid, girl. Focus.*

With a final twist and heave, she broke through into the clear and got her first glimpse of the situation. Dev pushed the last of the crowd toward the exit and faced off against an older woman in tight white leather. Curls of fluffy white smoke drifted up from his clothing.

This is so not good.

Four bodies littered the ground, limbs sprawled, skin gray as ash. The woman held a beautiful young starlet in a slinky black dress by the back of her neck. The girl flailed her arms and kicked wildly, but couldn't break free.

"Let her go!" Dev charged, but didn't get five feet before he bounced off a wall of shadow that sprang up from the pools of darkness at his feet.

Stunned, Wren watched Dev juke and shift in his attempt to get around the wall, but nothing worked. Shadow blocked his every move.

Wren dove through the opening in the bar to her right and crawled around to a spot about five feet from Dev. She had never seen anything stop him before. Once he charged, he won. Period. Although, she'd never seen him in an actual fight before, only sparring matches against the other Knights.

From the nearby bar prep station, Wren grabbed two small paring knives. Not much of an arsenal, but it would have to do. What she wouldn't give for her throwing knives.

With her back against the outer curve of black marble, she peeked over the rim.

The woman sneered at Dev over the starlet's shoulder as the girl's movements became sluggish and stopped. The color bled from her skin like the unfortunates already on the floor. With a nonchalant flick of her wrist, the woman dropped the body and stepped over the ungainly heap to face Dev.

With the girl's death, he prowled behind the wall like a caged tiger. Wren saw the signs of his mounting rage—tight jaw, hard eyes, hands alternately clenching and unclenching.

He's losing it. With a glance toward the front door, she verified that the last of the guests had made it out. *Good. No audience.*

"How does it feel, Knight of Flame, to know you let these people die?" The woman spoke, her voice a sultry purr.

He would never just let people die.

Dev responded with a murderous stare. He tested the shadow wall with a punch, found it strong, unyielding. Smoke billowed out of his suit jacket.

This close, the woman seemed much younger than Wren originally thought. Long white hair framed beautiful, pale features. The skimpy white leather skirt and vest accentuated her glamorous curves. She could be a porcelain goddess of lust, until you found her jet black eyes.

Wren shivered at the hate that emanated from those twin onyx orbs.

"You are mine, Fire Knight." The woman raised her hands, palms out, fingers up. Hundreds of misty, translucent forms slithered from the shadows all around. Within their first seconds of quasi-life, they solidified into long, gray snakes.

Wren clapped her hand over her mouth to stifle her scream, grateful for the two feet of rock bar separating her from the summoned serpents. Deeprooted fear froze her limbs.

Snakes. Why did it have to be snakes?

A multitude of forked tongues flicked in an out, searching for the scent of their prey. They converged on Dev. He continued pacing as the reptile army drew near, paying them no notice, eyes riveted to the woman.

Within striking distance, the first of the attackers reared back—mouths open, dark fangs bared.

Wren couldn't turn away. She wanted to scream at Dev, urge him to do something, but the words locked in her throat.

Dev frowned and stopped pacing. A wave of orange flame rolled out from his feet and over the snakes. They writhed in the conflagration, flipping and coiling back on themselves until the fire burned them down to crisp black husks.

The flames didn't reach her, but the scorching temperature of Dev's pest control washed over Wren, melting her fear and freeing her to move.

The woman in white pulled more darkness from the shadows, gathering it into her hands.

Dev ripped off his smoking jacket and tossed it to the side. His eyes remained glued to the figure before him. Wisps of smoke rose from his shoulders. Most of his shirt had burned away and a dagger hilt, angled down, stuck out of the worn chain harness strapped to his back. His pants smoldered. Patches of Armani wool burst into flame. Charred ends of fabric disintegrated, opening a window to the pink skin underneath.

The heat he gave off was oppressive. Between the bonfire behind her and Dev in front of her, Wren felt like a rotisserie chicken. Sweat rolled down her arms and between her breasts. Despite the swelter, she inched closer, and looked for an opening.

Knees bent, weight on the balls of his feet, Dev twisted his right arm behind his back and grasped the hilt of Cinder, his elemental dagger. As his fingers closed around the ancient weapon, the amber crystal at the base of the blade sparked to life.

The woman unleashed a smile—frigid and fierce. The shadow wall dropped.

Dev ripped Cinder from its sheath and leaped forward, halving the distance in a blur.

The roiling shadow in her hands surged forward, knocked Dev back, and wrapped his arms and legs in murky restraints.

"Dev." Wren blurted, concern overriding her caution, then ducked back behind the bar.

"Ah, there you are little one." The statuesque woman spoke, voice calm, untroubled. "I was wondering when you'd come out to play."

"Run, Wren." Dev whispered. He strained against the bands that circled his arms and legs. "Get the car. Pick me up out front."

"But I can help you."

"By all means, Develor Quinteele, let her stay." The woman gazed at Wren. "I don't know your name, child."

"Never mind her. Just go." Dev urged. "I'll handle this."

All that was left of his pants were a few fast-burning threads that clung to the curve of his butt. Wren couldn't help but stare at the ripple and play of taut muscles that strained against his constraints. Then she imagined the view from the evil albino witch's perspective.

That bitch.

Even though Dev was wrapped in shadowy ropes of energy that, for all she knew, would squeeze him into sushi, all she could think about was how that nasty slut had a prime view of her Knight in all his glory.

Wren growled and pinched the tip of the paring knife in her right hand. *If I distract her, Dev can get free.* Heart thumping, she exploded up, over the edge of the bar. Line of vision clear, she sighted on her target, aimed and threw. Despite the improvised weapon's awkward balance, the blade speared the corpse-like flesh of the woman's forehead.

She didn't even flinch.

In her peripheral vision, Wren caught Dev's horrified expression.

"What the hell are you doing?" He spat the question out of the side of his mouth.

"Um," Wren's eyes grew big, "Rescu—ing you."

"Nice job." Dev frowned. "Well done."

Casually, the woman grabbed the knife stuck in her forehead and drew it out. A tiny spurt of gray dust puffed from the wound, but no blood.

"Gogogo." Dev urged.

"But…"

"Now, child," the woman's patronizing tone a sharp slap to Wren's ego, "that was not very nice." With one arm holding the shadow bands tight around Dev, the other clenched into a fist. She punched the air, striking out toward Wren.

The air crackled as it solidified into a large round mass that streaked across the room, gathering size and dark density from the pools of shadow in its path.

"Move!" Dev ordered. A single cut with his diamond-bladed dagger dissolved the shackles. Freed of his bonds, he leaped to intercept the attack, Cinder held before him like a talisman.

Wren ducked behind the bar, scrambled around to the opening she originally came through, and peered around the corner as the shadow struck. It smashed into Dev with the strength and speed of a semi-truck. His brow drew down and in a flash his eyes blazed from dark gray to the deep red of burning coals as he rocked back with the impact. Wisps of steam escaped from his nostrils. Cinder gripped tight, his bloodless knuckles stood out against the rest of his pink skin.

Wren felt the clash, heard him grunt under the strain, and watched the give and take as he struggled against the woman's will. Body rigid, arms outstretched, eyes focused on her opponent, she stood between Wren and the entrance.

Wren wanted to help, but Dev ordered her to get the car and she wasn't going to let him down. If anything happened to her Knight, she didn't know what she would do. Stomach in knots, she ghosted through the shadows, keeping one eye on her path and one eye on her Knight. After every few steps, she reminded herself to breathe.

She circled the combatants and got behind the woman, whose attention focused on the battle. Escape through the main doors lay mere feet away, but she couldn't bring herself to leave.

He told me to get the car. Wren's heart fluttered. *But I can stop her. I can help him.*

Shouts sounded from outside.

Wren whipped around to the door. Two sets of footsteps pounded on the pavement outside. She rushed to the side of the entrance, out of sight, and waited. The first guard burst through, gun immediately centering on Dev.

Wren tripped the second guard, rode him to the ground and rammed his head against the grated floor. She caught Dev's eye and he nodded, once, reinforcing his order to leave.

"ENOUGH." Dev roared.

From her perch atop the guard, Wren wiped stinging sweat from her eyes as a thick rope of fire snapped loose from the bonfire and struck Dev in the back.

Knight joined with element in a brilliant flash that incinerated the shadow magic and burned dark spots behind Wren's eyelids. When her vision cleared, Dev stood unfettered. Corded arms hung ponderous at his side. His chest heaved with each breath. A bright yellow flame flickered and danced over his skin, leaving his head untouched. He glared at his opponent with eyes transformed to the color of the sun.

Magnificent. Powerful. And gloriously naked.

"You, witch, demon, or...whatever,. Dev's breath washed over the room like a scorched desert wind. "By my honor, I am forced to give you one chance to repent. However, if you refuse this offer, and I hope you do...you're toast."

Wren watched the hatred play out in the woman's features. Prominent ridges appeared across her cheeks with tightened jaw muscles and her eyes scrunched up, small and harsh. The guard at her side trembled, the tip of his semi-automatic pistol wavering like a pennant in the breeze.

Dev stepped onto the oily stain left behind when he obliterated the shadow magic.

"We'll see." She raised both arms over her head. "Awake and destroy." Gray ash gushed from her open mouth, covering the ground and bodies near her in a dense, low-hanging cloud. The corpses twitched and rose gracefully to their feet. They turned, dead eyes clamping onto Dev. As one, they sprang.

Dev's flame flared and enveloped his head in a blazing helm. His wavy brown hair burned away, filling the air with an acrid aroma.

Wren's heart threatened to beat out of her chest as she hopped up and sprinted for the door. She had to get the car, had to be ready.

She paused at the wooden doorframe and poked her head out. *No guards. Maybe fifty yards to the parking lot.*

A surprising number of cars remained in the lot considering the frenzied exodus that emptied the club a short time ago. Their owners clustered in groups, talking and laughing as if the insanity inside had never happened.

Are they crazy?

After a finger-rake through her hair and a dress adjustment, Wren stepped out into a too-bright night. She cursed with each sedate step as the moon shone down on her like a spotlight.

Nothing to see here.

She found the guards interspersed with the criminally stupid patrons in the parking lot.

Are they looking for me? Her eyes darted from side to side and she sipped her breath in tiny morsels as she maintained her slow, maddening pace.

Some...*thing* flew past overhead, blocking out the moon's glow for the span of two heartbeats. Goose bumps broke out along her arms and legs and a palpable dread buckled her knees. The sensation vanished quickly, but she couldn't shake the fear.

Screw this.

Head down, she sprinted to the car.

₧Ω

A hungry smile stretched across Dev's face and his fire-laced spirit soared as Wren disappeared through the doorway.

She's safe. Game on, zombies.

Gray-skinned shapes leaped and charged. To his fire-enhanced perception, their movements seemed slow and ponderous. He dashed between the bodies, stabbed Cinder hilt-deep into the chest of one and caved in the face of another with his burning fist.

The guard opened fire as the rest of the animated corpses pounced. Dev channeled his element, boosting his temperature to the extreme. Waves of blistering heat radiated from his skin and melted the oncoming bullets into tiny bits of slag that bounced harmlessly off his bare chest.

Two zombies, flashy clothes smoldering, charged high and attacked with fingers twisted into claws. The third lunged at Dev's legs. He slashed Cinder up and across in a sweeping arc, scoring a deep wound across one attacker's chest and severing the other's hand. The third he met with a straight-arm to the chest. The fiery contact ignited the shadow-man's clothes.

Some deep-seated fear of fire must have remained in that decaying brain for, as the flames spread, the attacker flailed, trying to put himself out.

Dev drove Cinder through him, severing his spine, to finish him off.

With the last reanimated corpse down, Dev grinned a promise of sharp edges and crippling pain at the guard. The guard bolted, clearing the doorway before his spent, semi-automatic clattered to the floor.

Dev spun, expecting another attack, but none came. The woman stood frozen in the same position in which she cast her spell. Cautiously, Cinder poised and ready, he closed the distance. Four feet...three feet. No reaction. Her arms stayed above her head and her eyes remained closed. If Dev hadn't seen her before, he might have mistaken her for a classic sculpture. But he knew better.

Dev cocked his arm back to deliver the coup de grace, but a sense of familiarity stayed his hand. He studied her face.

Where have I seen you before?

A high-pitched wail pierced the night. Dev jerked around and searched for the source of the tortured sound. It came from outside. He thought of Wren, hoped she made it to the car. Another noise, low and faint, whooshed, moving the walls of the tent in and out, like the lungs of a great beast.

"He comes, Knight." The woman's cruel lips barely moved to form the words.

"Who co—"

A second wail, like the sound of an air raid siren, cut his question short. Dev estimated its location just above the rear of the tent. Below that, the ceiling bowed until the leather split. Green sparks flared along the rift. The edges curled back and dissolved, expanding the opening until a large section of the roof had been eaten away.

Moonlight sneaked in…so did something else. Cloaked in a dense pocket of midnight, it defied the moon's pale light and touched down across the club.

Dev felt the vibration as it landed, tried to see through the dark veil, but failed. Something watched him. He could feel it in his bones. If he had any hair left on the back of his neck, it would be at full attention.

Jackpot. The suit of flame coating his body flared. *Oh yeah, baby.* He shifted his weight from one foot to the other and back, adjusting his grip on his elemental blade. *Bring it.*

From out of the lightless void appeared a man. Dressed in a sharp black business suit, he strolled across the floor to the far side of the bar and rested his hand on the massive bone foot of the mastodon. A shifting patch of shadow shrouded his face.

"Welcome to my club, Knight of Flame." A powerful voice carried across the distance as if he were no more than two paces away. "I see you have met my daughter, Triessa."

Dev looked back at the frozen figure. Her limbs trembled.

Is that fear? What could frighten her here?

"You have disappointed me again, my dear." An overly dramatic sigh leaked from his pursed lips. "Do you have anything to say for yourself?"

Triessa dropped to the floor as if someone had cut her strings. She struggled to her hands and knees and glared at her father. Her lips parted. Before she got the first word out, a translucent tentacle, big around as Dev, whipped out from the darkness and smashed her to the floor in a cloud of dust.

He killed his own daughter?

The Knight of Flame reeled from the charnel stench of that arm. Old death and rot clogged his nostrils. Breathing through his mouth seemed little better since the desiccated air tasted stale and musty, like it had recently blown through a crypt. That nervous flutter in his gut returned. Glancing to either side, Dev assessed his options. The exit was close, but that tentacle struck like a viper.

Having dispatched his daughter with as much ceremony as ordering take-out, the man turned to Dev and shook his head, "Children. A crippling source of disappointment." He brushed non-existent lint from his crisp lapel. "Do you have any children, Knight?"

Dev sensed a low hum, below the range of hearing. It would have escaped his notice if he hadn't been in the full embrace of his element. The under-current of subsonic vibration thrummed through the air and assaulted Dev's equilibrium, leaving him queasy and unsteady.

"Nothing to say? So be it." He slapped the huge bone leg and shouted, "Shreetok," in a deep, guttural rumble.

Dark magic washed through the room and over Dev, coating his skin with a noxious film. The filth turned his stomach and blurred his vision. He wanted to attack, to rip this guy to shreds, but for the first time his instincts screamed that he was in over his head.

Above him, bone scraped on bone with nails-against-a-chalkboard intensity. Dev looked up. *You have got to be kidding me.*

The enormous mastodon lowered its head. One of the tent peaks came down with its tusks, but snagged on a granite pillar before it fell more than a couple of feet. The creature touched down, shaking the ground with its impact.

Dev gaped at the new obstacle standing between him and freedom. What kind of power did it take to reanimate a dead creature the size and age of this behemoth? He'd dealt with zombies and other flavors of undead, but this was different, colossal, and required power on a scale he'd never faced before.

"Beautiful, isn't she?" The smug tone jerked Dev back to reality. "And much stronger than when she was alive. Oh, yes. So much stronger." A thin smile flitted across the man's predatory features. "But I'll let you be the judge of that."

The dead beast's eye sockets flared green and fixed on Dev. The ground trembled under the weight of its first ponderous step in his direction.

Oh, sure, 'bring it on'. Dumb ass, now what are you going to do? If he ran for it, either the undead heap of bones or the tentacle would take him out.

In a sudden burst, Dev sprinted for the entrance. A second tentacle struck from the shadows, met him halfway. It swept him up and threw him across the tent where he bounced off the far wall and crashed to the floor.

Unfazed, he popped to his feet, sucking air back into his deflated body.

Nothing broken, a couple of bruises. I'm the Knight of bloody Flame, not the Knight of freakin' Air.

The short flight landed him closer to the back of the tent, and his well-dressed assailant. The same sense of familiarity he experienced with the daughter tugged at his brain.

On tree trunk-thick legs, the mastodon advanced, blocking Dev's escape route.

Wait a minute…what am I doing?

Dev called the fire from the closest torches. The flames already licking across the surface of his body intensified, changing from yellow to a deep azure blue. He backed against the leather wall and melted open a new door. The singed edge of the opening expanded quickly as the fire ate the oiled skin.

Once outside, he didn't have more than a second to check his position and get moving. He had a good idea of where he burned through and, more importantly, where he hoped Wren waited with the car. Heedless of the low scrub and brush snagging his feet, he tore around the curve of the tent. The parking lot and a cluster of clueless lingerers appeared on his right and he cursed Wren again for forcing him to wear that suit instead of his usual Quinsteele-lined leathers.

Being naked wasn't a problem. Being on fire wasn't a problem. However, being naked and on fire and running from a giant monster in front of a crowd of people wasn't his idea of a good night. To top it off, small fires erupted wherever he set his feet and blazed a clear trail for anyone or anything to follow.

The mastodon crunched into the dry brush in pursuit. Its heavy footfalls picked up the pace behind him.

Dev felt the tremors through the soles of his bare feet. He had a big speed advantage. If Wren waited out front with the car, they'd make it. If not...

She'll be there. By his reckoning, she should be coming into view any second.

Another few yards brought Dev around front. His arrival generated a few catcalls and much finger pointing from the peanut gallery in the parking lot.

"Run!" Dev yelled and waved his arms. "Get out of here."

A few people in the crowd waved back.

Dev shook his head and hoped the beast followed him, ignoring the clueless crowd.

Wren waited at the curb with the rental. Her anxious eyes lit up and she bounced in her seat to urge him on. When her eyes grew big and terrified screams erupted from the crowd, he knew the beast turned the corner.

The man in the suit emerged from the Club's entrance, crossed his arms over his chest and frowned. Two tentacles burst out of the doorway in a hail of splintered wood. One swiped at the running Knight while the other streaked toward the idling car.

Dev put on an extra burst of speed. Flame-coated legs churned. A blue tinged comet-trail thinned in his wake. The tentacle swept in low, but he hurtled it easily.

The Jag's front tires spun, kicking up a cloud of dirt and loose gravel, until they bit and the car accelerated backwards. Wren avoided the onrushing limb by inches, but barreled straight for Dev.

He narrowly avoided the Jaguar-shaped bullet and glimpsed Wren's terror-masked face as she raced by. He'd help her if he could, but he had his hands full.

The mastodon rammed the back of the car. Aluminum crumpled against bone. The trunk caved in and the car's momentum stopped dead.

Dev spared a glance for Wren and saw her struggling with the gear shift. *She's got this.*

He dodged to the left as a tentacle hurtled by, but the second one, having abandoned the attack on the car, slammed into his calves and flipped him onto his back. A quick roll to the right took him out of danger as the first tentacle smashed down.

As the tentacles passed close, he scored a few deep gashes with Cinder, but the wounds closed immediately. His effort earned him a few cheers from the audience. Instead of fleeing like they should have, the left-overs watched what they thought was a staged show.

The tentacles attacked mercilessly, chasing Dev every which way. He lost track of Wren and the car. He knew he couldn't keep this up forever, needed to get to the man controlling these things.

Dev feigned right then jumped left and sprinted for the front of the tent, to the man pulling the strings. *Faster.* He channeled the dwindling elemental power at his command and boosted his speed.

Just...another...few...feet.

A tentacle hammered into his waist, doubled him over. He coughed and dropped to his knees. His lungs burned with each breath. It had been a long time since he'd pushed himself like this. The life giving energy and rage of his fire sputtered.

He got to his feet in time to duck another swipe. The wind from its passing whipped the flames on his head.

Where's the oth—

It drove into his side. Ribs shattered. Flames died.

The massive blow knocked him across the gravel drive. He slid through the stones and came to rest face down in a smoking heap. Blood, road dust and small rocks filled his mouth. He groaned, tried to lift his head out of the dirt and stones, but it weighed a ton.

Get up...get up. Can't stay in one place. MOVE.

His spirit growled and spit and cursed and yelled until the body finally listened. He rolled from stomach to back as a tentacle blasted into the earth where he'd lain, clipping him in the shoulder. His left arm went numb and the side of his body felt like it had been flattened by a steamroller.

Dev closed his eyes against the pain and took a second to catch his breath.

The harsh screech of tortured metal parted the clouds over his brain and his eyes sprang open. He jerked up into a sitting position. The pain of his tortured shoulder and broken ribs made breathing excruciating, but he couldn't give up, had to keep fighting.

Cinder lay just out of reach. He knew the crushing weight of the next attack would nail him at any second and had to be ready. He dug his right hand into the gravel and pushed. Body screaming in protest, a tidal wave of nausea threatening to drown him, he fought through it, grabbed Cinder, and surged to his feet.

An odd whistle sounded off to his right. Twin midnight missiles streaked toward him.

"I'm sorry, Wren." Dev braced himself for this final impact.

Gravel popped as the car slid to a halt in front of him and the passenger door flew open.

It took him a second to realize what happened, that Wren was in front of him with what was left of the car and that it sputtered in a heap between him and the tentacles. Hope gave his rubbery legs the strength to propel him into the seat.

Wren punched it. The tentacles slammed into the driver's side, smashed the back window and lifted the car up onto two wheels. With a curse she eased off on the gas and tweaked the steering wheel to keep them from flipping over.

Once all four wheels touched down, she gunned it. The engine revved like a racecar, but the battered vehicle only limped away to the sound of grinding steel and the smell of burned rubber, carrying them barely far enough to take them out of immediate danger.

Applause and whoops of encouragement from the onlookers turned to howls of terror and pain. Gunshots rang out. Dev glanced in his side-view mirror and watched the guards open fire on the witnesses. He wanted to turn back and help, but he knew there was nothing he could do. Feeling sick and useless he sank into his seat.

Chapter 5

A N ANGRY, BLACK CLOUD LOOMED IN THE NEAR DISTANCE OFF THE INTERSTATE JUST beyond Cassidy's exit. If she were lucky, Club Mastodon had been destroyed in a fire. She'd write a quick story about how sad it was to lose the club, but how wonderful it was that no one was hurt and then be off to bed.

Yeah. Right. It better not rain.

She smacked the turn signal when it refused to shut off and slammed on the brakes at the light across from the club. *Eight point two miles in forty-five minutes. Are you kidding me? I should be home by now.* She'd ask the first person she met two quick questions and get the hell out of Dodge.

Stopped at the streetlight across from the club entrance, she checked her makeup in the rearview. An orange glow peeked from around the mirror's edge.

Holy sh—Club Mastodon really is on fire. The sight of the fire clued in the rest of her tired senses. Smoke hung in the air and the scent of old, charred meat filtered through her open vents.

A mangled Jaguar rolled to a stop, sputtered and died next to the club's drive. A car door slammed.

Eyes focused on the bright flicker through the trees, she drove onto Mastodon property.

A shiny blur ran in front of the car. Cassidy swerved and tensed in anticipation of the *thunk*, but thank goodness, it never came. Pulse throbbing, she opened the window. *Where'd it go?* She checked out the front and leaned to the other side. Nothing.

Craaaap. Must have hit it. She opened her door. With one foot in the air, a shimmer hurtled from behind the wrecked Jag and shoved her over to the passenger seat.

"Move it."

Oh hell no. Cassidy swung her left arm with all the strength she could muster. A girl in a sequined dress dipped and returned a punch of her own that split Cassidy's lip. Blood filled her mouth and dribbled down her chin.

Cassidy screamed and launched a two handed barrage of slaps, scratches and hair grabs that would have made her self-defense instructor cringe—two years of martial arts and judo classes out the window. Her haphazard flailing continued until the tiny, sparkling girl captured her hands.

"Quit it." Sparkles said. *Great. I named her like she was a new kitty.*

Her grip was like iron. Cassidy pulled and twisted, but couldn't break free.

A warm tingle of honor, desperation, and fear flowed into Cassidy as she sensed the girl's emotional state through their skin-on-skin contact.

Empathy. Cassidy's grandmother had smiled at her in that private, knowing way whenever she talked about her 'gift.' Curse, more like. It had done far more harm than good through the years, and she didn't want any part of it. She'd much rather take people at face value and know them by their actions than to get a true sense of how they felt from a simple touch. Sparkle's actions should have sentenced her to a car ride of desperate fighting and escape attempts. Instead, she'd get a big dose of wait and see.

The back door opened. A heavy weight flopped into the car, shifted around amidst a chorus of groans, and closed the door.

Now what? She twisted around, caught a glimpse of a bald, dirt-streaked head, but Sparkles yanked her back before she got a better look.

"Who is...?" Cassidy asked.

"Get out." Sparkles nudged Cassidy toward the door.

A raspy male voice spoke from the back seat. "No."

No?

Sparkles ignored the croak and shoved Cassidy toward the door. "Out."

"No, too, dangerous. Drive." The voice from the back countermanded Sparkle's insistent shoving.

"Too dangerous? What, the fire?" Cassidy asked, her curiosity getting the best of her. Her grandmother had warned her about that too.

Is he afraid I'm going to ID the girl?

Sparkles rolled her eyes. "I got this," she shot over her shoulder then turned to Cassidy, her demeanor dripping in syrupy sweetness. "The Club is on fire and the bad guys are coming. We need to leave. Right now. I can't drive if you fight me." She batted her eyelashes. "So please sit there and be quiet. When it's safe, you can go."

Please? "Look, Sparkles—"

"Wren."

"What?"

"My name is Wren." Her eyes shifted to the front then back again. "Tick tock. What's it gonna be?

"What bad guys?"

"Wren..." The voice from the back cracked, sounded like he was in pain.

"We don't have time for this." Wren released Cassidy's arms and turned the car around.

Cassidy lunged for her door handle and cranked it down. The door swung free and nobody stopped her.

"I wouldn't do that." Wren said.

"Why?" Cassidy asked, one foot already out the door when the car shook. "What was that?"

"In or out?"

It rumbled again. Cassidy's head whipped around to Wren. "What *is* that?"

Wren pushed gently on the accelerator while Cassidy dangled on her decision point. "Last chance. In or out?"

Cassidy pulled her foot inside and shut the door. The shiny woman intrigued her and she was dying to know who was in her back seat. Plus, she liked this car and didn't want to hand it over to a carjacker, no matter how polite they were.

Wren took the ramp for the interstate and merged into traffic heading south towards the Sunshine Skyway. Within three car lengths, their progress ground to a halt.

"Oh, yeah. By the way..." Cassidy deadpanned, "Traffic is all backed up."

Wren closed her eyes, took a deep breath and lowered her head.

"But it'll clear up at the bridge, at the end of the construction zone." Cassidy pointed up ahead. "Yeah, see, we're almost out of it." She nudged Wren's arm. "Hey, we're moving."

Wren opened her eyes, checked the mirrors and drifted the few feet to catch up. "You, uhh, you probably won't believe this, but I'm sorry. I don't normally do this kind of thing." She dragged shaking fingers through disheveled black hair.

And an "I'm sorry?" I didn't realize they made carjackers this polite. That blows the whole image for me.

Cassidy buckled up and decided to play along for now. Who knew? This could turn into a great story.

Detached reporter mode engaged. She tried to mentally capture everything as if she were watching the events unfold in a movie. Spark—*Wren* obviously came from the club, based on her fancy dress, but she was coated in dirt and blood. Also, her eyes contained a wildness, a desperation that you normally didn't see after a fun night out with your boyfriend. Cassidy had covered enough police calls to recognize the look of someone who had been in a fight, a bad one by the looks of it, and this girl reeked of fear and shock and danger.

Dang it. My recorder's in the back seat.

Wren looked in the rearview way too often, like she was expecting someone to be following. Cassidy checked the mirror too and saw a long line of traffic, but nothing out of the ordinary. Something blocked out the stars up ahead for a split second then disappeared. The hairs on the back of her neck danced as a chill shook her body. She looked for it again, but failed and chalked it up to her imagination.

"Who are you looking for?" Cassidy asked. Since she was given the choice to come along, she'd make the best of the situation. When she was in Wren's grip she'd felt her integrity and honor. For the first time, her empathy worked in her favor. Whatever happened, she believed that Wren meant what she said about letting her go when it was safe.

The car rocked as the mystery-mister in the back moved around with a lot of grunting and groaning.

Ooh, forgot about him.

Cassidy sneaked a glimpse while Wren checked the mirrors for the thousandth time. When she saw him, her eyes flashed to Wren, then back to the guy, then back to Wren.

"Wren." Cassidy fought to keep her voice neutral and gripped her knees to steady her hands. "There's a naked man writhing in my backseat." Forget the warm fuzzies she got from Wren a few minutes ago, this new development kicked the credibility of her gift in the teeth.

Maybe this wasn't such a good idea.

"That's Dev."

A muffled, pained, "Hi," drifted into the front. "Kick up the heat, please."

Wren fumbled with the knobs on the strange console. The cool air came on. She turned the dial. It got cooler.

"*Fakku!*" Wren pushed another button and the airflow stopped. She punched the console and shouted, "Turn on the damn heat."

Cassidy jammed her finger onto the correct button and whipped the dial to red. Hot air blew out of the vents, increasing the heat in the already warm car.

"Thanks," Dev whispered.

Cassidy twisted in her seat to get a better look at her suffering passenger. Dev lay on his side in the fetal position facing toward the trunk with half his naked body hanging off the seat. Covered in dirt and blood, he took quick, shallow breaths. His skin was pink, except for his left shoulder and torso, which showed mottled grays and brown. The gigantic knife strapped to his back threw her for a second, but the EMT side of her discarded that as less important than assessing the damage to her patient.

No, not a patient, just a passenger. Get the story. Get the car. Get the heck out. But she couldn't help herself, and assessed the injured man.

Right side of his torso caved in, indicating severe trauma with probable internal injuries. A dislocated shoulder with possible bone and muscle damage. She couldn't be sure without x-rays and an MRI, but that's what it looked like. The guy was a mess.

"He needs a hospital." Cassidy touched Dev's arm, but recoiled as if burned. "He's burning up."

"He'll be alright." Wren paused, hand raised for silence. "Did you feel that?"

Wren's nonchalance about her boyfriend's injuries bothered Cassidy. She opened her mouth to tell her so when she felt it.

Boom. The tremor was back.

Looking away from Dev, Cassidy was shocked to see the other cars obscured by fog or smoke. When did that happen? She could barely make out the tail lights of the car ahead of them. The wind must have changed and blew the smoke from the burning club over the highway.

It shouldn't be this thick.

When the traffic jam cleared, the vehicle ahead of them zoomed forward, disappearing into the gloom.

Boom.

"What is that?" Cassidy asked again.

Boom.

"You wouldn't believe me if I told you." Wren checked the mirror even though there was no way she could see anything. "Dev, it's getting closer."

They'd made it to the bridge. Cassidy couldn't see it, the tall yellow spires and thick suspension cables having been eaten by the fog, but could tell by the change in the car's pitch as they started the climb.

Boom.

The vibration rattled the windows.

Boom.

"Dev?" Wren's tone raised an octave.

The roadway rumbled and shook. The frequency of the vibrations increased until it was a constant thrum through Cassidy's bones.

Boom. Boom. Crash.

Something exploded behind them and faint, disembodied screams floated on the fog.

"Keep going, but slow down when you get to the top." Dev's voice sounded stronger.

Boom. Boom.

Cassidy stared straight ahead, fingers crimped against the dash. She jumped, smacking her head into the roof, as the back end of a yellow VW Beetle crashed down in front of them. Wren yipped and jerked the wheel. Parts scattered, smoke rose from the overturned engine block and the bumper bounced over the bridge's guardrail.

Boom. Boom. Boom. Boom.

At any moment she knew it was going to get them. Maybe she should have gotten out of the car when she had the chance. But what if this thing came from the club? What if it started the fire down there? Cassidy's brain sang through a what-if medley while with every muscle tense and hard, she waited for the crash, the collision that would destroy them. Even though she expected it, it took her by surprise.

The back end of Cassidy's sedan lifted and crashed down with a jarring bounce. A second impact hammered into the back of the car and spun it round one hundred eighty degrees. She caught a glimpse of a giant, bone head with glowing red eyes before the mist swallowed it up.

Wren slammed the car into reverse and accelerated.

The skeleton charged. Ethereal streamers peeled away from bone as it broke cover.

With her first full glimpse of the beast, the rational side of Cassidy's conscious thought switched off. This couldn't be happening, but the horror show bearing down on them looked real, felt real, and generated such a palpable feeling of evil that she wanted to scrape it off her eyeballs. She couldn't help but cringe deeper into the seat, brace herself against the dash and hold her breath.

Wren's poise astounded her. Cassidy didn't know how she managed to keep moving, to keep just out of reach of that killing machine, but was damn glad she did.

At the apex of the tall bridge, they broke free of the mist. The sudden clearing took them by surprise.

"Let me out." Dev commanded. "It's me it wants." His voice sounded stronger.

"Are you crazy?" Both girls cried in unison.

"Certifiable." Dev grabbed the door handle. "But it's what I do. After I'm gone, get out of here. That's an order."

The thing pounded after them, its curved tusks shredding the mist as it broke into the clear not ten feet in front of them.

Wren slowed. The beast gained.

The back door opened and Cassidy heard a rustling from the back seat. *He's serious? He's going to jump out of a moving car to do...what? Fall over in front of that monster?* She refused to look. If she didn't see his face, didn't look into his eyes, she could maintain her distance and keep this impersonal. His would be just another corpse some poor schmuck had to scrape off the pavement.

Who am I kidding?

It had become personal the moment she let her guard down and put on her old EMT hat. While she assessed his wounds, she felt that old rush, the adrenaline spike that made her feel alive and kept her going through the worst of the carnage and destruction she'd balanced on a daily basis. But that was a lifetime ago.

Cassidy heard him jump, heard his body hit the pavement with a dull thud, and heard the air gush out of his lungs.

Once Dev was clear, Wren backed into the fog down the other side of the bridge. However, instead of following the road down, she stopped inside the concealing bank and shifted into Park.

"What are you doing?" Cassidy asked.

Tears streamed down Wren's cheeks. Cassidy nodded. Whatever happened, they would wait and watch. Either way, Dev would need a ride home.

ᏩᏅ

As the car slowed, Dev flopped out and rolled across the lane. A nice soft landing was out of the question, but the brutal joining of soft knight with hard roadway left him dazed. Though the ride had only lasted a few minutes, it was long enough to restore some of his energy. He'd absorbed the heat from the warm air and the hot engine to kick-start the healing process; but the harsh landing jarred his shattered ribs and injured left shoulder.

He gasped from the pain and struggled to one knee. Hand braced on his leg, he found his balance and rose to his feet. Jaw set in agony and building rage, Dev glared at his undead attacker charging across the clearing. The outcome of the battle was a foregone conclusion given the battered state of his body and dwindling elemental power. He only hoped to delay the beast long enough for the girls to get away.

The monster followed the car, unaware that its prey had thrown itself out of its hard shell.

Dev whipped Cinder from its sheath, squeezed her hilt and roared a challenge. The giant beast's hooves skidded on the smooth surface as it scrabbled to turn around.

Heat shimmered all around him—in the air, in the concrete of the bridge, in the wreckage that littered the interstate along the mastodon's wake. The Knight of Flame drew in his element.

Stripped of its warmth, the temperature of the roadway plummeted. Cracks fissured out from where he stood, jagged streaks cut across the concrete and asphalt mix. The air turned crisp and cold and the wind whipped across his face.

Blessed energy rushed into him, but his damaged body could only retain a small amount. The excess drained away like water through a sieve.

Not enough.

He called his inner flame to clothe himself and provide some measure of protection, but it wouldn't ignite. Too weak to support a sustained burn, he would have to fight unprotected. The fire-laced adrenaline that pulsed through his veins would allow him to move and put up a short fight, but no more.

The beast charged. Sharp tusks speared the air.

Before the sweeping weapons could impale him, Dev spun to his right and slashed his elemental blade at the base of one thick tusk. To his surprise, the dagger sheared through and the heavy bone clattered to the street. He smiled grimly. A shred of hope sparked in his soul.

Dev waited for the beast's charge again. His heartbeat hammered against his broken ribs, and his shoulder throbbed with each ragged breath.

It charged and swung its remaining tusk like a scythe.

Dev twisted away, but the creature still grazed him with its ribcage, knocking him off his feet. Agony jolted from his injured shoulder, but he fought off the black net of unconsciousness.

Heavy thuds drew closer. He rolled out of the way of those thundering hooves and saw the bone structure from a new perspective.

A sudden idea burned new life into his limbs. Painfully, he struggled to his feet.

This is ridiculous. When was the last time I ended up on my ass this many times?

With Cinder held in front of him at the ready and his legs flexed, Dev once again waited for death to charge. The massive skeleton slowed and made a ponderous turn amidst the wreckage.

Thank goodness that thing has the same turning radius as a freight train.

Head and torso finally aligned, the mastodon charged.

As the beast closed, Dev leaned to his left and swung his dislocated arm like a pendulum to build up momentum. The pain was incredible, but he stuck to the plan.

A spear-like tusk leveled on his midsection. Dev spun to the left as it grazed his hip, jammed his injured arm between the ribs of the beast and grabbed a fistful of bone.

The creature continued its charge, jerking Dev from his feet, but he held on despite the excruciating pain. He hacked through several giant ribs while the beast bucked and kicked until he had carved an opening large enough to crawl through then climbed into the belly of the beast.

The mastodon reared. Dev swung from one arm inside its chest cavity like a gorilla until the beast landed. Feet planted against the bottom curve of its ribs, he wedged the tip of his diamond blade between two of the shadow beast's vertebrae. The dagger slid through the mineralized connective tissue and severed the creature's spine.

Dev jumped free as the monster's skeletal structure snapped, folded in on itself, and collapsed in a heap of brown bone.

Left arm twisted behind his back, Dev lay on the roadway and stared into the nighttime sky. He'd won. He'd defeated the undead spawn, but damn he hurt. He didn't want to move, didn't want to breath. But he had to, had to get out of there before the police or medics or whoever else showed up.

He'd ordered Wren to drive away. Despite the searing agony, he laughed as he imagined himself, a naked, wounded man wielding a big knife and lying next to a mound of old bones hailing a cab at the top of the Sunshine Skyway.

I bet they don't see that every day.

A slow applause drifted out of the fog. He didn't turn to the noise, didn't move at all while he tried to place its exact location.

"That was quite impressive, Knight of Flame." The deep voice oozed condescension.

Aw crap.

Dev rolled onto his good shoulder and leveraged himself to his feet. The melody of distant sirens rose out of the haze and reminded him of his quickly shrinking escape window.

Got to make this quick. Where is he?

"I didn't expect you to defeat my pet."

The voice had moved. It sounded like he was over the water, but that wasn't possible.

"Show yourself, coward," Dev said.

A jet-black reptilian visage from out of the darkest fairy-tale rose thirty feet in front of him. Large, coal-hued eyes regarded him with a lethal cunning. It hovered over the dead space between the north and south bound lanes of the bridge. The man from the tent sat comfortably on its back.

An engine revved inside the covering fog.

Dev wearily held Cinder before him like a shield to absorb whatever foulness this new creature would hurl at him.

The nightmarish face split, revealing rows of long, saber-length teeth, and sucked in a large breath.

A blue sedan ripped through the mist and skidded to a halt between Dev and the guardrail. Dev ran for the car.

The dragon roared—hatred and hunger given voice in an earsplitting cacophony.

The shockwave smashed into Dev's back, flipping him up onto the car. Desperate to halt his momentum before he flew off the side of the bridge, he plunged his dagger into the hood. The elemental knife punched through the thin metal like it was soft cheese and sliced a long groove across the surface until the blade bit and held firm.

Dev lay spread-eagle across the hood, legs dangling over empty air, and turned to the driver. *Wren.* He shifted to the passenger.

Two glacial blue eyes gazed at him.

He was lost as soon as he met that stare. A beautiful stillness claimed his soul. He stopped breathing. His limbs went numb. His rage evaporated and contentment filled him like nothing ever had before.

The dragon breathed an oily black cloud that engulfed Dev and the car. The gale force tore Dev's grip loose, sent him over the rail. His skin bubbled, split, and began to dissolve.

As he plummeted, the Knight of Flame's soul swelled with an emotion vastly different from his usual anger or rage. His vision swam with the image of those two miraculous blue eyes until the warm water closed over his head and stole his senses.

Chapter 6

A LEXANDER GRAY SAT BACK IN HIS LIMO, PUT HIS FEET UP ON THE LEATHER COUCH and sipped Krug '95 from a gold flask. It had been a wonderful night. The Knight of Flame was gone, smashed against the surface of Tampa Bay and flushed out into the Gulf of Mexico like so much pulverized offal.

After his victory, Alexander rode his dragon down to the surface of the water in the hope of finding the mangled body, but nothing floated up. He dredged the bottom with tendrils of shadow to find proof of the Knight's demise, but there was nothing. Not a head. Not a leg. Not even a little finger. He was simply gone. Vanished.

Alexander smiled and took another sip. Yes. It had been a very good night. He closed his eyes, swished the perfectly chilled champagne across his palette, and let it sparkle down his throat.

For the first time he welcomed the scheduled call with his father, even considered initiating it early to share his news. It wasn't every day that a member of the renowned Knights Elementalis met their demise.

The Gray Lord will be pleased. He pictured his father's gnarled and wrinkled visage split in an evil mockery of a smile, with the twinkle of affection alight in those tomb-dark pupils.

Who am I kidding? Not even his own imagination could envision the all-powerful Bestok Molan uttering a word of praise for his third son, let alone allow something on his body to twinkle.

"Wake up, boy." A high-pitched version of his father's voice filled the cabin.

Ah. The grim image speaks. Alexander raised his flask and toasted the leering vision in his mind.

"To victory." Alexander upended the container and drained the remaining liquid in two loud gulps. "To me."

"Drunk, I see."

Cold dread congealed in the pit of Alexander's stomach. His eyes blinked open and he stuffed the flask behind a cushion.

The Gray Lord's avatar paced across a serving tray on the other side of the cabin. Ten emaciated inches of malice and ego wrung its swollen hands and glared. The glare was the same, but the nervous attitude was new. Something troubled his father and he hoped that his good news would be well received, maybe even rewarded.

Bestok Molan, evil incarnate in his Ken-doll frame, stopped dead in his tracks, ear cocked toward his son.

"No, Father, but I have been celebrating." Alexander suppressed a giggle at seeing the Gray Lord in this diminutive form with a helium-esque voice, which threatened to blow his moment. "The Knight of Flame has been destroyed." He led with his big news, but would keep the part about the club's destruction to himself if possible. No point in bringing up that minor loss to tarnish his glorious day.

"What did you say?" The figure lowered his brow and stared, one side of its mouth twitching. Claw-like hands grasped the air.

Alexander clamped his hand over his mouth as the image of a Darth Vader bobble-head teetered in his mind. The temperature in the limo's cabin dropped. Condensation formed on the one-way windows.

"Do not push me." The little Gray Lord spat.

The limo jumped a speed bump too fast. The rear axle bounced up and threw the Gray Lord into the air. He landed awkwardly, backside first, followed by the loud click of boot heels against a thin sheet of aluminum.

Alexander laughed, on the inside, at his father's rise and subsequent fall and waited for the intense reaction.

Slow, ponderous movements marked the Gray Lord's ascent. Back on his feet, he arched his back and grimaced.

The laughter escaped, deep, gut-busting howls that grew more uncontrollable when he looked at the rage painted across his father's minute face. For the first time in his life, tears formed and blazed a trail down his cheeks. Amazed, he collected the flow on one finger and flicked it at the tiny gnome of evil in front of him.

Bestok Molan destroyed the tear before it got close.

A pang erupted behind Alexander's left eye, a sharp needle that jabbed and twisted and chased away all sense of levity. The enormity of his indiscretion settled in. He didn't need to see his father to know what he was feeling.

"You were saying." Civility. A dangerous sign.

"I said the Knight of Flame has been destroyed." Alexander gained control of himself.

"Where? When?" The Gray Lord's avatar took two eager steps forward.

"Gothrodul and I defeated him last night after he came to the club."

"Bah. You cling to that old dragon like a wet nurse. Do you have the body?" The Gray Lord searched the car. "Let me see it."

"No, Father. I did not recover the body."

"Of course not, for that would have required thought."

The last drop of champagne tasted like ash on the back of his tongue as his triumph turned to manure within seconds. This thing dressing him down was an aspect of his father, a communication tool controlled by the Gray Lord. Its capacity was severely limited. If his father tried to manifest too much power through the link, the device would fail.

"We searched the water. There was nothing left."

"There's always something, a toe, an earlobe, something. But you have nothing." The figure paced across the tray and clasped his hands behind his back. "Were you recognized?"

Alexander shrugged. "I was not wearing a name tag."

"Curb that tongue, boy."

Don't call me boy.

"That I was the owner of the club was no secret. However, any who saw me there last night are dead."

"What do you mean *was* the owner of the club?"

Alexander cursed his careless language. "The club was destroyed in the fight along with many of the patrons."

"Another failure." The Gray Lord raised his hand, fingers splayed wide, and muttered a word Alexander had never heard before. A gelatinous green mass the size of a baseball appeared and spun before the Gray Lord. He pointed a bony finger at Alexander. The slime ball picked up speed. The hum of its rotation filled the cabin like a swarm of agitated bees.

Alexander held his ears, but the sound was everywhere—in his skin, in his bones, in his brain. It wormed beneath his palms and burrowed into his eardrums.

This was what he was waiting for, the punishment for his insolence. He collapsed on the soft bench next to him and clasped has head against the very real possibility that it would split open.

The green ball inched toward him.

Unable to look away, he watched its approach, certain that its touch delivered death. It reached the edge of the tray and the Gray Lord's avatar looked on expectantly.

Alexander froze.

As soon as the ball spun out over open air, it and the Gray Lord winked out. Most of the pain vanished along with the Lord, except for the prick behind his eye. His father left him that as a reminder.

Like I could forget.

He slid across the bench seat and recovered his flask. After one whiff of that celebratory drink, he chucked the container against the front metal shield.

The intercom crackled. "Is everything alright sir?"

Absolutely not.

"Fine, Simmons, just fine. Take me to the office."

Chapter 7

DEV SNORTED A STRONG DOSE OF WARM SALTWATER THAT BURNED HIS NOSTRILS and flipped his brain's switch to 'On'. Awareness flooded back in a series of images. The disjointed pieces came together in a collage that depicted the fight on the bridge and his fall.

Am I dead? He tried to open his eyes, but they stuck. He strained to hear something, anything, but only the steady thump of his heartbeat registered.

If I have a heartbeat then I'm alive. And, by extension, that means my brain is working. Right?

Dev tried his eyes again. This time he managed to pop the salt-crusted seal. Still, though, movement was progress. Heartened, he lifted the thing that should be his arm out of the water. It felt heavy and awkward and dripped liquid all over his face. He rubbed the crust from his eyes and stared into a clear night punctuated with a million stars.

A large swell broke against the side of his head, splashing brine across his face. He blinked away the sting and took a deep breath. Bone grated on bone. Pain slammed into him like a wrecking ball. His body's pain receptors hadn't kicked in until he tried to breathe. Then, not only his chest, but his shoulder, legs, hips, and back vied for attention.

Overwhelmed by a deluge of synaptic input, his brain overloaded and plunged him into a dream-like state of semi-consciousness where his past and present collided. Memories of a centuries old pain replayed in his head.

꙳

Filth, old straw and fresh blood covered the stone floor of his prison cell. From his fetal position against the wall, Dev eyed the boots of the man he'd learned to hate. Every day they shuffled into his cell behind a cart with squeaky wheels that served fresh torment. And for what? To force him to confess to heresy—to admit that upon orders from the Grand Master, he and his Templar brothers renounced Christ upon initiation into the brotherhood.

It was all a lie. No matter how many times he told the truth, screamed it as loud as he could, they continued to cut and stab, twist and snap. He wasn't even a knight, by God, but an artisan, a weapon-smith. His jailers didn't care.

His tormentor, mindful of where he set his boots in the muck, lifted his blue and gold tabard, and bent low. "Tomorrow." The word oozed out of the fat guard's mouth smelling of onions. "Tomorrow, *hérétique*, I bring fire for you." He kicked Dev in the chest and squelched out the door behind that squeaky, infernal cart.

Dev hated that squeak, hated the man, hated all men wearing the arms and colors of King Philip of France. For it was by the king's order that he and the

Templars were falsely imprisoned. No matter what they did to him, he denied their accusations, refused to disgrace the Quinteele name by being weak. This last session was brutal, worse than the previous one, but he held strong.

Alone again…alone with the constant pain and cold, niggling thoughts of how he got there, Dev curled into a ball.

Blood ran from dozens of new wounds. His body twitched from the chills brought on by the high fever that ransacked his weakened body. The stench of his own waste mixed with newly spilled blood broke through his normally numb senses—a horrid reminder of how his life had changed in so short a time. At least he thought it was a short time, but couldn't be sure. Time lost all meaning in the dungeon and served no purpose other than to fill the void between agonizing sessions with the torturer.

Torchlight flickered through the slats in the tiny window set near the top of the cell door and danced with the shadows on the bare block walls. Fire. He missed the heat and the light and the smells of the forge. The ring of hammer on metal was the song of his heart. He'd spent long days and nights working on new swords or axes to martial perfection until Véronique pulled him away.

Beautiful Véronique. Long, auburn hair. Brilliant blue-green eyes. Tanned skin. Only she had the power to drag him from the fire and forge.

Soon, my dear. I'll speak to your father when I get back from Paris.

This separation from his two passions hurt more than any physical torment. In these black moments of despair, when life lost its meaning, the flame from the torch outside his cell whispered to him.

At first he thought the guards had invented a new way to punish him. The unknown language wafted through the cell on a warm breeze. He peered through the slats to find the speaker, but saw no one. No guards. No prisoners. Just him and the flickering torch outside his cell. As the days wore on, the hiss and crackle started to make sense. That's when he thought his senses had fled. On some basic level, the flame's message resonated, gave him hope, promised that the end was near. End of what, he didn't know and didn't care. His body near to breaking, he no longer possessed the strength to fight back and considered any end, no matter its shape or purpose, a blessing.

I'm ready.

‽ 

Dev woke with a mouthful of Tampa Bay. The saltwater had sneaked in while his head lolled to the side. With his good arm, he clamped down on his chest to hold it together during a coughing fit to clear the alien element. He lay back in the water and eased a few dry, shallow breaths into his system.

Once sure his chest wouldn't burst, he opened his eyes and looked around. Dawn's faint glow pinked the horizon to his left. A row of houses huddled along the distant shoreline to his right. The moving tide had carried his unconscious body across the shallow flats to the mouth of the bay where his heels snagged on a sand bar. To keep him alive, his body automatically drew the heat from the water through his pores. The process made him itch.

Magic called to him from that row of houses, something familiar, elemental. He felt the strain in his soul, the need a separate ache from the rest of his shattered body. He willed his arms to paddle, to follow the call, but they wouldn't obey. Exhausted, thoughts muddled, limbs numb and lifeless, he surrendered to the magic's pull.

A strange stinging sensation circled his chest, traveled up his spine and out through the base of his skull like an invisible rope tied around his torso. With a gentle tug, his body stopped and reversed course, but his heels remained firmly locked in the sand.

The "rope" tightened around his shattered ribs and pulled. Intense pain blurred his vision, threatening to knock him out again. His trapped body slid through the grasping sand a few inches then stopped. The pull increased and squeezed the air out of his lungs. He tried to lift his legs out of the sand, but they refused to listen.

The tension on the line increased, he could no longer draw breath and the pain blocked out the world. The last thought he had before the stars winked out was a vivid memory of another restraint across his chest.

೮ಿಶ

King Phillip's men placed Dev on a sturdy oak table and held his arms out while a wide iron band snapped into place over his chest.

Thunk. Thunk. Thunk.

His torturer hammered long spikes into the band's eyelets at each corner to secure him in place for the day's event. He'd promised fire, but Dev hadn't seen or felt it yet.

After one last pound that mashed the head of the spike against the hole, the torturer stood back from his handiwork.

"Stand him." He motioned for the guards to hurry.

They pushed one end of the table to the ground and angled the other toward the ceiling. Strapped in and helpless, the restraint's rusted edges bit into Dev's slack, pale skin. His arms and legs hung down and swung free.

The torturer's tongue darted between the gaps in his teeth like an adder, and a thin trail of saliva leaked from the corner of his mouth. Fever bright eyes slid over Dev's trapped body. Rough, grimy fingers grabbed him by the chin and forced his head to the side.

"You see, *hérétique*, I keep my word. Fire, he comes."

The cart squeaked closer. Before Dev could see the fire, he felt it. A wave of heat covered his body like an old, comfortable blanket. After countless days locked within cold stone walls, the warmth felt wonderful against his ravaged body. He would have smiled if his ruined lips could move without breaking.

Fire entered the room contained in a large brazier. Various prods, poles and tools stuck out of the burning coals. Dev had to squint in the presence of the light after too long spent in gloom.

The flame spoke.

Not in words, not in signs, but in raw emotion on a direct line to his soul. It offered freedom from his current pain and suffering. It offered power, a melding of man with element. It offered righteousness, an opportunity to fight against darkness. His spirit rose with each offer made.

The flame offered him a choice.

"It's time, *hérétique*, you kiss the flame now."

A brand, its letter 'H' buried in the center of the coals, was the first selected. The torturer lifted it out, spit on the molten tip, and savored the resulting hiss. "Everyone will know you are *hérétique*." To his men he said, "Hold his face."

The guards rushed to comply. Dirty fingers pressed Dev's cheek to the wood and held him fast while the other man bounced the rod against his palm.

Dev watched him come, watched this loathsome wad of humanity position the fiery symbol over his upturned cheek, watched his little piggy eyes flash as the brand descended.

Dev made his decision.

There was no pain in that initial touch. No sizzle. No smell of seared flesh.

But the contact ignited a maelstrom inside. Dev's body arced off the table, popping the nail heads holding the iron band. It banged to the floor and his torturers jumped back. The flames burning in the torches around the room and nestled in the brazier leaned toward him, reaching out to their new elemental brother. As one, they leaped from sconce and coal to man in a fiery conjoining of life, spirit, and purpose.

Fire ripped through Dev's veins and fused with his bone and sinew. The pain dwarfed anything he felt before, ripped a primal scream from his throat as his fire-laced body transformed. Within minutes it was over and a new strength coursed through his system.

The flames were there, inside, an integral part of him now. Their heat warmed his belly. Still weak from months in captivity, from the daily torture, he knew the fire would heal him. He also knew it would respond to his call.

The room dimmed and the rest of the world resumed its pace. For the first time in as long as he could remember, Dev took a step under his own power. His battered body protested, but he could move.

His fire had incinerated the guards and his torturer, reducing them to piles of ash on the stone floor. With a rush of satisfaction, he scuffed his foot through the piles and scattered their remains among the muck and filth.

Booted feet pounded down the hall.

Dev faced the door, stood straight.

Three guards charged into the room. They took one look at Dev, crossed themselves and tripped over each other to get out. He thought he heard one of them mumble something about a demon.

It was time to leave, to go back to his old life. No more Templars. No more Paris. He wanted to go home and be a simple blacksmith, marry Véronique, raise a family, and live out his life in peace.

Dev stumbled to the door, his foot bumping into a steel helmet one of the guards dropped in his haste to get away. He picked it up and examined the stranger reflected in its polished surface. Dirt and dried blood marred his gaunt features. And his eyes…they were crimson.

I am a demon.

Chapter 8

Wren prowled through Cassidy's house, picking through the relics of another person's life. She was exhausted. The fight, flight and frantic search for some trace of her Knight had wiped her out. The soft leather couch in the living room called her name, begged her to take a load off, but her whirling mind refused to rest.

At the center of her mental vortex lay Dev. *Where is he? Is he alive?* As she tried to fill in the blanks, her body roamed from room to room and banished the early morning shadows with the flick of a switch. After her first circuit, every light in the house shone bright, but one.

Wren refused to believe Dev was lost to her. She half expected him to walk through the front door at any minute. But that was silly. He had no idea where Cassidy lived, and would most likely head for the Cradle or the condo.

She called home earlier and got the machine. She wanted to call one of the other Knights to help, but without the scrying mirror locked inside the condo, contacting anyone in the Cradle so far underground would be impossible.

I told her to make the mirrors portable. But did Cyndralla listen? No. Made cards instead.

Wren stood over the sleeping loose-end in the bedroom. Cassidy Sinclair lay curled on her side with a pillow clutched to her chest. Petite snores punctuated her deep breathing and a thin line of drool connected her split lip to the pillow.

Wrong place at the wrong time, lady. I should have made you leave. What do I do with you now?

Wren didn't understand why Cassidy made the decision to stay. If it were her, she would have kicked the carjacker's ass and gone out for ice cream. But Cassidy didn't have the same level of training as Wren, so the physical solution wouldn't have worked for her. Yet this chick chose to stick it out, even proved helpful and somewhat comforting during the crazy search along the south shore of Tampa Bay. She could have left at any time, but she hung close. *Why?*

Cassidy rolled over.

Wren shook her head, sighed, and resumed her restless journey through the house. Stalking down the short hallway, she ignored the closed door on her left this time. During her first trip, she'd opened every door and gone through all the closets and drawers, except for this room. It seemed different. The moment she'd stepped in she felt out of place, an intruder into the realm of the sacred. A quick glance at the thick layer of dust coating everything— stuffed animals, Barbie's Dream House, pink and frilly bed sheets—and the way each and every item was arranged just so told her that the room hadn't been used in quite some time. A red satin pillow lay across the top of the bed with "Amy" stitched in clumsy pink lettering.

Arranged across the child-sized desk, a large collection of photographs of all shapes and sizes captured the life of a dazzling child with startling blue eyes, chubby pink cheeks and an unruly mop of blond hair from infancy to maybe, five or six. A curly lock of hair tied with a pink ribbon and preserved in a little baggie lay in front of the pictures.

That one visit was enough. Wren had turned off the light, closed the door and never ventured back.

The hallway opened into the living room and that tempting couch. The first hint of morning outlined the panels in the closed vertical blinds as she navigated the furniture and stopped before a group of shelves she'd passed by all night. Trophies, medals, and newspaper articles covered every square inch of the central bookcase's four shelves.

Cassidy Sinclair, first place, fifty meter free style. Cassidy Sinclair, first place, one hundred meter backstroke. Cassidy Sinclair, first place, two hundred meter free-style. First place. First place. Champion. First place. Yeah, yeah. I get it.

She picked up a worn newspaper clipping.

Let me guess. It's about Cassidy Sinclair. The article started out, "Cassidy Sinclair sets new record…" *Yep.*

Wren continued to read.

Whoa, that's crazy. I've held my breath for maybe thirty seconds, but six minutes?

"What are you doing?"

"Waah," Wren jumped, dropped the article and reached for her knife, but came up empty. "What did you do that for?"

Cassidy yawned and rubbed her eyes. "Do what?" Her innocent, sleepy voice diffused the situation.

"Never mind."

Cassidy padded across the lush brown carpet to the kitchen.

"Want some coffee?" Not waiting for a reply, Cassidy grabbed the carafe and filled it to the line. "So what's the plan?"

Wren climbed onto one of the old-fashioned bar stools that lined the kitchen counter and dropped her head into her hands.

"I need to check the north shore." Wren said.

"I know, but the place will be crawling with cops and reporters and pretty much every other agency imaginable. Hell, I should probably be there." After spooning in ground coffee, Cassidy flipped the switch and leaned across the counter on her elbows.

Wren palmed her eyes. "Sugar. I need sugar."

"Sorry, I don't really have anything."

Wren went over to the pantry closet and pulled out a package of donuts that had fallen behind the boxes of pasta.

"How did you know...?" Cassidy's brow lowered.

Wren ripped open the box, took a big bite of chocolate covered goodness, and held up one finger to buy time.

"I, uh, I've been through your house." Saying it out loud, Wren felt like a steaming pile of crap. It hadn't occurred to her, aside from entering the little girl's room, that her actions were inappropriate in any way. New places could be dangerous and she needed to get the lay of the land. At least, that's what she told herself as she pawed through drawer after drawer.

"I see," Cassidy said.

The coffee maker coughed and wheezed. Cassidy plunked down mugs and fixings, and poured the coffee in silence. Wren upended the sugar container over her cup and watched a waterfall of crystals disappear beneath the dark surface until it threatened to overflow.

"Seriously?" Cassidy shook her head and cupped her mug in both hands.

Wren opened the drawer and self-consciously grabbed a spoon. She didn't want to do anything to remind Cassidy of her invasion, but she needed the spoon.

"What are they saying on TV?" Cassidy asked.

"What do you mean?"

"This is big news for Tampa. It's probably on every channel. Didn't you check?"

Stupid girl. Wrapped up in her own little world of misery and planning, she hadn't thought of checking the news.

Cassidy pulled her into the living room and turned on the television. "Let's see what they say."

"Tragedy at Club Mastodon. Details when we return."

They sat on the edge of the dark leather sofa. Wren jiggled her left foot and cracked her knuckles while the commercials wasted her time.

"Information is still coming in about the tragic fire and murders at a local hot spot last night." A news anchor read from the paper he held in his hand.

The word 'murders' didn't sit well with Wren. Her stomach tossed the half-eaten donut and sugar-sludge coffee around.

"Over eighty people were killed at Club Mastodon last night when a man, whom police have not yet identified, set the club on fire, killed five people and the manager inside, then opened fire on other patrons waiting in the parking lot. In the hope of identifying the man, the police have asked us to show the following video. But I warn you, the footage contains disturbing images."

৪০৫৪

Cassidy held her breath as a black and white security video played out. A bald, naked, well-built man stabbed a number of club patrons before turning on the club manager. The camera never found his face, but she knew it was Dev. Had to be.

He's a killer and I helped him escape.

She stared unseeing at the television as the reporter went on to say that the killer headed south on I-275 over the Sunshine Skyway. On his way, he killed another six people as he plowed into and over them during a freak onset of fog.

"But...Dev was attacked." The color drained from Wren's face. "Those people were already dead."

Cassidy felt sick and used. "Get out." She had enough. Her gift must have been wrong. "Leave before I call the police." Cassidy grabbed the phone.

"Ms. Sinclair." Wren's voice was calm and quiet as she stood up. "Please, wait. We didn't do it. You saw what happened on the bridge."

Cassidy dialed nine. "That was your boyfriend in the video." She pressed one.

"Boyfriend? You think he's my boyfriend?" Wren blushed and an uncomfortable giggle bubbled out.

Cassidy imagined a lot of things that could have happened at that moment, but a murderer's accomplice giggling in her living room like an awkward ninja schoolgirl wasn't one of them. She imagined Wren pulling a gun from somewhere under her dress, or lunging across the room. Not...that.

Without all that serious end of the world shit stressing her out, she looks like a kid.

"God, I wish." Wren flopped onto the sofa and smiled shyly. "He doesn't see me that way." She paused then raised her eyes to Cassidy's. "Please, don't finish that call."

What just happened?

Cassidy realized she wasn't facing off against a hardened criminal, but a young girl with a crush. It made Wren seem more human, fragile.

She didn't hang up the phone, though. She wasn't ready to do that and only one digit remained between rescue and the unknown.

Wren stared at the floor. Cassidy stared at Wren.

Quiet minutes slipped by.

"Wren." Frustration made Cassidy's voice sound hard, so she cleared her throat and started again.

"Wren?" This time her tone softened. "Did you and Dev kill those people?" It was a silly question. How could she believe the answer? Of course the killer would say, "No."

Wren paused for a moment, head down, hands resting on her knees.

Cassidy got the impression she was thinking about how to say whatever it was she was going to say.

"Cassidy Sinclair." Wren stood, tone and expression serious. "We didn't kill anybody. You have nothing but my words and actions to convince you of the truth. Yes, we borrowed your car, but you may have that back once we find Dev. And yes, I searched your house, but only to ensure there was nothing lurking about." Wren clasped her hands in front of her chest and bowed at the waist. "I apologize for the invasion of your privacy."

"Give me your hand." Cassidy held hers out and waited.

Wren titled her head and raised one eyebrow, but crossed the room and placed her hand in Cassidy's.

"Repeat what you said," Cassidy said.

Through her gift, Cassidy felt the girl's sincerity, embarrassment, and concern as Wren reaffirmed her statement.

Cassidy hung up the phone.

"Let's find him." She could really use that swim now to calm her nerves, to chill out, but it would have to wait. At least she had something to look forward to at the end of this ordeal—a nice warm swimming pool in her backyard.

Cassidy zipped the blinds, pulled open the door and stepped out into the chilly September air. Beyond the pool and grass, her back yard opened onto a choppy Tampa Bay glimmering in the early morning sunshine. The gray slate tiles beneath her bare feet were cold, freezing cold. She shivered, arms covered in goose bumps, and hopped back in the house.

What the...?

A layer of ice coated the entire patio floor and extended out to the surrounding grass. The privacy fence to either side of her property prevented her from seeing the neighbors' property, but she imagined their yards to be frozen as well.

"Um, Wren, check this out."

Wren took a quick look and shouted, "He's here!"

"What?"

"Let me out." Wren bolted through the doorway and charged across the ice-rimed tile. Arms whirling, feet sliding in different directions, she half ran, half fell into the wrought iron patio table. She glanced back to Cassidy as if to say, "Are you coming?" before venturing further into the yard.

Cassidy stepped into a pair of flip-flops, grabbed a jacket for herself and one for Wren, and eased onto the ice.

Ice? In September?

In Florida, winter didn't bother to appear until late January. And when it did, it only hung around for a couple of weeks. After frosting a few lawns and sending the blue-hairs into a tizzy, it traveled north to colder climes.

Cassidy knocked several icicles from the swoop of the ladder leading down into the in-ground pool. *So much for that swim*. Frozen solid, her favorite place in the world had been transformed into a skating rink.

Wren had already disappeared down the back slope of the yard towards the water and hollered for her to hurry up.

Within three steps, Cassidy's toes were numb. Thank goodness she brought a jacket.

Wren bobbed up and down on her toes in a circle of charred grass. Cassidy tossed her the other jacket and bent to inspect the area. *Still warm*. Steam rose from the burned grass. It looked like someone had started a fire, but there were no ashes or wood or remnants of anything else that might have burned.

Through chattering teeth, Cassidy asked, "What do you think?" Her breath misted in the cold.

Wren looked to the water. "I think Dev came ashore, rested here then dragged himself...." She pointed to a trail of brown grass that led away from the circle, around to the side of the house, "There." She took off.

What's this got to do with Dev? The wicked cold air bit Cassidy's cheeks, but at least the warmth of the path kept her toes from freezing. *I'm such a wimp. Wren's barefoot and barely covered in that skimpy dress and she doesn't even look cold.*

Cassidy wrapped her jacket tighter and jogged after the girl who had already disappeared around the side of the house. She caught up to Wren, who looked down at a figure on the ground.

Cassidy stopped dead. *No way.*

Wren hovered, wrung her hands, bit her lower lip.

The closer Cassidy got to the body, the hotter it seemed. By the time she got close enough to recognize his face, sweat beaded on her forehead. She took off the jacket.

"Is he...?"

"Yes," Wren bit back a sob, "but not by much."

Oh. How did he get here?

Dev lay face down in a circle of blackened earth, the grass having already burned away. Yet outside his hot zone, the frost reached out in all directions.

In Cassidy's expert opinion, he was broken—legs shattered and bent at unnatural angles, one arm dislocated, skin a sickly pale white except for the extensive purple and black bruises that generously coated his back and chest. There could be massive internal injuries. His shallow breathing whistled in and out like a punctured bellows.

She wanted to touch him, probe his torso to feel for other injuries, but his skin was too hot. Heat shimmered and rose off his body in waves, making it impossible to get close. She'd never seen anything like it.

Wren couldn't get close either, but continued to circle.

"He needs a fire." Wren said.

Cassidy's stomach knotted. "Are you crazy? He's burning up. We need to cool him down, not add more heat. I'll get the hose."

Wren didn't listen and mumbled. "We need to move him."

"Move him?" Cassidy sputtered. "That could kill him."

Lost in her own thoughts, Wren continued. "Get him away from here and onto the patio. We'll build the fire there."

"No way. I'll call an ambulance. They'll have the right equipment to stabilize and move him safely." The heat made her eyes water so she took a step back. Her skin felt tight, like she'd spent too long in the sun, and thought of the pool again. *Oh wait, it's frozen solid. Sweet.*

"Are you crazy? We can't call anyone," Wren said.

"But they can help."

"We don't have time." Wren spun Cassidy toward the neighbor's house. "Look." She pointed to the frost climbing up the privacy fence a few feet away. "He is sucking the heat out of the ground and the air to stay alive. If he stays in this spot much longer, it'll spread to the neighbor's yard."

Cassidy scowled at Wren. "He's doing what now?" *Sucking the heat...what kind of voodoo is she selling?* She hadn't noticed the frost on the fence before and, as she watched, it climbed another inch.

"Trust me. Please," Wren said.

There she goes with that whole 'please' thing again. Something had to be done, but this seemed...reckless.

Wren stepped closer. "We need to move him now. If we don't, in a little while the neighbors will wonder why their pipes are frozen and their backyard is covered in frost, like yours. They'll make some calls and, before you know it, we'll have lots of company."

"Fine." Cassidy met Wren's stare. "Kill him if you want to."

"He'll be fine. He's tough like that." She reached down to grab what looked to be an uninjured arm, but yanked her hand away before she made contact and blew on her fingers.

"Too hot." Wren stepped back. "I can't touch him. We need something to push or pull him."

Cassidy could tell he was too heavy and awkward to push through the grass, but since she didn't have anything better to offer, kept her silence.

What can we use? Cassidy looked around for a solution. She spied the hose connected to the spigot.

"No hose?" Cassidy asked.

"No hose."

If we can't cool him down, how do we move him hot. How do you handle something hot? Gloves? No.

Wren paced. The frost rose. Dev roasted.

"I've got an idea." Cassidy raced to the house, taking it slow on the frost, and ran into the kitchen. She grabbed the Hello Kitty oven mitts from the drawer next to the oven. But there were only two and both she and Wren needed to work together.

She rifled through the remaining drawers and scoured the pantry, shifting stacks of cans and boxes until she knocked a large box off the top shelf. It dropped to the floor with an ominous crash.

There go my Christmas plates.

She had to know the extent of the damage and opened the box. The top three plates had shattered into several big pieces, but the rest of the set looked okay.

Hey, forgot about these. From between the bowls she extracted two Christmas potholders. One a jolly Santa, the other a Christmas tree. Tools in hand, she ran back to Wren.

I hope this works.

Chapter 9

ALEXANDER RESTED HIS ELBOWS ON HIS DESK, STEEPLED HIS FINGERS IN FRONT OF HIS face, and willed the stabbing pain behind his left eye to vanish. He had played this wishing game several times today, but to no avail. Whatever hold his father had on him was beyond his power to defeat.

Bastard.

He rubbed his temple. Resorting to more mundane remedies, he had turned off the fluorescent lights and had lowered the blinds against the harsh intrusion of the sun. The blasted sunlight still leaked around the edges to contaminate his darkness.

Click. Click. Click.

Curse that woman and her infernal heels. Perhaps I should not have killed the last temp. At least she was quiet.

The stench of spring flowers, deodorant and her obvious attraction preceded her person by three feet.

"Mr. Gray." She leaned over him, flashing her ample cleavage.

"What?"

"The gentlemen from Deep Services are here for the meeting."

The damp heat of her whisper tickled his ear. Silk brushed against the back of his hand.

Move away, vermin.

"Thank you." Alexander snapped his arms to his desk. The move cost him as the needle behind his eye sunk deeper into his optic nerve, but it was worth it. She jumped back. Fear washed the sexual confidence off her heavily made-up face and compressed her thick lips into thin red lines.

"See them in."

"Ye…yes, sir." She doubled-timed it out the door, her steps clacked like chattering teeth.

Alexander grimaced and rose to greet his newest visitors.

Two short, round men in brown jumpers and steel-toed, hard-worn boots clomped to the desk. Bald, pale, and stinking of filth, they stood at rigid attention.

Alexander pinched the bridge of his nose. *The humans have declared war on my olfactory senses.*

The men could have been twins except the one on the right had more lines around his squinty eyes and, with the hard set of his jaw, carried himself with more confidence. *Older and younger brothers, then.*

"Sit." Alexander's civil façade had chipped and cracked two meetings ago. All that remained was a conscious decision not to eviscerate everyone who walked into his office. A decision he re-evaluated on a minute-by-minute basis.

"Do you know why I bought your extermination…company?" Alexander hesitated calling two men with a few spray cans of insecticide a company.

"Yes, suh." The older one took the lead.

Ah, the fabled southern gentleman. This should be good.

"Explain." Alexander eased himself into his seat.

"Well." The elder brother licked his lips. "We been in tha business for generations." His words came out in a slow drawl. "My gran'da, he started killing rats and bugs and things when he was a kid and just kept doin' it. In fact, my little brother Enos here, he spends more time down below den he do in the sun."

Enos nodded and smiled.

"I do not have time for your family history. I own you now."

Two bald heads nodded.

"How long would it take to deploy a new pesticide through the sewer system?"

"Well, we ain't nevah put new stuff through tha entire line at one time." He looked to Enos, who shrugged.

"How long?"

"Well, we don' know."

Alexander's temple throbbed with each slowly uttered word. He yearned to jamb his hand down the older brother's throat and yank all the words out at one time.

"Can you figure it out?" Alexander barked.

"Well, suh, I—"

If he 'Well suhs' me again… "Yes or no."

"Yes."

"Bring me the answer in twenty four hours." Alexander turned his back on them and listened for their clopping exit.

The older brother cleared his throat. "Excuse me, suh, but why?"

"Do you see those?" He pointed to a huge stack of paper in the far corner of his desk. "Those reports detail hundreds of vermin and insect problems throughout the city."

He stood up and paced to work off his aggravation. His head pounded with each step, but if he sat there any longer, he would leap across the desk and throttle both men.

"Roaches, rats, snakes and other nasty creatures are escaping from the sewers. This must be stopped."

The brothers looked at each other then back to Alexander.

"But, Enos was jus down there yestuhday and he didn't see no critters. Didja Enos?"

Enos shook his head.

"Are you calling the Mayor a liar? He told me himself no less than an hour ago."

Both brothers, eyes big and shiny, shook their heads in unison. "No, suh. We ain—"

"Of course not." Alexander's words took on the sweet texture of honey. "I have a new type of pest control that I want you to spread through the sewers." The nice approach made him gag, but he gutted it out. "No one knows the sewer system like you two, so you are perfect for the job. I need to know how long it will take. Can you figure it out by this time tomorrow?"

Egos properly inflated, chests puffed out, the brothers stood. "We'll figure it for you."

"Good. Until tomorrow then. Good day, gentlemen."

Enos waved, his brother lifted his fingers to tip an imaginary hat and they scuffed their way out. Alexander followed right behind and shut the door in the face of the receptionist as she shifted her breasts to maximize her cleavage before speaking to him.

With the deadbolt fastened, Alexander strode to his desk, pushed his chair out of the way and faced the portrait of his toad-faced brother. He hated Thargen, hated all his brothers, but he needed the grotesque's help.

He concentrated on those tiny, black eyes and felt his body stretch and thin. The colors deepened and swirled to form a gray curtain over his vision. He sent his awareness through the paint and canvas, over the leagues, to the lair of his brother.

A woman's terrified scream greeted him at the other end and dug that needle into his eyeball. The suddenness of the assault almost made him cry out, but he held strong. Trapped within the confines of a painting, Alexander stifled his sudden feeling of entrapment.

Must not show weakness. Calm. Emotionless. In control.

"Ahhh, Thargen, I see you are entertaining. How…nice. Might I steal a moment of your time?" *You disgusting pile of vomit.* Alexander felt flat, two-dimensional, and pushed harder on the barrier holding him in place.

"Keep still. You'll tear the canvas with your wriggling." Thargen's raspy warning came from outside Alexander's line of vision.

Grateful for the canvas separation, Alexander surveyed his brother's house and decided he did not want to visit in person any time soon. Grime and dirt coated everything except for a blood-stained stone table in the corner of the room. Atop the table squirmed the source of the scream. A naked young girl with wide, terrified eyes jerked her head from side to side, struggling futilely against her hemp restraints. Her spastic movements did nothing but tighten her bonds and jiggle her breasts. Thargen liked that.

Whatever you do, girl, do not flip your long hair. He'll play with it for hours, pulling out strands and clumps like he was picking weeds from a garden.

She flipped her hair. *Bad move.* Alexander chuckled and sought his brother in the dark recesses of the room.

"I see you have a nice day planned," Alexander said.

An old-school torturer, Thargen believed the simple tools of the trade were best. Give him a rope and a sharp knife and he was a happy psychopath. Alexander did not agree with his father on much, but keeping Thargen out of the public eye was a smart move.

Where is that maggot? Alexander watched the corner and the girl. His brother would not leave his plaything alone for long. A dark shape fluttered over and landed on his portrait. He blew at it, but it only ruffled its semi-transparent wings.

Bugs. Alexander hated bugs. Always had. Having one this close, crawling across his painted image, made his skin crawl. He scrutinized the insect's hairy mandibles and spiked legs while it skittered over his nose.

He froze, imagining the clawed legs catching hold and digging into the creases of his skin, inching down his face, looking for a way in. Long antennae caressed his painted lips, traced the artful outline and illusion of depth.

Get it off. Alexander held his breath.

The roach slid down, planted its six legs across his mouth.

"What do you want, brother?" Thargen's bent form dragged a wooden crate into view, leaving greasy black smears on the floor.

Alexander wanted to respond, needed to get his brother on the case, but moving his lips to speak was out of the question. His body craved air, but he refused to draw breath.

Killed by an insect. How ironic.

His sight dimmed. His heart hammered and strained in his chest.

"Alexander?" Thargen looked at the portrait and doubled over in laughter. "Some things never change." He coaxed his little friend from Alexander's mouth. "Come here, baby."

On command, the roach climbed onto Thargen's palm. As soon as he took it away, Alexander sucked in great lungfuls of air.

Thargen left him in peace to recover, occasionally glancing over and chuckling to himself. He pulled the crate next to the girl on the table. She watched his every move and screamed when he placed Alexander's tormentor near her pierced navel. The roach scurried up her body, covering the distance quicker than Alexander believed possible.

Her screams echoed off the stone walls. She did not understand, would not keep her mouth closed. *The more you scream, my dear, the more he likes it. Besides, the noise attracts the bug.* As she opened her mouth to scream again, the roach jumped in. She coughed and gagged, but eventually swallowed.

"Good," Thargen patted her arm then licked his fingers. "Mmmm."

Alexander sympathized, having been on the receiving end of one of Thargen's little friends in the past. But the emotional anomaly lasted only a moment before he moved on.

"I need your friends."

"Oh?" The hunched man turned and focused his dark gaze on the portrait. "That seems odd considering..."

"I want you to unleash your worst in Tampa's sewers."

A wild, toothless smile spread across Thargen's squat face.

"It can be done, little Alex. Oh yes." He rubbed his hands together. "When? When?"

"Now."

"Some today, yes." He patted the girl's chest between her breasts and a bump appeared under her skin like it had been summoned. It slid across her ribcage and disappeared into her abdomen. "But more tomorrow...many more tomorrow." Business concluded, Thargen turned toward the crate and opened the lid to get on with business.

This favor would cost Alexander. Thargen never did anything for free. But, whatever the cost, he'd pay it. With that thought in mind, he imagined his office and closed the connection to Thargen's vile place. Satisfied that his plan was in motion, he leaned back in his chair, laced his fingers behind his head and took a deep breath.

"Well, what do you know?" Alexander said aloud. "The pain is gone."

Chapter 10

AT ANY OTHER TIME, SKATING ACROSS THE WINTER WONDERLAND OF HER BACK-yard would be a wonderful experience. There wasn't much chance of a white Christmas in Florida, so when it did drop below forty degrees and thin-blooded Floridians donned their flannel pj's, Cassidy's dad had dragged the old wood-burning fire pit out of the garage and lit it on the patio. She and Amy, who was no more than three at the time, had singed marshmallows while her mom and dad shared an ancient bottle of Merlot. Every year Amy asked to see snow and every year Cassidy promised to take her next year.

I ran out of years. Like her family, the fire pit and all the flammable items were long gone.

No time for those thoughts. Back to business. Cassidy jammed a mitt on her hand and tossed the other, along with one of the potholders, to Wren.

"Try this."

Wren examined the items as if they were alien artifacts. Evidently cooking wasn't one of her ninja skills.

"You're sure about this?" *Please say no.*

Wren nodded. "Let's pull his legs." She took up position over his right ankle while Cassidy stood over his left. Both ankles were fat as overripe melons with no sign of actual bone structure beneath the bruises.

The heat from the knight-shaped furnace baked her skin. The thought of pulling on his shattered legs didn't appeal to her in the slightest. It would probably do more harm than good. Although, they did need straightening so the bones would set properly. By the way they bent and curled, they needed surgery and pins and rehab and everything else modern medicine could throw in there to get him up and around. But if his spine was injured too, all bets were off.

"We pull on three." Wren said. "Ready? One. Two. Three."

Dev's ankle squished in Cassidy's hand, grossed her out, but she'd dealt with worse. Wren, though, dropped it like a hot potato and heaved her partially digested donut onto the lawn.

Poor kid.

"Sorry." Wren wiped away the sick and looked pitiful.

"Hello the house." A tenor male voice hailed from the back yard. "Is anybody home?"

"It can't be." Wren brightened and took off around the corner.

"Wait, are you expecting someone?" *I'm going to tie this kid down.*

Cassidy caught up in time to see Wren leap at a man in the yard. Blond hair, beard and mustache, average features, average height, a little on the thin side, he caught her in a one-armed bear hug. Obscenely baggy clothes hung from his spare frame and he carried a guitar case that looked to be as big as he was.

"How did you know?" Wren asked.

"Stillman. Said you might need some help. Gave me this address a week ago."

"I thought you were touring in Japan."

"*Ja*. Had to cancel some dates. The band's not happy. May give me the boot."

Cassidy cleared her throat.

"Oh, uh, sorry. Cassidy, this is Magnus."

Magnus set his giant guitar case to the side and offered his hand. "Pleased to meet you. I am called Magnus Siggurdson."

Shaking hands with the man was like grasping a rock—strong, hard, and rough. From the touch she sensed his concern and unease, but no aggression or danger.

"Likewise, Mr. Siggurdson. Do I detect a Scandinavian accent?"

"*Ja. Jag kommer från Sverige.*" A mischievous smile lit his face.

Wren smacked Magnus in the arm. "Be nice."

"*Aj.*" Magnus rubbed the spot where she hit him. "Sorry. I said that I was from Sweden." He looked around the frozen yard. "I see our boy is in bad shape."

"He's over here." Wren led the way.

Magnus dropped to one knee next to Dev. "Damn, Sparky, you look like hell." He slid back, his only concession to the intense heat. "So what's the plan?"

"We were trying to move him to the back patio so we could start a fire for him." Wren said.

"*Ja*, fire is good." He shook his head. "But to drag him there…would have caused more harm."

Wren flipped a side-long look at Cassidy.

Score one for the EMT.

"What choice did we have?" Wren asked. "Look at the fence. We couldn't leave him here." The frost had nearly reached the top and would soon invade the neighbor's yard.

Magnus grunted. "Where did you want to build this fire?"

Cassidy had heard the word too many times now to take a chance. There would be no fire in her house. None.

"There won't be a fire."

"Ms. Sinclair. He needs a fire now or he will not survive the day," Magnus said.

"No." Cassidy shook her head and crossed her arms. "Not here. Take him and go."

Magnus glanced at Wren.

"Dev needs that fire." Wren approached Cassidy, hands out, palms up. "We can't risk moving him very far. We don't need to take him inside, though. He can stay on the patio. But he needs that fire."

"What's the fire going to do for him? Do you honestly think there will be anything left of his brain after that body temp?" She pointed at the heat shimmering off Dev's body. "A temperature over one hundred seven degrees causes brain damage and his temp must be like three hundred to eat through these oven mitts. What kind of cognitive ability will he have left after this?" Cassidy ran her fingers through her hair. "His body is nearly destroyed and you can forget about him ever moving around again."

"She doesn't know, does she?" Magnus asked.

"It wasn't for me to tell her," Wren said.

Magnus rose, put his hand on Wren's shoulder as he passed, and walked over to Cassidy.

"Ms. Sinclair. You've seen strange things in the past twenty four hours, *ja?*" Magnus's voice was low, intense, but not condescending.

You might say that.

"Yeah. And?" Cassidy asked.

"You're about to see more." He turned to Wren. "Can she be trusted?"

"I believe so."

"Wait. Trusted?" Cassidy backed away from the three of them. "Look, I don't want to be brought into anything crazy. I'm a simple reporter who writes fluffy little articles for a small time weekly press."

"Reporter?" Magnus frowned at Wren.

Wren shrugged.

Magnus studied Cassidy, evaluated every inch of her five foot seven frame. Whatever they were concerned about, she didn't want any part of. She was in the wrong place at the wrong time, that's all. The sooner they got out of here, the better.

Magnus's scrutiny made her uncomfortable.

"Look, tell me or don't tell me. But please, stop staring at me like that." Cassidy shuddered and put on a brave front while her insides quivered. "You're creeping me out."

Magnus smiled. "Okay. I ask you not to report on anything you see or anything about us at all."

"I know. I know." Cassidy brushed him off. "You'll kill me if I do."

"No." Magnus's tone turned serious. "We don't work like that. The Knights Elementalis are an ancient order formed to defend humanity against the forces of Shadow. We don't kill unless there is no other way."

"We're the good guys," Wren chirped.

"Knights who?"

"Elementalis." Magnus turned to Wren. "Where are we going?"

"On the patio, by the glass doors." Wren moved to Cassidy's elbow.

"I'm going to move him now." He paused to collect his thoughts. "As you can see, Dev is…different." Magnus paused again, searched Cassidy's eyes. She nodded for him to continue.

"I, too, am different. Dev's element is fire. He can control, shape, and wield it. My element is earth. I'm telling you this because in order to move my brother, I need to become the earth. I need to change."

Cassidy's fear spiked at that last comment. "What do yo—?"

"You'll see."

Magnus squatted, untied his Doc Martens and kicked them to the side. Barefoot, he wriggled his toes in the frosted grass and sighed. The joy in his face at that simple pleasure surprised Cassidy. Despite only having known him a few minutes, she liked him. He seemed open and genuine.

Magnus turned to her. "On my honor as a Knight, I vow that you are in no danger from me."

Cassidy's pulse rate jumped even though she believed him. It wasn't every day that a total stranger came into her life and told her he meant her no harm. That only happened in the movies, right? Still, she backed away a step, just in case.

Magnus smiled, stood up straight and closed his eyes.

Cassidy's skin prickled and she felt a slight tremor through the rubber soles of her flip-flops. The cold air hung tense and still.

Magnus changed, grew until he stretched the seams of the t-shirt and jeans that used to hang off of him. His face and beard filled out too. Gone was the meek, average Joe. In his place stood a Norse giant—seven feet tall, long blond hair and great bushy beard, sculpted face, bulging muscles.

My god. Mouth open, Cassidy couldn't help but stare. She placed her hand on Wren's shoulder for balance as her notion of reality teetered.

"That's phase one," Wren whispered in her ear.

The giant's skin, at first tan and smooth, began to change. His color faded— dark tan to tan to white to cream to a dull gray. Small rough patches, pock marks and odd whirled patterns formed on his surface.

She could feel Wren watching her for signs of distress or fear, but if any- thing, she felt…alive. Magnus's transition was magic, pure and simple. She was a witness to the spectacular that she'd only read and dreamed about growing up. No way would she do anything to interfere. Instead, she watched in awe.

Magnus crouched, stone scraped against stone. With a father's tenderness, he cradled his friend's hot, limp body against his granite chest.

Dev moaned. His loose limbs slumped around those bulging granite arms. *How the hell is he still alive?*

The stone man turned and took one gentle step, trying his best not to jar his feverish passenger, but as Cassidy noticed Dev's tight eyes and clenched jaw she winced.

Another step, another wince. Cassidy followed behind, focused on Dev's face. She couldn't look away.

Half-way to the patio, his eyes flashed open and his crimson eyes lanced into Cassidy. She didn't think he actually saw her, but reacted more to the movement.

"He opened his eyes," Cassidy reported.

As soon as the words came out of her mouth, Dev closed his eyes and mashed his lids shut. A second later, he burst into flame.

Cassidy screamed before the world collapsed to a pinpoint of vibrant color and winked out.

₧ℴ₹

Cassidy woke to a darkening sky, a comfy position on her couch, and a clear view out of her glass doors. Back to normal, Magnus squatted over the flaming body on her patio.

Fire!

Cassidy jumped up and ran to the garage. She grabbed the fire extinguisher, raced back to the patio, and whipped open the door. "Move!" she shouted.

Magnus twisted around, a stick raised in his hand. Wren slouched in a wrought-iron chair she pulled over from the table, one leg draped over the arm.

"Get out of the way!" Cassidy squeezed the handle and the foam shot out, but Magnus grabbed the hose and pointed it away. Instead of gushing all over Dev, it blew into the air, coating the hot dog at the end of Magnus' stick in a blanket of white.

"Stop." Cassidy fought against the misdirection and tried to realign her hose. "Can't you see he's burning?" *Can't let him burn. Not again.* She couldn't breathe. "Let me go."

"Can't do that." Wren uncoiled from the chair, came to her side and placed a hand on her shoulder. "It's okay. You can stop that now."

"He's burning," Cassidy cried, "Don't you see that?"

She fought harder than she'd ever fought before. Tears streamed down her cheeks. As the spray sputtered and stopped, so did her strength. Though she gripped the handle and willed more flame-smothering foam to burst forth and coat the burning man, nothing came out.

Magnus released the hose and Wren pushed her arm down. Cassidy collapsed to her knees on the hard tile.

She couldn't look away. Morbid curiosity kept her riveted to the whirls and snaps of the devouring yellow flame. Soon his skin would blacken, bubble and melt away from the bone. She sniffed for the scent of roasting meat, but didn't smell anything except...hot dog.

Hot dog?

Magnus and Wren had set a barbeque grill on its side and lit the propane burners, which blazed at full strength. Blue flames reached out for Dev's bald head. She searched his face, looking for...what? Signs of pain? The expression on his face wasn't one of intense agony, but of peace.

Oh my god. He's dead. They're cremating him. On my patio. They're getting rid of the body.

"I won't tell anyone." Cassidy whispered and backed toward her door. The spent extinguisher dropped with a clank. A thin arm covered her shoulders in what was probably meant as reassurance, but felt more like a trap.

This whole thing was a trap—the rescue, the loss and subsequent discovery of their protector, the appearance of the giant and now the immolation on her back patio. It was all some twisted way for life to mess with her again. Taking Amy wasn't enough. Just as she started her climb back, it knocked her back down.

"I think it's gone." Magnus said.

How could he refer to his friend as an "it" when a short time ago it looked like he cared so much?

"Yep. It's a goner," Wren said.

You little bitch. I thought you cared.

"How can you be so callous about this?" Cassidy blurted. "You're friend just died and during his cremation you act like he never mattered. I thought you loved him."

Wren had the decency to flash a deep red across her cheeks and her eyes got huge.

Magnus laughed. "I knew it." He pointed at Wren and held his belly. "Wren's got a cru-ush. Wren's got a cru-ush."

"Shut up." Wren crossed her arms and pouted. "Shut. Up."

"Ms. Sinclair," Magnus said, "You don't understand. I," he looked to Wren, but she turned away, "...*we* apologize for putting you through this nightmare. If there were another way of ensuring our friend's survival, rest assured we would have done so." He laid down the stick with the white-washed hot dog speared on the end. "I said before that we were different, that Dev had an affinity with fire. *Ja?*"

Cassidy nodded.

"It goes beyond that. In essence, he is fire. It cannot hurt him, but he can use it to heal. The hotter he gets, the faster he heals. That's why the fire was crucial." He gestured to the patio and surrounding grass. "See? He pulls the heat from the grill instead of the ground and the air like he did before."

It seemed plausible, in a way, but too fantastic to believe. *I canna' change the laws o' physics, Captain.* Mr. Scott's catch-phrase played in her head.

"Where did you get the grill?" Cassidy asked.

Magnus shrugged. "Your neighbor," he pointed to the Murphy's house next door, "Donated it for the cause. We'll return it when we're done."

"I see." The things she'd witnessed in the last twenty four hours rocked her belief system, and she did her best to hold it together. *Fire. Earth. Knights. What next, dragons?*

She stared into the flames crackling over the body of the man—*no, sorry, Knight*—on her patio. Fire flickered over every single inch of him like the Yule log her father lit on Christmas day. That never seemed to get eaten by the fire either. Though it went against her idea of the natural rule of the universe, she had to admit he did look…better. His breathing came easier and his legs weren't nearly as puffy as they were earlier.

For the first time, she looked beyond the flames and the injuries, to the man beneath. Strong arms. Muscular chest. Handsome face. Tight bu—

"Hey, why didn't his eyebrows burn off?" Cassidy asked.

"What?" Magnus asked.

"All his other hair burned off, right. Why does he still have eyebrows?"

"They did." Magnus seemed pleased to spill another of Dev's little secrets. "What you see now is a tattoo. He had them inked in Hong Kong a long time ago after he saw his reflection without them. He looked pretty goofy and, well, *wrong* I guess is the right word."

"No way." Cassidy bent for a closer look. "Wow. They look so…so real." She straightened and turned to Wren. "Now what?"

"We wait." Wren flopped back into her chair.

Magnus flicked the ruined dog from the end of his stick and speared two more from the package next to him. With a wink at Cassidy, he lowered the pink tube steaks over Dev's forehead. It didn't take long for the classic aroma of a summer-time barbeque to fill the air.

"Here. Take a picture." Magnus flashed a cheesy smile. "He'll love this when he wakes up."

"Oh, Magnus, stop," Wren said, but laughed at the sight.

"What? He'd do the same if our roles were reversed."

"True."

Cassidy listened to the friendly banter. It reminded her of the clambakes she and her friends used to have on the beach, sitting around giving each other crap while the water boiled and the campers in the group insisted on burning s'mores.

"Hottodoggu ga dekita. Hoshii?" Magnus said.

What language was that? I hate when people do that, makes me think they're talking about me.

"Hai." Wren sat up and caught the dog that Magnus threw, but it was too hot and she juggled it until it cooled.

"That's rude, you know," Cassidy said.

Both Wren and Magnus looked her way.

"To speak in a language that we don't all understand, and on my patio, and after what you people have put me through." Cassidy couldn't stem the tide and the words kept coming. "Are you talking about me? What did you say? I'm right here. Just come out with it."

As Cassidy scolded, Magnus's and Wren's eyes grew bigger and bigger.

"Cassidy," Wren stood up, clasped her hands in front of her chest, and bowed from the waist. "You're right, and I apologize. We spoke out of habit and without thought to you."

"I, too, apologize," Magnus said. "I like to practice other languages when I have the chance and, since Wren speaks Japanese, I spoke without thinking."

Somewhat mollified by their apologies, Cassidy relaxed. "What did you say?"

"I said, 'Dogs are done. Want one?'" Magnus answered.

"Oh." Cassidy felt the warmth creep into her face. *Nice one, Sinclair.* "I'm sorry, too. I didn't mean to bite your heads off. It's just…it's been a long day." She looked away. "So, um, how many languages do you speak?"

"A few," Magnus said, "I've traveled extensively. I could have asked in Russian or a few dead languages. Now they were someth—"

"Magnus." Wren drew out the second syllable.

He laughed and stuck a couple more dogs with the end of his stick.

Cassidy dropped into the chair next to Wren. "So Magnus, you're from Sweden. Wren, Japan. Where is Dev from?"

"France, though he very rarely talks about it." Magnus said around a mouthful of food. "Bad memories, I guess."

"France?" Wren choked, "I thought he was a Brit."

"No. Like me, he's lived in many different countries, but never for very long." Magnus looked over the face of his unconscious friend. "I've never met anyone who could adapt so quickly to a new environment. Give him a week, and he's speaking the language. Give him two, and he's blending in like a native. It's a gift, I tell you."

"France?" Wren shook her head.

"Don't tell him I told you."

"Nothing wrong with France," Cassidy said. "I've wanted to visit Paris since I was a kid. See the Louvre, the Eiffel Tower and the Bastille. Eat snails and drink wine at an outdoor café."

"Tastes like snot."

"What?"

"Snails." Magnus said. "They taste like snot." He touched one of the charred hot dogs. "Dog?"

Both Wren and Cassidy shook their heads.

"Suit yourself. Now, how about that picture?"

Chapter 11

THREE PAIRS OF EYES STARED DOWN AT DEV—GREEN, BROWN AND CRYSTALLINE blue. Familiar faces watched him, their expressions an odd mix of concern, relief and...*amusement?*

I'm alive. Memories haunted his thoughts, but he pushed them back. Some small measure of his strength had returned, thanks to the heat source near his head. The flames cavorting over his body took the edge off, but the pain remained firmly in the intense category.

He tried to speak, but after working his lips and tongue, nothing emerged. He would have sat up, but a granite hand on his chest convinced him to remain still.

"You're busted up pretty good there, Sparky. Lie still."

I hate it when he calls me that.

Wren stood close, still dressed in that sparkling dress, so he couldn't have been out for too long. He turned his head. The effort cost him a few major hammer strokes on the inside of his skull.

Mental note, don't turn head.

After the hammering ceased, he gazed into those blue eyes that had so captivated him before. He was expecting it this time, so the serenity didn't take him by surprise. Even so, he wanted to dive into that stare and absorb all it had to offer. He could not afford to do that yet.

Stillman was right. Shadow had returned, and it was strong, stronger than the Knight of Flame alone, that's for sure. Dev's ego cringed, but the state of his body proved otherwise. He'd gotten his ass kicked for the first time and it ate away at his soul.

Words. He needed to form words again. Swooshing his tongue around his mouth, he wrangled enough saliva to moisten his throat.

"Where?" Dev croaked.

"The lovely home of Ms. Cassidy Sinclair," Magnus said.

Right. That was her name. Cassidy.

"How long?" A little clearer this time.

"About twenty four hours," Wren replied.

Only twenty four hours.

"Cinder?"

"Safe," Wren said.

Dev nodded. On cue, the hammers beat him up.

Right. Keep still.

"I feel her...there." Dev lifted his arm in the direction of the house. Now that his brain was operating on more than one cylinder, he recognized the elemental force that had pulled him toward shore. He'd heard stories of other Knights losing their weapons only to have them turn up the next day. In his case, his elemental weapon had lost him and pulled him back within reach. He would have chuckled at the reversal, but didn't want to set the hammers in motion again.

"We'll get Cinder later," Wren promised. "How are you feeling?"

"Like cream in a butter churn. I told you dancing was a bad idea."

Wren teared up and smiled in relief.

"You up for a trip to the Cradle?" Magnus asked, and flipped open his guitar case. "I've got a few of Cyndralla's toys in here." Instead of a guitar, the case held a giant battle axe nestled firmly into black felt. He tilted up the blade and grabbed a bundle of oversized playing cards from underneath. In the hands of the Knight of Earth, the cards glowed a faint blue and the swirling pattern on their backs came alive, spinning down into the center of a vortex. The rubber band holding them together snapped as he thumbed through the deck. "Studio. Studio. Maui. Ooh, Amsterdam. Want to go there?"

"Magnus, please," Wren said.

Magnus pulled a different card from the stack. Its face showed the opening to a cave carved into a forested mountainside. A shimmering path of emeralds began at its mouth and led back into the darkness toward a symbol carved into the rock floor—four silver triangles contained within a golden ring, their tips connected at the center. He handed it to Wren.

In her hands, the magic died. The card lost its luster and resembled nothing more than a giant-sized ace of clubs. A wistful expression crossed her face at the abrupt change.

"Let's get this over with." Dev doused his flame. Movement would hurt, big time, but he needed to get back to the Cradle. It was the only place he knew he was safe. And leaving now would remove the danger from Cassidy. On the downside, it would also remove him from her.

When Dev first looked into those eyes, he found a peace he hadn't known since before his time as a Knight. And there was something more, something he couldn't identify at their core that captured his will.

"Help me up." Dev reached up an arm for help in fits and starts. The muscles weren't responding like they should.

This sucks.

Magnus leaned down and lifted his friend like a baby.

"You're loving this, aren't you?" Dev asked.

"No." Magnus nodded his big toothy grin in Dev's face. "Where do you want to set up?"

"Let's use the doorway into the garage." Wren shifted the barstools to make a clear path for Magnus, who followed with Dev, and opened the door. The

light from the hallway glinted off the mashed front fender and tire rim of
Cassidy's car.

Cassidy picked up the guitar case Magnus left by the door in both hands,
lugged it over to Wren, and backed out of the way.

Magnus eased his friend to the ground. "Can you stand on your own?"

"Of course." Dev assumed his feet touched when his downward momentum stopped, but he couldn't feel anything below the waist.

"You sure?" Magnus asked. "I'm going to let you go."

"Go for it." Dev gritted his teeth and hoped for the best.

Magnus let go. Dev crashed to the floor. Wren and Magnus rushed to his
aid, but Cassidy remained distant. He couldn't blame her. *She'll be glad to get
rid of us.* The thought stung.

"Okay." Dev grimaced. "Maybe I don't have this."

"You have the right of that, my brother." Magnus picked him up off the
floor and held him facing the open garage doorway.

An elemental force tugged on Dev, the same magic that had pulled him in
to shore.

Cinder.

"Wait. Cinder is in the garage."

"I'll get it," Wren said, pushing past Magnus. "Move it, Sasquatch." She
stepped through the door and flipped the light switch. Fluorescent tubes
flickered before they shed their steady glow on the remnants of Cassidy's car.

Magnus whistled. "I assume Wren was driving."

"Oh, shut up."

The front end of the car looked like a melted block of Swiss cheese. Hood
gone. Holes burned into the engine. Jagged rents eaten into the chrome. Tires
melted.

"I didn't think we'd make it here," Wren whispered.

From amidst the metallic carnage, Cinder stood tall and unblemished.
Firmly embedded in the engine block, the dagger survived the fight and the
ride home. Wren grasped the hilt and tugged, but the blade wouldn't budge.
She yanked with both hands, but still nothing happened. After vaulting up
and bracing her feet on the engine block, she pulled with everything she had,
but Cinder held fast.

Wren hopped down and stormed through the doorway. "You can get your
own damn knife." She stomped out onto the patio and stared out at the water.

Dev cringed at her passing. She wanted so much to be selected as a Knight,
to be graced with an elemental power, to truly be one of them. Perhaps someday she'd get her chance.

Magnus carried him to the car. Dev wrapped his fingers around Cinder and
she came away from the metal with a whisper and flash from the orange gem.

"Anything else?" Magnus asked as he carried Dev into the house.

"Yes." Dev smiled at Cassidy. She stood in the background with her arms crossed and an anxious expression on her face. He wanted to tell her that he would be back. That he wanted to get to know her. That she was pretty. But the fluttering butterflies in his stomach eroded his confidence. Here he was, the Knight of Flame who'd faced and defeated countless enemies—timid in the presence of this intriguing woman.

He wanted to say so much, but all that came out was a breathless, "Thank you."

"That's it?" Magnus stifled a laugh. "Let's get you home."

Wren rejoined them, her expression cold and aloof. She handed the card to Dev.

Once again, the magic sprang to life, only this time the card's face showed the same cave set into the side of a volcano with bright lava flows to either side of the entrance. The path to the Order's symbol was paved in fiery rubies. Heat rose from the flat surface.

Delving into his elemental bond, Dev formed the trigger in the primal language of fire that would activate the gateway. The word hissed and crackled on his tongue. He flicked the card into the doorway. As it crossed the plane from one room to the next, he spoke the word.

"Journey."

Dazzling golden light exploded from the card's edges, expanding to fill the doorway with its brilliance. As it faded, the cave mouth depicted in the card's artwork filled the doorframe. A ruby path wound into the darkness and beckoned Dev home.

Wren embraced Cassidy before setting her hand on Dev for safe conduct through his elemental portal.

"Hold tight." Magnus said.

Dev craned his head around the bulge of Magnus's shoulder to get a last look at Cassidy before his brother stepped through and the cave swallowed them up.

Chapter 12

ALEXANDER PUSHED BACK FROM HIS DESK AND WATCHED THE SHADOWS EAT THE dying rays of the setting sun through his penthouse windows. The incident with the Gray Lord that morning had set the tone for another dismal day among the human cattle.

Meeting after meeting with unimportant corporate minions set him on edge more than usual and he'd fired his secretary this afternoon for clicking her heels too loudly on the wood floor.

I should have eaten her instead.

He stood, knuckled his lower back, yawned and stretched. The fight with the knight had drained him more than he realized and he needed to recharge.

Gothrodul's mental knock brushed against his mind. The intimate touch of his friend's thoughts was a balm to his seething spirit.

Welcome, my friend. It has been a long day. Alexander did not try to hide the sincerity behind his thoughts. He did not have to present a false front before the mind of the dragon.

You need a break. The dragon's thoughts seeped into his consciousness. *And I need to feed.*

That is a great idea. Come to me, Alexander responded.

I'm already here. Open the door.

In the outer corner of the office, Alexander pushed a hidden panel lost in the intricate pattern of the wallpaper. Seams opened in the wall. They crept from floor to the ceiling then continued across for another fifteen feet until they met in a large wedge. The walls folded in and the ceiling slid open to form a giant doorway big enough to land a Chinook helicopter.

Gothrodul landed heavily, talons gouging deep grooves in the soft wood floor. Only the front half of the dragon fit into the penthouse. The other half stuck out the side of the building, back claws dug into the cement ledge to hold him in place. Armored scales the color of an empty night sky covered the magnificent creature from tail to snout. Cold obsidian eyes regarded Alexander with eager amusement.

"If the mortals could see you now, what would they think?" Alexander asked.

But they can't, so what does it matter? My magic cloaks my true form unless I wish it otherwise.

Gothrodul's form wavered, began to change. Great sheets of the dragon's black mass sloughed off, pooling on the floor of the penthouse until it evaporated in a puff of black smoke.

"Why are you doing that? You know I find the process revolting." Alexander turned away.

The dragon's laughter rumbled through the mental link. *On very rare occasions, Alexander, I like to mix it up.*

In less than a minute, a tall, thin man dressed in black jeans and a black, long-sleeve shirt stood in place of the massive beast. A silver medallion, two dragon silhouettes hovering over a miniature globe with a rune carved in the center, hung from a chain around his neck. His too-narrow face and pointed chin would have earned him many puzzled stares, but not enough to mark him as anything other than human.

"How do you tolerate this form?" With his deep, scratchy voice, Gothrodul injected malice into every syllable. He held out his human-shaped arms. "I forgot how weak and soft and ugly it is."

"It has been a while since I have seen your human form." Alexander grimaced. "It is ugly."

Alexander preferred his dragon as a dragon. This human shape was disturbing and not suited for tonight's planned activity.

The dragon-turned-human pranced over to the leather chair and dropped into its embrace. With a push, he spun the chair, but stopped it after only a few revolutions as a green sheen overtook his already pale complexion.

"Weak." The dragon spat and held his stomach.

"You mentioned a hunt." Alexander hoped to distract the dragon from being sick all over the floor.

"Yes. Meat."

"Let's go." Alexander walked to the open corner of the office and looked out over the roofs of lower buildings to the bay beyond.

"What are you in the mood for? Blonde or brunette?" Gothrodul jumped from the ledge and transformed. *Much better.*

"How about a nice red? I could go for something spicy." Alexander climbed onto the dragon's back and pressed the secret external button to close the massive doors. With a few strong beats of the dragon's giant wings, they gained altitude.

"Your pick. They all taste the same to me. The usual split?"

"You get the body and me the life force." Alexander dug his knee into the dragon's flank and it banked left. "I crave a younger vintage tonight."

"Where?"

"Northeast. Ybor City."

Yes. A nice, young red head will suffice. The smell of abject terror as Gothrodul makes himself known has a unique, heady aroma that adds a touch of ambiance to the meal.

Chapter 13

GLOWING WHITE CRYSTALS CAST THEIR LIGHT ACROSS THE SMOOTH STONE WALLS and rounded ceiling of the hallway outside the Cradle's forge. They lined the natural corridor beyond the limits of Wren's vision. She shuddered and listened for the inevitable creak and scrabble of loose rock that signaled the cave-in she believed was only minutes away.

What was that? She paced, rubbed her arms, flicked another glance to the ceiling.

"When will you accept the Cradle as your home, my little bird?" The gentle tone belonged to Stillman, Precept of the Knights Elementalis. Ruffled white shirt tucked smartly into slim black pants, which, in turn, were tucked into calf-high black leather boots, he could have stepped off the set of one of those old black and white swashbucklers.

Alchemist by calling, he'd taken up fencing to keep in shape and dressed like Tyrone Power in his younger days. She had no idea how old he really was since he refused to come clean with the digits, but he was up there…way, way up there.

He gazed into the dim interior of the forge.

"When it's not five miles underground," Wren answered with another look to the ceiling.

Back straight, shoulders squared, hands clasped behind his back, Stillman waited for Magnus. Straight, salt and pepper hair brushed the tops of his shoulders. His sharp brown eyes never strayed from the forge doorway, but the old man noticed everything.

"He'll be fine in short order," Stillman said. "The Knight of Flame is as tough as they come. Give him enough fire and a little time, and your Knight could probably grow back a limb." He rocked back on his heels. "Or, if he didn't grow one, he'd make one out of that Quinsteele he perfected." Stillman chuckled to himself. "Marvelous invention that."

Wren sighed, allowed herself a breather. *He'll be fine.* The sound of Stillman's voice always made her feel better. He had this fatherly way about him that made her want to curl into his lap and let him stroke her hair, like he did when she was twelve and afraid of dark places.

Magnus shuffled out of Dev's room. "By Odin, it's hot in there." Sweat streamed down his forehead, plastered his long hair to his face and stuck his shirt to his thin frame. "I thought I would pass out."

"How is he?" Stillman asked.

"Sir." Magnus snapped to attention.

"Relax, my boy. Relax."

"Almost lost him." Magnus stood down, hands clasped in front. "But he'll be fine after baking in that oven for a few days."

"I see." Stillman eyed Wren. "What happened?"

"We went to a club." Nerves bubbled up, made her voice quiver like a child caught with her hand in the cookie jar.

"Why?"

"It was my idea. Dev didn't really want—"

"That was not my question." Stillman spoke his rebuke quietly with an awareness toward Wren's growing distress.

"Yes, sir. We went there to celebrate. It's been two years since you assigned me to him."

"So it has."

"Dev was attacked at the club by some chick wielding magic."

"Did you see the attack?" Stillman's faced showed no distress at the mention of a magical confrontation.

"Ye—"

"Were you in his presence when the attack started?"

"No, but…"

The Precept nodded. "I knew this day would come. Saw it in a vision. He's becoming the danger I feared he would."

Danger? Dev?

"I must consider the next steps carefully." Stillman turned away and walked down the hall. "Maybe it's time."

Time? Time for what?

"Sir?" Wren asked, but Stillman didn't respond. "Sir?" She spoke a little louder this time, following him down the hallway. Still no response. "Father." She grabbed his arm when the switch in tactic failed to get his attention. "What danger?"

Magnus pulled her back with a cautionary, "Wren."

Stillman shook his head. "The Knight of Flame may be lost to us."

"What does that mean?" A sense of doom weighed her down as Magnus gripped her arm in support.

"Fire is the most volatile and corrupting of all the elements." Stillman lectured, his features softened as he looked at Wren. "Sometimes, its influence is too great for the Knight to control and leads down a violent path. With Dev, I believe that is only part of the issue, a very small part in fact. There is something else that drives his self-destructive actions. From what you have reported—"

"From what *I* reported?" Wren blurted.

Magnus's grip tightened around her arm.

Stillman continued. "Dev's actions and attitude have taken a more lethal turn."

"But the fights at the club and on the bridge weren't his fault." Wren pleaded.

"According to the news, more than eighty people died at that club because of the fighting. I deem that unacceptable."

"That's just one incident, though." Wren felt the bedrock of her argument crack.

"You have brought many others to our attention, no?"

This can't be happening.

Her personal reports to Stillman were matter of fact and honest. They weren't supposed to be used against her Knight, but as a means to chronicle events.

She couldn't breathe. The walls shifted in on her and the ceiling loomed closer.

"Some of the other Knights agree that Dev has strayed from the path." Stillman said.

"By some, you mean Dronor." Magnus spat out the Water Knight's name. "Sir. The Knight of Water has never liked the Knight of Flame. Ever. Dronor would do or say anything if there was some negative consequence for Dev. You know that."

"I have seen the enmity between the two. It pains me that our own team cannot get along as they should." Stillman addressed Magnus. "But that does not negate Quinteele's violent behavior. He craves it, needs it like we need food and drink. Can you refute this statement?"

Thoughts of Dev's black eye and the joy on his face when he ordered her out of the tent flittered through Wren's mind. *He loved every minute of it.* She thought he'd wanted her out for her own safety, but maybe there was another reason. Maybe he wanted her out so she wouldn't see what really happened.

No, that's wrong. Don't think like that.

Wren looked to Magnus for support, but he refused to meet her gaze. He probably had similar thoughts running through his head. *Could there be some truth to this whole out of control thing? Sure, the fight started when I was in the bathroom, but Dev was on the defensive when I got out. He didn't start the fight… did he?*

She looked up to the man in front of her, the man she called father when they were alone, and searched his lined face for the answer. She didn't like what she saw in those compassionate eyes.

If Dev is out of control, what happens to him?

Stillman responded as if she had spoken her thoughts aloud. "One more chance. If the forces of Shadow have truly returned, we need to be at full strength. We need our strongest fighter to lead the charge."

Yes!

"But," Stillman's tone hardened. "I will brook no other lapse. If Develor Quinteele loses control again, I will be forced to confine him. Shadow or no Shadow. I will not risk the safety of those our Order was founded to protect by allowing this volatile element to roam free." He leaned in close. "Need I remind you of your assignment, Wren Peterlin, or of your duty to this Order?"

Wren snapped to attention. Her body wanted to wilt, but she would not allow it. Duty, honor, loyalty—tenets drilled into every molecule of her being from birth, living off-base with her parents then with the street gangs, to joining the Order—trumped all.

Stillman had promised her a life of purpose and challenge. In return, he'd asked only that she remain true to herself and to her heritage. He knew her hot buttons and played them like a master. As a member of the Order, she would out carry her assignments without regard to the personal cost.

Dev, please, find the control. Don't make me do this.

With the eyes of Stillman upon her, Wren clasped her hands in front of her chest and bowed low, partly in acceptance of her fate, but mostly to hide the tears.

"Magnus," Stillman said.

"Sir."

"We need more information. If Shadow has returned, they do so with a plan. We need to know that plan."

"Agreed."

"Go to the club and snoop around, but be careful. Do not engage, if possible. We do not need escalation."

Magnus nodded, turned to leave.

"Sir? Might I go as well?" Wren needed to get out. "I know the layout and may be able to help the search."

"Are you sure you are up to this?"

"Yes, sir."

"So be it." He looked into the darkened forge doorway as if he could see the Knight of Flame from his position. "Quinteele is down for a time. Make sure you get some rest before he is ready to move again."

Stillman disappeared down the hall.

"Sparky will keep it together." Magnus smiled, wrapping his arm around her shoulders, and dragged her toward the portal room. "So he gets a little crazy once in a while. We all do. We'll just sit on him until we need that crazy bastard to go all fire and brimstone." He tugged on her earlobe and jogged ahead.

Magnus was being Magnus. He tried to lighten the mood, but she could not shake the sense of gloom. She wanted to believe him, wanted to smile and share in his well-meant optimism, but she knew it was only a matter of time before she had to choose between her honor and her love.

She faked a smile and laced her arm around his. "Let's go, you big goofball."

ഇറശ

A quick step through the portal to Dev's condo and cab ride through the early morning St. Petersburg streets brought Wren and Magnus to the Waffle House a mile away from the club. Magnus tossed the driver a fifty and waited until he pulled out of sight before jogging down the road. Wren followed close behind, glancing over her shoulder to see if anyone followed. At two in the morning, she thought it unlikely, but didn't want to take any chances.

A quarter of the way there, they ducked behind a parked car to avoid a patrolling police cruiser.

Police had cordoned off the area with crime scene tape strung between the trees and portable barricades across the half-mile driveway. The wrecked Jag sat off to the side of the gravel path, its hulk stripped of anything valuable. The scent of smoke hung in the air.

"Wren," Magnus called from the tree line. "Are you sure this is the right place?"

"Yeah. Why?" she asked.

"Look for yourself." Magnus raised his hand toward the field as Wren trotted over.

"It's all gone." Wren surveyed the lot. The tent, parking markers, power poles, and everything. Gone.

"This may be a little harder than we thought," Magnus said.

"How could they move everything so quickly? It's like it was never here."

"Money, bird brain. Money makes things happen and by the looks of it, our friends have plenty of that to throw around."

The moon shone bright on the empty field. As they moved, Magnus and Wren stayed low so their silhouettes would not give them away. When a police car pulled up, they dropped to the ground and waited.

Wren, face in the dirt, felt the minutes drag by. *Come on. They should be gone by now.*

"Can we—"

Magnus held up a hand for silence. Voices drifted closer and stopped at the trees. A beam of light from a high-powered flash light lit the ground to her left, on the other side of the Earth Knight.

"Don't move," Magnus whispered and dug his fingers into the ground.

Wren lay as motionless as she could and held her breath. Her heart thumped, the effect magnified by the hard ground beneath her chest. She stared at the stone-still form of Magnus. Eyes closed, he looked like he could be sleeping. The ground hummed beneath her seconds before a comforting warmth covered her body. Her vision grew fuzzy, as though looking through gauze, and where Magnus lay, a mound of dirt now showed.

The light swung toward them, shining over Magnus then directly over her own hiding place without slowing. At the end of its arc it winked out and she allowed herself to breathe.

Nestled in the cozy embrace of the earthen disguise, Wren didn't mind that Magnus played it safe and hunkered down for long minutes after the voices retreated and the car doors slammed. Despite the fact that she lay on the very ground where she almost died not too long ago, she felt…safe.

"They're gone," Magnus said, his voice at a more normal volume. "We have to make this quick."

"Man. That took forever," Wren said.

"I had to be sure they were gone. Waited until I could no longer feel the vibration of their passage." He jumped to his feet and followed the drive.

The earth magic retreated, leaving her chilled and with a strange sense of vulnerability—an entirely different feeling than the energy and aggression she got when touched by Dev's element.

Dev. Her mind never strayed far from her favorite topic. *Is he going to be alright?*

"Is he lost, Magnus?" Wren's worried question sounded loud in the early morning air as she kept pace.

"Don't be silly."

"No, Magnus, I mean it." She spared a glance in his direction. "He's done some…questionable things lately."

Magnus snorted. "I know. I've heard your reports."

My reports. My observations. If Dev gets in trouble it's because of me…

"What can I do?" Wren felt the tremor in her words, but couldn't help it. "I love him."

"I know." Magnus pressed his hands to his waist and shook his head. "*Dum flicka.*"

"What does that mean?" Wren asked, but could guess the meaning from the aggravation in his face.

"It means stupid girl."

Yep. That's what I thought.

"Spirits help me," he muttered. "You know there can be no relationship with Dev."

"Why?" Wren needed to know once and for all. The other Knights alluded to the fact that the Knight of Flame was alone for a reason, but they refused to tell her. She saw Dev's loneliness every day. It was right there, in every move he made and every word he said. He tried to hide it behind his gruff demeanor and dry sense of humor, but it was there if you knew what to look for.

And I know what to look for. Been there. Done that. Got the scars to prove it.

"I don't know." Magnus blew out a deep breath. "For as long as I've known him, say five hundred years or so, I've never seen him with a woman. I've asked him about it, usually after too many tankards of ale, but he never answered." He lifted his chin and looked toward the moon. "After I'd ask, Dev's mood would change, grow sullen. I know there is a story there; but, after a while, I stopped asking, left the man to his peace."

The distant wail of a police siren grew louder and they dropped again, but this one didn't stop.

"We need to move," Magnus said.

I wonder what Dev's story is.

Lost in speculation of Dev's possible past, Wren stumbled from the grass into a large barren circle of dirt and sand.

"Magnus," Wren whispered, "The main club was here." Using both arms, she traced an expansive gesture in front of her, delineating the location of the primary tent.

Magnus stepped close and tugged at his blond beard.

She pointed to another section off to her left. "The valets parked cars over there, and a small tent sat in the back, but I don't know what they used it for."

Magnus walked out onto the bare earth. "Keep watch. I want to try something." He began to take off his shoes.

"You should just wear flip flops or Crocs or something easier than those punk-rocker kicks."

He pulled off his boot with a grunt and threw it at her.

"Okay. Okay. Be quiet. I get it." She checked the drive and field. All clear.

Magnus buried his toes in the dirt and raised his face to the sky.

"Why do you do that?" She hoped that the questions would ease her back into his good graces.

"Shh."

Maybe not.

He sank into the ground to his knees.

"Are you alright?"

"Shh."

"Fine. Be th—"

"Shh." He raised his palm to her. "I feel something wrong…tainted." He slogged through the ground like he was wading through the surf. "It's coming from over here."

Wren followed after, sparing quick glances over her shoulder.

Magnus stopped near where the back section of the tent used to be.

"Something is out of place." He put his hands together, palms up, and muttered a string of noises that sounded like boulders tumbling down a mountainside.

Wren didn't understand the language, but felt the soil tremble in response.

The ground shook and the packed sand around the Knight of Earth's legs churned. Dark, moist soil rose to the surface, changing places with the dry surface crust. Along with the deeper layers of the earth, a foreign substance appeared. In minute amounts at first, the small white crystals soon covered the ground in a snow-like blanket.

The earth stilled. Magnus lowered his arms and stepped back.

"What is that stuff?" Wren asked.

Magnus scooped up a handful. "Perlite. A form of volcanic glass."

"What?"

"It's an insulating agent used in the phosphate and agricultural industries."

"What's it doing here?"

"That, my dear, is the question du jour." Magnus crouched, grabbed another handful only to let it sift through his fingers. "It could be a coincidence, is all. And have nothing do with the club."

"But you don't believe that, do you?"

"No. Something doesn't feel right." Magnus walked to the other side of the white patch. He pushed his hand under the surface then jerked it away as if stung. "What the...?"

"What?"

"I found the taint." He patted his pockets and frowned. "We need to take back a sample, but...guess I need to do this another way." Careful not to touch the crystals again, he held his palm over the corrupted surface. Within seconds a ring formed, emerging from the ground to capture the sample in a natural limestone container. "Something is definitely wrong here. I can't tell you what it is, but I know the feel of Shadow, of evil."

Tucking the box under one arm, he picked up his shoes. "Here. Hold this." Magnus tried to hand Wren the sample, but she backed away. "It won't bite you. Please. I have to put my shoes on."

Wren took the container and held it at arm's length.

"Let's go." Magnus said. "I'll open a gateway. Any ideas on where to set it up?"

"How about the Jag?"

"That'll work." Magnus headed for the car, setting a much quicker pace than when they first set out. "I hope Stillman or Cyndralla can make some sense out of this stuff."

Wren's back stiffened.

Oh man, not her.

Chapter 14

Sleep ran from Dev like a hare from a wolf.
The woman in the club. Who was she?

The question dominated his thoughts as he lay on the stone cot in his forge and stared up at the fire-lit ceiling. The stifling heat from the banked lava chamber cocooned his body in its healing embrace. He closed his eyes, but the pale features, long hair and dead eyes of the woman haunted him.

I know I've seen her before.

For hours he struggled with the whos and wheres, but the effort yielded only frustration. His body needed sleep, but his mind thrashed on the images, keeping him awake and on edge.

This isn't helping.

He rolled to his side and sat up gingerly, waiting for the pain to knock him back down. It didn't and he gave a mental cheer at the small victory. The healing process progressed nicely; and, while he still felt a twinge with every twist and movement, it no longer kept him out of the game.

Okay leggies. Let's go. Dev held his breath while he shifted his left leg over the side of the bed. Unsure if they were ready to support his weight, he took it slow, slid his right leg over and off to dangle next to the other, toes an inch above the floor. Pins and needles attacked as the blood rushed to his feet.

It's nice to be upright for a change.

The next step would be tougher, so he planted his feet on the hot stone floor and waited for the tingling to subside. He rocked forward and pushed up on shaking legs, teeth set tight against the strain. His body felt too heavy. Arms out to his side for balance, he waited out the bout of dizziness that overtook him. The spell dissipated and his stance solidified. Standing hurt, but he needed to get off his ass for a while, move the old bones before they got used to lazing around.

Right. Now to walk.

Dev set his sight on the anvil across the room. If he could make it there, he was good to go.

It's only ten feet. I can piss farther than that.

He slid his right foot forward a couple of inches and took the weight on the ball of his foot. Scraping his left foot forward, he brought it even with his right. Confidence grew with each shuffle forward and he closed the distance four inches at a time.

Almost there. Emboldened, he tried a normal step and toppled forward, but caught himself on the anvil before his body and pride spilled onto the floor. He'd made it. It wasn't easy and as a reward, his entire body throbbed in victory, or pain, he couldn't tell which.

That wasn't so bad.

He winced and set his eyes on the doorway to the hall beyond. When he began this odyssey, he didn't have a final destination in mind. Having achieved mobility, he knew where he had to go. The woman's pale face loomed large in his mind.

Oh, man, this is gonna hurt.

He pushed off from the anvil, stiff-legged it the few feet to the doorway and propped himself against the jamb with a *woof*. The sweet smell of freedom blew across his face from down the corridor.

Thank goodness someone thought to throw a pair of drawers on him. He couldn't imagine shoving his legs through anything at the moment and he didn't want to go schlonging through the Cradle.

A quick glance left then right showed no mother hens or overbearing friends in sight. They wouldn't be happy with this adventure, but he needed answers. A leisurely stroll, or shuffle—a sharp pain jabbed his left thigh—or maybe even a crawl through the Hall of Ages might help. Leaning one shoulder against the wall, Dev pushed himself, inch by precious inch down the long hallway.

After the first few steps the pain leveled out to a nice dull roar. He set his shuffling gait on auto and returned to his ruminations.

I know her face. I've seen it bef—crap. Def stopped and raised his eyes to the ceiling as heavy footsteps came up behind him.

A deep voice said, "Help. There's a zombie on the loose. Somebody please save me."

Freakin' Magnus.

"You shouldn't be up yet, you know." Magnus circled around Dev.

"Bite me." Dev looked up at the towering figure of the Knight of Earth. "Why are you big?" Magnus usually trod the halls of the Cradle in his tiny musician body, but today he looked full-on Norse giant.

"Been working out. You stink."

"Been dead."

"Where you going?" Magnus asked.

"Hall of Ages." Dev didn't feel up to their usual banter so he opted for the truth out of the gate.

Magnus's brow creased and he humphed. "Haven't been there in ages."

Kill me now, he's in one of those moods.

"Mind if I tag along?"

"Uh—"

"Good."

Great.

"Feeling nostalgic, are we?"

Dev's left leg lagged behind. Moving it took more work than the right, and his limping shuffle grew more pronounced. He knew Magnus noticed, saw him look down. Neither said anything about it as they plodded on.

"The woman I…" Dev winced and stopped, finding it too difficult to talk and walk and breathe at the same time. "Fought in the club." He took a few deep breaths before continuing. "She said I should know her."

"Do you?"

"Yeah, I think so." Dev started moving again, but slower. Magnus dipped under Dev's arm and took part of his weight. A relieved sigh escaped before Dev could stop it.

"You think so." Magnus said.

"I know I've seen her before, but I can't place where." He would never admit it, but cornball routine aside, he was damn glad Magnus showed up when he did.

"So you thought to check the Ages room."

"Right."

Dev leaned harder into his friend, allowing the big man to take more of his weight. His chest ached. He leaned against the wall outside the Hall of Ages to catch his breath and give his body a moment to stop screaming.

"You should be in bed." Magnus said.

"I know," Dev said. "But she won't let me sleep."

"I know that problem." Magnus grinned and jagged his eyebrows.

"Shut up."

"You better hope Wren doesn't catch you…us."

"No shit. She'd kick my ass."

"Mine too, sister, so move it." Magnus adjusted his hold so he could take most of his friend's weight. "What are we looking for?"

They squeezed through the door into an airplane-hanger-sized room crammed with pictures, tapestries, statues, weapons, and other objects from the history of the Order arranged in museum-quality displays. Some stood free while others clung to the walls or hung from the ceiling. Glowing crystals lit the perimeter, but the room's primary light source shown down from several spelled gemstone candelabras. The air tasted stale, as if it hadn't been disturbed in many years, though the room itself was immaculate.

"I forgot how big this place was." Dev whispered, as he swiveled his head to find a good place to start.

"Me too." Magnus mirrored his hushed tone. "Where do you want to start?"

"No clue."

"Odds or evens." Magnus put out his fist. "Odds we go left. Evens we go right."

Dev chuckled and put out his fist. "What about the center?"

"Nobody starts in the center. Ready?" Magnus shook his fist and Dev did the same. "One, two, three, shoot."

He threw out two and Dev dropped three.

"Left it is." Magnus said.

Dev remembered why he didn't spend much time in this room. It focused entirely on the past while he looked to the future. The artifacts showed the Order's history of violence. He and Magnus limped past tableaus of every war in the history books and then some. Uniforms the Knights wore into battle or the weapons they wielded held prominence.

While they walked, Dev looked every which way for a glimpse of that pale face.

"No way." Magnus stopped short in front of a vibrant painting. "I can't believe we still have this."

"Oh geez." Dev smiled.

A grim-faced pirate with long black hair stared out from the canvas between two other rogues on the deck of the *Queen Anne's Revenge* amidst bales of rope and ancient wooden casks. Magnus stood to the Captain's left clad in a blousy tan pirate shirt, and red pants. A stiff sea breeze blew his long blond locks out behind him while a red-headed wench with bulging cleavage laughed on his arm. Dev scowled down from the captain's other side. In a half-buttoned gray shirt, tattered draw-string pants and shiny boots, he watched another pirate who hung his head over the side.

Magnus shook his head. "Dronor never forgave you for that, did he?"

"Nope. I had to do it. I mean, come on. The great Knight of Water seasick. Hell, I even paid the artist extra to paint Dronor mid-heave."

"No wonder he doesn't like you."

Dev shrugged. The movement jarred his shoulder, reminding him that they were there for a reason.

"And then we have this." Magnus's tone turned reverent. He steered them to a large, round table surrounded by gleaming suits of plate armor. In the center of the plain oak table, a golden circlet rested on a battle standard—three antique crowns on a field of azure.

"Arthur was the greatest of our order." Voice filled with awe, Magnus named his predecessor. "The greatest Knight of Earth the world has ever known."

"Yeah, but could he play bass for one of the biggest rock bands in the world?"

Magnus continued as if reading from an archaic tome. "And then he was betrayed by the then Knight of Flame, Lancelot, who ignited Guinevere's passion and—"

"Brought about the downfall of Camelot. Yeah. Yeah. Knight of Flame bad. I know." Dev needed no reminders about the darker side of his element.

Magnus gave him a penetrating look. His lips parted, as if he wanted to say something, but he shut them without a sound.

"No worries here, my brother," Dev said. "You don't have a queen for me to steal, remember?" An image of glacial blue eyes flashed across his thoughts.

"Dev," Magnus hesitated, averting his eyes. "There's been talk."

"About?"

"You. Stillman is concerned that you've lost control."

"What do you mean 'lost control'?"

"He thinks the fire has taken over and that you're a danger to yourself and everyone around you."

Anger spiked. The healing flame burning through his system flared, ready to lash out.

"That's crazy," Dev fired back. "What proof does he have? Why would he think that?" Dev stood under his own power, his elemental force lending him strength. "I haven't hurt anyone and I'm in complete control." The fire roared to life, blazed through his veins and heated his skin. He paced away from Magnus, the crippling pain receding to little more than a distant throb.

How dare he! Dev clenched his fists and spun back to Magnus who stood mute and wide-eyed.

"I. Am. Fine."

"Oh, I can see that."

The flame wanted to respond, to fight. Dev closed the distance, forcing injured muscles to react. He raised his arm back for the first strike and stopped.

"There she is," Dev's rage evaporated in a rush and with it, his strength. Without the rage fueling his element, he collapsed to the floor. The pain redoubled its intensity, but he didn't care. He found her.

"Help me up." Dev looked to his friend like nothing had been about to go down.

Expression bland, the big man grabbed Dev under the armpits and hoisted him up.

"Over there." Dev inclined his chin toward a group of sinister, gloomy paintings off by themselves in the center of the room. Five large family portraits brooded in a semi-circle around what looked like a black stone podium. Shrouded in darkness, four of the paintings showed only lifeless grays and drab greens. The last one, however, practically glowed with vivid, life-like color. It looked as if the subjects could walk right off the canvas. Light projected from the base of the podium onto this last painting, illuminating the members of the last family of Shadow.

Magnus manhandled Dev to the podium and encouraged him to transfer his weight to the dark, silver-veined marble. Across the platform's wide top gleamed five names etched in gold. They each lined up with one of the family portraits. The last one, Molan, faced the bright portrait.

"That's her." Dev whispered. He leaned over the podium and stared at the likeness of the pale woman he fought at the Club. "I knew I saw her before." His hand brushed the letters and Stillman's voice broke the silence.

"The family of Gray Lord Bestok Molan." Stillman's crisp, formalized intonation, coming from hidden speakers, rang through the hall. "Know these faces for they shall appear one day and attempt to smite all in their path. We must be vigilant." The light projection changed. Instead of lighting the entire family, the beam narrowed, zeroing in on the aged man in the center seated on a black velvet throne. "Bestok Molan, Gray Lord, Master of Shadow, Lord of the Darkness."

"If I'd have known there'd be a show, I'd have brought popcorn." Magnus crossed his arms.

"Zip it," Dev said.

The spotlight shifted to the far right corner of the painting, away from the woman of his search, and highlighted a big guy. Stillman's voice droned on, but Dev stopped listening. He focused on the bottom left where she kneeled elegantly in front of another man. Next to her, on the same level in the picture, was some kind of distorted, wavy image. Whenever he tried to make it out, it blurred even more and made his eyes itch.

Blinking away the uncomfortable sensation, he lifted his gaze to the man behind her. *Is that the guy who kicked my ass?*

The light dropped to the woman and Dev tuned in.

"...had twin daughters. In testament to his black arts, Bestok Molan ordered his son to turn his granddaughters, Triessa and Agridda, into powerful weapons of Shadow."

Footsteps halted behind Dev.

"Is it wise for you to be out of bed, Knight of Flame?" Stillman's real voice sounded exactly like the recorded one.

"Probably not, sir."

"I assume you have a good reason, yes? Is it her?"

"The resemblance is close. I believe it was her." Dev faced the Precept. "I fought and defeated Triessa. I was about to deliver the killing bl—"

Stillman's mouth twitched, eyes narrowing. Based on what Magnus said earlier, Dev wasn't sure if Stillman reacted to the news about his fight against a minion of Shadow or the fact that he was about to kill.

"So you killed her?" Stillman asked in a tone that indicated he already knew the answer.

Dev's element stirred inside him, but he stuffed it down. "No, sir."

"Then she still lives."

"No, sir. Her father killed her. He is the one who kicked my a—, defeated me, sir." *I am so sick of saying that.*

Stillman clasped his hands behind his back and paced to the painting. Moving from face to face, he studied each one before turning back to the waiting Knights.

"If what you say is true—"

"It is," Dev growled, flame burning hot.

Magnus rested a hand on his shoulder and Stillman raised one eyebrow.

"Stand down, Develor Quinteele." Stillman maintained his formal monotone. "I am not questioning your veracity. Your battle and positive identification proves that the Gray Lord is mobilizing his forces."

Dev relaxed.

"And they are powerful." Stillman continued. "As proven by your defeat."

Can we please stop talking about that?

"To clarify, you said her father killed her."

"Yes, sir." Dev slouched against the podium, strength and energy spent.

"So, the son of Bestok Molan has taken to the field. Do you recognize him in the picture?"

Dev struggled to keep his head upright. With the mystery woman indentified, exhaustion sought to bring him down.

"No, sir. His face was masked in shadow. But I would know him if I saw him in person. I'd sense his power."

"I don't see how that would be possible."

"Excuse me, sir," Magnus chimed in, "The Club was owned by Alexander Gray. Perhaps we can start with him, ask some questions."

"Gray is it?" Stillman shook his head. "Seems too obvious, but sometimes that's the best place to hide."

"Alexander Gray operates out of the Daegon Gray office in Tampa," Dev said.

"We cannot act unless we are sure." Stillman paused, eyes lowered as if deliberating his choice of words. He looked up and met Dev's gaze. "We need verification. Rest tonight. On the morrow, observe him without letting him see you. Is that possible?"

"Hold on," Magnus jumped in. "Can't it wait a couple of days until Dev gets his strength back?"

Shut up, Magnus.

"No. We have no time. The Gray Lord knows we are here. I sense something different about this one. The other Gray Lords," Stillman gestured to the darker portraits. "their tactics were simple. Amass an army large enough to swallow the world and attack. They lacked subtlety, finesse. Though powerful, we found ways to defeat them in time. Bestok Molan, on the other hand, has remained elusive. I believe he's had a hand in human tragedy for centuries—striking from cover, manipulating leaders, shaping events. He revels in turning humanity against itself."

"Why haven't you shared any of this with us?" Dev asked.

"I believe, I sense, I think...all conjecture." Frustration crept into Stillman's voice as he walked over and gripped the podium. "I need facts, Knight of Flame. There have been too many examples of human cruelty over the centuries for Bestok Molan not to have been involved. Robespierre, Pol Pot, Amin, Hitler, Stalin...the list goes on. Their despotic actions reek of Molan's influence." The old man's piercing gaze lanced Dev then Magnus. "These names are not unfamiliar to you. Both of you have run missions against them, helping to bring them down. Have you encountered any evidence to suggest Shadow's involvement?"

Dev and Magnus slowly shook their heads.

"We need clues, proof, a trail to follow. I can strategize based on supposition, but I cannot act. Until now, that is. Go. Prove this Alexander Gray is the man we believe him to be."

"I'll go with him," Magnus offered.

Thanks, man.

"No. I have something else for you. Wren will take him."

Magnus inclined his head.

"Get your rest, Knight of Flame. We need you at full strength." After a nod to Magnus, Stillman strode from the room.

Magnus frowned, slipped his arm around Dev and hoisted his weight.

"Hssst, be careful."

"Ya big baby." The Knight of Earth poked him in the ribs, sending a wave of agony through his torso. They journeyed back through the hall in silence.

Chapter 15

THE DAEGON GRAY LOBBY HUMMED WITH EARLY MORNING CELL PHONE CHATTER and the constant arrival of suit-clad professionals. Frigid air pumped out of the vent over Cassidy's head. She sat in the plush waiting area chairs and shivered. The black suit-jacket she wore was for style, not warmth, and the short black skirt did little to keep the cold leather seats from biting her legs. Arms crossed over her leather portfolio, she lay in wait for her target.

It had been four days since the club had burned down. Wren had kept Cassidy busy for two of those days and when Cassidy woke up on the third, she didn't have the gumption to leave her room. This interview scheme jump-started her reentry into the real world after the Knights flipped her beliefs on their sides. Besides, since she didn't get to the club before it burned down, she hoped to make it up to her editor with a face-to-face interview with Alexander Gray himself.

She'd called the night before to get on Mr. Gray's schedule and had been politely, but firmly, denied. It was time for plan B—stalk then pounce. The stalking part was easy. She needed only to wait for him to show. The pouncing might prove difficult since that depended on when Mr. Gray arrived and who he had around him. She could easily sidestep a secretary, but security guards presented a different problem.

She'd chosen her spot well amongst the array of deep-backed chairs in the waiting area. She could keep an eye on the bank of elevators and the front doors within the building's glass walls.

Damn, it's cold. Cassidy shivered. Across the street, the coffee house churned out customers. She would kill for a cup of hot coffee, or a blanket, or even a pair of socks, but she couldn't leave her post and risk missing her target.

Cassidy paced around the waiting area for the third time. She stretched and rehearsed the questions she planned to ask about the club. Even in her head, her voice cracked.

Relax, he's just a man. But not every man had the money and power of Alexander Gray.

Speaking of power, what if the Knights were right? What if Gray and his company were part of this Shadow Clan thing? If there was some secret war going on, she didn't want to get caught in the middle.

Carjacking and kidnapping aside, she'd grown fond of the Knights, but she didn't believe they'd given her the whole story. Even though she'd witnessed some crazy stuff both on the bridge and in her own backyard, she still found everything hard to swallow.

A chill shook her and her teeth chattered. *This is ridiculous. I need to move again.*

She walked around the small waiting area to get her blood moving and stared at the Dali painting for the third time. She liked his art, but after the second inspection of melted furniture and bent clocks, it lost its appeal. Next to the painting, a press release announced Daegon Gray's purchase of Seagren Chemical and how adding the agricultural giant to the existing corporate portfolio excited Alexander Gray.

Huh. How exciting can fertilizer and insulation be? She blew on her frozen fingers and rubbed her hands together. *Come on, Gray, where the hell are you?*

Mr. Gray strode out of the elevator and around the corner, heading for the main doors. *He's been here all along.* She straightened her suit and tucked a stray lock of hair behind her ear. *Only two lackeys and they're walking behind him. Time for the frontal assault.*

Folder in hand, she hustled to beat him to the door.

"Mr. Gray!" Cassidy shouted above the bustle. "Mr. Gray."

Alexander Gray did not take note, but the closest guardian put out a restraining arm to keep her at bay.

Amateur. She may not have been in the reporting business long, but even she knew how to avoid "the arm." She lunged, reached for the door handle just ahead of Alexander Gray. His warm fingers closed over her popsicles and sent a strong emotional jolt up her arm. Cassidy tried to pull away, but he refused to let go.

Furious brown eyes turned toward her as a wave of malevolence hit. Her hope for an interview wilted under that hateful stare, but in a flash it was gone, replaced by a gentler mien.

Whoa.

"I am sorry, Miss?" He unleashed his world famous smile.

"Sin...Sinclair, Mr. Gray. Cassidy Sinclair, with the Weekly." She reversed her grip and shook his hand, pumped it twice with purpose as her father had taught her.

"My goodness, Ms. Sinclair, your hand is an ice cube. How long have you been waiting down here?" His smooth baritone soothed her jangled nerves and calmed her down. She breathed easier and her heart rate slowed its sprint. *What was I worried about? He seems like a normal guy.*

"A little while, sir. Would you mind answering a couple of questions?"

Mr. Gray's two associates stepped between them, but he refused to release her hand. When he shifted his eyes, the men backed off.

Beat it, boys.

His heat stole into her, worked its way up her chilled arm, and made her skin tingle as the warmth returned. She didn't want him to let go.

"Not at all. In fact, I was just going to indulge in a cup of coffee. Would you care to join me?"

Cassidy nodded. *Awesome.*

Gray ordered his men to stay put and escorted her across the street.

෫෦෬

"Put these on the corporate tab, please..." Alexander read the cashier's name tag and winked, "Glenda. Thanks, sweetheart." The joyful barista couldn't take her big, doe eyes from his and fumbled with the keys on the register. Hiding his impatience, Alexander nodded and carried the drinks to the table the young reporter had chosen.

What was her name? Eh, it did not matter.

She was an odd one, though. Pretty. He detected a hidden strength when he touched her hand. Curious, he wanted to find out more.

Cups in hand, he wove among the tables to the one in the back. "Sorry that took so long, Ms.—"

"Please, call me Cassidy, and it's no problem." Cassidy wrapped her hands around the steaming cup.

"I hope you like the special blend." Alexander sipped first and suppressed a shudder as he choked down the nasty brew. He despised coffee, but jumped on the opportunity to get the girl into a less threatening setting. Taking this reporter out of the proverbial lion's den would help her yield her secrets. "Daegon Gray owns a number of coffee plantations in Colombia. We ship our brand to all our companies throughout the world."

Cassidy took her first sip.

"What do you think?"

"It's very good."

He lifted his cup in salute and forced down another bitter mouthful. "So, you have questions for me?"

Cassidy jumped and grabbed her pen. "Oh, um, yes, I do." Hand poised, she met his gaze.

Through those bright, blue windows, Alexander peered directly into Cassidy's soul. Even without the enhancement of shadow magic, he could tell this woman had seen her share of pain. It had left its indelible print upon her psyche. Nevertheless there was a resilience there, a strength of spirit he rarely encountered anymore.

As he invaded her mind, her face went slack.

Like an awl, he gouged his way through layers of experience, down to her earliest memories, and though his intrusion only lasted a few seconds, he extracted a lifetime of information.

He preferred to work his way out from the first day, fast-forwarding through the lives of his victims. The reporter's oldest memories had devolved

into emotion more than remembered fact, colored by retelling and the per-
ceptions of the people involved through the years. He got the impression of a
glorious childhood filled with wonder, support and love.

Disgusting. While he did not relive each and every remembered moment,
he gleaned a general sense of her personality. The memories of her father were
the worst—attending her swim meets, laughter, big hugs next to the pool.

They made him want to retch.

Where is that pain? He recognized its mark, knew it was there. Did he miss
it? No. There was no sign in her early days. He needed to search her current
memories. They were more distinct, easier to follow.

Here. Poor dear. And St. Matthew's, how fortuitous. Wait, what is this?
Alexander schooled his features, putting a damper on his emotions. He
grabbed the edge of the Formica table and dug his fingers into its underside.
Brutally, he ripped his consciousness out of her mind, planting the seeds of
an excruciating headache and the strong sense of being violated, though she
would never know of his transgression.

*The Knight of Flame lives. She has seen him. Helped him. Felt a fondness for
him and his fellows. I failed. Father was right to doubt me.* The thought burned.

No. Control slipping, Alexander called upon centuries of magical disci-
pline to ease his apoplectic mind. *Father was not right. So the Knight lives. I
can fix that.*

This woman was the key. Once he destroyed the Knight of Flame, he
would dine on her soul.

As he discarded her memories, he refocused on the woman seated across
from him.

"Ms. Sinclair?" He jiggled her arm. "Ms. Sinclair, are you alright?"

With a start, Cassidy broke the trance. Wincing, she raised her hand to her
head and grimaced.

Yes, the pain. Consider that a taste of things to come.

"Ahhh." Cassidy mumbled, "What happened?"

"What do you mean?" Alexander asked, feigning concern. "You were in the
middle of asking me a question when you grabbed your head."

"Oh god, it hurts." She dug her fingertips into her temples. "I feel like someone stabbed my brain."

"I am so sorry, Ms. Sinclair, but I need to get back to work." Alexander
stood. "My driver can take you home or to the hospital or get you an aspirin
perhaps?"

"No, I'll...ugh, I'll be fine in a couple of minutes."

"Speaking of hospitals...would you do me the honor of accompanying me
to the ribbon cutting ceremony at St. Matthew's this Friday?"

"St. Matthew's? I don—"

"Splendid. My assistant will get your address from your employer and I'll send a car for you at 8:30. I do hope you feel better."

Alexander left the shop wearing a twisted, confident grin.

Chapter 16

Fɪʀsᴛ ᴛʜɪɴɢ ɪɴ ᴛʜᴇ ᴍᴏʀɴɪɴɢ, Dᴇᴠ ᴛᴏʟᴅ Wʀᴇɴ ᴀʙᴏᴜᴛ Sᴛɪʟʟᴍᴀɴ's ᴏʀᴅᴇʀ ᴛᴏ ID Alexander Gray and she flipped, charged off to have her own confab with the Man. It didn't go her way and she fumed at having to drive Dev's broken ass into town to, maybe, catch a glimpse of this guy.

Dev wasn't too happy about it either. Riding bitch in her pink Caprice wasn't his idea of a good time. He wanted to take his Harley, but Wren insisted on her car, and he was in no shape to argue.

"You are in no condition to be out and about," Wren said.

"I know…I know." Dev frowned at his resident nag. She was many other things too, but that title fit best this morning.

"You can barely move."

Count to ten. Chill. It was true, but that didn't mean Dev wanted to hear it driven into his skull. Yes, he overdid it last night. Yes, his body scolded him mercilessly this morning. Yes, he freakin' hurt. *Shut up and drive.*

"And all the stupid walking around last night with Magnus." She smacked the steering wheel. "I'll deal with him later."

Heh heh. Poor bastard.

"Oh, and put up your hood. The police are still looking for you and you don't need to get turned in by some good Samaritan."

She dressed him this morning in jeans and a black hoodie with the swooping emblem of Magnus's band, Light's Keen Edge, emblazoned on the back. He made sure to strap on his armor underneath first. He wouldn't make that mistake again.

"Over there, behind the truck." Dev nodded at a parking space down the street from the Daegon Gray building behind a white truck with "Devonshire Catering" painted on the side in big red lettering. It was the perfect spot to wait.

Yeah. Wait. It's not like his body was up to anything else. Hell, it had taken all his energy just to port in to his apartment, slither down the stair rail with Wren supporting him and hobble into the car. He knew he shouldn't be out, but orders were orders. Actually, he needed to see Gray for himself and would have made the case for the recon trip even if Stillman had not.

Wren fought him, even after her conversation with the boss. In the end, though, after he threw out her buzz words like "duty" and "honor" she relented.

The man he fought in the club was Alexander Gray. He knew it. As soon as Stillman said that name in the Hall of Ages, he felt the truth of it in his bones. Still, he had to be sure.

Dev yawned like a grizzly. "Ooh, coffee." He spied the coffee shop across the street. "How 'bout a nice white mocha on me?"

Wren pursed her lips and placed her hands on her hips.

"What? I'm just going to sit here and watch." He sank into the seat and adopted a pathetic half-smile. "What trouble could I possibly get in to?"

"Dev…"

"I know." He would have raised his arm in surrender, but that simple move required too much energy.

"Do you have any money on you?" Wren asked.

"I, uh, left my wallet in my other pants?"

"Whatever. You owe me." She rolled the window down like he was a puppy that needed air and got out of the car.

"Make it a large, please." Dev shouted. "Oh and get me a blueberry scone too. Thanks!"

The shouting sapped his energy. He needed to keep his eyes open, but they grew heavy. He didn't want to succumb to the dark dreams of sleep, but he was losing that battle.

Hey. This was an older model princess car. He checked the dash. *Score. Cigarette lighter.* He pushed it in and yanked it out when it popped. The heat from the spiraled coils felt great as he held it up to his face and, before it cooled, he placed it on his tongue.

The hot wires sizzled, sent a jolt of fire down his gullet, giving him the boost to fight off sleep's minions. He did it again…and again…like chewing peppermints, while he waited for Wren to return with the caffeine.

A familiar voice plucked the strings at the fringe of his hearing.

Cassidy.

He could never mistake her voice. *What's she doing here?*

Cassidy's voice got stronger, closer. He sucked on the lighter and scoped out the coffee shop. *Come on, Wren. What the hell. How long does it take? Why is Cassidy giggling?*

Dressed to the nines, Cassidy approached the shop with a man at her side. When they got close to the door, he sped up and opened it with a flourish. She smiled at him as she entered.

No way. That wasn't him, *was it? Why would she be with him?*

He spat out the lighter. Anger fired across his heart. Energy flooded into his limbs. He had to move, had to get out of the confines of this car.

Grabbing the lighter off the floor, he slammed it into the socket to power up again. The car door handle cracked, but held firm as he swung the door open. After one last hit of the heat, he fell out to the curb. If he could get to the catering truck, he'd pull himself up. From there it was a straight line to the coffee shop.

On his hands, he dragged himself around to the front bumper and slid up the hood on his left shoulder. Pushing with his fractured legs was not smart, but the only way he knew to get up. He held his breath and shoved. A wall of pain crashed down, but he managed to get to his feet.

It was him. Had to be. She should not be with that…thing.

Snarling, the corner of his mouth lifted uncontrollably under the strain. He leaned forward, caught the back of the truck and pulled himself over.

Where is Wren? Shit. Did Gray have her too? He hung his head, waited for a bout of nausea to pass, and imagined the Shadow ripping Wren and Cassidy to bits.

Have to see the shop. He rocked his shoulders, and rolled his body across the truck's back doors so he could lean over to see the coffee shop door.

What's happening in there? No sirens. No screams. No explosions. People walking out with coffee cups in their hands.

"Hey, man." A harsh, reedy voice called to Dev. "What are you doing to my truck?"

Dev turned. A wiry man in blue coveralls struggled toward him under the weight of a chafing dish. His Einstein hairdo added a couple inches, but he stood much shorter than Dev.

"Get off my truck, dirtbag."

Heat rippled from the smoldering Sterno canister under the dish where a small flame burned. Dev called and it responded, feeding him a trickle of energy.

"Back off, Zippy," Dev said, "I'll be done in a minute."

The little man set the dish in the grass off to the side and swaggered over.

This isn't going to end well.

"You got two options." The little guy tried to look fierce, but barely managed put out. "One, I t—" He squinted. "Do I know you?"

Damn.

"Nope."

"I know I seen you somewhere."

As Dev shook his head, his hood fell back. With his bald head on display, he watched the light bulb go on behind the guy's eyes.

"Hey," the caterer's eyes grew big, "you're that guy on the news." His volume grew with each word. "The one that killed them rich folks at the club." He jumped up and down and waved his arms.

Dev called the small flame, but there was more Sterno in there than he thought and it roared into his system. The borrowed strength raced to his limbs, pushed his wounds to the background like the night before. He'd pay for it later, but that didn't matter right now.

He clamped his hands over the agitated man's mouth and pulled him close. "Be quiet if you want to live," Dev whispered in the guy's ear, pumping in as much Dirty Harry menace as he could muster. "Nod if you understand me."

The smaller man nodded vigorously.

"Good. Keep still."

The boost from the small flame expended, Dev held onto the caterer as much for his own support as it was to keep him quiet. Luckily, the caterer didn't know that.

Damn, where is that girl? What's going on in there? Is Cassidy okay?

Dev ventured another peek at the coffee house. No change. Distracted, his grip loosened. The small man called Dev's bluff and fought for his freedom. Dev barely managed to hold on. In the struggle, he lost his balance and fell on top of the little guy.

"G'off, m—" The little guy wheezed. "C'nt bre—Help. Heeeeeelp."

Dev had to stop the pathetic screams before they drew attention. Hands trapped beneath the smaller man, he smashed his head into the caterer's face.

The little guy sucked air in with a whistle and screamed louder. "Heeeeeelp."

"Stop it." Dev bashed him in the nose. Blood gushed everywhere, coating the man and Dev in its crimson wash. And still he screamed.

Shut up. Dev butted him again. *Shut up.* And again. And again. And again.

Two cups of coffee hit the pavement. Arms snaked under his pits and hoisted him back. The body under him was still, head cocked to the side. Blood flowed from his ruined face.

"Dev," Wren's voice held equal parts concern, anger, and disappointment. "You promised." She leaned him against the car hood and bent to examine the unconscious man.

"He's breathing." She pulled her cell phone from her back pocket. "Barely."

"Who are you calling?"

Wren ignored the question, punched in three numbers and waited for an answer.

"We have to go," Dev said.

She held up one finger. "Um, yes, hi. There has been an accident and we need an ambulance outside the Daegon Gray building in Tampa." Without further explanation, she hung up and helped Dev back into the car. Poised, as always, she walked around the back of the car and got in.

People started to notice that something was happening and ambled over. As they got a look at the man on the ground, they shot frightened glances at Wren and Dev then quickly uncorked their cell phones.

Wren eased the car through the building crowd. Once clear, she hit the gas, but jammed on the brakes to avoid a man in a dark suit who walked out in front of them. He spun on the offending vehicle, fists braced on the hood of the car, face carved with deep lines of hatred. Mouth open to shout, his eyes grew wide when he locked stares with Dev.

I knew it.

"Run him over." Dev shouted. "That's Alexander Gray. It was him at the club. I'm sure of it."

"I can't do that."

"He killed all those people at the club! Take him out."

"No."

Wren punched it, tried to steer around Gray, but still knocked him off his feet. From his side-view mirror, Dev watched people run to the fallen man's aid. *If they only knew they were helping a murderer...*

Wren barreled through multiple intersections without regard to the color of the stop lights. Tires screeched. Cars swerved or stopped. When they were safely out of the downtown area, she slowed to a more legal speed.

"Nice driving." *She should have run him over. Ended this before it got too out of hand.* "The cops are probably after us already. They tend to frown on the whole running over corporate executives thing."

"It's over, Dev."

"I know." Dev checked the mirror, intentionally misinterpreting her meaning. "We got out of there quickly. Good job."

"You know what I mean."

Yeah. I do. Maybe Stillman is right. Maybe I am a problem. I could have killed that little guy. He slammed his head against the headrest and closed his eyes.

Chapter 17

ALEXANDER STORMED THROUGH THE WAITING ROOM OUTSIDE HIS OFFICE. *The Knight of Flame was here. I could have had him.* A sizzling glare locked the new secretary in her seat before she had a chance to move. He slammed the door behind him, threw his jacket on the lounge chair in the corner and smacked both palms into the thick glass of the window. Head lowered, heart pounding, breath hissing in and out, Alexander raged.

The audacity, coming here.

He spun back to the room and blasted the chair with a stream of black shadows that stripped the varnish and ate the wood, reducing it to a pile of dust and splinters.

Gothrodul's laughter intruded upon his mind. *You are behaving like a child. Get a hold of yourself, Lord of Shadow.*

Lord of Shadow. The title calmed him slightly, but the rage burned inside. He lowered his arm, took a deep breath and willed his body to relax.

There. Isn't that better?

Do not mock me, lizard. Alexander said, in no mood for Gothrodul's sarcasm or condescending wit. *Where are you?*

Elsewhere, but I heard your mental screams.

Blast. He hated to show weakness in front of anyone—his father, brothers and especially his underlings. He must be strong, flawless, and, above all, powerful.

The Knight of Flame still lives.

Silence.

Alexander shielded his thoughts. Either Gothrodul was mastering his own twisted emotions, or he already knew about the Knight.

Gothrodul?

A loud knock interrupted his chain of doubt.

"Be gone." Alexander shouted.

"But, sir, the men from Deep Services are here." The muffled voice of his temporary secretary seeped under the door.

"Right. Send them in." Alexander unlocked the bottom drawer of his desk and removed a twelve-by-twelve wooden box. Parts of the slender walls had burned away, revealing the play of lightning streaks against the dark, curved surface of a shadow orb.

The doorknob jangled.

"Sir, the door is locked."

"Use your key!" Alexander blasted back and tucked the box under his arm. *Humans—what a monumental waste.*

The door opened and the temp guided the brothers in.

Alexander handed the box to the grubby-handed elder brother. From the sight of them—slumped shoulders, red, puffy eyes, mysterious dark smudges on their arms, cheeks and brown coveralls—and their offensive odor, the boys had spent the night doing their homework.

At least somebody takes me seriously.

"You was right, suh." The elder brother's voice sounded tired, weak. "There's all kinds a things crawlin' 'round down there." He rubbed a greasy hand across his bald pate. "We dropped more bait, but they ate it up like corn bread."

The younger brother nodded.

"We ain't never seen nothin' like it."

Thargen delivered as promised. Alexander read the elder brother's name tag.

"Randall, my friend, that box I just gave you contains the future. A vermin free future."

The brothers blinked at him.

"That box contains the new pesticide I mentioned. It contains one treatment only, and I need you to set it up in the sewer junction below St. Matthew's hospital. Tonight. The mayor requested this himself." He paused to let the lie sink in. "He said St. Matthew's is having a huge problem and wants it taken care of it before the ceremony tomorrow."

The brothers nodded. Killing small creatures in the sewers was something they could understand.

"I knew I could count on you two."

"Uh, suh?" Randall spoke up. "The answer is forty eight hours. It will take us a straight forty eight hours to bait the sewers."

Two days.

"Very good. I will collect the supplies. Be ready for my call."

A red-faced, older man in a tight brown suit and power tie charged through the doorway with Alexander's apologetic assistant in tow. Nudging his way between the brothers, he brandished a finger at his quarry as he brushed down his sparse white hair.

"Gray!"

"Mr. Tomasin. What can I do for the ex-CEO of Seagren Chemical?" The promise of death to come had lightened Alexander's mood, so instead of filleting this cretin on the spot, he viewed his hostility as comical.

Security guards emerged from the stairwell and flanked the blustering executive, but Alexander waved them off. He didn't need their muscle to deal with this situation.

"Why have you changed all my shipping orders, Gray?"

"*Your* shipping orders?"

The executive pushed into Alexander's personal space, met him nose to chin.

"Don't play coy with me, Gray. You've ground my business to a halt."

"You mean my business, Mr. Tomasin?"

Tomasin sputtered. A drop of spit struck Alexander on the cheek.

While his mood may have changed, he had his limits.

"The only reason I bought your excrement-producing company was for its global transportation system." Alexander poked the man in the chest hard enough to back him up. "I rerouted everything in support of another project."

"We are losing money."

"Not to worry, Mr. Tomasin. Your problems will be solved by tomorrow." Alexander laid a companionable hand on his shoulder and turned him toward the elevators. "Guaranteed." A gentle nudge in the right direction and he stumbled out the door.

There's a new entrée on the menu. Alexander thought to his ever-present companion.

Let me guess, Gothrodul replied, *fat executive.*

Take him and his family. Destroy the house. Leave nothing.

Mmmm. Sounds like fun.

Chapter 18

THE HEADACHE TO END ALL HEADACHES HAD CEASED KILLING CASSIDY AN HOUR earlier. She'd taken a cab home from the coffee shop, too embarrassed to take Mr. Gray up on the offer to have his driver take her home. She would have driven herself, but the sun hit her eyes like shards of glass. When she got home, she popped a couple of the special yellow pills she scored after her root canal, and slunk into bed with a cold rag over her eyes. The epic-fail interview with Alexander Gray replayed in her mind and kept her awake.

Nothing like that had ever happened to her before. One minute she opened her mouth to ask a question and the next, her head exploded. Gray must have thought her an idiot. He seemed nice though. Handsome. Deep, silken voice. Smooth, gentle hands. The medication took hold and she drifted to sleep.

Cassidy awoke pain free, but with a sick feeling in the pit of her stomach, like when she snuck out of the house to go skinny-dipping with her boyfriend and thought her dad found out. She also felt grimy, unclean. A shower wouldn't cut it, not this time. She needed a good long soak to wash the weird ick from her mind and body. The pool called to her.

Cassidy pulled on her favorite suit, grabbed a towel and dove into the deep end.

Swimming, wading, floating, diving, it didn't matter so long as she became one with the water. As a kid, her parents teased her about being a mermaid, descended from a long line of Irish mermaids on her mother's side of the family. During the summer, she even took her meals at the pool's edge while her parents sat on the patio.

The water was the answer to all her problems. Whenever she struggled with one of life's challenges, she found somewhere to dive in. Weightless and graceful, the realm of water seemed like a world away from the gravitational pull of a young woman's mundane problems.

Its lilting movement fascinated her, fueled her imagination. As a child, she pretended each drop was a separate little entity, and imbued it with emotions and dreams and goals until she wasn't swimming alone, but with a pool full of watery friends. She'd tried explaining her thoughts to Amy several times while they swam together, but it never panned out. Her daughter simply giggled and looked at Cassidy as if she had tried to sing *Raindrops Keep Falling on My Head* in dolphin.

Oh, Amy, I miss you.

It took a while, but the odd taint washed off. Relaxed, she closed her eyes, arms straight out at her sides, and floated.

He invited me to the ceremony. The thought disrupted her quiet time and she sank like a stone. *That's tomorrow morning.* While dealing with the pain, she had buried the fact away, but now it floated to the surface.

Mr. Gray had asked her to accompany him to the dedication of the new hospital wing. Excitement rippled through her.

The press passes had all been distributed weeks ago. *No one from my Podunk newspaper has been invited and now here I am, not only invited, but accompanying the guest of honor himself.*

Wait until she told her editor. She'd leave this last bit of news for when she dropped the bomb on not getting the other stories. It would more than make up for it.

Cassidy walked up the pool steps and grabbed her towel. Drying off was a melancholy event. It signaled the end of her sanctuary and return to the real world. This time she had something to look forward to.

On the patio, she bent over and dried her hair with the towel. As the ends of the towel swished and swayed, she looked at the scorch marks on the tile from the recent fire. An image of the Knight of Flame flashed across her thoughts and sparked a warm prickling sensation that percolated inside her.

I wonder how he's doing.

Chapter 19

THE MAN BEHIND THE UNCLUTTERED OAK DESK CROSSED HIS ARMS AND STARED AT Wren, brown eyes weary. Along with the positive ID of Alexander Gray, she reported the incident outside the coffee house. After giving her unbiased account, Stillman's crestfallen expression told her that while he knew what she came to say, he had still held out hope.

"One more chance, sir, please. He can control it." She wanted him to believe her, to give Dev yet another chance. *But for what? So he can kill an innocent next time?*

Stillman shook his head.

She'd made the only decision she could have. While not an elemental knight, she was still a member of the Order and, as such, had a duty to perform. Dev had stepped over the line...again. If she hadn't stopped him, he would have killed that man outside the coffee shop. And the worst part...he didn't even realize he was doing it.

I failed him.

Tears filled her eyes. The figures in the tapestry behind Stillman blurred. The normally distinct figures of Merlin, Arthur and his mounted knights smeared together in a riot of brilliant colors against the stark white fortress backdrop.

Dev's going to hate me.

Wren swallowed the sobs that threatened to topple her composure. Quiet tears were okay, maybe even expected, but losing herself to a full-blown emotional meltdown in front of her superior officer was not acceptable.

"Child." Stillman's deep, gentle voice filled her ears. "This violence has been building in the Knight of Flame for a long time." He stood and walked around to the front of his desk.

What will Dev think of me?

He clasped her shoulders. "Your courage and honor in doing what is best for the Order is commendable."

Is this really the best thing for the Order?

Wren remained at attention—head back, shoulders straight, arms locked at her side.

"What happens now, sir?"

Stillman sighed and for the first time that she had witnessed, for all she knew the first time ever, he let his shoulders slump, allowed the years to bow his resolve.

"What indeed." Stillman smiled wistfully and leaned back on the desk.

Footsteps sounded outside the doorway. Stillman stood, squared himself, and once again assumed the too-heavy mantle of leadership.

"Come."

Magnus nodded to Wren and snapped to attention in front of the Precept. "You wished to see me, sir?"

Stillman moved back behind his desk, inserting a layer of formality between them. "Did the sample from the club yield anything useful?"

"Cyndralla detected the resonance of exceptionally strong shadow magic. Unfortunately, without the source, she could not determine its purpose," Magnus reported.

"I expected as much. Obviously, we need more to go on. At least we can put a name to our enemy."

"Alexander Gray," Wren said. The name jarred loose a memory. "Cassidy mentioned something about a hospital dedication that he would be attending in the morning. Maybe we can learn something there."

Stillman shifted his weight, his expression thoughtful. "I want the two of you to check it out in the morn—"

"Check what out?" Dev hobbled through the open door. "I want in." He came to rest beside Magnus and straightened up with a wince.

Oh, my dear Knight, I'm so sorry.

"Not this time," Stillman said.

Dev glared at his commanding officer. "But I ca—"

Stillman met Dev's glare with compassion until the Knight of Flame looked away. "You all have your orders. Dismissed." He turned, walked to the other side of the long room and made a big production of inspecting the state of the blades on the wall next to the entrance to his personal library.

"What's going on?" Dev asked. He glanced at Wren, but she couldn't meet his gaze. Head down for fear he would see the tracks down her cheeks, she walked from the room. She wanted to bolt, almost gave in to her selfish desire to get away, but held to her dignity. Two steps beyond the doorway, free from prying eyes, she ran.

Stillman's voice carried down the hall. "Magnus, a minute if you please."

She knew what that was about. Magnus would fight for his brother, try to talk Stillman into giving Dev another chance, but it was futile. Dev was screwed and it was her fault. She had betrayed him.

A fresh torrent of tears flowed as she ran.

Dev called out to her, but she ignored him.

What have I done?

Her flight took her deeper into the Cradle, to her favorite room in the place. Alone and miserable in the front row of the theater, she curled into

tight ball and let her emotions run free. In her grief and self-loathing, she
returned to the same question.

What will happen to Dev?

ဆၺၺၖ

Head low, elbows resting on his knees, Dev sat on the edge of his stone
bench in a gloom tinted by the reddish glow from the lava trough next to the
forge. Stillman ordered him to stay put. Magnus couldn't be found. He'd lost
a fight to some wack-job in a bad suit. Oh, and he almost killed a man earlier
because the guy recognized him. All in all, things could be better.

Magnus warned him the other night, but he blew it off and acted like
everything was normal.

*Okay, maybe I was a bit overzealous with the caterer, but I wouldn't have
killed him.*

He wanted to believe that he would have stopped, but feared that if Wren
hadn't shown up when she did, he would have smashed the guy's head into
road pizza.

Ordered to await the summons in my room. What am I, ten?

He scrubbed his hands over the stubble growing across his skull, blew out
an anxious breath and got to his feet.

*What are they going to do? Make me scrub the floor, do the laundry, write on
the wall of the Womb 'I will not kick ass for no reason' like a million times? What?*

He roamed the twenty steps from wall to wall, repeatedly. The healing
process was almost complete. His upper body felt stiff, but strong. His legs
still ached, though, and he walked with a heavy limp favoring his left side. He
raised his arms over his head and stretched, snapping a few vertebrae back
into alignment. Twist right. *Crackle.* Twist left. *Pop. Ugh. I'm getting old.*

Standing in front of the forge, he traced the precise edges of the anvil's face
and the curve of its horn. The massive structure huddled on top of a flat shelf
Magnus coaxed out of the stone floor. A large square trough made out of the
same ultra-hard material as the anvil merged with the wall on its left. Heat
and orange light rose from the circular well in its base.

Blacksmith's tools lay on benches, in bins, and in specific holders along the
walls. Tongs, clamps and hammers of all sizes predominant among them. He
brushed his fingers over them, recalling the different weapons and armor he'd
created over his many years of crafting.

Finishing the tour, right hand lingering on the head of his four-pound
cross-peen hammer, his chest felt tight.

*What the hell am I doing? I just said goodbye to my freakin' tools. I'm going
crazy and it's only been a few hours.*

Big Magnus filled the doorway, solemn and quiet. Dressed in his Knight of
Earth finery—dark brown surcoat over thin, flexible Quinsteele hauberk that

hung to his knees, full-length tan cloak trimmed in the color of rich loam, and high-gloss, sturdy black boots. The handle of his elemental axe jutted over his right shoulder.

"Hey, man, what's the word?" Dev asked.

"The Order has convened in the Womb," Magnus intoned, eyes staring straight ahead, back and shoulders rigid. "I am to escort you there."

Dev licked his lips. This was big. Magnus only did the whole knight-in-armor thing for official occasions.

"Um, okay." Dev scrambled for a clean white shirt. It wouldn't do for him to enter the Womb half-naked.

"What's up?" As they walked down the hall, Dev finished buttoning his shirt. Magnus kept the pace slow so the injured Knight could keep up. The tempo of his heartbeat increased the closer they got to the Womb until, at the entrance to the command center of the Knights Elementalis, it thumped heavily against his ribcage. The Womb was open to all members of the Order at any time, but only official functions like new investitures or disciplinary hearings required the formality of regal dress.

Stillman stood at the head of a horseshoe-shaped table made of smoky quartz. Cyndralla and Dronor, decked out in their knightly regalia—white for Cyndralla, blue for Dronor—had already assumed their appointed positions to Stillman's left. To his right, Magnus's and Dev's seats remained vacant.

The magnificence of the Womb never failed to impress the Knight of Flame. Clear, luminous crystal made up the floor and ceiling of the circular room. The walls, black marble inlaid with veins of copper, silver and gold glittered in the perpetual light that prevented the existence of shadows.

Magnus marched Dev to the opening of the table then stood by his seat at Stillman's right hand.

Dev stared at a miniature model of the Earth that spun on its axis in the open space between the table's legs. Mountains stood out in variegated relief while invisible winds dictated the movements of dense cloud pockets. Four pinpricks of different colored lights—red, blue, brown, white—a different color for each Knight, clustered around a spot in central Wales.

Stillman, dressed in black surcoat, and cloak trimmed in jet-black fur, raised his hand and the globe floated up to the ceiling, so as not to obstruct anyone's vision. He cleared his throat.

"This official conclave of the Order Knights Elementalis has been called to address the flagrant aggression and disregard for the safety of those we protect by Develor Quinteele, the sixth Knight of Flame." With a rustle of heavy fabric, he flapped his cape behind him and sat down.

The other Knights followed suit.

A chill washed over Dev's skin at the formal opening, but the cold sensation was quickly banished by a flash of heat as his element stirred.

"Due to repeated, uncontrolled, violent outbursts as witnessed by members of this Order, you, Develor Quinteele, are hereby re—"

"This is ridiculous." The volume of Dev's voice increased with each word. "Repeated. Uncontrolled. Outbursts."

Dronor leaned forward, lent his swarthy voice to the mix. "Don't forget violent."

Magnus pinned the Spaniard back into his seat with a glare.

Dev growled at Dronor, who smiled in return.

"Granted, there have been some fights lately," Dev said, "But none out of control."

"The fights were not out of control, you were," Wren spoke up from the doorway. All heads turned in her direction.

Her words felt like a slap in the face. "You too?" Dev asked.

Against the other Knights, Dev would argue until his throat dried up and his tongue fell out, but Wren knew the truth, had seen everything. Even so, he never expected this.

The fight in him slithered away to die. *I'm doomed.*

Stillman addressed Wren. "I told you not to come." His tone was low and charged with a father's desire to spare his child pain.

"I had to, sir, and will present myself for disciplinary action when this meeting has concluded."

"As you will."

"Dev," Wren spoke to him as if he were the only person in the room, "I'm sorry, but you've left me no choice."

She recounted each and every hairy moment. From the shoving match in the express line at the supermarket, to the daily fights in the shipyards, to the near murder outside Daegon Gray this morning, Wren told them all with a matter-of-fact, news-anchor worthy delivery.

As she covered the countless dates and facts, Dev surveyed the others. Magnus looked bored, but chuckled when she described how the old lady in the express line beat Dev off with her purse. Stillman looked sad and old, the weight of his responsibility sitting heavy. Cyndralla stared at Dev, her lavender eyes cool and calculating. Did she support him or not? He never could get a good read on her. And Dronor, that bastard, devoured every condemning word like it was covered in custard. Today was probably the best day of his damp life.

At the three hour mark, Stillman held up his hand. "I think that's enough. Wren, your report has been thorough and unclouded. Thank you."

Wren bowed, turned stiffly, and marched from the Womb.

Stillman stood. The sound of his chair scraping against the stone floor echoed in the silent chamber. "Develor Quinteele, the evidence presented is incontrovertible." Stillman looked at each of the Knights in turn, and waited for a nod.

Dronor nodded with short, energetic bursts.

No surprise there, but I could do without the face-splitting grin.

Cyndralla's sharp features softened as she looked at Dev, commiseration shining in her purple-hued eyes and sad smile. She, too, nodded.

Thanks, Cyndy.

Magnus took a long time, but eventually closed his eyes and lowered his head.

You didn't have a choice, brother.

Stillman took a deep breath. "Knight of Flame, you are hereby restricted to the halls of the Cradle until such time as you have shown significant control of yourself and your element."

"You can't be serious." The air left Dev's lungs as fire filled them. "Shadow is back."

With the formal proceeding over, the Knights stood. Magnus stepped toward Dev, but Stillman waved him off and came around the end of the table.

"If you please," the Precept addressed Dev's peers, "give us a few moments."

On his way to the door, Dronor turned to Dev. "You have been defeated. We'll take it from here."

You smug son of a bitch. I'll kick your...

Dev lunged at the Water Knight, but didn't get more than two feet before an invisible force rooted him to the spot.

Cyndralla. She caught him by surprise. He fought her spell, but her control was flawless.

"If we fight amongst ourselves, the forces of Shadow win." Cyndralla released Dev only after the Knight of Water had disappeared from sight. On her way out, she squeezed Dev's shoulder.

"We'll catch up later," Magnus assured Dev as he left.

Dev stared through the empty doorway to the rest of the Cradle.

"What would you have done had Cyndralla not stopped you?" Stillman asked, his voice casual and calm.

Good question.

Dev turned to his commander. "I would have tried to hurt him." Just thinking about Dronor's comment stoked the fire in his soul.

"I believe you." Stillman studied Dev, watching the heat ripple across his face.

"Sir, you need me." The thought of his fellow Knights fighting Gray without him sent his element racing through his veins. "I'm a warrior. I fight. It's who I am." Anger gripped his heart.

Stillman shook his head. "I disagree. You are so much more than a walking battle zone, Knight of Flame. I need you to understand that."

I'm in no mood for games, old man.

"What more is there to understand?" Dev's words came out hot. His hands ignited and he curled them into blazing yellow fists. "Do not speak to me in riddles. If you know something, spit it out." He stepped toward the Precept.

Unconcerned, Stillman hitched one leg up on the table and folded his hands in his lap. "Are you going to attack me now?"

The question hit Dev like a fire hose, extinguishing his internal blaze.

"What?" Dev's hands winked out as his mouth opened wide. "Sir, I—"

I lost it again. Over what?

Stillman waved off Dev's shock and the apology forming on his lips. "I will help you any way I can, Develor, but I cannot give you the answers."

"Can you at least give me the question?"

Stillman gave him a small smile. "My son, sometimes that's the hardest part to figure out. Think on it. We will talk again soon."

Chapter 20

ONE FINAL SPRITZ OF HAIR SPRAY AND HER LONG AUBURN HAIR LAY PERFECT. A light foundation with a hint of blush, and lip gloss applied just right... Cassidy stepped back from the vanity mirror in her bathroom and gave herself an approving smile. It wasn't every day she got invited to a major event by one of the most powerful men in Tampa, and she wanted to look her best.

Fifteen minutes. Will Mr. Gray come to the door? No, probably not. He has people for that. Or, will the car simply stay parked at the curb until I deign to appear?

Silly thoughts like that had flipped through her brain all morning. She applied a second layer of antiperspirant, against the heat she told herself, but knew deep down that she was coating herself against the beehive of nerves buzzing around in her stomach.

What am I so nervous about? Alexander Gray is just a man. I've been asked out before. So, really, there is nothing to be nervous about.

The doorbell chimed. She ran to the door, patted her clothes and hair one last time, took a deep breath and opened it. Mr. Gray stood on her doorstep, one hand in his pocket, his other poised to ring again.

"Good morning, Ms. Sinclair." Alexander's beguiling smile brightened her morning. "You look lovely. Are you ready?"

"Uhhh...yeah." Cassidy stammered, "Just...let me get my purse and notebook." She found it difficult to focus as she grabbed her bag and stepped outside. She turned to close the door, but stopped when Mr. Gray cleared his throat.

"It would be a shame to ruin your beautiful ensemble by showing up to the event barefoot, my dear."

She expected to hear a sneer or some other condescension embedded in his tone, but she detected nothing. For everyone else, she got a sense of the emotions behind their words, but not with Alexander Gray. Ever since she caught that unguarded view into his fury when they first met, his emotions seemed blank.

"Duh. I'll be right back." She raced into her room and slipped into the conservative, yet sexy, black heels. With a final glance in the mirror—*why am I blushing?*—she headed out the door.

The limo ride to the hospital seemed to be over in an instant. Mr. Gray spent the ride on his cell phone making sure all was in order for the ceremony. He mentioned something about a package being in place, but she lost interest in the conversation when the façade of St. Matthew's hove into view.

Elegant Spanish archways, porticos and old stone marked the turn of the century construction. It looked more like an upscale hotel than the oldest hospital in the south. Not big by modern standards, it towered over Cassidy's life like the Empire State Building. An overflow of news vans, taxis and limos spoiled the quaint image.

Her heart dropped into her stomach when Gray's living room on wheels drove under the great stone archway and glided to a halt opposite the red carpet that led to the front doors. She'd made that same drive two years ago under much different circumstances, and hadn't been back since.

Seeing the place up close, the memories popped into sharp focus. The dread that had governed her prior visit closed in upon her. She had to get out, get some fresh air. Hand trembling, she pulled on the handle, but the door didn't open. She pulled again, harder, with similar results.

Why won't you open? The limo's tight walls edged closer. *Can't breathe.*

The door slid open and a white-gloved hand reach in to her. She grabbed on and let it pull her to safety.

Out in the open, she sucked in the sweet taste of Tampa, filling her lungs with its hot moist flavor. With it came a renewed purpose.

I can do this. Get the story and get out.

Distant clouds threatened rain, but over St. Matthew's the sun beat down on the media horde outside the shade of the covered walkway. They lined the red carpet. Jostling, butting shoulders, inching forward, they vied for position to get a clean pic or to shout their questions. The big guys, well-known reporters and local royalty, waited inside for the man of the hour to arrive and the tour to start.

"Come, my dear," Alexander offered his arm and led her through the gauntlet accompanied by the digital *chchk* of hundreds of cameras. Cassidy marched by Alexander's side, eyes downcast, matching her step to his.

"Smile and wave."

Not wanting to disappoint him or seem unappreciative, she painted on a broad smile, held her head high, and waved to the crowd. She looked everywhere except at those doors. With each step, though, they got closer. Her resolved flaked around the edges and her steps faltered until she felt a tug from Mr. Gray that pulled her forward.

I'm okay. I need to do this.

The doors whispered open at their approach. A blast of cold air escaped the confines of the hospital and charged up her spine.

Aside from the people, the lobby looked identical to the frozen image in her mind. Same white marble floor and spoiled cream colored walls. Same low, black leather and metal chairs and tables. Same seasonal collection of silk flowers sprouting from faux onyx vases.

How dare this place not change!

Even the nurses seemed the same. Cassidy recognized the one behind the counter—stern face, uncaring eyes, hair flipped back, starched white uniform. A modern day Nurse Ratched. But she knew better, knew it was all a big act put on for the circus that invaded the head nurse's territory.

Alongside her host, Cassidy ignored the mumbled discussion that buzzed around her as the tour began, but maintained the presence of mind to respond with an inane nod or vapid smile when addressed directly. For the most part, she kept her head down and focused on the shoes of the person ahead of her, stopping and starting when they did.

No landmarks marred the linoleum, just one anonymous square after another. She could almost imagine herself walking through Home Depot or the mall. Almost. When she hit five hundred, she stopped counting.

What? Her empty stomach turned summersaults. *Did someone say second floor?* The shoes ahead of her climbed the stairs. She had to do the same.

A wave of grief hammered into Cassidy. *Oh God. I thought I could do this, thought I was past the worst.* She turned around, but Mr. Gray tightened his grip.

"Please, I need to go," Cassidy whispered, trying to peel back the fingers around her arm.

"No. Stay. It will be over soon and my driver will take you wherever you want to go."

"But…"

Mr. Gray faced her. Did she just imagine that? Did his eyes flash black?

"You WILL see this through."

The clamp on her bicep hurt, but she didn't want to make a scene and prolong her time in this awful place, so she stopped struggling and let herself be guided through the halls.

Maybe they won't tour the whole floor. Maybe the new area is just outside the stairwell.

At the top of the stairs, Cassidy risked a glance. The Mayor walked ahead of her, talking over his shoulder to Mr. Gray who listened and nodded. She realized it was the Mayor's sycophantic mumbles she'd tried to tune out for the whole tour. *Figures.*

"Ah, Stephen," Mr. Gray spoke up, "Allow me to introduce the lovely Ms. Cassidy Sinclair. She works for the Weekly."

"Pleased to meet you, Ms. Sinclair." Mayor Stephen Green aimed his best vote-getting smile at Cassidy and stuck out his hand. "I'm a big fan of your publication."

She shook his hand and felt his lie through the contact. "Likewise, Mr. Mayor."

Obligatory action completed, he turned back to Mr. Gray. "Alexander, I've been meaning to…"

The Mayor's words drifted into the background clutter.

Down the hall, beyond the Mayor's bobbing head, she hoped to see some sort of temporary seating area, a place for the speeches and the blue ribbon cutting. But there was nothing like that, only walls and halls…five of them. Eyes down again, aimed at the Mayor's feet, she named each one as they passed its entryway and prayed the procession would stop before she called the fourth.

Radiology. Oncology. The names rattled off the top of her head without hesitation.

Cardiology. Cassidy felt cold, freezing, and so alone. Her entire being wanted to stop, turn around and sprint in the other direction, but Gray drove her forward with the rest of the media herd.

The Mayor stopped midway to the next hall. Cassidy had to put on the brakes or end up in his back pocket. Mr. Gray released the vice-grip that held her in thrall to clasp hands with Hernst Borgash, the Director of St. Matthew's, who promised that the ceremony wouldn't be disturbed.

Rubbing some feeling back into her arm, she spied the makeshift presentation area set up by the last wing. Neat rows of multi-colored plastic chairs and a portable lectern occupied all the available space in the north end juncture. Above the new wing, a freshly painted sign in large blue letters named it Neurology. Below that, a large blue ribbon with a giant bow stretched across the entranceway.

Platitudes exchanged, the men humphed, grumphed, patted each other on the back and moved on.

Don't look. Walk past. Ignore it.

Cassidy listened to her own advice. Head down, she followed the Mayor until the linoleum pattern to her right opened into a darkened hallway. Her feet quit moving and she raised her head.

Blah-gray doors stood silent sentinels at the end of the short hall. Above them "BURN —NIT" proclaimed the purpose of the room beyond in faded, blood-red letters. The "U" had lost its grip and fallen away from its brothers and sisters.

Please…no.

In the crowd, she focused on the blue pinstripe down the back of the Mayor's jacket while he walked and schmoozed the media reps, extolling the virtues of St. Matthew's.

Don't stop. Stick with the group. Get out of here.

She watched each and every one of those people ignore that hall. It wasn't bright. It wasn't new. It wasn't alive. They didn't even look down there, opting instead for the warmth and safety of the light. As they strolled by, oohing and aahing over the shiny new paint job and gleaming floors of the other wings, Cassidy flipped her private glances at those doors. She willed her feet to follow the mob of reporters and cameramen, but stopped and let the crowd pass her by.

She licked her top lip, bit down on the bottom. Heart jumping and pounding and twisting, her body remembered. She'd trod this path before, two years ago. Time is a harsh mistress. It sank its claws deep into Cassidy's brain, ripped out the buried memories, dusted them off and served them fresh and raw.

She hugged herself tight, tried to control the quake that savaged her limbs, and shuffled into the isolated hallway. Thirteen steps from the hallway to the doors. She'd paced it off a thousand times that night.

Thirteen steps, turn, thirteen steps, turn.

Cassidy counted them again, sucking in a tiny breath with each tentative footfall. The acrid smell of cleanser and sulfur clung to the walls and the linoleum.

Not again.

Thirteen steps. Hands clenched, arms rigid, she closed her eyes and leaned her forehead against the cold metal door.

Turn around. Just go.

Pings from the monitors of that long ago night ricocheted inside her skull. She'd stood in this very spot with her forehead pressed against this same cold door and listened to the rustling and frantic scuffing of comfortable shoes from the other side while her little one screamed.

Those bastards wouldn't let Cassidy in. A trained and experienced EMT and they wouldn't let her in to tend and comfort her own child—said she was too close and wouldn't be able to handle it.

Sobs burst from her as she slid to the floor against the peeled-paint wall; her legs no longer willing to bear her weight.

She knew what was coming as the memories replayed. Dreaded it, but welcomed the end to this revisited slice of hell. Silence. No movement, no machines, nothing. When she was here last, she was on her feet and peering through the small window when all went still. That's when the doctor turned to her and, with a slight dip and shake of her head, destroyed Cassidy's world.

The agony she thought secured in the depths of her heart flared up, boiled over, and left her a puddle of emotion to stagnate on the floor.

Slumped in the corner for who knew how long, she eventually stopped sobbing. Spent and numb, she clutched her knees to her chest.

Someone grabbed her arm and jerked her to her feet.

"I told you," Gray spat the words into her ear, "Not to leave my side."

"But I-"

Down the hall, the speeches continued. With his back to the rest of the hospital, Gray shook her. Black streaks zigzagged across his eyes, but they flashed and disappeared so quickly that Cassidy wondered if she really saw them. The burning hatred he communicated through his fingertips told her the real story.

"You can feel that, can't you, my disdain for your kind?"

It took a moment for the meaning of his words to register.

Feel it? How could he know?

"Yes," he tucked a strand of her hair behind her ear. "I see it in your face, in the way you look at me now." He traced her jaw line and bared his teeth in a cruel mockery of a smile.

"How did you like the tour?" His tone was offhand, casual, like he was talking to an old high school buddy. "Bring back memories for you?"

"You son of a bitch." Realization lent Cassidy strength. She yanked one arm free. "You set me up."

He sneered and checked his watch. "Come, my dear, time to go."

"I'm not going anywhere with you." She tried to jerk her other arm free, but he held on.

Gray's fingers chilled, sent an icy sensation into her arm. Cassidy tried to pull away, but her arm failed to respond. The cold spread quickly, jetting through her veins until she felt numb.

She wanted to scream, to run away, to kick this asshole in the nuts, anything, but her body refused her commands.

"Shall we?" Gray held out his arm like he was escorting her to a gala.

Her traitorous arm wrapped gently around his.

"Oh, stop scowling and smile."

Cassidy's lips curved. *Stop that!* Her mind fought off the frigid grasp of his control, desperately hanging on to her small bastion of rebellion.

Gray led them down the stairs and out the front door at a pace that suggested some urgent matter elsewhere. She railed at her limbs, pleaded with them to stop, but she matched him stride for stride.

While they were inside, the clouds had moved in. The promise of a downpour drove off all but the most desperate reporters. They eyed Gray and Cassidy's march down the red carpet. Some snapped pictures, while others finished their cigarettes.

Gray's hired goon opened the limo's back door. The interior was dark, a gaping black maw that would suck Cassidy into the oblivion found in Gray's touch.

I can't let this happen, can't go in there. Terror ate at her. Her heart should have been beating out of her chest, but its pace remained normal, untroubled.

A single tear escaped and rolled down the curvature of her forced smile.

Surprised, Gray gave her an appreciative look. "I knew you were strong." He caressed the moisture away with a brush of his knuckles. "I will enjoy this...relationship."

Cassidy's lips trembled.

"Get in the car." Alexander commanded through a tight smile as he watched the reactions of the reporters. She bent down, setting one foot in the car.

Cassidy focused her will, fighting against Gray's near-absolute control.

A photographer jumped out of line and shot a close-up. The flash went off, slashing Gray across the eyes. His control slipped.

"No." Cassidy pulled free and fell to the ground. Warmth and, more importantly, control rushed back into her system. Weak, she crawled a few feet away and opened her mouth to scream.

Gray's whisper cut her off. "You scream, you die. Right here and now."

Cassidy didn't doubt he'd kill her. He reached out a hand, presumably to help her up, but she knew it was only for show.

"Last chance. Get in."

"I will not." Cassidy spoke through clenched teeth.

"Ms. Sinclair, I am sorry you are not feeling well." Gray's raised voice carried to everyone in the vicinity. "Please contact my secretary to reschedule your exclusive interview." He leaned down so only she could hear. "Say hello to the Knights for me...if you live long enough."

The Knights? How? Why? Her head pounded with all the disjointed information.

Gray brought his hand to his mouth and coughed into his fist. It sounded odd, like a word in some foreign, guttural language. When he opened his hand, a small black fly with bright green wings took flight. Slow at first, it increased speed as it righted its course and flew toward the hospital.

The limo's back door slammed behind Gray and his driver peeled out.

What just happened?

Seated on the red carpet, Cassidy felt wrung out. The ordeal in the hospital shredded her emotions and Gray's crazy puppet-master act left her physically weak. Her limbs shook and she wanted to sit there and cry.

He drove off and left me. Just like that. Why?

One of the reporters came over to check, but Cassidy waved him off. She needed space, and a drink. Yes, a huge drink and a long swim.

What's with that fly thing?

She looked toward the hospital, searched for the fly. From this distance, she shouldn't be able to see anything so small, but she could. Clearly. It prowled along the edge of the front door.

A nervous flutter kicked up in her gut, but quickly transformed into a mounting fear that snaked through her intestines, growing stronger. With dread certainty, she knew if that fly got inside, something terrible would happen.

Desperation powered her legs. She surged to her feet and ran toward the doors. If they didn't open, it couldn't get in and she'd squish the little pest.

Within her first three steps, the door opened. It flew in.

Cassidy stopped and backed up a step. Everything seemed normal. The hospital didn't blow up when it got inside.

I'm going crazy. She turned around and walked to the end of the red carpet. Something clattered to the pavement behind her. Cassidy spun in time to see the reporter at the base of the stairs that led up to the entrance drop to the ground. Others rushed to the reporter's side, but when they got close, they too collapsed.

The hospital doors whooshed and the head nurse staggered forward, mouth stretched wide in a silent scream. All color bled from her skin, leaving it gray and lifeless. Hands, twisted and bent, pawed the air as she stumbled down the steps.

Too stunned to move, Cassidy watched the jerky movements of the nurse's arms slow, stop and hang limp. She fell forward, skull bouncing off the flag-stones. A crimson pool spread around her head like a dirty halo.

Cassidy had to do something, couldn't just stand there and watch this horror movie unfold, but the bodies of those who got close to the building hadn't moved.

What if I walk in there and the same thing happens to me? The question locked her in place. *On the other hand, can I live with myself if people die because I choose not to act?*

She knew the answer. Two years ago she buried herself alongside her daughter, giving up on the wonder life had to offer. Until she met the Knights, she hadn't missed it.

Her legs wobbled as she took her first step toward the hospital doors.

Chapter 21

THUNDER RUMBLED AS WREN SLUMPED AGAINST THE BOLE OF AN OVERGROWN OAK. The tree hadn't been tended in years. Its branches spread out too far, their weight causing them to dip down and brush the sparse grass.

"By Thor's fat arse, Cyndralla's good." Magnus craned his head around the thick trunk. "She put us down in sight of St. Matthew's hospital based on some old black and white photo from twenty years ago. Is that magic, or what?"

Stiff and drained, Wren rolled her eyes. "That bitch can suck it."

"Wren."

"Just…let's get on with this." The outline of the hospital showed through the leaves. She slid between the intersection of two major branches without disturbing a single leaf and started across the vacant field toward their goal.

Magnus thrashed through the branches like a yeti and when he caught up to Wren he draped his arm across her shoulder. "Look, I know you're upset about Sparky."

Wren snorted.

"He can turn it around." Magnus actually sounded hopeful.

Wren shrugged off his support. She didn't want to be comforted and she definitely didn't want to march across an open field toward who knew what.

"Why are we here again?" Wren asked. Magnus didn't deserve her attitude. He was the only one who stood up for Dev, arguing strongly against sanctions. Stillman ignored his protest and restricted Dev to the Cradle anyway.

Sure. Dev just needs to get control of himself. Good luck with that one. She tried to clear the image of Dev's fallen face as he heard the proclamation, but it stuck with her like a rash. The hurt look in those eyes broke her heart.

What's done is done.

"What are we looking for?" She asked, picking a path around the cars lining the drive to the hospital.

"You already asked me that."

"Well, did you answer?" He so didn't deserve her attitude.

"Yes. I said that I didn't know. Something suspicious, I guess." Magnus placed a hand on her shoulder and stopped. "I'm only going to say this one more time. The stuff with Dev is not your fault. You did what you had to do."

"I know that, but does he? Will he forgive me?"

He wrapped her in a hug. "In time, bird brain. In time. But, enough of this mushy stuff." He pushed her away. "Let's find us something."

"Something." She echoed and fell into step beside him. "How do you want to do this? Go in the front, or the back?"

"We should hit the back. Go in through Emergency." He cocked a grin at her. "Want a broken arm?"

"Want a kick in the bal—something's happening." On the red carpet in front of the hospital, a well-dressed man held his hand out to a woman on the ground while a line of reporters snapped pictures.

"Let's check it out." Magnus changed direction, trotting toward the front of the building to get a closer look.

"Do we have to? We have our own stuff to deal with," Wren said.

"It wouldn't hurt to look. She probably just fell. It's not like we can get involved with those reporters around anyway."

The reporters stayed clear of the pair near the limo, so Wren had a decent view. A little closer and she'd be able to make out faces.

"That looks like Ms. Sinclair," Magnus said.

"Magnus, that's Alexander Gray."

They picked up the pace.

What is Cassidy doing with Alexander Gray?

"He just cast a spell." Magnus shook his head. "I felt the release of his magic."

Gray got into his limo and drove off with Cassidy spilled on the ground.

Wren and Magnus reached the edge of the pavement, not far from Cassidy. If she yelled, Wren could get her attention.

"Do you taste that?" Magnus asked, working his tongue in and out.

"Uh uh."

"Ugh. That's foul." He gagged and dry heaved. "I can't even describe it."

The reporters outside the building fell and a nurse stumbled out the door. Cassidy stood up and leaned toward the hospital.

"Don't let her get any closer. That spell will kill her." Before he finished his sentence, Wren sprinted toward Cassidy.

"Cassidy!" Wren shouted, but Cassidy must not have heard because she stumbled toward the hospital.

ᑲᎧᏣ

Cassidy avoided the blood around the nurse's head and knelt near her shoulder. The skin of the nurse's face, neck and hands was a uniform, battleship gray. Cassidy pressed two fingers against her throat and recoiled. The texture was wrong, too hard, and her temp was off the chart cold.

Dead. Before she stood, Cassidy thanked the woman for her kindness two years ago and closed her milky eyes. The reporters looked to be in the same shape. Gray. Cold. Dead.

Oh my god.

A dull pain rooted in her stomach and slowly branched out, following her blood flow. Cassidy stared at the other corpses laid out around her.

Everyone inside can't be like this, can they? If they are, what can I do to help?
She shuddered, wrapped her arms around herself. Tears threatened. *No.* She
looked at the face of the head nurse. *I can do something. I have to try.*

Determined, she took another step toward the door and found herself on
her back looking up into the sky. A dark silhouette blocked the clouds and
small hands grabbed her under the arms.

"Pull her back to the curb."

Magnus? Cassidy's arms and legs throbbed.

"Aye, aye, Captain." Wren dragged Cassidy down the red carpet with ease.

"Wren? What's goi—?"

"Shh. Take it easy." Wren said. "You'll be alright."

The further away from the building Wren dragged her, the better Cassidy
felt. The pain receded from her limbs, centering once again in her belly until
it disappeared altogether.

"Her color is coming back." Magnus dropped to one knee at her side.
"Another minute or two and we would have lost you, Ms. Sinclair."

"Cassidy."

"Alright, Cassidy, how are you feeling?" Magnus helped her into a sitting
position.

"Much better now." Cassidy looked at Wren. "Thank you."

"You're crazy," Wren scolded, "Didn't you see those dead people? Why
would you head into the building?"

"I had to help."

Wren spun, throwing her hands in the air, and walked off.

"I think the magic is subsiding. That taste is going away," Magnus said.

"What taste?" Cassidy asked.

"Well," Magnus stood and looked to the hospital, "Our dear Mr. Gray made
a statement." He seemed to be talking more to himself than to either Wren
or Cassidy.

"What do you mean?" Cassidy asked.

Wren stomped back. "Gray unleashed a spell at the hospital. What you see
is a result of his magic."

"Yes, the spell is over, but..." Magnus walked toward the building. "I feel
something dark... rancid, like what we found at the club site."

"Are you sure?" Wren asked.

"Yes. It's inside." He closed his eyes. "Close. I need to get it."

Was that a...? Cassidy held her breath, straining to hear.

"I-" Wren started, but Cassidy raised a hand to silence her and focused all
her attention on a sound she thought she heard.

Wait...wait. THERE. Cassidy jumped up and bolted for the hospital doors.
At her approach, they shushed open and she ran inside. Gray bodies lay on
the floor, slumped over the reception desk, and sat upright in the leather and

metal chairs. Death's noisome aroma filled the room. Cassidy let it wash over her as she paused to listen. A low coo, off to her left. She ran. Magnus and Wren pounded after her.

A cough, louder this time. *Close.* Moving quickly down the hall, she hopped over bodies when she couldn't walk around them, ears straining against the hospital's white noise.

She turned left on instinct, passed the vending machines, and slowed her pace.

Where are you?

Magnus and Wren followed her silent lead. Outside the pediatric ward she stopped beside a child-sized kitchen play area complete with table, chairs, and Playskool appliances. A whimper behind the plastic refrigerator fixed the position. Cassidy gently lifted the plastic table out of the way and went around the refrigerator.

"Oh dear God," she breathed and dropped to her knees at the feet of a little girl. Eyes shut tight, the girl tossed her head from left to right. Short red bangs swished across her forehead.

"Magnus, pull the kitchen out. We need room."

The Earth Knight stepped closer and eased the kitchen pieces up and out of the way. Cassidy scooted up to the little girl's head. Her skin was too pale, nearly white, but thankfully not gray yet. A blue tint colored her lips.

"Wren, we need something to warm her up. Blankets. Anything. Go."

Wren ghosted away.

Carotid pulse faint, but there. Breathing shallow. Cassidy chafed the girl's arms and motioned for Magnus to do the same with her legs.

Wren appeared with an armload of blankets and a portable electric heater. Cassidy covered her patient, leaving only her head, hands and little feet uncovered, as Wren plugged in the heater and positioned it near her chest.

The girl shifted, kicked her left foot into Magnus's knee that sent the little pink and purple lights on her sneaker to twinkling.

Come on, baby.

The wheezing stopped. Cassidy felt for a pulse. Nothing.

No.

She flipped the blankets down to the girl's waist and started CPR. Thirty quick pumps. Two breaths. Thirty quick pumps. Two breaths. Cassidy paused, checked for a pulse. Nothing.

Don't leave me.

"Magnus, Wren, rub her legs."

Thirty pumps.

Come on, girl.

Two breaths.

Breathe, baby. You can do it. Cassidy's eyes welled.

Thirty pumps.

Not another one.

Two breaths.

Cassidy checked. Nothing.

She couldn't hold the tears at bay. They rolled down her cheeks and plopped onto her bunched hands as they pumped up and down on the ironed-on image of Dora the Explorer.

Two breaths.

Thirty pumps.

Still nothing.

She leaned forward and placed her forehead on the child's chest. A barely-there whisper tickled her cheek. Cassidy froze. It came again, stronger this time. Without moving her head, she slid her hand to that thin, fragile neck and felt a faint pulse beneath the skin.

Sirens sounded in the distance.

"Cassidy, we need to go." Magnus warned.

"She's alive." Cassidy said.

Magnus and Wren's mouths dropped open and they stared first at the girl and then at Cassidy.

"Take her." Magnus said.

Cassidy clutched the little girl to her chest. Magnus took the lead until they got back to the lobby.

"Go around back." He told Wren. "I'll meet you there."

Magnus pounded down the hall and turned into the stairwell. Cassidy followed Wren through the Emergency room exit and found a discrete spot to wait between two ambulances.

The sirens reached a constant volume and leveled out.

What will they make of all this?

The child stirred, whimpered. Cassidy rocked her, made comforting shushing noises in her ear and kissed her on the forehead.

You're going to be okay.

Magnus emerged a few minutes later carrying a bundle wrapped in a lead x-ray smock under one arm.

"Did you get it?" Wren asked.

"The parts I could find at least."

Cassidy interrupted. "How are we getting out of here?" She didn't have her car and she didn't know how Wren and Magnus had gotten there.

"Wren, do you know how to hot-wire a car?" Magnus asked, eyeing the vehicles in the staff parking lot.

"No."

Magnus cracked his knuckles. "I guess it's on me."

Chapter 22

D EV HALF-HEARTEDLY CLUBBED THE PADDED DUMMY WITH A WOODEN PRACTICE sword. *I brought this on myself.* He always beat the snot out of the blue one on the end, but his blows lacked their usual fire and energy. Its sewed-on buttons and crooked-stitched smile mocked him.

Dejected, he tossed the sword at the dummy's dangling feet and lumbered across the sparring circle. Past elliptical machines, treadmills and stationary bikes, he roamed to the racks of free-weights, plunked down on a bench and waited for his spirit to motivate him.

Grounded. Dev lay back, let his arms dangle free, and stared toward the ceiling. *Like a bratty child.*

"The mighty one has fallen, no?" Dronor's Spanish accent reminded him of Antonio Banderas minus the long hair and bad-ass cool in *Desperado.*

Dev groaned.

"See how he wallows in defeat, punished like a little boy." Donor *tsked* as he made his way closer.

Don't push me. Dev's anger ignited and he sat up.

The Knight of Water wended his way through the equipment, ran his hand along the rails of the treadmills, taking his time.

From under a lowered brow, Dev tracked the Water Knight's unconcerned movements, sizing up the situation. Loose navy-blue slacks, tight white polo, rubber soled shoes, George Hamilton tan, rapier strapped to his hip....

He's come to pick a fight. An accomplished fencer, Dronor relied on precise, lightning-quick strikes. For him, it was an art, not a martial skill. He spent long hours lunging and feinting and prancing in front of a mirror, admiring the majesty of his own form. But when challenged, he had business elsewhere.

"I'm not in the mood," Dev said.

"Oh, I am sure you are not ready for visitors." Dronor straddled a bench opposite Dev, and mirrored his posture. "The righteous have won the day."

Dronor's rolling 'R's set Dev's teeth on edge. He clenched his fists in his lap and let the flames build up strength in his gut. Rage. His friend for so many years had his back.

"If you're here to fight, shut up and get on with it."

A cocky smile spread within the boundaries of a carefully groomed van dyke. Arrogance sparkled in his hazel-colored eyes. With fluid grace, the Knight of Water gained his feet, drew his sword and leveled it in front of Dev's nose.

"As you wish, *gusano.*" Dronor spat out the last word.

Dev got to his feet, the steady tip of Dronor's rapier followed his movement. "If you're going to insult me, at least use a word I can understand." Empty hands raised in front of him, Dev emphasized his unarmed status.

Dronor lowered his sword and nodded toward the middle of the room where a twenty foot circle had been marked off on the floor. The Knight of Water strode into the center, rested his thin blade on his shoulder and waited.

Dev limped to the rack and eyed the vast array of weapons on display. Aside from his left leg, which still gave him some trouble, the rest of his body had pretty much healed. Days on his back left him feeling stiff and uncoordinated, so this fight should prove interesting.

The long knives piqued his interest, but the morningstar looked appealing. He imagined that big spiked ball smacking into the side of Dronor's smug face. The power of the fire burning under his skin flickered and danced at the image.

Nah. Don't want to kill the arrogant fool. The knives called to him. *Maybe just carve my initials in his uptight ass.*

Dronor tapped his foot and cleared his throat.

You can wait. Dev took his time, pretending to agonize over the decision he had already made, but eventually grabbed a pair of simple, straight-bladed daggers. Compared to Cinder, they were sad and clunky, a pair of beat up Pintos to a Ferrari, but they'd do the job. The choice gave Dronor a definite reach advantage, but Dev balanced that out with aggression and ability.

He twirled the knives and played up his limp as he moved into the arena.

Dronor adopted a classic fencing stance, complete with left arm bent and at his hip. "*En garde.*"

"Bring it, Drippy."

Lip curled at the insult, Dronor lunged. Dev blocked the blow, but it came in quicker than he expected, quicker than he thought the old Knight could move.

Another lunge, down and to the side. Dev barely knocked it aside.

Damn, he's quick. Dev crouched, weight balanced on the balls of his feet. He needed to take this fight more seriously.

Dronor noticed the attitude change and charged in with a furious combination.

Sweep high. Block. Slash low. Dodge. Dev forgot about his left leg and, as he twisted to avoid the latest strike, it gave out and he dropped to his knees.

Dronor capitalized with a stab to Dev's left ass cheek. It was a superficial wound, but stung all the same.

Son of a bi— The rage broke free of Dev's control. Fire roared to life and engulfed his hands. They became a blur in front of him as he rose and recklessly charged the Knight of Water.

Slash. Jab. Slash right. Slash left. Thrust.

Wild swings left Dev panting while Dronor danced out of the way unharmed. The older Knight seemed amused by Dev's fiery outburst and rage-inspired tactics.

"You are pathetic and should have been locked up long ago."

Fire screamed through his body. Dropping the knives, he threw himself at the Knight of Water, grasping for his throat. When his blazing hands came in contact with Dronor's skin, a torrent of steam rose into the air.

"You forget, stupid Knight of Flame, I am your foil." Dronor smacked Dev across the top of his skull with a bare palm that sent a gush of water down the Knight of Flame's face. It sizzled and separated into droplets that boiled down his cheeks. "Your fire means nothing to me."

The water cooled Dev's fury, left him wet and fuming. Dronor pushed him off and followed with a slap of his blade to Dev's chest.

"Pathetic." Dronor sheathed his rapier and strode toward the door. "You will be stuck here forever, Quinteele."

Pathetic. Dev sat down hard on the wet floor, landed on his new wound and quickly adjusted position.

Ass kicked twice in the same week. I know better. Why did I let that Spanish fossil get to me?

A glimmer of the rage he felt before stirred, but he immediately tamped it down.

If I can't control the fire and rage, I am going to be stuck here forever.

Chapter 23

THE ELEVATOR PINGED OPEN ONTO THE BRIGHT WAITING ROOM OF ALEXANDER'S penthouse office. Whistling, he stepped from the doors. It had been a good morning, despite that Sinclair woman's impudence. Alexander's new secretary scampered over with a fist full of post-its and "panic" stamped across her forehead.

"Mr. Gray, Mr. Gray." The blonde wheezed, her voice scratchy and annoying. Stale cigarette smoke clung to her polyester jacket and too-short-to-be-taken-seriously skirt. Thick brown hose and chunky shoes completed her comical ensemble.

She parked herself in his path, waving the papers at him. "Oh, Mr. Gray, thank *God* you're finally here."

Her breath lunged at him—a lethal mix of Marlboro and coffee.

"Calm yourself, Ms....?"

"Dorayis, sir. Kareena Dorayis." She smiled demurely. "The agency sent me over this morning."

"Calm yourself, Ms. Dorayis. Take a deep breath."

And, darkness prevails, a breath mint.

"I am sure whatever it is you are pushing in my face can wait for a few more minutes."

Alexander stepped around her, careful not to touch any part of her loathsome body, and rushed for the door to his office.

"Please see that I'm not disturbed." Alexander shut the door in her face and grinned when he heard the follow-up thunk and muffled curse.

"It's about time, little brother." A powerful voice, rich and condescending, greeted him. *Magdon.*

Surprised, Alexander schooled his features.

"Brother," Alexander approached the portrait of his eldest brother on the wall. Magdon glared from the canvas, his puffy red cheeks billowed in and out as if he'd run all the way through the magical link. "It has been too long. What brings your sentience here to my insignificant harborage?"

"Can it, Lexi."

Bastard.

"Why, whatever do you mean?" Alexander portrayed the innocent well, but his brother didn't buy it.

"What is going on down there?" Magdon's jowls flopped. "I've been getting condolences from CEOs and government officials about the accident at the hospital."

"Oh, that. It was just a little test."

"As the CEO of Daegon Gray," Magdon lorded his position over his younger brother, "I need to be informed of all 'tests' that could possibly affect our corporation's sterling reputation. Are we agreed on this...brother?"

"Reprimand duly noted. Has our business concluded then?"

"So, Alexander...," eyes shifting left and right, Magdon leaned forward. "What sort of test was this?"

Curious, are we?

It was only his brother on the portrait, not his father. He could be honest, to a small degree, without fear of major reprisal.

"I wanted to see the magic of the shadow orbs in action."

"And?" Magdon's expression grew eager, eyes bright and lustful. "What happened, little brother? Did the humans blow up?"

"Why would they do that?"

The fact that his eldest brother did not know how the orbs affected the humans was another surprise.

"I thought, hoped really, that they would blow up." Magdon's fat red cheeks sagged.

Interesting.

"Sad to tell, it was nothing so dramatic. Boring, truth be told. The weaklings changed color then died. No blood, no spectacle, no style."

"That's it? How...anticlimactic. They should blow up. I'll work on that."

"I was led to believe it was supposed to be boring and appear to be caused by some natural phenomenon."

"Where's the fun in that?" Magdon cocked his head like he was listening to something on his end of the line.

What an odd call.

"What is new with you?" Alexander asked.

"We're moving forward, little brother. Daegon Gray bought out the overseas manufacturing companies last week. A couple tweaks to the assembly line, add a touch of Shadow magic here and there, and voila."

"When will the first product be available?"

"Six months, maybe sooner. We've initiated a global recall of all baby products. Staged a few, one or two thousand, infant deaths around the globe to make the defects look real and serious."

Alexander nodded, impressed.

"You know how these humans get," Magdon continued, "Kill one of their young, and they go berserk." Looking up, he ticked points off on his blunt, sausage fingers. "We killed their larvae and framed the infant product manufacturers, what, six weeks ago? Their stocks tanked and Daegon, with the promise of fixing what was broken in the—" He placed his hand on his chest, "—interest of humanity, gobbled them up for pennies on the dollar."

"Well done."

"Once the recalled products are back, we'll repackage under the Little Ghost brand and send them back out. Pacifiers, nipples, chew toys, the lot. We have to gain their trust with a decent product before we can introduce Shadow into the mix."

Alexander bit his tongue.

Too long. If I had run that project, I would have had it done by now. But, no, this brainless brute gets to have all the fun.

"And Father approves?"

"Of course he does. We developed the plan together."

Together!

Magdon burst into laughter. "Every time I think about it, it makes me laugh. Building an army using their own young." He wiped a tear from his eye. "You have to love the beauty of it. Six months from now, a horde of little shadow beasts will be crawling or flying around on their itty, bitty bat wings. Ahhh, good times. We're almost there, Lexi. Father's glorious plan unfolds."

"Yes…glorious. So, brother, what is next?"

Magdon leaned forward, pushing out the painting's canvas a half inch. "The insect plague, knives in the dark, death and destruction. You know, the fun stuff. Get the different human factions blaming each other then sit back and watch the mayhem. It's been a long, tedious wait, but mankind has finally developed the tools to bring about their own subjugation. Once they've plunged their world into a state of permanent shadow, we will rule."

What is all this permanent shadow nonsense? No one has mentioned this to me! How do the orbs work into the plan?

"Ah, yes, the insect plague. So, Thargen, is involved then?" Alexander pretended to rub his chin to hide the building tension in his jaw.

"Of course. Has been since the beginning." Magdon turned his head and nodded to someone off screen. "Ooh, hey, gotta go. Seriously, though, let me know when you plan another one of your little stunts so I can be more prepared."

Little stunts?

"Are you not going to ask about the orb production and shipments?"

"Oh, yeah, right. The orbs. I'll ask next time." Magdon retreated into the frame, losing perspective and dimension until his fat, lifeless face stared from the canvas.

Alexander paced the length of his office. *My brother did not know the effects of the orbs, why? He did not want any information regarding their production or shipping schedule. Again, why? Why is father working directly with him? Knives in the dark? And Thargen knows about this grand plan? What is going on?*

Just put it out of your mind, Alexander, Gothrodul's thoughts intruded. *Think of something else. Or, better yet, put on the news to see if they are still talking about St. Matthew's. That'll cheer you up.*

Alexander shrugged and turned on the TV, looking for a report on St. Matthew's. Instead, a woman with long brown hair and an obnoxious voice cackled into the screen from the set of some strange kitchen.

Blast. Someone changed my channel. Alexander grabbed the remote and flicked through the stations. Judges, soap operas and talk shows dominated the daytime cable lineup. *What is all this tripe? Where is the ne—ah.*

"Have you seen all the bugs, Marianne?" The senior news anchor asked his pretty young colleague. "My goodness, they bubbled out of the sewer like a… like a…well, there were a lot of them and I've heard other reports about the same thing happening all across the city. What do you think?"

Marianne shivered. "I saw it too, Bob. This morning, my driveway was crawling with beetles. Disgusting. The way their little shells crunched when I drove over—"

"Er, thank you, Marianne. Coming up, a grisly discovery in Ybor City. But now, back to Sam who is live on the scene at St. Matthews."

"Thanks, Tom." Sam, with his stiff hair and brown suit, stood on the red carpet in front of St. Matthew's. "It's another dark day in the bay area. Two tragedies in the same week. First, eighty of Tampa and St. Pete's elite perish at the hands of a madman. And now, the St. Matthew's tragedy. The latest count is four hundred twenty eight," he pressed his fingers to his ear piece. "No, sorry, five hundred twenty eight doctors, nurses, patients, reporters and even our own Mayor, died in what police and experts are calling a freak natural gas leak."

Alexander sat back on the love seat, lacing his fingers behind his head. "Five hundred…not bad."

The camera returned to the senior anchor. "There was one bright spot, though. The Emergency Room's external camera caught a few survivors fleeing the scene." A black and white video flashed on the screen. For the first couple of seconds, it looked like a still picture of the back driveway then two people, one of them carrying a small child, emerged from the back door.

Alexander sat up, eyes glued to the women running from the hospital. *That whore.*

He rose to his feet and turned his back on yet another disappointment. *How did she escape? And who was that other girl?*

A knock sounded. Lowering his head, he yanked open the office door, grabbed the offender by the floppy collar of her cheap polyester blouse and pulled her into his office. With a thought, he slammed the door behind him.

"Mr. Gray," Kareena pried at his hands to no effect. "I am not that kind of secretary."

I cannot take that voice. Alexander slapped his hand over her mouth and drew her life force out in one massive surge. He dropped the ashen gray body and lurched back to the couch unsated.

Dragon, Alexander called, *I have a snack for you in my office.*

Gothrodul's laughter filtered through the link. *On my way.*

They replayed the video of Sinclair fleeing the hospital.

We cannot have loose ends. You are mine, Cassidy Sinclair. Tonight.

Chapter 24

Vision blurred by tears, Cassidy watched the All Children's hospital sign fade in the distance through the back window of the "borrowed" car. Leaving the little girl proved tougher than she'd expected though she knew it was the right decision. All Children's would provide the specialized care and emotional support the girl needed in the aftermath of St. Matthew's. Still, it broke her heart.

I miss the feel of a child in my arms. The gentle sway of Magnus's conservative driving lulled her to sleep.

Cassidy jerked awake as Magnus shifted into Park and opened his car door. The dome light flared and she covered her eyes.

It's dark? How long was I out?

Sleep fogged her thinking, but she remembered it being no later than two in the afternoon when they dropped off the little girl.

"Where?" Cassidy stretched.

"Your house." Magnus turned in his seat. "Remember the plan. After I check the place out, we all go in while you get what you need, then we port to the Cradle."

"Right," Wren said. "We're gone in fifteen minutes, tops."

The seriousness of her two companions dispelled the lingering effects of her nap. Wide awake, she peered into the darkness surrounding the car. As usual, the neighborhood was as silent as a grave.

"Do you really think Gray will try something?" Cassidy asked as she tried to look out of all the windows simultaneously.

"He killed a lot of people today and you are the only witness." Magnus said as he unlaced his boots.

Wren shook her head. "Nice work there, Captain Ominous. The only thing missing was the sinister laugh. Oh, and by the way, the boots ain't working. It's flip-flops for your birthday this year."

"Don't bother. Won't wear them."

"Whatever."

Cassidy didn't mind the bickering. She'd come to realize that's how they dealt with stress. In a way, it was comforting. She could imagine herself hanging with these people, the big brother and little sister she never had.

And what about Dev? She didn't know what to think about him. There was something there, but the fire thing...

"I'll be back in a minute." Magnus got out of the car then stuck his head back in. "Eyes open. Be alert."

"Oh, hey." Cassidy fished her keys out of her pocket and handed them to the Earth Knight. "You'll need these."

Their hands touched.

"Whoa," Magnus jerked his arm away and a strange I-knew-there-was-something-different-about-you look came over him. "You have a gift."

Holy shit. He felt my gift too.

"I...I."

"It's okay, Cassidy. You don't need to hide it."

"What's going on?" Wren asked.

"Nothing at all," he said. "Yell if you need me."

Wren gave Cassidy a speculative look.

Cassidy derailed Wren's question before she could give it voice.

"What was all that with the shoes?"

Wren frowned at the change in topic, but played along. "The shoes block his earth mojo, I mean, power. When he is in direct contact with his element, he can sense what's going on around him. Vibrations, movement, things like that. Comes in handy on recon missions like this one."

"Makes sense." Cassidy nodded and watched for anything out of the ordinary.

"Let's go. He's waving us in." Wren pointed to the front door. "Get only what you need. We're exposed here. The sooner we're gone, the better."

Only what I need. Right.

Cassidy and Wren hurried into the house. Wren ran for the back door and looked out from between the blinds. Magnus watched the front yard from the big window in the living room.

Cassidy grabbed her suitcase and filled it with the essentials—a few pairs of jeans, t-shirts, underwear, toiletries—to survive a few days away from home. Next stop, she rushed to the kitchen counter to grab her laptop. She still owed a major story to her editor and some time away would give her the chance to get it done.

Next to her computer, the answering machine flashed a red four. Unable to resist, she played the messages while she packed up the laptop power supply. Her editor left the first three messages. She winced at his rising level of urgency and concern in each one. In the last, he pleaded for her to contact him immediately. She'd told him she would be at the opening and he wanted to make sure she was alright after the accident.

That was no accident.

The fourth call was just wrong. As soon as Alexander Gray's silky voice purred through the speaker, she hit delete.

You've got to be kidding me. Is he really that stupid?

Her house phone rang. Cassidy looked to Magnus for guidance. He shook his head and turned back to his surveillance. After three rings, the machine picked up.

All packed and ready for whatever came next, Cassidy carried her bags to the front door while her digitized greeting played.

"I see you made it home safely." Gray's silky tone oozed out of the speaker. "I saw you on the news. Who were your friends?"

"Knulla." Magnus swore. "He's here. Wren?"

"Nothing back here. You?"

"No. Be ready." Magnus called on his earthen power and changed. His body grew and hardened to granite in seconds.

The sound of Gray's voice should have petrified her, should have dropped her to the floor in a puddle of whimpering slush. She growled instead.

I'm sick of this mother fu—

Gray continued. "No matter. They will share the same fate. Goodbye, Cassidy Sinclair. Our association has come to an end."

Teeth clenched, she placed her bags in the center of the room.

"What can I do?" she asked, her voice cold and grim. Anger ripped through her. She thought of those who died at the hospital, of the head nurse, of the girl who lived—all victims of this monster. He had to be stopped.

"Do you have—" In his big stone form, the Earth Knight's words came out in a gravelly rasp. Midway through the sentence, his voice quit. His lips moved, but no sound came out, like someone pushed his mute button.

"What's going on?" Cassidy heard the words in her head, but they never left her mouth.

A bright green flash lit the world outside her front window.

Chapter 25

ALEXANDER WAITED FOR THE GIRL TO RETURN HOME FROM HIS SEAT ON THE DRAG-on's back. Since nightfall, they had hovered a safe distance above the Intracoastal waterway directly behind Cassidy's house. The wind currents at that height allowed Gothrodul to remain relatively steady with nothing more than the occasional shift of his broad wings.

What if she doesn't return home? the dragon asked.

Alexander patted the sleek, scaled neck. "Patience, my friend, she will return. In the meantime, I have another matter to address." He pulled a cell phone out of his pocket, and tapped in a number. "The twit had better answer."

"H…he…hello?"

"Oh, man up, Revost. I have a job for you."

"Alex? Is that you? I hardly ever get a call."

Alexander rolled his eyes and the dragon's sides heaved in laughter.

"Yes, Revost, it is Alexander."

"Brother, it's been so long." Revost took a deep breath. "I haven't talked to you for ages. I didn't think this phone worked anymore. How is Florida? I bet it's nice."

"Revo—"

"It snows here every day and it's cold, but the cold is good for the machines. They like it. They told me they did. When are you coming to visit me?"

"Revos—" Alexander slid more power into his voice, tried to break through the ceaseless chatter.

"Fall is a nice time in the Yukon, Alex. You can come then. I'll turn up the heat a little, but not too much. The machines will be unhappy if I do. They don't work well if they're unhappy. Oh, I got another character to level ninety. A hunter. He has a big crab for a pet. I named him Cra—"

"REVOST."

"Yes, Alex?"

"I need your help."

"Do you need information? Money? Credit? A robot? I like to build robots."

Alexander bit his tongue. Dealing with Revost always took far longer than it needed to so he did it sparingly.

"We have an enemy."

"Ohhhhh, another bad person out to harm father's company?" A dangerous change came over the voice on the other end of the phone. "You want me to clean them, right?"

Clean. I would think erase or delete would be more accurate.

"Yes. One Cassidy Sinclair."

"C.a.s.s.i.d.y. That's a pretty name."

A quick series of clicks sounded through the phone.

"There are over four thousand Cassidy Sinclairs in the United States, Alex. Which one?"

"The one in Florida, Revost, near Tampa."

Alexander rubbed his forehead and checked the house for a sign that she returned.

More tapping. "Okay. Still have over two hundred references."

"She works at the Tampa Weekly."

"Oooh, that will help." *Click. Click.* "Got her. She's beautiful."

"But evil, Revost."

"The pretty ones always are, brother. Give me a sec."

Alexander pictured this odd shadow warrior concentrating with the tip of his tongue stuck out the side of his mouth, fingers flying over the keys. His ability to interface with machines of all makes, models, eras and technologies was nothing short of magic and his father and older brother kept him tied in to every aspect of the global business. He had a backdoor into every corporate system in the world. Revost, and therefore the Gray Lord, knew the major decisions made in every boardroom before the actual members of the board knew.

A car pulled into Cassidy Sinclair's driveway.

Why do you doubt me, dragon?

She's not alone, Alexander. The Knight of Earth is with her.

So? It does not change our plans.

"Squeaky clean, Alex. I deleted her credit cards, bank accounts, driver license, school records, social security number, tax ID, pr—"

"Good work, brother. Once again you have foiled the bad guys." Alexander felt his brother's pride swell. "Now I must go."

"So you'll come visit me, right? Soon?"

"Absolutely." Alexander terminated the call with his brother and placed one more. He left a short message on Cassidy Sinclair's answering machine then turned off his phone lest his lonely brother call back to chat.

"Destroy them."

The dragon banked its wings and dove. Shadowed bands of power strapped Alexander into place against the speed of the near-vertical descent. *I hate this part.* Air rushed past too quickly to breathe.

"Pull up you stupid beast." The hard reality of the water came closer. "You will kill us both."

This, Shadow Lord, is what it feels like to be dragonkind. Gothrodul unfurled his massive wings at the last possible instant and pulled out of the dive low enough to drag the knife-edge tip of its forked tail in the water, trailing a vapor cone in its wake.

Alexander swallowed his stomach, which tried to escape during free-fall, and marshaled his strength. As they'd done hundreds of time in the past, Alexander's magic would shroud the house in silence while their combined attacks leveled the place.

"On my mark." Alexander took control. The dragon leveled out ten feet above the surface of the water and closed in on ground zero.

Goodbye, Cassidy Sinclair.

"Mark."

Chapter 26

CASSIDY'S FRONT WINDOW EXPLODED INWARD, BLOWING GLASS SHARDS AND THE stone giant Magnus across the room. He reared up in front of Cassidy, blocking the majority of the sharp rain, but a few sneaked around, sliced her cheek and the exposed flesh of her arms.

Wren came up behind as another explosion rocked the house and caved in the ceiling over Cassidy's bedroom.

The Earth Knight dropped to one knee and pulled the women in close. Through the contact, Cassidy felt his frustration, his concern, and his joy as he drew on the power on his element.

The ground rumbled. The floor around them cracked and split into a ring around the huddled trio. Jagged rods of limestone shot from the ground at odd angles, creating a protective rock shelter over their heads. Magnus braced himself against the roof of the structure, bolstering it with his earthen strength.

Green fire tore the house apart around them. Chunks of the ceiling bounced off the top of the makeshift shelter and smashed to the floor. Cassidy shuddered with each strike. The rods bowed. The last hit tore off a chunk.

It's not going to last much longer.

With one arm holding up the limestone, Magnus dug a glowing card out of his back pocket. He held up the glowing picture of a cave entrance in the side of a mountain then to the garage doorway across the room. Raising five fingers, he counted down. Wren grabbed Cassidy's wrist.

Three...two...one.

The shelter shattered as Magnus released his power. He grabbed Wren's hand and indicated she should grab Cassidy's. Linked together, he leaped for the doorway. When they got close, he flicked the card. It expanded, opening onto a dark room with the seal of the Knights on the floor. The big man charged through.

Another blast rocked the house. The sounds of the disaster around Cassidy should have been deafening, but they happened in eerie, surreal silence.

Wren followed Magnus. A hot gust of air ripped Cassidy from Wren's grasp. Before tumbling away she glimpsed Wren's horrified expression as the girl reached back through the gateway. Her mouth opened around a scream, but the oppressive silence devoured it.

The garage doorway collapsed under the blow of a mighty shadow arm, taking the gateway down with it.

Cassidy slammed against the back wall and threw her arms over her head as the kitchen exploded. Through the gap between her forearms, she watched her matching appliances crash through newly made holes in the wall and ceiling. The counter top disintegrated. Glass doors and windows shattered.

She cowered under the remains of the bay window and wished for the nightmare to end.

Any minute now, I'll wake up. The sofa, covered in hungry green flames, smashed against the side wall, its ends stuck on either side of the double wide doorframe. Like dominoes, the interior walls collapsed into each other. The ceiling dipped and wobbled before it caved in on the front half of the house.

A cloud of dust, rock and splinters rolled through the still-standing portion of the house. Amy's princess pillow tumbled out of the churning mass. It flopped across the floor and bounced off Cassidy's shoulder on its way through a hole in the wall.

Cassidy coughed. Smoke stung her eyes, filled her lungs.

Can't anybody see what's happening? A crystal lamp smashed against the wall beside her head. She screamed, but nothing came out.

Only the shell of the kitchen and living room remained. A tremor shook the back wall and rattled her spine. *Gotta get out.* On hands and knees, she crawled toward the open doors into the backyard.

A large ball of luminous green splashed down in her living room floor. The force of the impact ejected her out the door and into the pool.

The cool water revived her spirits. She took a deep breath and dove under as heavy bits of stone, wood and rebar splashed into the pool around her. Grabbing the bottom rung of the ladder, she forced herself to stay submerged, dodging debris and watching the destruction through the distortion of the water.

Game time. Focus. Just like in practice.

On the bottom, Cassidy watched the outside wall of the house loom over the edge of the pool. It rocked toward her then away. *Oh no.* Hand over hand, she pulled herself up and broke the surface. Heavy fallout from the silent explosions fell around her, but she ignored it, too intent on the sway of the wall. It canted, towering directly over her head.

Fall the other way. Fall the other way. The wall toppled. She had just enough time to take a breath and dive before it locked her in.

Trapped, she floundered underwater in the pitch black. *Stay calm. Control your heart beat.* The words had the desired impact. She stilled her movements and the time between beats increased. Senses locked by the wet cocoon, the slow deep throb of her heart thumped loud in her temples and her chest.

There's gotta be a gap or a hole. She searched the edge, but met only concrete below the water line. The wall not only covered the pool, it had sunk below the surface. No gaps. No holes. No air.

I'm going to die. She tried on the idea for size. Would it be so bad, giving herself over to the loving embrace of the water? After Amy died, she'd lost her faith and hadn't looked back. But now, faced with the ultimate question, what did she believe?

Is this the end? When I drink in my last breath, will I just fade to black? No afterlife. No heaven. God, I hope not. I'm not ready for that. What about Amy? Is she waiting for me on the other side linked arm in arm with Mom and Dad? Seems too good to be true, but I'll take that plan thank you very much.

Another sound, above and beyond the slow thump in her veins, made itself known. *What?* She thought she detected words on the edge of her hearing. No, not hearing, in her heart or brain or whatever made her Cassidy. She tried to decipher them, but they remained out of reach.

Her chest tightened. Her lungs burned. She pictured the little girl from St. Matthew's, her own parents, Amy, Wren, Magnus, and lastly Dev.

She wanted to breathe, had to breathe, but to breathe meant to die. She clamped her lips shut and pinched them with her fingers. *Almost home, my angel.*

Spots swam all around her. Air. She needed air. That strange sound again. No, different this time. Light pierced the gloom.

She opened her mouth.

৪০৫৪

Alexander grinned as the wall crashed down over the pool, trapping Cassidy underwater. "Land." He commanded the dragon. "We will fish her out so I can end this."

If you leave my back, Alexander, my magic will no longer conceal you.

"Do it."

Gothrodul banked his wings and glided down.

The neighbors are coming.

"Kill them."

The dragon angled his descent to pass over the oblivious people and drew in a mighty breath. Before he unleashed his weapon, the whir of an approaching helicopter caught his attention and he veered off, turning away from the house and out to open water.

"Where are you going?" Alexander spun in his perch. "I need to get back there."

Too much going on. We'll be seen. You can't afford that. Not yet.

"We cannot leave this unfinished."

It is finished. She has been under the water long enough and is probably dead already. What more can you do? Now, let's get out of here.

Frustrated, Alexander stared down at the covered pool. The helicopter's spotlight criss-crossed over the wreckage, highlighting yet another disappointment. He wanted to take her life himself, drink in her fear and pain, watch the spark fade from those blue eyes.

"Fine. Take us home. No. Better yet, take us to Ybor."

Chapter 27

C*ASSIDY'S GONE.* W*REN TOUCHED DOWN IN THE* P*ORTAL ROOM AND YANKED ON* Magnus's arm. "We have to go back." Panic rushed her words.

The gateway winked out in a flash.

"Where's Cassidy?" Magnus asked.

"Back there. I lost her. Something pulled her out of my hand." Wren bashed her head against the Earth Knight's chest. "We have to go back."

"But Wren I…"

"Ah, so you have returned."

"Cyndralla." Wren spun to the lyrical feminine voice. "Send us back. Please. We need to get back. She's in trouble."

The Knight of Air, tall and austere, crossed the smoky quartz bridge at a sedate pace and stood upon the seal of the Order—four polished silver triangles contained within a golden ring, their tips connected at the center—engraved in the rock floor of the cavern.

"Calm down, child, and speak clearly." Cyndralla tilted her head, her long white hair swishing gracefully around her waist.

I am not a child.

"Cyndy," Magnus said, "We need to go back to Cassidy Sinclair's house immediately. Gray attacked and the doorway containing the gateway we just came through collapsed before Ms. Sinclair could make it through. I have not captured the image to make a card, else I would take us back myself."

"There. Was that so difficult?" The Knight of Air smirked at Wren. "Now I understand the situation. Thank you, Magnus."

*Grrrr…*Wren's hands balled into fists.

Cyndralla calmly walked to the brick archway built into the wall behind Magnus and laid her palm flat against the smooth stone. She closed her eyes and bowed her head.

"Yes. Destruction. I can see it through the residual trail of the last gateway. There are no longer any viable doorways upon which to tether a new one."

"There has to be something." Wren grabbed his shirt, eyes desperate. "What about the car?"

"Cyndy, do you see a car?" Desperation tinged Magnus's voice. "Can you anchor the gateway to that?"

"Hmmm…" Cyndralla squinted as she focused her concentration. "I believe…there. Yes." The stone shimmered beneath the Knight of Air's touch, spiraling into a gateway that looked out from the open car window on the devastation that used to be Cassidy's house.

Wren dove through, Magnus right behind. The smell of smoke hit them like a physical presence as soon as they emerged onto Cassidy's driveway. Though the attack seemed to be over, Wren scanned the grounds for Gray.

Sirens cried in the distance. Afraid to get too close, Cassidy's neighbors stood at the end of the driveway and watched the flames claim the structure. A helicopter circled overhead, shining its spotlight over the grounds.

"Ignore them," Magnus indicated the neighbors. "We don't have much time." Magnus picked his way through the rubble of the house. "I sense her."

Wren heard his words. "Hey, the weird silence is gone. What about the chopper?"

"Take out the light, I'll see what I can find." Following a trail only he could see, the big man stepped over fallen, splintered A-beams, shattered glass, and segments of furniture with jagged gashes in the fabric, impervious to the skin-damaging material beneath his bare feet. Tendrils of smoke lazily drifted up from smoldering sections of carpet.

Wren raced around back, took aim with one of her knives at the low flyer's beacon and threw. The glass shattered and the spotlight went out. Mission accomplished, she reconnected with Magnus.

The big man came to a halt at the front edge of the patio and moved his head from side to side, searching. With a fallen expression, eyes round and moist, he shrugged.

"I lost the trail. I sense her in the house." He walked to the rim of the wreckage and pointed to a spot where her kitchen used to be then walked to the pool's edge. "Another hint of her is over here. But then the trail just… vanishes. It's like something picked her up and flew away with her. There is no trace of her upon my element."

"Do you think Gray took her?" Wren asked, stepping out onto the patio. "She can't be gone." She tripped up onto the slab of wall covering the pool.

We just left her a few minutes ago.

"She's gone." Magnus moved alongside her and rested one bare foot on the downed wall. "Wait." He dropped to his knees and placed his palms upon the slab. "I sense…"

She's in the pool.

"Check the pool." Wren's voice sounded loud and strident.

"If she were in the water, she would have drowned by now."

"We don't know that."

"Wren…"

"Please, Magnus."

"What about those around us? We are exposing ourselves. "

"Who who cares! Just pick up the wall."

"Okay, Wren, okay. Stand back." Magnus jabbed massive fingers under the slab, leaned back and lifted. Shoulders, thighs and back bulged, straining the simple fibers holding his shirt together, but the slab remained firmly in place. With a growl, he pulled more from the earth, added to his mass and strength. Big before, now he topped eight feet and his skin darkened to the color of freshly turned soil. His clothes ripped along the seams.

Another massive effort and the slab shifted, inched upward.

"You're doing it." Wren watched his face lose distinction, features flattening as he absorbed more of his element until his face resembled a vaguely human grouping of crags and outcroppings upon a rocky summit. No longer that of a human man.

The wall lifted clear and, with a last intense heave, he shoved it out of the way. Cassidy stared unblinking into the night sky, lips curved in a restful smile. Wren dove in, lifted Cassidy's face out of the water and swam over to the side.

Magnus, heavily under the influence of his element, stood still as a mountain.

"Help me." Wren gasped, struggling to keep herself and Cassidy afloat.

He lifted Cassidy out with one hand and yanked Wren out with the other like she was a sodden rag doll.

Taking Cassidy in her arms, she laid her flat and felt for a pulse. Nothing. "We need to do CPR." Wren mimicked what she saw Cassidy do to that little girl earlier, found the spot on her chest and pumped thirty times then breathed twice. "Do something, Magnus," she screamed. "Don't just watch me." *Come on, Cassidy, breathe.*

"She was under too long." His words came out slow and ponderous.

Thirty pumps. "No, Magnus, she was a swimmer." Two breaths and pump. "She held some kind of record for holding her breath. We can bring her back." Two breaths. "Now get your big ass down here and pump."

Come on.

Patio tiles cracked under his weight as he slowly knelt next to Cassidy. Placing his giant hands across her chest, he prepared to push.

"Not there. You'll break her. Lower." Wren puffed two breaths into Cassidy's mouth then pointed to the right spot. "There. Go. Pump."

Magnus pumped harder than Wren, and slower, affecting Cassidy's entire body with each mighty push.

Wren puffed again and received a mouthful of water. Cassidy sputtered, coughed and rolled on her side.

"Odin be praised." The Earth Knight's features regained their more human definition. "Good job, kid."

Wren rubbed Cassidy's back while she expelled what seemed like a third of the pool water. A more natural color returned to the Earth Knight's cheeks.

Police cars pulled into the driveway. Their flashing lights bathed the wreckage in alternating flashes of blue and red.

"We're outta time," Wren whispered. "Need a gateway, like, now."

Magnus searched for a suitable spot. "We can use the pool."

"What? That's not a doorway."

Beams from the officers' flashlights cut across the yard and the chatter from their radios burst through the night.

"It'll do. It's a transition point between elements." He snaked his arms under Cassidy and lifted .

"Hey." One of the officers spotted them. "You in the yard. Stop."

"I'll buy you a minute." Wren stood and raised her arms in surrender. "Hello, officers. We are unarmed."

"Get down on the ground." Weapons drawn, the police officers scrambled through the remains of the house.

"Hurry up," Wren whispered. "They're coming."

"Downdowndown. Now." An officer commanded.

Magnus fumbled then drew a glowing gateway card out of his back pocket and flicked it onto the surface of the water. Gold tinted ripples radiated outward and formed the edge of the gateway. As soon as the seal of the Order came into view, Wren dove through. Magnus followed right behind.

Chapter 28

Faces swam in the light. Familiar faces locked in expressions of desperate concern looked down upon Cassidy. Wren. Magnus. Rhythmic pressure on her chest. Warmth on her lips. Wind in her mouth.

A voice in the distance. "She's gone."

The pounding on her chest ceased; but a different beat, this one generated from within, picked up the pace. Her skin felt tight and heavy.

A pressure began in her lungs. It spread to her stomach and leaped into her throat. Water gushed from her mouth and nose. She coughed and gasped as the taste of sweet air reached her starved lungs.

More. She needed more. As the water fled her system, she replaced its absence with the invisible life all around her, breathing in the scents she'd grown up with—grass, salt water, sand. Her insides tingled, tiny pinpricks of pain-laced pleasure brought her back to the moment.

I'm alive. Someone, it must have been Magnus, picked her up and cradled her against his soft, grainy skin. He smelled like her grandfather's cornfield after a summer rain, rich and fertile. Cassidy buried her face against his chest and drank in his scent.

"You're safe now," he murmured in her ear and pressed her close.

She had the impression of walls closing about her and, for a split second, every inch of her skin itched like an army of centipedes marched across her body. Her surroundings changed, the familiarity of a moonlit night in her own backyard replaced by a black field of glimmering orange stars. Alarmed, she raised her head, but Magnus pushed it back into place.

"Shshshhhh," he whispered, dropping his chin to the top of her head, offering some measure of comfort. "It will be over before—"

Another eye blink, another setting change.

Cassidy stared up at a rough stone ceiling adorned with the mismatched peaks of stalactites aglow in a pale white light.

"Can you stand?" Magnus asked.

Cassidy nodded and he set her down, but held her close for support. The warm stone floor soothed her bare feet. They'd brought her to some sort of underground chamber that reminded her of her trip to Carlsbad when she was fourteen. The caverns there were beautiful, but this one put those dank holes to shame.

Three strangers, dressed in odd outfits like a cast from a diverse time-travel movie, stood atop a silver insignia carved into the stone floor. They held back, giving her time to find a measure of comfort in her new surroundings.

The chamber stretched out before her. Midway through, a stream burbled across the floor. It flowed from under the wall on her left to disappear beneath the stone on her right. Spanning that stream was a magnificent bridge made of a black crystalline material that reflected the light from the glowing crystals mounted evenly along the chamber walls. On the far side of the bridge, an opening led further into the rock.

Where is the door I came through? She turned. Against the wall, outlined in glittering gold, shimmered a gateway to…chaos. The setting looked like her backyard, but the wreckage…and her house?

Gone.

Two policemen popped their heads into view.

Her strength fled. She would have fainted, but for the Earth Knight's support. As she watched, the gateway collapsed, shrinking in on itself until, with a final twinkle, it closed on her past.

This is a mistake. It has to be. How can it all just be gone? Cassidy stared at the blank stone wall, lip quivering, and willed the gateway to open, to show her house and yard and pool and life whole and back to normal.

"I am sorry, Ms. Sinclair." A deep, sincere male voice broke the silence.

So am I.

Cassidy didn't want to move, didn't want to turn from this spot, didn't want to acknowledge another abrupt change in the course of her life. Hadn't she been through enough already?

Apparently not. She took a deep breath, squared her shoulders, and slowly spun to face the others in the room. Wet clothes peeled off her skin. She shivered and clasped her arms around her still soaked body.

"Oh, for the sake of…Magnus, could you not get the girl some dry clothes?" A tall, whip-thin woman with waist-length white hair streaked with faint lavender highlights, left the confines of the symbol on the floor. She crossed the distance in a hurry, stripped off her long white cape and draped it across Cassidy's shoulders. "That will do for now. My name is Cyndralla." She smiled in welcome, showing long white teeth.

*Those eyes…*Timeless. Critical. And a sparkling shade of violet.

Cassidy couldn't help but stare. While the woman was attractive, there was something about her that seemed…off. Maybe it was her face—high cheekbones flared wide then tapered into a thin round chin. Or, it could be her teeth. When she smiled, there seemed to be far too many to fit comfortably in such a narrow mouth. And her voice… The strange lilt and cadence to her speech was musical. She'd never heard anything quite like it. The way Cyndralla extended each syllable, as if savoring the feel of the words on her tongue before releasing them, struck Cassidy as beautiful.

"It's not polite to stare, dear," Cyndralla said.

"Oh, sorry." Cassidy shook her head to erase her lapse in etiquette. "Sorry. And, um, thank you for the cloak. I'll return it soon." She pulled it tighter about her. The heavy, sumptuous fabric engulfed her body in its warm embrace.

Beyond Cyndralla, the others waited their turn to greet the newcomer. A swarthy man dressed in baggy trousers and a loose fitting, blue button-down glided forward.

"Dronor, at your service." The man bowed, clasped Cassidy's fingers and kissed the back of her hand. "Welcome." He raised one eyebrow and stroked his moustache down to the tip of his manicured goatee.

Cassidy didn't like the way he eyed her, and the lecherous echo of his touch made her shiver. She wanted to pull back, but figured it would be impolite and didn't want to offend. Instead, she offered a polite nod.

A second gentleman, dressed in tight black pants, ruffled shirt and shiny black boots, stepped forward. His long white hair hinted at an age his youthful physique and sparkling eyes contradicted.

"Cassidy Sinclair, I am the Precept of the Knights Elementalis. You may call me Stillman."

Cassidy sensed his authority without having to touch him. Here stood a man used to giving commands and having them obeyed without question. Under the scrutiny of his measured stare, she stood a little straighter and held her breath.

Stillman's smile banished the tension and her mounting nerves.

"Be at ease, child. You are welcome to this place, the Cradle of the Elements." He strode forward and wrapped her in a tight, grandfatherly hug.

At first contact, Cassidy sensed genuine affection, gratitude, and ageless serenity. He stepped back first and held her at arm's length. "I believe some measure of thanks are in order."

"For what, sir?"

All heads turned at the scuff of leather on stone from the opening at the other end of the room. Dev stormed in, arms cutting back and forth in time with his steps.

Cassidy overheard Magnus whisper to Wren, "Here it comes."

Dev thundered across the chamber and stood over one of the triangles in the Order's seal.

Wow.

He looked great dressed in form-fitting leather pants and sleeveless leather vest, every bit the primitive warrior.

"Another meeting without me?" Dev's nostrils flared, anger flashed in his crimson-flecked eyes. "I've been restricted to the Cradle, not kicked out of the

Order. The least you can do is include me in—" His mouth quit flapping the moment he locked eyes with Cassidy and his posture radically changed from one of anger and violence, to one of self-conscious embarrassment.

Cassidy watched the other Knights exchange baffled looks, except for Magnus, who grinned. Wren shifted away, quickly turning the crushed expression compressing her features to the floor. Cassidy had the decency to look away before Wren realized she had seen.

"I...I...I'm sorry, Ms. Sinclair, I didn't know you were here." Dev bowed.

"Cassidy, please, and it's no problem. Really," Cassidy said. "How are you feeling?"

"Um, much better, thank you." Dev took a step back. "I guess I'll...be... seeing you around. Bye." With that, he turned on his heel and hustled out of the room.

Stillman cocked a glance at Cassidy then at the retreating Knight of Flame.

"Interesting," he said. "Magnus will see to your accommodations. Make yourself at home, my dear." With a nod, he followed Dev, but at a much more leisurely pace, hands clasped behind his back. The other Knights took their cue and filed out after saying their own farewells with a wave or a nod.

Wren slipped away at some point, leaving Magnus alone with Cassidy.

That was weird. Dev looks better though. Amazing.

"Let's find you a room. I think there's one over by the Knight of Air."

"That's not the creepy guy, is it?"

Magnus chuckled. "Who, Dronor? Nah. He's the Knight of Water. Cyndralla is the Knight of Air."

So, she is a Knight.

"She seems nice." Cassidy said.

"She has her moments." Magnus led the way.

What does he mean by that?

Chapter 29

*T*HUNK. *THUNK.*

Wren hit the center of the target, the knives spaced no more than a half inch apart. The old-school paper targets were set at different heights along a densely packed sand wall, peppered with the results of earlier throws.

She grabbed another bunch of practice blades from the half-full bin, rolled to her right, aimed, threw. Another one in the middle.

Of course he wants Cassidy. Who wouldn't?

She tumbled left. Balanced. Threw. Center hit on the high target.

He hates me now.

Executing a perfectly balanced back-handspring, she landed, sighted low and threw. Bull's-eye.

I ruined it.

From sixty feet out she drilled one knife after another into the center circle. Each throw slammed into the target harder than the last, sinking in as far as the rounded handle, until the bin emptied and the targets looked like pin cushions.

Her mind raced from one incident to the next with Dev at the center of her maelstrom. Hungry, exhausted, she needed sleep. She'd been on the go for nearly forty-eight hours straight and needed to put it in "park" for a little while.

But when she got like this, with crazy, self-mutilating thoughts screaming around in her head, she had to move. Trying to fall asleep only made the situation worse. She had to push herself until both her mind and body were too exhausted to function. At that point, she'd collapse and sleep it off.

Been there. Done that. Need to do it again.

The knives weren't cutting it. She needed a challenge, one that would knock her out for the night.

Gauntlet.

Wren headed for the darkened doorway in the back corner of the room where the mats ended and the floor resumed. The cool stone barely registered on bare soles toughened through harsh practice sessions over the years, but was enough to center her in the moment. Pushing thoughts of her betrayal, and the light in Dev's eyes when he saw Cassidy, out of her immediate thoughts, she focused on the task at hand—survival.

As she stepped through the doorway, the crystals in the Gauntlet room flared to life, illuminating the blades, mallets, open pits and other, more insidious, challenges that packed every inch of the room. To make it through to the open door on the other side required total concentration and fearless execution. Hesitation only got you thumped, or worse.

She inhaled a deep breath and blew it out slowly. The first time she'd run the course, Dev coached her through, offering words of encouragement and goading her to perform better. His voice echoed in her head now, "Only run the gauntlet when your mind and body are fresh."

Whatever.

She pulled off the loose t-shirt and faced the challenges in her sports bra and form-hugging pants.

You can still chicken out. No one would know. She bent and stretched, loosening tired muscles. *I'd know.* Toes behind the safety line of the first obstacle, the room sprang to life challenge-by-challenge, until the scrape of stone and metal reached a sustained crescendo.

I forgot how loud this place got.

The first iron-mounted obstacle whirred and clacked. Metal bars as thick as her wrist and as long as her arm swung above her head, at waist level and near her ankles at varying speeds. No two passes were the same.

She watched the moving bars, gauged the timing, and looked for the pattern that would keep her safe. Blowing the air out of her lungs to shrink her profile, she dove under the first bars. She twisted, lifted her left foot, dipped her shoulder, jumped up, grabbed the frame and vaulted beyond the last bar's reach.

Clear. Easy.

Another agility-based obstacle squatted in front of her. Pillars of stone swung ponderously from side to side, overlapping and sometimes smacking the one next to it with a sharp report. She didn't want to get caught between those two. Again, speed, timing and total concentration led to success here. Dev had told her not to touch the stone with her fingers or risk getting them squished.

Yeah. No shit, buddy.

The stones, some taller and wider than her, swung through and returned, whistling as they picked up speed. The breeze from their passing blew her short hair around.

Dev would have sai—stop. Forget what he would have said. Just do it.

The stone rushed by, she jumped in and slid between the passing monoliths. *Dev said to—*

A stone grazed her butt, shoved her forward into the path of another. At the last moment, she slid between the last two and squeaked through to the other side.

Bent over, hands on her knees, heart pounding, she caught her breath. *Too close.*

If she could, she'd have turned around, skipped the rest and gone back to her room. Better that than get hurt when the Order needed her the most. But the Gauntlet was a one way ride. Either finish or...well, finish. There was a panic buttoned mounted near the entrance that would shut this bitch down, but she wasn't in a position to hit it.

That's why you always ride with a partner.

She eyed the next obstacle, the one that gave her nightmares. Great gears meshed, driving the pistons that stabbed swords into the metal frame from the bottom and sides. At the top, a large fan, spiked with additional blades, spun lazily. Its slow pace didn't deceive her. She knew it would descend upon her once she entered, forcing her to quickly place her feet and slide around the other prodding points.

She nearly lost her hand the first time she went through, but Dev saved her. He jammed Cinder into the mechanism to stop the blades before they nailed her.

Who's going to save you this time?

Determination pushed through her veins, adding a little extra bounce in her step.

Sword blades flashed and jabbed throughout the frame.

The first time she braved the Gauntlet, she had asked Dev why the blades were dull. His response made perfect sense. He told her that the obstacle tested a warrior's concentration and reflexes. It wasn't supposed to kill anyone; but, and he made sure he had her attention, if you get hit with one of those blades it will definitely ruin your day.

She stepped up to the whirling, shining steel and wiped her palms on her pants.

Analyzing the pattern, she waited for it to restart and leaped in. Her foot slipped out from under her and she went down on one knee, throwing her out of position. The blades at the top of the frame dropped fast, scything the width of the obstacle's cage.

Wren flattened herself against the floor, hoping that the blades would stop before they thwacked against her breasts and ribs. If they could slice off a hand, they could do some major damage to other, more tender, parts.

Six inches...the blades whirred closer. Their breeze kissed her face. She clenched her eyes tight, grabbed the legs of the cage and braced for the impact.

Who will be the one to find me?

The first sword grazed her breast. *Oh man, oh man.* She clenched her jaw, but the blades stopped and the entire room wound down. Bars, blades, and stones reset to their starting positions.

"You know better."

Father.

The pressure on her chest let up and Wren opened one eye to see the blades rise to the top. Heat flooded her face and hot tears fell.

"Come out of there."

Her lip quivered. "No." Her voice sounded wet and miserable to her ears.

"Please come out from there. It's safer to talk over here."

Avoiding his eyes, she retraced her steps through the obstacles. Stillman sat on the floor near the entrance and opened his arms wide. Wren melted into his embrace. The fit had changed, but in his arms she still felt like a little girl.

"It's okay." Stillman stroked her hair and rocked back and forth. "Everything's alright, little bird."

Her heart swelled when she heard his special name for her.

"He hates me, Father."

"He doesn't hate you."

"Yes, he does, and I don't blame him."

"I need to tell you something and it's not going to be easy for you to hear," Stillman said.

Wren swallowed the lump in her throat and sat up, putting a little distance between them. The dark circles under his eyes were new and the seams of his face like wide cracks in his armor.

"I've seen things." His voice was no more than a whisper.

"You've had more visions?"

"I always have visions, Wren. Knowing what they all mean is an entirely different matter, I'm afraid." He licked his lips. "Catching a glimpse of the future without knowing the full circumstance is more curse than gift, but I'll take any edge I can get in the battle against Shadow."

"What have you seen?

"I saw the rise of Shadow in Tampa. I saw Dev losing control, but I didn't know when it would come to a head."

"I know. That's why you put me with him. To watch him."

Stillman nodded. "Yes...and no. While I am the head of the Order, I am still a doting father. I may not have given you physical life, but I love you no less for that. I saw the adoration in your eyes whenever he entered the room. We all did." He shook his head. "I thought it nothing more than a passing crush. And, by having you work closely with him, I thought you would outgrow it."

"But I didn't."

"No." Stillman's face softened into a sad smile. "Please, forgive an old soldier his short-sightedness. I may have lived for a long, long time, but I still make mistakes, and I feel that I made a, how do they say it now, a 'doozey' in this case."

Wren lowered her head, letting his words sink in. He didn't reveal anything she didn't either already know or had suspected. It also didn't do anything to alleviate her feelings of betrayal and desolation.

"There's something more," Stillman continued. "I see this Cassidy Sinclair playing a larger role in the coming events, but exactly how..." He shrugged. "She will change things. Of that, I am certain. It is good that she is here with us now." Stillman lifted Wren's chin with two fingers. "Know that you have done nothing wrong. The Knight of Flame was too far down the path for you to save him. That was never your responsibility. It needed to come to this. You did your duty. Remember that." He got up to leave. "You should get some sleep. I see long days in our future."

Wren got to her feet. "Even I can see that."

Chapter 30

THERE WERE ONLY TWO WINGS OF THE CRADLE WITH EMPTY ROOMS AND DEV strolled through the first one, poking his head into all the doorways.

Where did Magnus take her?

Pace nonchalant, hands in his pockets, he ambled along. If he ran into her, he didn't want it to be so obvious that he'd just spent the last thirty minutes tracking her down.

I can't believe she's here. What happened? The last room at the end of this hall was empty as well. *Figures. She's on the other side.*

He retraced his steps and turned down a side hall.

Hi, Cassidy. No. Hi, Ms. Sinclair. No. Hey, Cassy. Dev shook his head. *Hello. Remember me?*

"Will this be enough?" Magnus's question drifted out of Cyndralla's room.

"I do not know yet," Cyndralla said. "You just gave me the new sample."

"I thought you were magic."

Dev sauntered in as the Knight of Air walked around the purple metal table that stood near the center of her cavernous purple room. Everything was purple—tables, chests, shelves, even the stone walls shone a pale shade of purple. Smaller tables, arranged in a semi-circle behind the main work space, held containers and vials filled with different colored powders, crystals and liquids.

Toward the back of the room, a flattened mound of loose silk, cashmere and fine, treated furs spilled out over a large area big enough to park a small plane. Above the heaped fabric, hung a large tapestry depicting two dragon silhouettes encircling a miniature version of the world. A golden rune sparkled in the center of the globe. Dev had asked about the piece years ago, and Cyndralla told him it was based on a myth her father told her when she was a youngling.

"Damn, Cyndy, what's with all the purple."

"I like purple. Now, hush."

Magnus nodded to his friend as Dev took a spot next to him and leaned his elbows on the table. The usually cluttered surface had been cleared to make room for a lead-lined x-ray smock they'd spread across it. Six jagged segments of what looked to be a broken ostrich egg made of glass lay in its center. Whatever it was, Cyndralla wasn't taking any chances. She'd covered it in a blue suspension field. Blue was stronger than yellow, but not as intense as pink.

So she is concerned, but not crazy scared.

"Where's Cassidy?" Ignoring the shield, Dev reached for a curved shard. The glass was at least an inch thick, the inside blackened.

Cyndralla smacked his hand. "That is not for touching."

"Alright. Alright." Hands at his side, he peered at the specimens through the magical haze. "What are they?"

Austere in her sleeveless white dress, she grabbed a long crystal rod from her desk and flipped over one of the charred pieces.

"New samples of that shadow magic." Magnus said. "I grabbed these at the hospital this morning."

With the snap of her fingers, Cyndralla called a beam down from the ceiling that penetrated the shield and bathed the shards in bright light. As she concentrated on the shadow orb remnants, she chewed the inside of her cheek.

"You know, Cyndy," Magnus's voice came out as a deep rumble, "You look pretty when you work."

Her eyes flicked up, then back to her work. A hint of a smile played across her lips.

"What happened?" Dev asked.

Magnus moved in close. "Your friend Gray opened up a can of whoop ass on St. Matthew's this morning." He whispered so as not to disturb Cyndralla. "Lots of people dead. Cassidy was there and she saved a little girl."

"She must have been covering the story for her newspaper."

"Yeah. Let's go with that."

"What's that supposed to mean?"

"She was there with Gray. As his guest."

Anger sparked. Dev clamped his teeth together to stop the loud curse from interrupting Cyndralla's research. "You're wrong."

"Sorry, brother, but that's what she told us."

Rage boiled. Dev felt an overwhelming need to attack, to fight something, anything. His friend was close and could take a good beating. He pulled back his fist.

Magnus eyed him, one eyebrow raised.

What am I doing?

Cyndralla murmured a phrase that prickled his skin. She waved her palm over the shards in a slow circular pass. A thin, black tendril rose up from the largest piece. When it hit the magical blue light, it fizzled and disintegrated.

A horrid stench wafted from the orb.

"What is that smell?" Dev covered his nose with both hands, but it didn't keep out the foul reek. At least he wasn't raging anymore.

"Man, I hate that taste." Magnus stuck out his tongue.

Cyndralla pursed her lips as she studied the two of them. "Interesting. I triggered a latent shadow element that clung to one of the shards."

"Bleh. Warn a guy next time, will ya?" Magnus swallowed hard.

"So, Develor, you smelled the shadow magic?" Cyndralla asked.

"Are you sure that wasn't Magnus?"

Magnus backhanded him across the shoulder.

"And you, Magnus, tasted it." She tapped her chin with a slender fingertip.

"Yeah. It's happened a few times now, at the hospital and in Cassidy's neighborhood."

"And this all means…what?" Dev asked.

"It means that the same shadow magic that Magnus felt at the club site was the cause of all the deaths at St. Matthew's."

"Can you counter it?"

She sighed and tossed her tongs on the back table.

"No. I need more to go on. I need a whole one."

"That's what I was afraid of." Magnus said.

Cyndralla waved her hand over the shards and both the intense spotlight and the magical field winked out.

"They are safe now." She paced across the lavender floor. "This is new magic, boys, and nasty. I have never felt anything like it before. I wish I could do more, but I am stuck without the source."

"We'll just have to find you one," Dev said.

"What's this 'we' stuff, buddy? You're grounded," Magnus teased.

"Yeah, yeah. Don't remind me."

"Oh, and Cassidy is sleeping down the hall," Magnus threw over his shoulder as he headed for the door. "I set her up in the spare quarters next to our illustrious mage here. Come on. I'll fill you in on what's been going down in groove town."

"Groove town, really?" Dev asked.

Magnus shrugged. "I'm in a mood."

"You're always in a mood." Dev followed the big man out. "So, the hospital?"

ಚಿಂಡ

Dev listened intently to every word out of Magnus's mouth and had a hard time not exploding on the spot. The rage burned inside him at the thought of Gray attacking people, his friends, and especially Cassidy. After the Earth Knight finished explaining about how she almost died, flames crackled from Dev's hands, but he fought the spread to the rest of his body.

After a quick check on Cassidy, he slapped Magnus on the back and charged down the hallway to Stillman's office.

He has to listen. I need to be out there.

Dev burst through the doorway and snapped to attention. "Sir, this cannot stand."

Stillman, bent over a parchment unrolled across his desk, held up one finger for silence. Dev steamed, little white wisps escaped from his nostrils and rose to the ceiling. His blood boiled. Wavy lines of heat shimmered off his bare arms. If Stillman didn't acknowledge him soon, he would immolate that desk and all the books in the room.

"Yes, Knight of," Stillman looked up and frowned, "Flame."

"You need to rescind your decision. Reinstate me."

"No."

The pressure in Dev's chest soared.

"We almost lost her today."

"Lost who?"

Are you kidding me? "Lost Cassidy. Sir. I—We can't afford to lose her."

Stillman crossed his arms, face locked in stern annoyance. "We did not lose her and now she is here. Safe. Allowing you free access would accomplish nothing."

Dev shook under the strain of keeping his element at bay. *How can he be so blind? I need to be in this fight.*

"With all due respect, Sir," Dev's voice trembled. The fire inched up his arms. "We need to hit Gray now, before he kills again."

"How do you propose we do that, champion?" Dronor's odd inflection and macho arrogance fueled Dev's flame. He hadn't heard the wet knight enter the room and didn't know how much Dronor had overheard.

The Knight of Water passed close enough to brush against Dev's arm on his way to Stillman's desk. They sizzled.

"Look at you," Dronor sneered from Stillman's side, "You are out of control, a disgrace to the Order."

"Sir," Dev ignored Dronor, focused on Stillman. "I can control it."

"Is this the control you speak of?" The Knight of Water barked out a laugh.

Dev growled, took half a step toward Dronor.

"That's it, Knight of Flame, give in to the fire," Dronor said.

"Enough," Stillman slapped the desk, "Both of you. Quinteele, you are dangerous. The decision stands. Dronor, Cyndralla needs an intact shadow orb. She can't negate the magic without it. Find one. Search the waters of Tampa Bay and the surrounding areas. If you don't find it in the water, search the land."

"But, sir, I—"

"See Cyndralla for details on what to look for. Dismissed."

Dronor clicked his heels together and strode from the room, glaring at Dev the whole way.

"You, Develor Quinteele, need to find balance." Stillman stood and walked over to stand before his Knight. "There are more emotions inside there," he poked Dev's chest, "than anger or rage. Find them. Use them. You are strong, but you can be so much stronger."

"This waiting for some miraculous epiphany is killing me. I need to do something. What can I do from here to help?" His anger burned, but the rage subsided along with his flames.

Stillman stared into Dev's eyes for a long time. "Look within yourself. Find that balance. For I fear that, if you do not, we are all lost."

Beaten again, Dev walked from the room. By the time he reached his quarters, the anger that normally bolstered his soul was replaced by a cold sense of dread. He sat on the stool in front of his anvil.

His forge had been cool for too long. Wielding an acetylene torch at work gave him enough of a daily fix that he didn't miss it, at least, not until he stood before it. Then, the absence gnawed at him like an abscessed tooth, reminding him how much he missed the act of creation. Patching up old hulls with a slab of mystery metal was okay, got him by, but didn't come close to the elation of forging a new sword or axe or spearhead from a cold lump of metal.

Speaking of metal.... At least a dozen ore samples—gold, iron, copper, silver—lay atop the anvil—gifts from his neglected friend.

Where is the little guy anyway?

"Jester? Come on out, bud." He searched the floor for the telltale bubble, but it remained flat and firm. "Jester?" Nothing.

Odd. Dust billowed and filled the air as he brushed a hand over his ore cabinet. *I guess it has been a while.* Piece by piece, he put the samples away in their appropriate drawers. *I hope the little guy is okay.* He grabbed a block of Quinsteele. *He's a tough nut. He'll turn up.*

Dev stepped up to the trough beside his anvil and looked down the center opening to the burnt orange glow near the bottom. The long shaft tunneled deep into the planet and tapped into the magma near the Earth's core.

Find the balance, Stillman says. Look inside. What does that mean?

With a thought, Dev sent his need down that hole in the trough, into the bowels of the primal fire, and waited. The response came quickly. A hot breeze sighed from the opening, suffusing the room with moist heat. The immediate rise in temperature took his breath away.

It has been too long.

The normally faint orange glow intensified until it bathed the entire forge with its festive color and lava spilled over to fill the trough. Eyes never leaving the swirling mass of quasi-liquid fire, Dev backed to the doorway and pushed the button Magnus had installed. A stone door ground into place and sealed him into his crucible. Working this forge, born of the elements and shaped by the power of the Knights, was like stepping into the heart of fire itself. Only he had the power to withstand the extreme temperatures his work generated.

Find the balance. Stillman's words banged around his skull. *What will balance my rage?* He knew the answer.

Love. Love conquers all, right? Bullshit. Virgil was an ass, and love is for dreamers. He tossed the Quinsteele into the lava. *Quinsteele. Geez, I was hungry back then, curious. It took me years to figure out the perfect combination of metals and heat. But it was worth it.*

Dev grabbed the four-pound hammer and medium length tongs and placed them on the face of the anvil. Bare-handed, he extracted the softened metal from the lava. The super-heated Quinsteele mass glowed.

Pinching the sides of the malleable blob, he struck the first blow. The ring of hammer on hyper-diamond anvil sang out, bouncing off the stone walls of the small room. Centuries of swinging a hammer had deeply ingrained the proper speed and angle into his muscles so that he quickly worked into a rhythm, alternately striking the metal and anvil with precise, measured strokes.

"What will you be?" Dev whispered to the flattening mass in front of him. After a few minutes of hard pounding, he threw the chunk back into the lava to reheat. Cooled, Quinsteele proved impossible to work with.

While he waited, he gazed at his vast collection of smithing tools, some of which he made himself. Next to the diamond-edged chisel he made for the fine work on that Prince's dagger in Austria, stood a swath of fabric locked behind a glass frame. Lace. Lavender. Véronique.

Long auburn hair. Soft, tan skin. Eyes a vibrant blue-green—the essence of the Mediterranean Sea.

The old ache stirred in his chest—guilt, anger, regret, fear.

He tried to bury the memories and the pain beneath a thick layer of anger; but, once open, the insidious thoughts clung to his psyche like a tick whose head was rooted deep in his soul. *Fire kills ticks. Everyone knows that. But what if this tick was born of fire? How do I kill it then?* He scooped the glowing metal from the lava, splashing a few smoking droplets over the side, and slammed it on the anvil.

"Balance."

He swung the hammer hard and fast.

"What does a demon need with balance?"

Reckless, he caught the near-molten lump on the edge. It flipped off the anvil and splashed into the cooling vat with a violent hiss. Ruined. The hammer went next, whipped against the wall only to bounce off in a flurry of stone chips and land in the bubbling lava.

"Shit." Dev rescued the tool from a fiery demise and tossed it back on the bench.

Balance. Yeah, that'll happen.

Chapter 31

CASSIDY WOKE WITH A START. *THIS ISN'T MY ROOM.*
The light hit the wall in the wrong place. The obnoxious green numbers of her alarm clock didn't flash at her from the nightstand. Without moving her head to show that she was awake, she took in as much of the room as she could. There wasn't much to see in the dim light. Wall. Desk. White cloak draped over the back of a chair.

Cloak. Knights. It wasn't a dream after all. Magnus brought me here, to a room near Cyndralla.

She kicked off the soft blanket, got up and peeled the still damp t-shirt away from her skin. Maybe Cyndralla could scrounge up something else for her to wear. She fastened the cloak around her neck, padded out into the hall, and looked around for someone.

They don't expect me to just stay here, do they? She didn't want to intrude or put anyone out, but she really wanted out of these damp clothes.

Wet panties suck. The idea of taking them off and going without crossed her mind, but it felt disrespectful to go commando in someone else's house. And if the pig, Dronor, should come along, she wanted as much fabric between her and him as possible.

If she remembered correctly, Cyndralla's room was right next door. The Knight of Air was a little taller and markedly slimmer, but she probably had something that would get her by until she could get home and...*oh, right.*

"Hello? Cyndralla?" She poked her head into the Knight's room, but it was too dark to see anything.

"May I be of assistance?" Cyndralla appeared from around the closest intersection.

"Oh, um, hi," Cassidy said. "Sorry. I didn't mean to pry. I was looking for you."

"And I found you." Cyndralla walked past Cassidy and, with a casual wave of her hand, lit the room with soft white light.

Holy lavender, Batman. Somebody likes purple. Cassidy checked for a closet or armoire or dresser or even a cardboard box that might hold clothes, but found only books and scrolls and some wild, satiny nest thing in the back by the tapestry.

Maybe I can get something from Wren. I'll probably have to stitch a couple of things together, though. That chick is tiny.

"Tea?" Cyndralla waved her hand and produced a steaming hot decanter and two beautiful teacups, white porcelain with a riot of little purple flowers. "Sit. Relax. You have been through a great deal."

Cyndralla poured, her movements fluid and graceful. She turned the commonplace act into a work of art. With equal poise, she swirled her white dress and sat in a cushioned purple chair that hadn't been in the room until a second ago, crossed her legs at the ankle and tucked her feet under her chair.

Cassidy plopped into a chair that definitely was not there when she came in, but felt like a moose in comparison to the Knight, all fat ass and elbows.

"What can I do for you?"

"I was hoping to trade your cloak for something more substantial, maybe a dress, or, pants and a shirt." Cassidy sipped her tea. The nectar caressed her taste buds with the flavors of chocolate, peanut butter and vanilla wafers ground together with a dash of cinnamon. *Heaven.*

Her grandmother had served a version of tea at Christmas, but it tasted like she'd poured hot water over her scruffy, old dog. Her mother made her choke it down anyway.

Cyndralla's liquid perfection went down smooth, warming Cassidy from the inside out. She cradled the cup in both hands and savored the rich aroma.

"You like?" The Knight of Water studied Cassidy's reaction. "I do not take the time to entertain."

"What about the other Knights? Don't you guys get together?"

"Guys?" Cyndralla's eyebrows drew down. "Cassidy, I am female. I thought my gender obvious, and why you came to me."

"Wha-? Oh, no, I mean, yes. Of course you are. I meant guys as in, you know, one of the guys." *Yeah, that explained it.* "Sorry. Let's start this over. Do you and the other Knights get together?"

"On occasion, but not for tea."

The image of Magnus and Dev sitting down and sipping tea from dainty cups with their pinkies out made her giggle.

"So, you would like something else to wear."

"Um, yes, please. If you have something you think will work."

"Stand up. Let me see you."

"What?" Cassidy tilted her head.

"Stand up and take off your clothes. How can I find you something to wear if I cannot see your figure?"

Yep. That's what she said. Well, didn't this just get awkward?

"Um, look, Cyndralla, I don't..."

"Oh." Cyndralla's face brightened in recognition. "Shy, is it? Here, I will close the door so no one else can see." She murmured something under her breath. "We are alone."

Cassidy spun. All signs of the doorway had vanished. The wall was smooth, as if there had never been an opening there at all.

Oh boy. She bit her lip as the butterflies swarmed in her belly.

Cyndralla strolled around to her side of the table and reached to unfasten the clasp at Cassidy's neck, but Cassidy stepped back and raised her hands in front of her.

"I'm sorry, Cyndralla, but I don't work that way."

"You do not get undressed?"

"No." *She's going to make me say it.* "I don't like girls...in that way."

"Ms. Sinclair." There was an edge to her voice. "In order to get the proper fit, I need to know your measurements." She barked a command and Cassidy's clothes, what little there were, vanished.

"Wah." Cool air tickled Cassidy's skin. "Hey." Hands rocketed to the appropriate places.

From her toes to the tip of her head, Cyndralla gauged every inch of her body. The inspection lasted no more than a minute, but under that kind of scrutiny it seemed like forever. Partway through Cassidy relaxed and took it for the clinical exam that it was.

The Knight of Air finished, closed her eyes and murmured.

"You will find what you need over there." She pointed to a table in the far corner. "And for the record, I do not recognize members of your kind as acceptable mates."

Good one, Sinclair. Way to piss off your new friends.

"I will leave you to get dressed in peace. Please do not touch anything in here other than the clothes." Cyndralla walked toward the wall. By the time she reached it, the door had reappeared and she left.

My kind? What does that mean?

The clothes the Knight of Air conjured—silk bra and panties, sleeveless silk dress, silk hose, silk slippers, all a beautiful shade of lavender—whispered against Cassidy's skin as she slid into the luxurious outfit.

Dressed in such finery, she felt ready for a ball, not traipsing around dusty old tunnels and caves. But, if she wanted to check on Dev, that's exactly what she had to do. She hung a right out of Cyndralla's room and walked for ten minutes. The stone hallways looked the same—open doors leading into room after room after room.

One of these damn rooms must be Dev's.

The beautiful sheath dress swished around her knees with each step. *Magnus said to make the second left then walk until I start to sweat. Doesn't he know that women don't sweat? They glisten.*

Finally, the second left came up. She followed another hall filled with more freaking doorways. The change in temperature told her she was on the right track, rising from pleasant to uncomfortably warm within twenty feet.

I hope I don't glisten all over this dress. She wiped the moisture from under her eyes and across her forehead. Condensation beaded and ran down the walls into growing puddles on the floor. Evidently it had been hot in here for a while.

To continue down the hall was like walking into a furnace. Her normally loose, curly hair hung limp over her shoulders. Dark splotches marred the beautiful dress. Sweat beaded on her arms.

Why am I doing this again?

She had to check on her patient. As much as she wanted to believe she could remain distant, she cared and had to know how he was doing. The quick glimpse in the Portal room showed that the healing had progressed, but she'd feel better hearing him say it in person with no one else around.

So close, but so damn hot. Each step seemed like too much work, even breathing became a major effort. Like a fragile lavender rose in the desert, she wilted.

I can't do this. I'll catch him when it's cooler. What's up with this place? Light flickered out of the doorway up ahead, but she was well done and ready to go. She leaned against the wall before making the trek back to her room.

Boots shuffled into the hall up ahead.

"Véronique?" It was Dev's voice, but in a tone she'd never expected to hear from him. Fear. "Véronique, attendez. Je vous dois une explication."

Was that French? Cassidy felt the Knight of Flame's hot hand on her shoulder.

Shirtless, chiseled pecs flexing with his agitation, he faced her, eyes thrown wide in shock.

Damn, he looks good.

Dev spouted another few sentences in a foreign language.

What's he saying? "Dev, it's me, Cassidy." She didn't move and watched for the spark of recognition. "Who's Véronique?" Whatever it was, her gift told her that he was terrified and terribly sorry. *What set him off like this?*

"Oh, um, Cassidy, hi. Don't mind me." He scratched the stubble on his scalp. "Sometimes the forge messes with my head." Dev smiled, awkward, uneasy, and tried to brush it off as nothing, but Cassidy knew there was far more to this story.

"No worries. I wan—"

He held her shoulders and shifted past, reversing their positions in the hall. "I'd love to catch up, but I need to take care of something. Can we hook up, I mean, get together later?"

His confusion transferred through the hot touch of his fingers.

"Sure, sure. Whatever," Cassidy said.

"Good. Great. See you later. Oh. Hey, I like your dress." He hurried away, practically tripping over himself to get out of sight.

"Well, that didn't go as expected." Hands on hips, she waited, hoped he was just embarrassed and would recover in time to come back to her.

The hallway had returned to a normal temperature, but the dress was ruined. The doorway through which Dev had emerged seemed to call her name.

Well, what do you know? An open door. I wonder what's inside.

She slipped into his room. It was still hot, but not so warm that she had to get away.

Typical guy. Tools. Tools. Tools. They were everywhere. On the bench, hanging on the wall, scattered on the floor, everywhere she looked, tools. Dev lived in a small, functional room taken up mostly by the forge. A stone bench stood against one wall near the back next to a simple armoire and basin. Another table held a collection of bladed weapons—axes, swords, knives. Never a fan for weapons of any kind, she had to admit they were all stunning.

One knife in particular, with a dull orange crystal embedded in the base of the faceted–*that can't be diamond*—blade, hung in a chain harness from a peg on the wall.

Power emanated from that knife. She traced the tapered hilt with a finger, marveling at its sleek lines. It was beautiful, sacred. She wanted to hold it, feel its weight, but to do so without Dev's approval overstepped the bounds of her curiosity.

"Cinder," spoke a reverent voice from the doorway.

Cassidy yelped and grabbed her chest as her heart threatened to explode. "Holy hell, you scared me."

Without a word, Dev took down the harness. His face seemed calm, but she couldn't see his eyes.

Is he angry that I'm snooping around? Cassidy waited for his lead and hoped he didn't draw the knife.

He drew the knife. In his touch, the crystal flared to life, pulsing with a sharp orange glow.

"Look, Dev, I was just poking around." She backed away and knocked over the stool, but caught herself before she fell on top of it. "I'm so—"

"This is Cinder. She was created and presented to me upon my induction into the Order. Each one of us received an elemental focus. Magnus got that big axe, Cyndralla has her crown, and Dronor has that flimsy stick he thinks is a sword." He twisted the diamond blade so that it amplified the dim crystal-light, reflecting bright pinpoints onto the wall, the floor and Cassidy. There was no hint of fear or nerves or anything but cool confidence in his voice and bearing

"It's amazing." She reached out to touch the long curved blade, but he snatched it away.

After a few seconds, and what looked to Cassidy to be an internal struggle, he reversed the blade and offered it to her.

She reached for it, but hesitated. "Are you sure?"

"Go ahead."

As she took the blade, the crystal's fire winked out. Across her palm, the handle felt warm and smooth. Feather-light, it seemed a natural extension of her arm. She looked to Dev, asking permission to swing it with a glance. He took a giant step back and nodded.

This is crazy. Look at me with a big ol' knife in my hand.

She adopted her best hero pose—body turned, right leg forward in line with the blade, left arm back and bent up for balance, but before she could do anything else Dev stepped in behind her, his strong presence comforting despite her earlier scare.

"That stance is good if you are fencing." He squared her shoulders, put her back arm down and brought her feet almost even. "But will get you killed in a knife fight."

He picked up another knife from the rack on the wall and showed her the position he was looking for. She had it right the first time, except for the arms. He shifted them to chest level, elbows slightly bent.

Dev's uncomfortably hot hands glided over her skin.

She endured the pain and bit her lip to hide her wince. When he backed off to demonstrate the proper pose, she sneaked a look at her forearms. No burns, but they were bright red and tender.

"Balance on the balls of your feet, like this." Dev crouched, weight forward, and rocked from side to side in perfect balance. Cassidy caught a glimpse of his strength and could imagine his ferocity. As he moved, the muscles across his entire body flexed and relaxed in beautiful, lethal harmony.

Oh, yeah.

Dev must have detected her switch in focus. He stood up, put the knife back, and held out his hand for Cinder. Their fingers met during the transfer and she caught a hint of resignation and…sadness?

What's that about?

"I'll see you later, okay? You can look around some more if you want." Dev backed out of the room, smacking into the doorframe on the way. "Duh." He let out a self-deprecating laugh, and spun out the door, leaving Cassidy open mouthed and wide-eyed.

Chapter 32

Through the security gate and past the Port Authority administrative offices, the driver followed the main road to the dock. Separated by his tinted window, Alexander watched the grungy dockworkers gawk at the passing limo and vowed that if their drool left spots on the limo's immaculate black finish, he would feed them to his dragon.

"Berth 257," Alexander said.

"Yes, sir."

Anonymous behind the dark glass, Alexander marveled at the size of the moored vessels. Huge supertankers capable of transporting several hundred thousand tons of oil sat in line with cargo ships piled high with blue, red and white shipping containers. Further down, a cruise ship reached into the sky taller than his father's black-walled fortress in Eastern Europe. Even the smallest of these maritime behemoths dwarfed the largest boats Alexander had sailed on through his many years.

Overhead the ship-to-shore cranes loaded and unloaded massive crates and boxes as if they weighed no more than a man, and set them down amidst the throngs of workers. A steady convoy of forklifts and loading vehicles ferried goods to and from enormous warehouses and dry goods silos hunched along the landward side of the dock.

The steady stream of human traffic drizzled to a stop once the last of the big ships shrank in the distance behind them. Ahead, Alexander spied the rusted deck of the barge he'd purchased. Compared to the ships he'd just seen, his boat appeared small, insignificant, and perfectly suited to his needs. A few old crates and a cargo net littered the wide flat deck. Across the stern hunched a dilapidated steering cabin. The glass had been broken out of its windows.

On land across from the barge leaned a rusted iron building. Surrounded by weeds, the small warehouse had disintegrated under the tortuous Florida sun. Glass-free windows gaped from partially collapsed walls and more than half the roof had fallen in.

Neither the barge nor the shed looked to have been touched in months, if not years; and, judging by the neglect and general disrepair of the dock, the workers stayed well clear of this area.

Excellent.

They rolled up alongside the derelict, opposite the gangway. Not waiting for the driver to open his door, Alexander got out and tapped the roof for the driver to pull away.

The less people who notice where I stop, the better. Although, in a few days, it will no longer matter.

Much like the rest of the immediate area, the plank bridge over the gap between the dock and the ship had rotted. Boards were missing or falling apart, and as he watched it pitch and roll with the flat deck, a support beam broke off and splashed into the water below.

Charming.

After a last check for curious souls, he layered a cushion of shadow across the bridge to ensure a quick, dry passage. But the effort cost him. Calling and controlling shadow under the inferno people called a sun in this cursed state required far more power than he anticipated.

Once across, he entered the ship's small cabin and paused to soak up what small shadows he found. The stifling, thick air clogged his lungs. He was out of the broiling sunlight, but the reek of salt, rust and dead fish punched him in the nose. And, like the rest of the vessel, the pilot house appeared abandoned and useless.

Anxious to be out of the stench, he strode the four steps to the far side, jabbed his finger into a rusted gap within a swiss cheese array of nearly identical holes, and triggered a mechanism. The thin façade of blank wall rose into the ceiling, behind which loomed a state-of-the-art bank vault door.

Alexander shielded his eyes against the sunlight reflecting off the stainless steel surface as a digital keypad and biometric scanner unfolded from the burnished surface. Once he entered the code and rolled his thumb over the scanner, the door clicked multiple times and swung wide on silent hinges. Wasting no time, Alexander stepped into the cooler, pitch-black interior and closed the door.

Much better.

At home in dark places, he descended ten steps to the first landing and marveled at the vastness of his creation—a storage hold of magical construct beneath a shallow-hulled wreck. When Shadow moved to this remote location, he needed someplace secure to store the orbs.

And what better place than one that did not yet exist.

He purchased the vessel, summoned this great hole and tied it to the barge via the vault door.

In the darkness below, deadly magic hummed—thousands of shadow orbs waited for deployment. He planned to ship most to choice targets across the US, but retain a small number for local use.

"Agridda." Alexander's whisper echoed in the darkness.

A pair of yellow eyes appeared in the air beside him. "Father." The word filled the space around him with a palpable malevolence.

"The orbs are to be shipped tomorrow. I will have a crew here later today to pick them up."

"My ssssister is gone." Thin black slits bisected pale yellow orbs and regarded him with cool detachment.

"You are aware?"

"Yessss. Felt her death."

"She was killed by the Knight of Flame."

Agridda charged around him, bestial eyes swimming in jagged circles through the darkness.

"The Knights know we are here and may try to stop us," Alexander warned.

"Let them come," Agridda hissed.

"If they do, hurt them. Kill one or two if you can, but not all. I want their annihilation to be at my hands."

"Yes, Father." The yellow eyes vanished.

Alexander sensed the latent power of the orbs and reveled in the might amassed beneath his feet. Never in the history of the Gray Lords had such a cache of raw shadow energy been harnessed in such a way.

I will kill them all and take my rightful place at the head of my father's organization.

Alexander left the darkness, locked the vault door and dropped the fake wall. He called his driver to pick him up then placed another call.

"Pick up the orbs at the dock. Send two hundred to Deep Services and the rest according to the shipping manifests of Seagren Chemical."

Tampa dies in forty eight hours.

Chapter 33

A WORKOUT HADN'T BEEN ON DEV'S AGENDA, HADN'T EVEN CROSSED HIS MIND until his steps brought him to the gym. Who was he to question his subconscious?

I shouldn't have gone back in the first place. Almost lost it. Oh man, and I called her Véronique.

Not in the mood for the weights or cardio, he eyed the heavy bag—a couple rounds with the blue dummy should cure what ailed him. Donning the Quinsteele-lined gloves from his locker, he rolled his neck, shrugged and approached his dangling opponent.

"I'm such an idiot."

The first few punches at half-strength warmed him up. He hadn't seriously worked out since before the fight at the club, and he welcomed using his muscles for something other than recuperating. Left and right, slowly at first, he attacked.

It felt good to hit something again, to feel the bag close around his fist as he drove the punch home. Pity the bag didn't fight back. He thought of the fight with Dronor and how his leg gave out, costing him the match. He would have kicked that Spaniard's ass if he'd been at full capacity.

But then Dronor would never have challenged me at all.

Dev pictured the bag as the Knight of Water and went at it full force. All thoughts of his latest embarrassment flew out the window as he pummeled his enemy. High, low combinations rocked the bag then he hammered the imagined Knight with a barrage of rib cracking upper cuts.

Bastard. Mid-roundhouse, Dev called on his elemental reserves. Molten energy screamed through his system, fed him strength and speed. He redoubled his efforts. Pace and power increasing with each strike.

Soon his fists weren't enough, and he changed style. Boxing morphed into Krav Maga. Open handed strikes, chops, and powerful front kicks sent the bag jangling at the end of its steel chain.

Lost in the moment, he forgot about the Knight of Water, forgot about the recent defeats, forgot about the restriction placed upon him by the Precept. All that existed, all that was real, in this place, at this moment, was the fight. No anger. No anxiety. No hesitation.

Krav Maga flowed into kickboxing. Fists on guard, legs battered the canvas. Left, right, high, low, all delivered with perfect balance and timing.

Dev roared and delivered a final straight kick that sent the bag flying back. It swung high and smashed into the ceiling.

Breathing fast, arm and leg muscles humming, Dev straddled a bench. It felt great to move again, get his blood surging and heart racing. Body strong, fit, and fully healed, Dev longed for the next meeting with Gray and his minions.

He's mine.

"Not bad, but your kicks are sloppy," Magnus said.

"Bite me." Dev lay back, still trying to get his wind back, and rested his arms across his forehead. His hands and feet throbbed. "How long you been there?"

"Long enough. What's up with you?" Magnus stood over him. "I've never seen you like this."

"Man, I'm losin' it. One minute I'm raging and the next I'm fumbling over myself." Dev sat up, elbows resting on his knees. "It's crazy...I'm crazy."

"You're not crazy. Psychotic, yes. But not crazy." Magnus mounted the stationary bike next to Dev.

"And then Cassidy came along," Dev said. "I don't know what to make of her. When I'm around her I feel awkward and foolish." Dev searched the gym for any one lurking around. "Off the record?"

"Yes, and bound by our friendship."

"On the bridge I was pretty messed up, at the end of my strength. I'd pulled all the fire I could hold and still got my ass kicked." Dev inched forward on the bench. "I was in full-on rage mode, you know, like when we found the torture chambers along those tunnels in Afghanistan, remember?"

Magnus snorted. "Yeah."

"I don't know if I can describe this." Dev locked stares with the big Swede. "When I met her eyes for the first time, it all...vanished, like she snuffed me out. The rage, the fight, all of it, wiped clean. I felt at peace, whole, for the first time since..." Dev stopped abruptly and looked away.

"So you like her," Magnus said.

"No, that's ridiculous. I don't like her." *I can't like her.*

"If you're going to waste my time, I'm going to go."

Dev knew he meant it, could tell from his tone that he wasn't going to put up with half-truths. Not this time.

Maybe it's time.

"I need you in this fight," Magnus said. "I don't believe we can win without you."

Dev drew a deep breath and thought back to his home by the sea. *Here goes...*"I'm a demon."

Magnus's lips teased a smile. "A demon?"

"I'm not joking around here. Straight up."

"Sorry."

"I hurt her, you see. I burned her, Magnus. Who but a demon would do something like that? It haunts me, replays in my dreams." Dev shifted on the bench. "The bastards almost broke me in that prison. Almost, but I took the element, accepted the fire and burned my way out." Dev watched Magnus's face for a reaction, but found only concern.

"Who did you burn?" Magnus asked.

"Véronique. We were pledged to be married before I went to Paris. But then I came home…changed." Dev's voice dropped low. "I was raw. Body shattered, emotions in tatters. But my spirit, Magnus, my spirit was alive." Dev saw the sparkle in his fellow Knight's eyes, saw that he'd experienced a similar feeling. "Before that prison, before the Templars, I had a life—a growing trade, and the love of a beautiful woman. I thought a year or so with the most skilled artisans in Christendom would take me to the next level, teach me something I didn't already know." Dev shook his head. "Véronique and I agreed, and so I left with Grand Master DeMolay the next morning.

"She was beautiful, Magnus. Tall, slim, long auburn hair, full lips, skin the color of honey, eyes the color of the Mediterranean." Describing her aloud for the first time in more years than he could count brought her image alive. With it came the buried truth he'd run from for centuries.

"The first few days were the worst. After escaping from the prison, I hid in a dress shop. Weak, hungry, and broken, I lay on the wooden floor and waited to die. I thought of her often, of how she would find another and follow her dream of a family. It hurt, but it was better that than her seeing me in such a diminished state."

Dev scraped his hand over the stubble on his head. "When the sun shone in my eyes through the front windows that first morning, I expected the owners to walk in and find me. I imagined the shriek at the blood stains on the floor. But they never came. As the day wore on, my inner fire burned and my body healed."

"How did it feel?" Magnus asked. "The fire?"

"Glorious. Like the sun shone from my soul."

Magnus nodded.

"By the end of the second day, I was up and about. Lucky for me the rats insisted on inspecting the newcomer. When they got close, I snatched them up and choked them down raw. I found some stale water in a rain barrel out back. It was gritty and tasted of tar, but got me by. By the third day, the rats stopped coming. Either they smartened up or I ate them all. I took the miraculous healing of my wounds as a sign that it was time to go home."

"I've had to eat rats myself." Magnus said. "They're not bad in a stew, but raw and squealing…"

"I killed them first. Didn't just suck them down alive."

"Don't be embarrassed. You did what you had to do." Magnus squirmed.

"Believe what you want. Anyway. That evening I tied a rough-spun skirt around my waist, stuffed an extra shirt into a burlap sack and struck out for home. I kept to the shadows until I was out of the city since I expected the soldiers to be out in force looking for me, but didn't see a one."

"Maybe they didn't realize you escaped," Magnus said.

"More likely they thought I burned up with the guards in the room. Regardless, I made it out and each day I felt better and better and better. The fire spoke to me, not so much in words, but in feelings and intentions. I still wasn't sure what kind of agreement I had made, but if the flame could be believed, it would serve me well. I travelled on foot for weeks, avoiding the main roads and villages, living off whatever I could catch or pick until I reached my home."

Dev's voice grew thick and husky. "It's hard to describe the feeling of coming home when you never thought to see it again. My heart melted as I saw my parent's inn; but, before I could go home, I needed to find Véronique, had to tell her I was back. The hour was late, well past midnight, with long hours yet before dawn. Not being able to run right over and grab her in my arms near killed me, but I took the opportunity to wash up with a dip in the sea, and to change into the spare set of leathers I kept in the forge."

"Did you burn through your clothes often back then?"

"More than I should have."

"Some things never change." Magnus smirked.

"The coals were cold, but my tools lay exactly where I left them. It gave me hope that what I'd hidden under the anvil a year before would still be there—a pouch with two gold rings. They were far from perfect—even though I spent weeks trying to get them just right before I left.

You know what's funny, Magnus?"

"What's that?"

"I can make perfect weapons, but when it comes to everything else, I fail. Why do you think that is?"

"I don't know, you tell me."

"You trying to pull a Freud?"

"*Ja Ja*. Lie back *und* tell me about your mother."

Dev ignored him and continued. "Rings in hand, I waited outside her window until the sun rose. As soon as her curtain moved, I was up and running. I listened at her window while her beautiful humming graced my ears, then risked a glance inside. She sat and brushed her hair on the edge of her bed. 'Véronique.' I whispered, but she didn't hear me. 'Véronique.' I called a little louder and she turned. I guess she didn't expect to see my face in the window because she inhaled to scream. I dove in the window and clamped my hand over her mouth before she got the sound out."

He waited for a sarcastic comment, but Magnus kept quiet.

"Her eyes were frantic, and though she looked directly at my face she didn't recognize me. I tried to calm her down, said her name over and over, but she struggled in my arms. She bit my hand and woke the fire. It crept through my system, bringing with it anger and more strength than I'd ever wielded before. It felt amazing. I was a god. I squeezed her chin and held her still until her wriggling ceased and I saw the recognition spark in her eyes."

Magnus nodded.

"She said my name and touched my face. I can't tell you how much I'd yearned for that moment. My heart pounded so hard I thought she might hear it. Her tears rolled over my fingers and she told me she thought I was dead."

"You were," Magnus said.

"Huh?"

"You were dead. The fire brought you back, gave you life."

Dev rejected the concept. *Fire destroys.* "No. It only gave me the power to get free. I exploded and killed those guards. That, to me, sounds like destruction."

"Let me ask you this." Magnus paused, tone serious and low. "Had you given up? Did you lie in your cell and want it all to end?"

How could he know?

The big man closed his eyes and dipped his head. "Your body was broken. You'd given up hope." His eyes opened, vision focused on an image from long ago. "You wanted it to end, longed for the freedom of death."

He's been there himself. "Yes." It was barely a whisper.

"My friend, fire gave you life much like earth gave it to me."

Could it be? No, he doesn't know the rest. Doesn't know what I did to Véronique.

"Wait, Magnus, let me finish." Dev took a steadying breath. "I cupped her face in my hands, but I couldn't control myself. I was so happy to see her. So excited to be home, to get on with our lives together. 'Your hands are hot,' she told me. 'Dev, you're burning me,' she told me. But I didn't get it, I wasn't listening, and all I could see was her pulling away from me. She slapped my hands. I felt rejected, I felt angry. Why would she do that? I loved her, thought of little else but seeing her gorgeous face and kissing those soft lips. Yet now that I was finally home, she was pushing me away."

The emotions came back hard. His hands smoldered. "The fire rose inside me, fanning my anger until it boiled over. I couldn't control it. My hands burst into flame. I don't know who screamed first. Me, at the shock of seeing my skin aflame or her at the pain I caused her."

He remembered the smell, that uniquely sweet aroma of burning skin.

"I released her, but the damage was done and our combined screams woke the rest of the house. Loud footsteps pounded down the hall outside her door. Fire spread to the rest of my body, engulfing me from head to toe. The heat must have been intense, but I didn't notice until the flames rolled across the bed linen and climbed the curtains. Véronique curled up in the corner farthest away from me and the spreading inferno, mouth frozen in terror. I saw myself reflected in her eyes—a monster, a demon, a destroyer. I wanted to stay, to assure her that this was all a mistake, but the door burst in on the foot of her father. He took one look at me and crossed himself. I leapt from the window and ran off into the dawn, away from the screams, away from what I'd done, away from the only woman I ever loved."

With his tale finally told, his emotional secret born in words and unleashed upon the world, Dev felt a release. Like a muscle cramped for centuries finally relaxing.

I guess I've been running ever since. No roots. No past. No pain.

"When did Stillman find you?"

"Two weeks later. Naked, lost, and shivering under a tree on the outskirts of Genova, Italy. I was convinced I was a demon and wanted to die. I hadn't eaten or slept in days, kept off the roads and out of sight. When Stillman caught up to me, I was on the verge of charging into a monastery and demanding they put an end to my blasphemous existence."

"Are you a demon?" Magnus gaze pierced into his soul.

"No." Dev's quiet response didn't convince either of them.

"What kind of bullshit answer is that?" Magnus pushed. "Are you a demon? Because it sounds to me like you were a kid who didn't know any better. A kid who unwittingly caused an accident."

"I burned her, Magnus." Dev's hands shook. He met Magnus's stare reluctantly. "Her face melted in my hands."

The Earth Knight's features hardened. "Did you mean to do it? Did you mean to hurt Veron—"

"Of cours—"

"If your answer is yes, Develor Quinteele, then I will kill you myself." Magnus stood and called on his element. It answered quick and hard, increasing his size and turning him to granite in seconds.

If my answer is 'yes' then I deserve to die.

Magnus wrapped Dev in a bear hug. "Which is it, Develor Quinteele?" He squeezed, lifting Dev off his feet.

"No. I didn't mean to do it. I loved her. Wanted to marry her." The air rushed from Dev's lungs as the pressure increased, but he had one more thing to say. "I would have given my life for her." Dev fell to the floor as Magnus released him.

Eyes closed, the Knight of Flame drew in a deep breath. The stillness of the moment and his brother's words settled into his soul.

"Well?" The menace was gone from Magnus's voice.

"No, Magnus. I am not a demon." No puffed up bravado. No delusions. Only truth, plain and simple. Dev climbed to his knees and bowed his head. His heart-felt admission worked its way through his conscious and subconscious mind, bringing order to the chaos wrought by long years of guilt and self-loathing.

Magnus placed his hand on the back of his brother's head.

"Tomorrow begins a new life, my friend. Accept it."

ꝏ

Dev's head swam from the revelation as he headed back to his room.

A new life? What about this old one?

Exhausted and emotionally drained, he wanted to hit the stone and wind down for a few hours. Disconnect from all the emo shit and take a breather.

It's not a new life I'm looking for, my friend. I just want my own life under control. Balance. It all comes back to that. Maybe Stillman knows what he's talking about.

Speaking of the old guy…

Dev stopped outside Stillman's office. The reception area was dark and empty, but a glow shown from the library door. Normally he wouldn't dream of intruding, but his instincts drove him forward into that light.

Books, books, books.

The place smelled…old. Moldy tomes filled dozens of freestanding bookshelves in perfect rows and columns through the center of the room. Two walls were reserved for parchments and scrolls that required special treatment or wouldn't fit into the regimented world of bookcases. The others housed cabinets with thousands of drawers and cubbies for storage of powders and the other crap alchemists needed to do their thing.

In the floor near the front of the room, another seal of the order gleamed, its triangles done in gold and onyx joined by a mother-of-pearl ring in the center. Above it hung an elaborate tapestry of Arthur and his knights.

He'd stood in Stillman's office a million times and never once ventured back here.

So why now? Looking for something, but not sure what, Dev walked the lanes. Crazy geometric symbols with arcane lettering decorated most of the available wall space. Even the ceiling sported mystic artwork, but nothing grabbed his attention. At the back of the room he found more of the same.

There's nothing here. On his way out, he noted the tapestry. Similar in subject to the one in Stillman's reception area, this one was taller than Dev, and displayed a far greater level of exquisite detail than he had seen in a tapestry before.

It's like a high-def version. Arthur, Lancelot, Merlin. There was something familiar about the graybeard. Up close, he looked a lot like Stillman. Same nose. Same facial structure. Same eyes. *I wonder if they're related.*

"So why do I care? Why did you call me in here tonight?" Dev asked, but the tapestry didn't respond.

Great. Now I'm talking to cloth. Arthur was, well, Arthur. The greatest of the Earth Knights. Lancelot, Knight of Flame, based his power on love.

"Lancelot, too, was out of balance."

Dev didn't turn at the quiet voice of Stillman, but continued his inspection. The Precept placed a comforting hand on his shoulder.

"That's why he betrayed his King and the Order."

"Out of balance."

"Right. Where you find your power in anger and rage, he found his in—"

"Love," Dev said.

"Yes. The balance you seek lies somewhere in between." Stillman leaned back on his desk. "I know you, Develor Quinteele, I know what you're made of."

Great. Another head job. I think I've had enough for one day. Sleep. I need sleep. Stop all this sniveling. A couple hours downtime and I'll be good to go.

"Once again, sir, you've given me much to think about. Thank you." Dev bowed and left the room.

Love. Beauty. Intimacy. They all went hand in hand. I went all flame-on over Véronique, who's to say it won't happen again?

Chapter 34

Frustration fueled the tension in the Womb. Dev paced across the open end of the table, shooting glances to the spinning globe. Red, white and brown lights in Wales, blue light in Florida. Dronor had been gone too long without checking in.

What the hell is he doing?

Stillman, Magnus and Cyndralla sat in their appointed places around the table while Wren and Cassidy occupied other seats brought in for them.

He should have been back, or at least reported in. Freakin' waste of an element.

"We can't just sit around here and wait for Gray to make his next move," Magnus said.

Dev slapped the table. "What choice do we have?"

"We do not have enough information to formulate an appropriate strategy," Cyndralla commented.

"I'm sure Dronor will be back soon." Stillman's confidence and calm demeanor kept the room from erupting.

Dev eyed Cassidy then Wren. Both women stared at the agitated Knights, their eyes bright as stars, and kept their mouths shut.

No help there. His relentless pacing continued, but when he checked the globe, the blue light had joined the others. "He's back."

As one, everyone shot to their feet when Dronor stumbled into the room. Dripping wet, breathing hard, he held his tongue until he fell into his seat with a theatrical sigh.

Drama queen.

"I...found...them."

Everyone spoke at once until Stillman held up his hand. The room fell silent except for the labored breathing of the Knight of Water.

"Well done." Stillman took the lead. "What did you find?"

"Shadow magic, a large concentration, must be the orbs." Dronor gasped and his chest heaved.

Spare me.

"Where?" Stillman asked.

"Near the port, run down barge." The Knight of Water's breathing evened out. "At first glance, I thought it abandoned, but found a new security door behind a false wall in the pilot house."

"Any guards?" Dev asked.

"None on the outside, but I don't know about inside."

"We can't take a chance." Stillman's voice held the edge of command. "We strike tonight. Midnight. Use the time between now and then wisely." He turned to the Knight of Air. "Cyndralla, we need something to get through that door and a gateway. Magnus, Dronor, Wren, get your kits together. This should be straight, hard and fast. In and out. Bring a few samples back, destroy the rest. Kill any shadows you find. Sinclair, you're with me."

Cassidy jumped when he addressed her directly.

Dev waited for his orders, breath held in hopeful anticipation, but the Precept didn't acknowledge him.

Stillman held the gaze of each of the participants until they nodded.

"We meet in the portal room at twenty three hundred for a last minute check and brief. Dismissed."

"Sir. What about me?" Dev rushed over to block Stillman's departure.

"You have your orders, Quinteele."

"Yeah, yeah. Get control. But you need me out of control against Shadow."

Stillman tried to push by, but Dev grabbed his arm.

"The team can't do this without me." Dev held his anger in check before he doomed his cause with a fiery outburst. "Someone could get killed."

Stillman moved in, nose to nose, brown eyes hard and resolute. If he noticed the knife-edge upon which Dev balanced, he gave no indication. "Dismissed."

Dev backed down as the group filed out. Cassidy squeezed his arm as she passed.

Inside, Dev raged. His warrior's spirit railed against the decisions made against him. Right or wrong, he needed to be in that battle. The Order needed him to fight, not sit around a freakin' campfire singing Kumbaya and discovering himself. He was there, he was healthy, and he was ready to kick ass.

The old man had to change his mind.

§

Fired up from the meeting, Dev prowled the hall looking for an outlet. He hoped Dronor would cross his path so he could give him a pre-mission pummeling. It wouldn't be too bad, just enough to shut his smug mouth up. But no luck.

Dev made it to his quarters unmolested, blocked out the rest of the world and fired up the forge. Pounding out his frustration on some innocent metal seemed like a good idea. It didn't matter what he made, so long as the creation made a lot of noise and allowed him to swing a heavy hammer.

With a thought, he called the lava. A whuff of scalded air escaped before the molten core bubbled out of the well and filled the trough. He grabbed a few chunks of Quinsteele and tossed them into the churning inferno.

I promised I would protect Wren.

He bare-handed a glowing lump of metal and tossed it onto the anvil. Grabbing it with the tongs, he took up his hammer and struck the first blow.

The blacksmith's song reverberated off the stone walls. Finding his rhythm, he lost himself in his craft.

The act of creation, of shaping and molding, burned away his anger and cleared his mind.

Ping. Ping.

This restriction wasn't Wren's fault. It was mine. I didn't listen.

Ping. Ping.

I was out of control. Out of balance.

Ping. Ping.

This must be shocking admission week. Last night I accepted the fact that I wasn't a demon after only seven hundred years.

Ping. Ping.

The Wren betrayal thing only took me a couple of days. I must be getting better at this.

The sarcasm made him smile. He fitted a sharp-edged chisel to the flattened metal and, with a few expertly placed blows, cut it into half-inch thick strips then set them aside. Like a machine, he did the same with the other two lumps of softened Quinsteele until he had a dozen strips in a neat pile.

Grabbing the lot, he chucked them into the lava to heat up for stage two. Some landed flat while others jutted out of the smoking orange mass.

Magnus will keep her out of trouble. She's his little sister, too.

Dev plucked one of the metal flats from the heat and checked its flexibility. Judging it acceptable, he laid it down and, choosing a lighter hammer, banged out the leaf-shaped blade. He worked through the others quickly. Years of training and practice combined with a clear head prevented any mistakes or false hits. Within an hour, a pile of rough throwing knives lay stacked before him. The blades thin and curved, the handles slightly thicker with an uncut flat circle at the base.

But there was something missing. For Wren, they needed more, something different, unique. Calling the fire, he pushed the responding energy to his hands and they burst into flame. A smaller measure of heat was needed to finish the job. He pinched the blade between his fingers to taper the edge then filed it to razor-like precision as it cooled. Using this first one as a prototype, he reversed the knife and focused on the circle at the end.

Something special.

A picture formed in his mind—short thin beak, dense feathers, ferocious eyes. He rubbed the circle at the end of the handle between his thumb and index finger enough to soften the surface and memorize its texture and contour. Satisfied and focused, he worked a diamond-tipped engraving tool to shape the head, its sharp beak pointed down. The eyes came next, the outline gouged deep to stand out. And last, the feathers. Delicate cuts and twists of the tool scored the metal while he fed it a trickle of heat to keep it malleable.

Wren deserved his best work. She deserved perfection. The blade delivered, but the bird…not so much. It was the best he could do. He twined a double layer of gold thread around the handle to finish the piece.

He inspected the completed knife one final time—keen edged, detailed, perfectly balanced.

One down, eleven more to go. Dev smiled and got down to work on his peace offering.

Chapter 35

A NEAT STACK OF JEANS, T-SHIRTS, SOCKS AND UNDERWEAR WAITED FOR CASSIDY when she returned to her room. Apparently, the clothes fairy made deliveries. Nothing said comfort more than a worn pair of Levis and a loose cotton T. *Ooh,* except for the pair of old-school Nike's with the light blue swoosh gracing the floor next to the bed. *Sweet.*

She had clean clothes, but could really do with a shower. Glistening was a good thing, a noble sign of hard work, but that sweat lodge Dev lived in was a bit over the top.

The room Magnus had stashed her in was modest, but clean and functional. A small bed and dresser dominated one wall. Over on the other sat a small writing desk and hard wooden chair. Beyond that, in the far corner, a—

What is that?

The lines in the corner didn't match up. From one angle, it looked perfectly fine, but from another it was off. She ran her hand along the wall and found the corner three feet sooner than she expected. It slid into another, smaller room.

Cool.

A small shelf built into the wall on her left held towels and a collection of toiletries. Further in, she noticed the slant to the floor. It angled down only a few inches to a squared off shelf with open slots cut throughout its surface. Above her head, the ceiling contained row upon row of small holes.

So how do you turn this puppy on?

No visible knobs or levers adorned the walls. As soon as she stepped under the holed ceiling, a deluge of clear warm water poured down. Cassidy yelped and jumped back. The downpour stopped.

She looked down at the mass of ruined silk hanging heavy off her shoulders and shrugged. If it wasn't dead before, it definitely was now.

She shimmied out of the sodden mess, kicked off the limp wet slippers, and peeked around the corner. Seeing no one lurking about, she padded to the collection of new duds, grabbed a promising ensemble and headed back to the watery bliss in the other room.

Half-way through her shower, a deep bass rhythm thrummed through the walls. The music continued to throb through the floor as she toweled off and dressed. The beat changed tempo, becoming more frantic.

Another mystery.

Cassidy left the growing comfort of her home away from home to find the source. At the end of her hall, she finally heard what she had been feeling, and put a name to it—bass guitar.

Magnus. All the halls looked the same, but the music seemed to be louder to her right. She turned and followed the sound. Her instincts proved correct.

The Earth Knight wore the guise of that wiry musician she'd first encountered in her backyard. His blond hair flipped in counterpoint to the bang of his head as he plucked a ferocious riff. She'd heard it before, buried in a song, but without the other instruments and vocals she couldn't place it.

Though his eyes were closed, he acknowledged her entrance with a dip of his guitar.

An elaborate amp and speaker system filled an entire wall, and explained why the whole Cradle rocked out with him. An array of guitars propped up in stands stood next to a large desk crammed with stacks of sheet music. Posters of Magnus's symphonic rock band, Light's Keen Edge, papered the walls next to other greats such as Kamelot, Iron Maiden, and Mozart. Lutes, dulcimers and stringed instruments she'd only seen in movies stood among a vast collection filling the back of the room. A great feathered cloak of many colors draped the bed.

Aside from the covered bed, the only seats were several giant beanbag chairs. Cassidy didn't think Magnus would mind an audience so she picked the fluffiest one, which coincidentally occupied the space farthest from the pulsating subwoofer, and squished into its cool vinyl.

Fingers dancing over the strings, Magnus opened his eyes and smiled at her. He dropped to his knees and finished with the opening riff from Queensrÿche's "Jet City Woman." As the last note faded, he raised his right arm, stuck out his tongue and flashed the heavy metal horns on his fingers.

Cassidy laughed and clapped enthusiastically.

"Thank you, Cradle. Good Night." Magnus put the guitar in the open case behind him, powered down the sound system and dropped into a beanbag chair next to her.

"You're awesome." Cassidy admired musicians. She couldn't play a lick, and to see an obvious master left her awestruck.

He flipped his hair and assumed a superior, rocker attitude. "Would you like my autograph?"

"I hope you don't mind that I made myself at home."

Magnus waved her off. "Don't be silly, you're more than welcome. Would you like something to drink?"

Her stomach grumbled loudly enough for Magnus to hear.

"I'll take that as a yes." Magnus placed his palm on the floor and spoke a single word, "Bob." Turning to Cassidy, he asked, "What would you like?"

"Whaddya got?"

"Ask him." He smirked and flicked his head toward the other side of the room."

"Ask who, whaaa-" Cassidy gaped at the patch of stone floor not five feet away that started to churn.

Two stone hands, a little bigger than her own, reached up through the floor on spindly arms. Stone scraped and scrabbled against stone as fingers rooted for a handhold. With a solid grip, they eased the rest of a stubby body through the floor until a little rock man stood on blocky feet.

"I believe you were going to ask 'what?'" Magnus said. "That, Ms. Sinclair, is Bob. He's a homunculus, an elemental being, and lives in the stone of this room. Think of him like a house elf from Harry Potter only without the bondage and clothes fetish. The care and upkeep of this room and its occupant are his responsibility. He'll get us what we need."

Cassidy, too stunned to speak, gawked at the improbable creature. No more than three feet tall, Bob stood with his stone knuckles resting against the ground and regarded Magnus out of dime-sized, sapphire eyes. Aside from the sparkling gems, and shallow groove for a mouth, his head and face were flat and featureless—a solid slab of rock.

"Hey, Bob." Magnus held his fist out to the little guy.

The groove on Bob's face turned up in a smile and his right eye twinkled. Quick, agile steps carried him over to Magnus for a knuckle touch.

"Bob, this is Cassidy. She's a new friend." From out of the corner of his mouth, Magnus whispered to Cassidy, "Hold out your fist and say hello."

Cassidy held out her fist. "Hi, Bob, it's a pleasure to meet you." Cassidy put on her best unthreatening smile, like she did when meeting a new puppy, and felt silly. She resisted the urge to whistle and cluck her tongue to get him to come over. The tiny stone man was adorable and she didn't want to hurt his feelings.

Wait...does it-he have feelings?

Bob looked her way, his mouth-groove a leveled line across his block. Cassidy couldn't tell if he was checking out her fist or her face or what, but she felt the assessing weight of that precious stare. It went on and on. Bob staring at her, she holding out her fist with that inane grin stamped across her lips.

Geez Louise. Stillman didn't check me out this long and he runs the place.

With no warning, Bob smiled and tottered over to her for their first knuckle bump. She expected his skin to be hard and cold, like a brick, but he was just the opposite—warm and smooth. He hit her soft, tentative, as if he realized she was different than Magnus. When their hands touched, she picked up a sense of agelessness. Or maybe a deep wisdom, she couldn't tell. She knew it was vastly different than anything she'd sensed before. Based on that touch, she believed things would have gone horribly wrong if the little guy hadn't accepted her.

Bob crawled into her lap with the grace of a capuchin monkey, all long arms and nimble strength, and made himself at home. The little bugger was heavy, maybe forty pounds or more.

"Looks like you made a new friend." Magnus grinned from ear to ear, evidently quite pleased with Bob's assessment.

Bob grasped Cassidy's arm and pulled it around his blocky torso. She didn't know what to make of it, but let him do as he pleased.

"Yo, Magnus, have you see—" Dev popped his head into Magnus's room. "Oh, hey Cassidy."

Cassidy waved and Dev didn't stumble or retreat. She didn't need to touch him to sense a new peace within him. It shone about his eyes and in the set of his face. Something major had changed.

"What's up?" Magnus asked and Dev lugged the rest of himself into the room.

"Is that Bob in your lap?" Dev squatted next to her and put his knuckles out. "What's shakin', buddy? Have you seen Jester?"

Bob tapped his knuckles.

"Please tell him I miss him and would like him to come home. Okay?"

Bob gave Dev a thumbs-up.

"I need to catch Wren before you guys head out. Have you seen her?" He stood up and switched the bundle he held from one hand to the next. "We need to talk."

"It's about time," Magnus scolded. "You've been an ass and put that poor girl through hell."

Dev had the good sense to blush. "Anyway, Wren?"

"Try the gym. You know she throws when she's nervous."

"Right. Thanks." Dev left with a wave and a crisp turn.

Bob played with Cassidy's hair, rolling it between two of his thick, round fingers. In the silence left by Dev's interruption, Cassidy's gut sang out, making Bob look down.

"So…" She laughed as the little guy poked her belly. "What's for lunch?"

Chapter 36

I N THE GYM, WREN MEASURED THE DISTANCE BETWEEN THE TWO KNIVES IN THE
center of the target with her little finger.

*An inch apart this time. I was aiming for a quarter. Must be the nerves. Need
to do better.* She plucked the slim blades from the wall, counted out ten paces
across the floor of the gym and turned.

*Paces. I've been hanging out with these old geezers too long. Fifty feet. That's
my mark. Not paces, feet.*

"Quarter inch this time." Eyes on the target, she grabbed the knife, blew
out her breath and threw. Dead center.

Okay. Same throw. Aim. Blow. Rel—

"Miss!"

The knife hit wide, still in the center, but off her mark by two inches.

She spun to the door, mouth poised to ream. "What the—oh, Dev. Cassidy's
not here and no, I have not seen her." *Not you. Not now.*

"I taught you better than that." Dev plucked the knives from the target
and slapped them against his palm as he strolled over. "I remember when you
could scrape the metal your throws were so close."

Wren frowned. *Does he have to mock me like this right before a mission? One
that he won't be going on.*

Dev tossed the practice throwers in the bin and approached, head down,
new leather harness slung across his shoulder.

This can't be good. Wren's stomach sank, like it did on the Tower of Terror
when the seat dropped out. Her emotions were in free fall and she was unsure
if Dev would pull the cord on her parachute or let her drop like a rock.

Sad eyes met hers. He looked vulnerable like this. Without saying a word,
he took her hand. He placed two knives across her palm and closed her fingers
around them.

"Try these." His voice was low, soft, tender.

Wren opened her hand. The crystal light reflected off the newly minted
blades. She admired the artistry, traced a calloused finger over the rough carving at the bottom. *Is it a dog? Ice cream cone?* They were heavier than she was
used to, but perfectly balanced and crafted to fly true.

"They're beautiful." She stroked the tightly wound gold threading. "But I
don't deserve them." *Please, Dev. Don't do this.*

"Yes, you do." Dev handed her the leather harness with the rest of the
knives stuffed into the loops. "Do you like the Wren at the bottom?"

Ohhhhh. She looked again, flipped the handle up. *Now I see the bird. That's
a beak?*

"It's beautiful, but..."

"Wren, I'm sorry." He brushed her cheek. "For so many things."

She waited for him to continue, watching him struggle for the right words, and held her breath.

"I was out of control and you had the courage to do what needed to be done." He smiled ruefully. "I wouldn't have taken it from anyone else. Would have kicked their ass, but not you."

"Why, because I'm a girl?" Wren couldn't stop herself.

"No. Because I trust you. I respect the young woman you've blossomed into. I'm proud of you, Wren. And I take great pride in knowing that I had a hand in that."

"You big ass. I tried to warn you."

"I know." He wrapped her in a hug and squeezed tight. "I know."

"I thought you hated me." Her words came out all wet and whiny. *Stupid, leaky girl.*

"I could never hate you. You're my little sister. I love you." His voice was husky as he rested his chin on her head. "That may not be exactly what you wanted to hear, but it's the truth."

Well duh. But no real surprise either. I guess I'll take what I can get. "I love you, too."

"We good?" Dev stepped back.

Wren nodded, but wasn't ready to meet his eyes. She didn't want him to see her disappointment.

"Good. Wipe that snot away and throw the knives. Let's see what you've got."

"Dev." Wren snorted.

"What's the matter? Afraid you won't hit the target?"

Wren wiped her eyes and nose on her arm with an exaggerated slurp.

"Yuck"

"Shut up." She took her position, and hit the target dead center.

"Better."

All her focus on the target, everything else in the room drifted into the background. Sighting along the path of the first throw, she blew out a breath and held. She wanted it as close as possible to the first knife, wanted to scrape the metal.

Smooth, controlled, her arm whipped forward. The knife sank hilt deep, scraping the blade of the first knife and nipping the golden thread.

Yes!

"That'll do."

Wren beamed, collected her knives and jammed them into the empty slots of her vest.

"I better get ready."

"Right, right. You go ahead. I'm going to hang out for a few, maybe work off some energy."

"See you at the gateway?" Wren smiled big, full of hopeful enthusiasm as she backed out the door.

₧&#x3; &#x3; &#x3;

"Wouldn't miss it." *Not now anyway.* Dev did his best to slap on a sincere smile and hoped he succeeded. He didn't need to bring her down with his own issues or send her on the mission second guessing either her ability or the strength of the other members of the team.

They'll be fine without me. The place will probably be empty and make Dronor look like an idiot...again.

"The throwing knives are beautiful." Cassidy's voice filled the room. "Magnus filled me in on a couple of things."

Startled, he swung at the heavy bag, more to hide his embarrassment than to make a dent in the canvas, and caught the curve to send it twirling.

Cassidy laughed, an infectious trill that made him smile. "That was pathetic," she said and shouldered him out of the way. "Step aside, rookie."

Eyebrow raised, he gave her room and watched as she set her feet and punched. Jab. Jab. Right hook. Jab. Upper cut. She bobbed and weaved and dodged imaginary strikes while landing some solid body blows.

Good form and balance. Power behind her punches. Graceful. He nodded. *Nice. She must have had some training at some point. Straight forward, toe-to-toe, can probably take a hit too. Hmmm, reminds me of someone.*

Out of breath, knuckles pink and raw from the rough canvas, skin glistening in the crystal's pale light, Cassidy winked. "Now that's how you do it."

"Is it now?" Dev sidled over, raking her warmed up figure with an admiring glance. "I've seen better. The bag doesn't hit back."

A left jab fired to his chin. He knew it was coming, watched her casually shift her feet to get in position for the strike while pretending to focus on something across the room, and slapped it away before it got close.

Game on. Excitement fired his element and little pinpricks of energy raced across his skin. "You'll have to do better than that, lady."

She squared off, a different stance than she used against the bag—weight on her back foot, hands open.

Nonchalant, Dev stood within striking distance and made a show of buffing his nails against his leather vest. Then he stretched, exposing his torso for an easy hit. Too easy. He even yawned, a big stretching affair that took his eyes off his opponent.

She struck, punching him low in the gut and following with a round house kick, waist high, in anticipation of where his head should be.

But it wasn't there. The punch was stronger than he expected, but not enough to bend him over the way she intended.

Sound tactic though. He brushed off her follow up kick. "Is there a draft in here?"

Dev's temperature rose, along with his amusement. Sparring with Cassidy felt different from the life and death matches with Magnus, exciting in an entirely different way that made his spirit tingle. He didn't want it to end.

Cassidy wrinkled her nose and bared her teeth. If her eyes were lasers, they would have burned a hole through his waist. She circled, forcing him to turn to keep her in sight.

Anticipation of her next attack spiked his flame. He watched her subtle movements, waiting for the twitch or bend or lean that would give her away. Well balanced, she was obviously comfortable in her own skin and didn't care that her shirt had come untucked allowing an inch of tender skin to peek out.

Round and round she glided. Body crouched, ready to spring.

This is crazy. What is she doing? Mind wandering, he blinked and jumped at an imagined attack. Cassidy remained poised, ready and on the move.

"Getting jumpy are we?" Cassidy smirked.

She's playing games now. Fine. Let's fire this up.

Dev stopped following her movements. She continued until directly behind him then stopped in his blind spot. He lifted his arms out to his side, inviting her to attack.

Cassidy screamed, flung herself on his back, locked her legs around his waist, and flailed her arms like a maniac. As if he she weighed no more than a flea, he stood firm and waited for her energy to play out.

Changing tactics, she wrapped her arms around his neck in a choke hold, but he slid his hands through before she cinched it tight.

"You need to try harder than that," Dev said, maintaining the block on her stranglehold.

"Don't worry," she tried to wedge her hand under his block, "I'm just getting started."

"And here I thought you were almost done." Dev refused to let her past his guard. Breathing hard, her chest heaved against his back, sending his element into a frenzied surge to combat the unprecedented chill that prickled his flesh.

Her weight shifted to the right and she bit his ear.

"Ow." Dev jerked his head and tried to swat her away, but she dodged his swing. "That hurt."

"What's the matter, you big baby, did I surprise you?"

Dev heard the smile behind her words. *So she is enjoying this too.*

"My turn." He spun in her grasp. Too fast for Cassidy to adjust, they ended up smile to smile. Surprise and mischief twinkled in her eyes.

"That was a bold move, sir," she whispered, her breath tickling his nose. "When did you think of that one?"

Bad idea. Acutely aware of her legs clamped tight around his hips and her heels pressed tight against his butt, Dev felt the heat flare in his breast then flash to other parts of his body like wildfire.

"I…uh…didn't…," his voice faltered. "…mean to…" He needed to move, to get free of her before something happened. But he didn't want to. *She feels so good.* His body trembled.

Her lips quivered as if she tried to hide her amusement, but that only made her more adorable.

Dev gazed into her eyes, desperate for the same tranquility that quenched his rage during that first glimpse on the bridge. Instead, he found something else. Like gasoline poured on a roaring fire, Dev went up with a whoosh. Throwing Cassidy clear, he bolted from the room as flames coated him in their elemental embrace.

Chapter 37

THE WARREN OF HALLWAYS IN THE CRADLE CONFUSED CASSIDY, ALMOST AS MUCH as did the Knight of Flame, and turned what should have been a short stroll back to her room into a major ordeal.

What was that all about? One minute we're getting to know each other and the next he's tossing me across the room and pulling a Houdini. I didn't even see him leave.

After leaving the gym, she reversed the directions and thought she took the right path, but must have turned right when she should have gone left or zigged when she should have zagged.

Where the hell am I?

The hallway she trod looked just like all the others. *They should put up signs with those 'You are here' stickers and nice arrows pointing to the important places. But nooooo, just more freakin' rock walls. Ah, hell.* She leaned against the wall and looked first left then right.

A song, barely in the range of hearing, played from down the hall. She couldn't make out the words, but the tune…*Where have I heard that before?*

Faint strains of mumbled voices grew into recognizable lyrics as she got closer to the source until she stood before the black felt curtain drawn across the doorway through which it played. She poked her head into the darkened room lit only by bright images on a screen.

Are you kidding me? Rows of plush seats faced a large screen on the front wall where the characters in an animated film trained for medieval warfare.

Amy used to watch this one all the time, the one with the Chinese girl who takes her father's place in the army.

The chairs were empty, but she noticed someone sitting on the floor up front, bobbing her head in time with the music.

Wren.

She thought to leave the girl alone, let her watch the movie in peace, but hesitated when she remembered the devastated look on Wren's face in the portal room, a look that she herself had worn many times over the years.

Cassidy slipped inside. "Want some company?"

Wren started. "Uh, sure…sure." She rubbed her eyes and started to get up, but Cassidy joined her on the floor.

"Shouldn't you be getting ready to go?" Cassidy asked.

"I am ready." Wren pointed to her leather armor and new brace of throwing knives slung across her chest. "I was nervous and this is one of the things I do when I'm nervous."

Cassidy turned her attention to the screen. "My daughter really liked this one. Watched it a couple times a day for like two months straight. At the time it drove me crazy, but now…I donated all of her movies when she died."

"How long ago?"

"Two years."

"I saw her pictures. She was beautiful."

"Yeah she was." Cassidy blinked back the tears.

Wren turned down the movie's volume, but kept her focus on the screen. "I lost my parents when I was six. A helicopter accident over Tokyo Bay."

"I'm so sorry, Wren. I can't imagine what you went through."

"Things were okay for a while. My mother's friend in Tokyo, Emiko, took me in."

"Didn't you have any other family?" Cassidy asked.

Wren snapped her gaze to Cassidy. "You researching a new article or something?"

She's young and upset, let her snipe.

"Sorry. It's my nature to ask questions," Cassidy spoke in a warm, friendly tone. "I didn't mean to pry." She started to get up. "I just thought you might like a little girl talk. I'll leave you to your movie."

"No." Wren grabbed Cassidy's hand, pulled her down. "That's okay. You can stay."

"Are you sure?"

Wren nodded, and returned her focus to the screen. "I don't know about my father's side of the family, but I did on my mother's. Not that it mattered. Once Mom married an American sailor, they wanted nothing to do with her. Mom, Dad, and me, we lived off-base at Yokosuka, and my Mom's older sister lived right across the street. I never met her, but I might have seen her once or twice." She huffed. "Look, Cassidy, I'm not really good with this whole *friend* thing."

"I think you're doing fine."

"So, what now?" Wren wiggled her fingers. "Are you gonna do my nails?"

Cassidy laughed, glad the young girl was opening up. "We'll save that for after the mission."

Wren leaned back on her hands and kicked her legs out front. The flashing lights from the movie glinted off her new knives.

"I'm glad you and Dev made up," Cassidy said.

"He's stubborn."

"Just like you."

Wren smirked. "Whatevs." She waved her feet in time with the beat.

"So how did you two meet?" Cassidy inched closer.

"Really? You want to hear about that?"

Absolutely. "If you're up to it."

"I guess." Wren sat up, pulled her knees in tight to her chest. "After my parents died and Emiko took me in, life was okay for the first year or two. I went to school, but there was no true place for a half-breed. Kids can be vicious little assholes."

Cassidy remembered Amy coming home with a bloody nose, and how furious she'd been. She'd raced back to Barden Heights Elementary, lambasted the principal as only a protective mama bear could. After, we went out for chocolate chip ice cream to make it all better.

If I knew where they kept it, I'd get Wren a big dish right now.

"On the upside, I learned a lot," Wren said. "I learned how to run, how to hide. After the first broken arm, I learned how to disappear into a crowd. Got pretty good, actually, settled into the rhythm of life on my feet, but then the bottom dropped out. Emiko died of a drug overdose."

Wren sniffed, and wiped her nose on her sleeve. "She was good to me. Helped me through some tough times."

Do I reach out to her? Touch her arm? Offer some level of comfort? Cassidy moved her hand, but pulled back when Wren continued in a stronger voice.

"A little bit older, maybe thirteen, fourteen, I could have made it on the streets. I was quick, knew some people, but they put me in an orphanage. Everyone who came in was looking to adopt a cute baby or an adorable toddler. They didn't want an older half-breed. I found a way to make life bearable. Once my chores were done, I had some freedom. I snuck out, got into trouble. Over time, I found a group of kids like myself, fellow outcasts. We called ourselves a gang, but compared to the real thing, we were just a club." She shook her head. "We thought we were so tough. Smoked, drank, picked the pockets of gullible tourists." Wren chuckled. "Actually, that's how I met Stillman."

"You picked his pocket?"

"Yup. Old man. Pin stripe suit. Cane. Looking all around like he was lost. I did the old bump and run then disappeared into the crowd. Easy. Big take too. Three hundred American. When that ran out, I headed back to the same spot, found another old man. This one seemed more alert, but still an easy mark."

"It wasn't Stillman again, was it?"

Wren nodded sheepishly.

"Oh, geez."

"I know, right." Wren's eyes opened wide. "What were the odds? Back then I didn't sweat the small stuff like, you know, faces and details. Only this time, when I peeled off to a side street, I had a tail. Two blocks in, a strong hand grabbed my arm, spun me around."

"Dev?"

"Yeah. Tall, bald and beautiful. I looked into his ash-gray eyes and melted. Then he smiled at me. Oh Cassidy, I couldn't breathe. I'd never seen anyone like him before. He had dimples, and perfect cheek bones, and...uh. He held out his hand and said, 'You're good kid. Quick. Embarrassed my...friend. You could be so much more.' Without a word, I put the stolen wallet in his hand and watched him walk away. Well, 'walk' isn't the right word. Prowl. Stalk. A panther doesn't walk through the jungle, it glides—agility and violent potential sheathed in muscle. That was Dev."

Can't argue with that.

"When I got back to the orphanage, I saw a police car parked outside. That was nothing new. They came out pretty often. Then I saw the old man's silhouette in the window, and I knew they were there for me."

"That's when Stillman adopted you?"

"I wish that were the end of the story." Wren's face turned to the floor. "When I saw him, I panicked, and ran. Made a few too many turns and ducked into a building without realizing where I was. I found one of those other gangs, a real one that didn't play around." She twisted a string that stuck out from the end of her pant leg. Her voice softened. "There were five of them, older, bigger, used to getting what they wanted. When they saw a young girl lost and alone, they decided they wanted me."

Cassidy didn't like the turn of Wren's story, wanted her to stop before a cruel reality crapped over her illusion of innocence.

"They grabbed me, dragged me deeper into their world. I was too scared to scream. It wouldn't have mattered if I had because there was no one around to hear it."

Oh Wren.

"I knew what was coming. But still, I didn't think it would really happen. I hoped it was a bad dream, that I'd fallen asleep watching one of the princess movies with the little kids and Sister Momoko was going to wake me up the way she usually did, with a smack on the back of the head. Little girls and their dreams, right? They always wanted to watch the princesses sing and dance and get rescued by their handsome princes. I thought it was a bunch of garbage."

"What *did* you dream about?" Cassidy asked.

"Huh. Good question. I knew there were no princes out there, not for the likes of me. When I got some time to myself, it wasn't often mind you, but as a reward for babysitting the younger girls, I got to watch something just for me. I always picked this movie." Wren looked back at the screen as the girl donned her armor and prepared for battle.

"She was tough. Learned how to fight, to defend her family's honor. I don't remember much about my parents, but one of the clearest memories I have is one in which my mother is talking to me about our family, that we were descended from one of the traditional samurai families of old. She even had a katana mounted on the wall. I wonder what ever happened to that old blade. Supposedly it was my great, great, great grandfather's or something like that. I don't know. But you know what's funny? Despite the fact that her family cast her out, she clung to her heritage. Honor and loyalty, they are the two words that sum up my ancestry."

Cassidy knew Wren was ditching the talk about the building, taking her down another path, but she felt there was something important going on. And while she didn't want to cause this girl any pain, Cassidy believed Wren needed to talk it out.

"After watching the movie," Cassidy said, "Amy would grab a whiffle ball bat and chase the dog pretending it was her duty to protect the house from evil creatures."

Wren laughed. "I practiced the moves outside when no one was looking. I wanted to be as tough as her. Thought I was."

Cassidy heard a sniffle, but kept her eyes on the screen.

Wren continued. "The leader, he wore sunglasses and a red bandanna, and sucked on a straw while the others tossed me around between them. I fought back, but they were stronger and faster. After a few minutes, he must have got tired of the game because he came into the circle and ripped my dress down the front. I remember thinking that the Sisters would be furious as I stooped to pick the buttons off the ground. That's when I noticed the sharp, sour smell, like old milk."

Cassidy took Wren's hand, expected her to pull away, but instead she gripped it tight.

"The other guys took the hint. Two held me while the other two tore off the rest of my clothes. I was twelve, so, you know, certain things were starting to grow and sprout, right."

God, I remember twelve. I was too self-conscious to change in gym class. I couldn't imagine going through this.

"And it was summer so I shouldn't have been cold, but my arms and legs were covered in goosebumps and I was shaking so bad I could barely stand."

"Oh Wren."

"When the leader approached me, he wasn't expecting a fight, came in all gentle like he was my boyfriend or something. After the first kick in the balls, his attitude changed. I held my own for the first minute or two, but then the rest of them grabbed my arms, bent me over the trash can. I told myself not to cry, to be brave." Wren sniffed, wiped her eyes. "I don't know why I'm telling you all this. I've never told anyone the whole story before. Not even Dev knows the truth."

"What do you mean?"

"Before the leader…took me, I had one fleeting hope. For a moment, I was just like all those seven year olds back in the home looking for their prince, hoped to see that white horse and handsome rider appear from around the bend in the road. I put all my heart and soul into that single desire, but then the pain blocked everything else out. I bit my tongue to keep from screaming, but I couldn't help the tears."

"I'm so sorry, Wren."

"It's okay. It all worked out. You see, my hero did come that day. In a glorious blaze of fire."

"Dev?"

"Yeah. He followed me home, but I lost him when I fled the orphanage. He thought he got to me in time, though."

"Why didn't you tell him?"

"After he dealt with the others, made sure they wouldn't be able to do anything like this again, he draped his shirt over me, gentle as a lamb, and carried me back to the orphanage. It must have been two, maybe three, miles. The whole time he said that I was safe, that he would take care of me, that I would come live with him and his friends in a wonderful place, and go to fancy schools, and learn all kinds of neat stuff. I didn't want to risk losing everything by telling him that my honor had been stolen. I was afraid they wouldn't want me anymore and what he promised sounded so good. So, I kept my mouth shut."

"That wouldn't have changed their minds."

"I know that now, but to a twelve year old half-breed…you didn't do anything to risk a good thing. In time, there was no need to tell anyone." Wren shook her head as if to reroute her train of thought. "Eh, not like it matters anymore." She stood up and stopped the movie.

"What do you mean?" Cassidy's stomach plunged at the abrupt change in Wren's tone.

"He's got more to worry about than just me." Wren pushed around her, but Cassidy grabbed her arm. "I gotta get going."

"Wait," Cassidy said. "Please."

Wren paused, keeping her back to Cassidy.

"He loves you," Cassidy said.

"I know that. Just like I know he will always look out for me. But, now there is someone else."

"Who?"

Wren turned, cocked an eyebrow, and gave Cassidy her best *are-you-really-that-dense?* look.

Holy hell.

Chapter 38

Nervous energy sparkled around the gathered Knights. Cyndralla, Dronor, Magnus and Wren stood at attention over the seal of the Order before their Precept. Cassidy stood out of the way at the base of the quartz bridge while Stillman walked the line-up.

Anxious for the Knight of Flame to show, she glanced at the doorway every few seconds. Wren's last minute revelation aside, she hoped Dev would at least have the honor to wish his fellow Knights well. Maybe he figured they wouldn't find anyone in the barge at all. The Knights didn't know what they were walking into. All they had to go on was Dronor's word that he felt the orbs in that ship.

Not taking any chances, they planned to go in force.

Good. She hadn't known the Knights very long, but she'd come to like and respect them.

The jury is out on the Water Knight, but the rest are cool. And Dev, yeah, the jury is still out on him too, but for a totally different reason.

Hands clasped behind his back, Stillman paced up and down the row of anxious Knights. His shiny black boots scuffed across the stone floor.

Cyndralla stared straight ahead, resplendent in knee-high boots and a pristine white combat dress, slit up both thighs. She'd bound her long hair in a tight braid. Circling her head, a silver coronet with delicate golden filigree held a flawless white diamond the size of an orange.

Dronor, dashing in his sculpted body armor and floor-length cape that mimicked the deep blue-black of the ocean at twilight, smoothed his goatee and smirked in that insufferable, cocksure way of his. A golden hilted rapier rode his hip.

Armored in Quinsteele mail, Magnus towered above them all, his golden mane hanging below his massive shoulders. He'd bulked up since the impromptu concert, regaining the height, breadth and muscle mass he'd shown at her house. The hilt of his double-bladed battleaxe stuck up over his left shoulder.

Wren stood at the end of the line. Black leather covered her lithe body from head to toe. Cassidy bet Dev lined it with Quinsteele. A brace of gold-wrapped knives crisscrossed her chest. She scanned the room.

"They look impressive, don't they?"

Cassidy jumped as Dev whispered in her ear. Preoccupied with the other Knights, she hadn't noticed him come up behind her.

"I should be going too." Dev's voice held no bitterness or anger this time, only resignation.

Cassidy didn't know what to say to that, but noticed a sharp spike in tension as the other Knights noted his presence. Stillman turned and eyed Dev expectantly.

"Well, here we go." Dressed for battle in jet black leathers lined with his Quinsteele armor and Cinder strapped tight to the center of his back, Dev approached the apprehensive Knights. The muscles in his bare arms flexed, probably in agitation, with each headstrong step.

I hope he doesn't make a scene.

Dev dropped to one knee before his commanding officer and lowered his head. "Sir. Permission to address the troops."

Stillman raised an eyebrow and grinned. "Permission granted." He stepped aside to make room for Dev. Magnus smiled and Dronor frowned.

Dev kissed Cyndralla on the cheek and hugged her close. She seemed bewildered by this unusual action.

"Try not to get everyone killed, Drippy." He said to Dronor and held out his hand. Dronor glared, but clasped Dev's hand firmly.

Dev punched Magnus in the chest and nodded once. Magnus returned the nod.

With Wren, he adjusted her straps and tapped her on the shoulders. She flung herself at him, launching herself off the ground, and wrapped her arms around his neck.

"Group hug!" Magnus bellowed and joined in.

Cyndralla looked on in bewilderment for a second before tentatively placing her arms around Dev and the others. Dronor sneered, but his eyes told Cassidy a different story, told her that he wished things were different. But he didn't close the gap, didn't join in.

Stillman smiled indulgently.

Sensitive to the undercurrent of emotions in the room, chills coursed over Cassidy's body. She hoped nothing happened, that the mission went off without a hitch, but she had a bad feeling slinking around inside her. She kept the unease to herself, afraid that giving it voice would make it real. So, instead, she cracked a brittle smile and played along.

Everything will be okay.

"Right." Stillman cleared his throat. "You all know what to do. Safe journey, my Knights. Wren?" He moved close to his daughter, pulling a small jar from his pocket. The scent of jasmine wafted through the room when he unscrewed the lid. "Close your eyes, little bird." After dipping one finger into the potion, he drew it gently across each of her closed eyelids. "This will help you see in dark places." He held her cheek with one hand and kissed her forehead. "Go in peace, my daughter."

The Precept stepped back. "Cyndralla?"

The Knight of Air handed a gateway card to him then touched the diamond above her forehead. A shimmering oval took shape in front of her.

"Based on Dronor's description, I opened this portal to an abandoned warehouse across the dock from the barge." She eyed the travelers for questions. "After you go through, step aside and make room for the next."

One by one, the Knights stepped into the portal and disappeared.

Cassidy bowed her head, saw that Stillman and Dev did as well, and offered a silent prayer for the Knights' safe return.

ଧ୦୯ଌ

The globe spun on its axis down low in the Womb—three lights in Tampa, one lonely crimson blip in Wales.

"How long has it been?" Nerves twitchy, Dev jumped up and paced from one end of the room to the other.

"About three minutes later than the last time," Cassidy replied.

I should be down there. Dev threw himself in the chair. *This sucks.*

"How about a glass of wine to calm you down?" Stillman asked.

"No."

"Fine. But I'll have it on hand in case you change your mind. Garison."

A spot on the floor near the wall roiled, the stone liquefied in a two-foot circle. Large hands pawed the air and slammed down on the solid stone to either side of the hole as the flat, black marble head of Garison emerged. Citrine eyes latched onto Stillman as soon as they crested the surface.

Garison wasn't one of Dev's favorites. Cold, aloof, he held himself apart from the Knights and didn't try to work with them like Bob, or his room's muncle, Jester. *Muncles—Magnus came up with that one.* Too lazy to say homunculus, he shortened it to muncle and it stuck. It worked well for Jester and Bob, but Garison just seemed…rigid. And while he had the same type of grooved mouth as the rest of the muncles, it never varied from a straight, flat line.

Clear of the floor, Garison ambled directly to Stillman, stone block feet clopping sedately across the bright crystal floor, and bowed at the Precept's feet.

"Garison. Some wine, please. And perhaps bread and cheese." Stillman looked to the others for approval. Cassidy nodded and Dev stared at the lights on the globe.

The stern muncle bowed again and, without a look to either Cassidy or Dev, left on his mission.

How can they eat at a time like this? Stomach in knots, jaw clenched tight, Dev launched to his feet and lapped the table for the hundredth time.

Chapter 39

Heart in her throat, Wren stepped through the gateway. After the bright glow from the transition, the darkness she walked into seemed absolute. She stumbled to the side, tripping over something on the floor, to make room for the others.

Her intrusion stirred up years of accumulated dust and dirt. It rose in a cloud, coating her tongue and throat. A light breeze drifted through the glass-less windows and carried with it the metallic tang of rust mixed with the stench of low tide.

By the time Cyndralla came through, Wren's sight had adjusted to the darkness. The salve Stillman rubbed on her eyes sped up the process dramatically. The moon provided enough light for her to find a path through the wreckage of the grimy warehouse, but not to penetrate the gloom to either side. She couldn't see the walls, but the rectangle a lighter shade of dark ahead must be the door. Trusting her instincts and sticking close to Magnus's hulking presence ahead of her, she made it to the door without another stumble.

Wren paused at the doorway and checked the scene. No signs of life and the only movement the slow rise and fall of the moored barge as it rode the bay's swells. A rickety gangplank, spanning the distance between land and dark vessel, creaked and scraped fresh furrows in the old wooden planks.

"I don't think the bridge will take Magnus's weight," Wren said.

Dronor turned to the earth giant. "Can't you just shrink yourself until you're over then get big again?" he asked, annoyed that the plan already hit a snag.

"I can shrink down, but I would take three times as long to re-grow over water and I don't want to take the chance of being attacked during my transition. Any other ways in?"

"No." Dronor jumped in as the authority on the subject. "Only the planks."

"I can make you lighter." Cyndralla offered.

"Why didn't you say that in the first place?" Dronor huffed.

"Probably because you were sucking up all the available air space with your babbling," Magnus said.

"Boys." Cyndralla's hiss cut Dronor off before he could respond. "We don't have time for this." She turned to Wren. "You're the quickest."

Was that a compliment? She must really be nervous.

"Sneak up the ramp and check out the deck." The Knight of Air leaned in close. "Wave to us from the rail when you're done. If something happens, scream."

Wren nodded.

"Careful, bird-brain," Magnus whispered.

She grinned and poked her head out of the empty doorframe. No signs of movement. Traitorous hands trembled as she leapt from cover. Her first few steps tentative, she crouched low, waiting for any sound or movement to indicate she'd been seen. When nothing happened, she bolted across the dock, sprang up the rickety gangway, and stopped just shy of the deck.

Blocking out the thumping of her heartbeat, she focused all her attention on the darkness ahead of her, looking for something out of place—movement of shadows, a strange light, anything that might alert her to someone else's presence. Other than the creaking of the ship itself as it rode the minor swells, the deck appeared clear.

Crouched low, she crawled from the gangway onto the deck and scampered from one hunk of cover to the next. Clearing the deck, she moved into the pilot house, ears straining, eyes darting.

A flutter, off to her left, like the pages of a book in a stiff breeze. She hit the floor behind the steering console and waited for the sound to happen again. It moved closer with another flutter and small thud. Then another.

What is that? No breeze. The floor isn't creaking under its weight. It can't be much.

She peeked around the side. Nothing. In a crouch, she crept around the console. A small dark shape jumped. Wren drew, aimed, and threw in the space between heartbeats, spearing the unfortunate to the wall.

The *thunk* of her knife sounded loud. She held her breath and waited for a response. All quiet, she examined her kill.

A gigantic bug. Nice. She yanked out the knife, slid the corpse off and wiped its juice on her pants.

Satisfied that she was alone, she waved to her companions on shore and met them at the ramp. "Don't step in the middle, use the supports on the side."

"Well done." The Knight of Air gave Wren a satisfied nod.

Wren caught her jaw before it dropped open. *Two compliments in one day. I must be dreaming.*

Cyndralla and Dronor made it up with no problem. Magnus waited until the Knight of Air waggled her fingers and whispered that it was safe for him to cross. Mimicking his predecessors, he braced himself on the supports. The bridge groaned under his weight, but he made it across and joined them on deck.

Dronor led the way through the small cabin and jabbed his finger into one of the rusted holes on the back wall. He triggered the mechanism and a false wall receded to reveal the promised security door. Cyndralla laid her palm on its surface.

Now that's a big door.

"Wait a minute." The Knight of Earth stepped outside the cabin, walked around, and came back in. "That's what I thought. That door is against the outside wall and there's nothing on the other side except blank wall. There is nowhere for that door to lead. Be ready for anything."

Wren looked around for somewhere to sit while Cyndralla worked the complex lock. It was going to be a while.

"It is done." Cyndralla said as the door swung wide onto a forbidding wall of darkness. Thin metal steps led down.

She is good.

"You can feel that, can't you?" Dronor asked, hands held out as if feeling the flames from a hearth fire.

Nope. Not a thing.

The other Knights nodded and peered into the black.

"I noticed Shadow's hint before, but the full extent of its evil was masked by the door. Do you sense anything else?" Cyndralla stepped through the doorway and vanished down the steps.

"Just the orbs," Magnus answered. "But I doubt that's all we'll find."

Dronor moved next. Magnus motioned for Wren to go, so he could bring up the rear.

"I thought barges were flat," Wren said as she paused in the doorway and tried to pierce the dark.

"They are," Magnus answered. "But this one is decidedly…different."

Dizziness, nausea, fear, panic, she felt them all until the comforting bulk of Magnus pressed against her back and scared them away. Licking dry lips, she put her arms out in front of her and took the leap of faith. Inside, her eyes tingled. Shapes resolved from the darkness. Dronor's, and further down, Cyndralla's forms glowed a pale yellow as they descended into…*what?* Wren's enhanced vision couldn't penetrate the gloom more than fifteen feet.

"How about some light, Cyndy?" asked a grumbly whisper from over head.

"Yes. Close the door, but not all the way." Cyndralla's voice emerged from the darkness ahead.

"Done."

A light flashed as Cyndralla took the point. She stood at the first landing of a steep iron stairway that led into the midnight abyss of the ship's hold. The small globe at her shoulder shed a dim light that barely lit a five-foot circle around her, but it beat feeling around in absolute darkness.

From what Wren could see, the stairway dived into a fathomless black. Against the farthest edge of the light, the darkness roiled. They descended slowly. Wren stretched her senses to the limit, on alert for that tiny sound, that small scrape that warned her that they weren't alone. In this darkness they wouldn't have much time to react, but even a second or two could mean the difference between life and death.

Aside from the creak of the stairs, she walked in silence for what seemed like an hour until the light down below leveled out, followed by Cyndralla's, "Found the bottom."

A few more steps and Wren touched down on what must be the floor of the ship's hold. She got the impression of a vast open space, although she couldn't be sure since the light didn't penetrate the gloom for more than a few feet,.

"This is crazy," Magnus growled. "What are we doing?"

"We're here for the orbs," Dronor said.

"No, I mean, what are we doing right this minute?"

Dronor bristled. "Don't start with me, you ignorant Viking brute."

"We're looking for little black balls in the belly of a pitch black ship with little more than a lit match to see by. Do you see a problem with that plan?"

"What do you propose?" Cyndralla asked.

"Light this bitch up," Magnus said.

"But then the forces of Shadow will see us." Dronor spoke as if to a two year old who'd lost sight of the obvious.

"I got a newsflash for you, buddy. Anyone hiding in the dark can see our light. But, guess what, we can't see them."

Damn. I hadn't thought of that. The impenetrable wall around them took on a sinister persona. Wren thought she saw a pair of yellow eyes watching them from the shadows, but chalked it up to a dose of paranoia brought on by Magnus's comment. To be sure, though, she checked again and they were gone.

"Cover your eyes," Cyndralla said.

"Let her rip, Cyndy."

Wren threw her arm across her eyes as a shield against the spell's flash. Now was not the time to be stumbling around with spots in front of her eyes. She opened her eyes a slit and looked over the curve of her forearm. A globe of dazzling white floated in the air twenty feet above their heads like a miniature sun, dispelling all but the farthest shadows. The end of the hold lay beyond the reach of Cyndralla's light, but what Wren could see surprised her—a big bunch of nothing. No boxes. No crates. Nothing.

This thing is like a black hole in the water. Where are the orbs?

"You…you all felt them too," Dronor stammered and pulled away from the group to begin his own search. "They are here. I know they are."

"Dronor, don't go off alone." Magnus barked the order, but the Knight of Water walked on, muttering to himself. "We can't let the fool wander off into the darkness. Let's see if there's something at the other end of this pit."

Cyndralla hurried after, increasing her pace to keep Dronor within the circle of light.

"I see something. A room of some kind up ahead." Excited, Dronor trotted back to the group. "I feel the orbs in there, but it's too dark to see anything. I need your light, Lady."

Magnus muttered something in another language, but loud enough for Wren to hear. She watched Dronor's expression to see if he noticed. The Water Knight's eyes flicked upward.

Half a second later, Dronor dove at Cyndralla and pushed her out of the way as a slab of midnight detached from the ceiling and crashed to the ground. Cyndralla fell clear, but the shock broke her concentration and her sun blinked out.

Caught beneath the descended darkness, Dronor screamed. His agonized wail reverberated off the steel walls and bounced his pain back at the team from all directions. It was almost loud enough to drown out the hideous series of cracks, snaps, and crunches.

"Cyndy," Magnus roared.

The floor shuddered. Dronor's screams faltered.

Without Cyndralla's light, Wren found the yellow outline of Magnus. He hacked away at the black slab on top of Dronor. Another glowing shape, away from the others, stirred on the floor.

Cyndralla. Wren rushed to the side of the downed Knight of Air and helped her to her feet. Cyndralla shook her head and gently moved Wren to her side.

Dev, I wish you were here.

A flare streaked up, trailing a line of yellow sparks. At the apex of its climb, it exploded into another mini sun. One last, wet gurgle slid out from under the nightmare slab before it shattered into a million jots of black and skittered out of the light like an intrusion of roaches. Laughter hissed all around them.

Magnus knelt at Dronor's side, and set his axe on the floor within easy reach. Wren's first step toward the men splashed into a spreading puddle of watery blood. The Knight of Water's pulverized body lay nearly flat against the bottom of the hold, his skull a mash of skin, bone and brain matter.

What could have done something like this?

Terror streamed through Wren's veins like ice water, stealing her warmth and her control. Her limbs quaked, her stomach flipped, she stumbled a few steps away from the ravaged Knight and wretched.

Dev, we need you.

"Oh, Dronor." Cyndralla limped over, a thin line of blood leaking down her forehead.

"Did you see what it was?" Magnus tried to look in all directions at once.

Cyndralla shook her head.

"I heard laughter," Wren said.

Magnus grabbed his axe and got to his feet. "Me too."

Yellow eyes floated lazily beyond the circle of light. Magnus saw them first and hefted his axe, murder ablaze in his righteous glare. "We've got company."

"So the Knightsssss are mortal." An amused female voice rasped from the darkness. "Are you ready for me?" Yellow eyes blinked, but did not reappear.

Wren pulled two knives from her harness, fingered the little birds and wished with all her heart that Dev were there.

A dark glob swallowed the light and the shadows rushed in.

Chapter 40

DEV SWIVELED AROUND GARISON, DODGING THE SINGLE-MINDED MUNCLE AS HE marched into the Womb bearing a tray laden with assorted white and yellow cheeses, breads and two bottles of wine. Half way in, he dropped the tray and pointed to the globe. The blue light representing Dronor flickered and went out.

No. No. No. This can't be happening. It was supposed to be a simple mission. Wren...

Dev glanced at Stillman and watched the color drain from the Precept's face. *What do you think of your decision now, old man?* The flame in his soul stirred in response to his growing anger.

"What's going on?" Cassidy looked from commander to soldier.

"The Knight of Water," Stillman dropped into his seat, "is gone."

This should not have happened. I should have been there.

He wanted to rage at Stillman, lay the blame at the old man's feet, tell him he had been dead wrong. But that would accomplish nothing so he kept his peace and took some solace in the horrified realization he read in Stillman's eyes.

"Sir."

"Go," Stillman ordered, hand trembling as he waved Dev away.

Free to kick ass, Dev was already down the hall when Cassidy's shout caught him.

"Wait. I'm going with you."

"Absolutely not," Stillman responded, but Dev hesitated, drifted back toward the Womb.

"You need my medical training. I can help."

Dev nodded once.

"Garison," Stillman said. "Please get the kit for Ms. Sinclair." The muncle melted into the floor and returned a moment later with a large case that barely fit through the hole he came through. "That should have everything you need to stabilize most wounds. Anything serious and they'll need to be brought here immediately." Stillman approached her and grabbed her arm. "Stay out of the combat. You are there as a medic only. Understood?"

"Yes, sir."

"Here." Stillman tossed the gateway card to Dev as he rushed in. "This will open on the warehouse across from the barge."

The Knight of Flame caught the card, grabbed Cassidy's hand and the medical kit, and pulled her down the hall. After the first few strides, she yanked herself free of his leading grasp.

Strong. Independent. She left him holding the bag. *And smart.*

He picked up the pace, taking her by the shortest route to the Portal Room. After a moment of concentration, he threw the card into the archway carved on the wall and the gateway opened.

"Are you sure about this?" Dev paused to give her one last out before he jumped them through the portal. He knew the answer, but had to ask the question. She wasn't a Knight, wasn't even a member of the Order and deserved the chance to change her mind. And yet, he knew what she would say.

"Absolutely."

Dev squeezed her hand and led them through.

In a blink, the Portal room vanished, replaced by the moonlit, dilapidated warehouse. Cassidy doubled over.

"Vertigo." Dev rubbed her back. "The nausea will pass in a second. Hang in there." He eyed the open doorway then turned back to his ailing companion. *Come on. Come on.*

Breathing heavy, Cassidy straightened and swallowed hard.

"Gogogo. I'm right behind you."

That a girl. Dev ran, but his warrior instincts forced him to stop before he charged blindly through the doorway out into the open. He reached out for heat sources. Only small dots of warmth, the usual wildlife, bugs and small fish in the water, came back. He hoped to sense his friends, but the barge's hull most likely masked their heat signatures.

Cassidy tapped him on the back to signal she was good to go. Dev broke from cover and sprinted across the dock. In two quick leaps, he vaulted up the gangway and landed on deck.

Security door. Where the hell is the security door?

Cassidy made it to the deck behind him.

"Look for the security door," Dev said.

Cassidy found the partially open vault and gave a low whistle. Dev rushed over, swung the door wide and plowed into the darkness to the first landing. Once inside, he heard the shouting. Cyndralla's light blazed far below. It wasn't strong enough to reach them, but it gave him a target.

Dev unleashed the fire within. It roared through his body, ignited his blood, and energized his muscles. Heat shimmered from every pore and his skin glowed red.

Cassidy stepped back.

Dev couldn't look at her, didn't want to see the fear, disgust and hatred in her eyes as she shrank back. Fire took her daughter. To her, his element, his very being, personified the force of destruction—an evil that ate little girls. He knew different, but couldn't deny her feelings.

Hell, for centuries he too believed he was a monster, a demon. But not anymore.

I am the Knight of Flame. A soldier of power and light.

He charged down the stairs. Each step closer to his friends and their danger fueled his building rage. Faster, he leaped the stairs three at a time. By his third leap, his skin ignited. Bright orange flame caressed his body and he grinned, grim and fierce, as his light consumed the shadows.

Like a comet, he blazed across the space of the hold. Cassidy trailed somewhere behind him, her heat sign steadily following his fiery trail.

Almost there.

Magnus waved him on. Cyndralla stood next to him, hand on her diadem. Wren crouched low by his side.

A shape, black and insubstantial, swooped at Dev's head, but his fire repulsed it, sent it back into the gloom. Another shape, or maybe the same one, he had no idea, dove at Cyndralla.

"Cyndy," Dev shouted, but Magnus was closer. With a single-armed swing of his axe, he severed the dark talon that tried to take her head. The creature attacked a few more times, but retreated when it got too close to Dev's fire or Magnus's axe.

"What's the scoop?" Dev asked.

"It's the sister," Magnus said.

"Who?"

"The other Maven, sister to the one at the club. The one with the yellow eyes in the painting. Agridda." Magnus spun his axe in his grip as he scanned for movement. "Dronor's down." His voice deepened, hollowing out as he called upon his earth power. His skin changed, hardening to iron from the hull and turning a dark reddish brown.

"Dev!" Wren got as close to the Fire Knight as she could, "Thank god you're—"

Running footsteps pattered behind them. Four sets of eyes turned to the sound. A knife appeared in Wren's hand, her arm cocked and ready to throw.

"Wren…" Dev started as Cassidy stumbled into the firelight.

"Here. Oh, you brought Cassidy." Wren stepped away from the Knight of Flame.

"It wassss good of you to come, killer of my ssssister. Develor Quinteele." Dev's name echoed through the open space.

"You're a popular guy." Magnus searched for the source of the voice.

Dev spun and drew Cinder. "Face me." Rage sundered his last shred of control. The orange crystal flared to life. Thin hairs of piercing light radiated out from the gem's facets.

An agonized scream surrounded them. Dev caught a flash of baleful yellow before it disappeared.

"This is ridiculous," Cyndralla complained. "Am I that out of practice that I cannot deal with a single foe?" She adjusted her outfit and fixed her hair. "I don't know about you, but I've had about enough of this bloody shadow hatchling."

"You're preaching to the choir, sister." Magnus spun in a slow circle, eyes scanning the hold's remote dark corners. Axe at the ready, he wrung the haft.

"Where is she?" Dev had been through dire battles with his friend, but the menace he felt in Magnus's voice spiked a chill into his molten core.

"Anybody hurt?" Cassidy asked and moved into the center of the Knights' impromptu diamond formation, each facing a different direction.

"Dronor's gone. Any sign of the orbs?" Dev took charge.

"No," Magnus answered. "But we haven't searched the whole place. Dronor mentioned something about a room at the far end of the hold."

"Let's check it out. Keep alert. Watch the shadows. We'll pick Dronor up on the way back."

"Got it."

As one, the group moved out in the direction of Dronor's phantom room. Dev on point, he led the advance slow and steady. His light augmented Cyndralla's spell, gave it a little extra bite to shred the shadows around them.

Come on, bitch. Bring it.

He thought of Dronor. They never liked each other, even went out of their respective ways to make the other look bad. But Dev knew, when it came down to it, Dronor had had his back.

And I should have had his.

"Hey, there's a room up here." Dev approached the open doorway cautiously and looked in. The room was shoddy, made of thin metal sheets riveted at the corners and poorly welded to the floor, with no ceiling.

Dev shook his head—*amateurs*—and guarded the front while Magnus stepped inside.

"There's a ton of perlite, the same material we found at the club," Magnus reported. The sounds of shifting material and muttered curses drifted over the relatively short walls.

"No orbs. Damn. I think they were here, but they must have moved them." Magnus roared after he spoke, a deep howl of frustration that rattled the walls. A huge fist punched through next to Dev's head.

Hello.

Dev peeked through the new window and saw the top of Magnus's head, hands pressed against the wall, shoulders bunched and strained. *Crack.*

He's not really...

Magnus growled and grunted. The wall bowed. Rivets popped.

Dev moved out of the way and warned the others, "Watch it."

With a final heave, Magnus toppled the entire wall. It crashed to the ground as a single long piece.

Chest heaving, eyes lowered and dangerous, hands curled into five-pronged meat hooks, Magnus stood over his handiwork.

"Better?" Dev understood the big man's need to vent. Dronor had been killed on his watch. He didn't envy the first few shadow people that crossed Magnus's path.

"A little." Magnus kicked the granular pile of insulation at his feet and sent a dark glass orb flying. It narrowly missed Cassidy's head and rolled beyond the edge of the light.

Dev couldn't help but smile at the sheepish expression now coating Magnus face. It was a complete one eighty from the insane killer mask he wore a minute ago.

"I got it." Out of reflex, Cassidy jogged after the orb. The further away from Dev she traveled, the less distinct her form became, until, as she bent to the ground to pick it up, she was little more than a dark, blurred mass.

Wren exploded into motion, wind-milling three daggers toward Cassidy. As the last left her fingers, she sprinted after.

Dev saw it then, the thing that triggered Wren's desperate actions—a pair of sickly yellow eyes atop a dark sinuous body wrapped around Cassidy. The daggers struck, distracting the Maven from her victim.

Legs pumping, Wren closed the distance.

Agridda uncoiled, relinquishing her hold on Cassidy, and reared up, the hood of a giant cobra fanning out around her yellow eyes.

Wren froze.

Throwing all he had into his element, Dev tore across the intervening space.

Nonononono.

Agridda struck. Curved black fangs pierced Wren's chest, lifted her into the air.

"Wren!" Dev shouted.

The shadow snake melted into the surrounding darkness, but somehow Wren remained aloft.

As Dev got close, his light illuminated the poor girl. She dangled above the ground like a butchered hog. Two black spikes jutted from her chest. Blood ran from the wounds, flowed down her back and legs and dripped onto the floor.

Wren...

Disbelief slowed Dev down. The other Knights ground to a halt at his side.

A woman peeled herself out of the dense wall of night. Formed of lithe, muscular limbs, perfect feminine curves, and long, flowing hair all the color of tar, she basked unafraid in Dev's fiery glow. The spikes holding Wren aloft grew out of her shoulder blades.

Wren moaned.

"Hold on, Wren. I'm here," Dev called.

"Shhh," Maven Agridda cooed. "It will be over soon." Wren's blood dripped on the Maven's face. A thin, snake-like tongue lapped it up. "Sssssweet and young."

"Let her go." Dev tried to keep the desperation out of his voice, but it crept in anyway.

"I will let her go, killer of my sssister. I will." The evil face grinned. "But not just yet."

"You can have me instead." Dev ignored the shocked looks from Magnus and Cyndralla.

"Mmmmm, tempting." She tapped one delicate finger against her chin. "I think…no. Thisss isss better. Hurtsss more."

Dev's guts twisted, and his mind whirled in a frantic search for a solution. *Where's Cassidy?*

There. At the verge of the light. She'd crawled away from the scene, close to Magnus.

"Wren?"

"Leave me and go." Wren strained to get the words out.

Hearing her pain, Dev flared to blue and advanced.

"Uh uh uh." Agridda waggled her finger and bounced the helpless girl. Her wounds tore open and Wren gasped. Bright red life rained down.

It stopped the Knight of Flame cold.

"Cyndy, can you do something?" Dev whispered.

"Not without killing our girl outright."

Agridda looked up at her prey. "Yesss. That should do it." The spikes retracted and Wren fell hard. Agridda backed away. "You may have her now." The shadow elements holding the Maven's form together dissolved and floated away, except for the eyes. They didn't move and her voice sounded from all sides.

"My father sends his regards." The yellow eyes blinked and were gone.

Dev rushed to Wren's side and dropped his flame, Cassidy and her bag right behind. She pushed him away from the wounds so she could take a look. Dev grabbed Wren's clammy hand. Her face crinkled in pain and her blue lips quivered.

After a quick look at the gaping holes through Wren's chest, Cassidy turned to Dev and, with the first tear rolling down her cheek, she shook her head.

No.

Cyndralla knelt at Wren's shoulder.

"Cyndy?"

"I'm sorry. She is beyond my power to heal, but I can ease her suffering." She placed her lips on Wren's brow and breathed a little magic into her. Immediately, Wren's features softened and she opened her eyes.

"Hi guys." Wren's voice was barely there.

"Save your strength," Dev whispered.

"For what?" She tried to smile, but only one side lifted. "Cassidy?"

Dev nodded. He couldn't speak. A wisp of steam rose from the corner of his left eye. Magnus knelt by her shoulder and answered.

"You saved her, bird brain." His moustache quivered as he wiped his tears away.

Her eyes lit up at Magnus's voice. "Block head."

Cassidy knelt at Wren's hip and took her other hand.

"Cass," Wren's voice little more than a vibration on the air, "Take care… of…him for me."

"I will."

Dev, Magnus, Cyndralla, and Cassidy huddled around the young girl that had become an important part of their lives, their friend, their sister. They sat with her, offering some small comfort in their touch.

"I love you." Dev's voice cracked.

As she took her last breath, her lips curled up.

Dev bowed his head over his fallen sister, gripping her slack hand in both of his.

I'm so sorry.

He'd lost too many people in his life—parents, friends, brothers-in-arms. *And now Wren.* His gaze drifted to Magnus, Cyndralla, and finally Cassidy. *Who's next?*

"Develor, we need to get back." The Knight of Air looked around her. "I don't know if Shadow's minion is gone, but we cannot chance it."

Cyndralla, ever the practical one.

Numb, he picked up Wren and laid her head against his chest.

So cold.

The others moved about, presumably taking care of business, but Dev was beyond caring. He moved and did what he was told, plodding along behind Magnus, stopping long enough to collect what was left of Dronor and for Cyndralla to create a gateway back to the Cradle.

A grim faced Stillman waited for them on the other side, eyes hidden in sad shadows.

Sadness, but no shock. He knew!

Dev fought every fiber of his being to keep the flames from incinerating the old bugger on the spot. There'd be time for questions and a barbeque later. But for now...he gazed down on the peaceful face resting against his chest. Unlike bullets or fire or blades, Wren's cold seeped through his armor and chilled his soul.

Tiny shuffling steps brought Stillman over. Hands shaking, body trembling, he reached out to his adopted daughter, but Dev turned away, refusing the old man that last contact.

The bastard knew and sent her anyway.

"Come." Stillman turned and struck off down the hallway alone. "The Chamber has been prepared."

Chapter 41

THE SOLEMN PROCESSION MARCHED DOWN THE HALL TOWARD A SILVER DOOR etched with the emblem of the Knights Elementalis. Stillman led, his steps measured, dignified. Magnus bore Dronor's remains while Cyndralla carried his elemental rapier—golden hilt with an oval, sea-green sapphire in the pommel—presented at chest level.

Cassidy walked with Dev who cradled his lost sister like a sleeping babe. More than once he caught her concerned glance as they traversed the Cradle in respectful silence. But he was under control now. For Wren, he had to be. This was her moment. The reckoning with Stillman would come later.

The silver door swung silently inward to reveal the majestic Chamber of Reflection. Dev had only been here once before, when his former assistant, Milosh, passed away. A vast round vault, the Chamber served as the spiritual center of the Order. A wide rock shelf circled the perimeter of the room, providing access to memorials of the past. Bas relief sculptures of former Knights and supporting members of the Order, stacked up as far as the light touched, watched over the ceremonies performed in this room.

In the center of the chamber, beyond a chasm spanned by a slim bridge of obsidian, rose an island. Aside from a rock platform at the terminus of the bridge, and four stone pillars rising mere feet above its mirrored serenity, a lake of quicksilver covered the island's flat surface.

Stillman led them onto the shelf and halted before a troop of golden muncles.

Regal, captain of the Cradle's defense force, and his honor guard of muncle warriors blocked the entrance to the obsidian bridge. Far larger than Bob and Garison, the golden warriors reached as high as Dev's chest with shoulders as broad. The blades of their golden halberds glinted above their heads. In addition to the long-weapon, each wore a short sword at its belt.

The captain bowed to Stillman and handed him a long golden staff. The Precept accepted the offering and nodded in return as Regal and his troops moved aside.

The slender bridge forced them to travel in single file. There were no guard rails and Dev felt Cassidy come up close behind him during the crossing.

On the platform, Stillman took up position a little apart from the others and bade Magnus and Dev come forward. "Lay Wren and Dronor on the surface," he directed.

Dev kissed Wren's forehead before placing her atop the reflective lake. The quicksilver didn't stir, supporting Wren's weight as if she lay on a mirror. Magnus laid Dronor out as well. Duty complete, both Knights stepped back.

"Cyndralla," Stillman intoned, "Please lay the rapier on Dronor's breast."

Cyndralla did as commanded, then stepped back.

Staff gripped tight in his right hand, the Precept raised his arms and faced the quicksilver to begin the rite. The Knights snapped to attention, hands clasped tightly behind rigidly straight backs. Cassidy followed suit, observing their ceremony with the same level of respect and honor.

"Lords of the Elements," Stillman's deep voice boomed across the lake. "Many centuries ago my brothers and I devoted our lives to the search for knowledge. Some of us soared in the light, while others delved in the dark."

Brothers? Light and dark? I don't remember that from the previous speech. Dev glanced over at Magnus who returned his quizzical expression.

"In my quest, I found a way to communicate with you, the prime elemental spirits of our world. Against the massing forces of Shadow, we forged an enduring alliance."

Stillman paused. Unease crept over the Knight of Flame, as if he were being watched. He wanted to drop into a crouch, and scan the area, but this situation was far from normal. Nothing here would hurt him or his fellows, but that didn't stop his skin from itching or fill the hollowness in his gut.

Power built around them, a pregnant expectation that something momentous would happen any second.

Cassidy sidled closer. She must have felt the effects as well.

Stillman set the end of the staff on the platform and let it sink a few inches into the stone.

"What's going on?" Cassidy whispered out of the side of her mouth so only Dev could hear.

"He's invoking the Elemental Lords."

"I call to you now, Lords of the Four Elements, to attend this gathering and accept one of your own. As you manifest, and it please you, speak in the common tongue of man so that all may benefit from your wisdom." Stillman drew a perfect upside down triangle, cutting through the hard rock of the floor as if it were water, and crossed the tip with another straight line. A single, rumbling word issued from his mouth. To Dev it held the power of a rockslide and carried the scent of grass and rich soil. Earth. The ground shook.

Magnus stood a little taller.

From out of the first pillar over the lake climbed a large figure, similar in shape and definition to the much smaller muncles. Only this version had a fully realized face with deep-set blue topaz eyes and full lips.

"Cernusen ap Gwyddno, I hear your call." The voice of the Earth Lord rumbled through the chamber. Its abyssal bass rattled the walls, the floor, and the ribs of those attending.

"Cernu—?" Cassidy leaned over and asked as quietly as she could.

"Cernusen ap Gwyddno," Dev whispered. "Stillman's real name."

Stillman bowed from the waist, a reverential acceptance of the elemental lord's presence. The floor smoothed out of its own accord, ready for the next symbol. Again, Stillman placed the staff's tip into the rock and slashed with precise movements. He drew another triangle, this one right-side up. With a finishing flourish, he sliced the pinnacle with a horizontal line. Air.

His lips formed the word of summoning. Soundless, a burst of power emerged, gained strength and careened around the chamber as a storm gale. Cyndralla smiled and her eyes glistened. The tempest reached a crescendo and funneled over the second pillar in the pool.

"Cernusen ap Gwyddno," the words of the Lord of Air streamed across the distance, buffeting the Knights and Cassidy with their blustery power. "I hear your call."

Stillman bowed to the elemental lord and drew the next sign—a perfect upright triangle. Fire. Dev opened himself to the presence of the Lord of Fire and Stillman spoke the word. It blasted from his mouth like the eruption of a volcano, filling the vast chamber with intense heat.

A gout of flame burst from the third pillar, changing color from orange, to red, to blue to the purist white.

How did he reach white? This embodiment of the Fire Lord rocked him. Dev had mastered the range of temperatures, from soft, warm amber all the way through the deep indigo inferno. Until now, he'd thought a flame so pure that it burned white nothing but a myth. The power of the Fire Lord filled his diminished reserve, its righteousness coursed through him in a cleansing scourge, dispelling any lingering doubts of his nature or purpose.

The other Knights shielded their eyes from the radiance until the lord dimmed his aspect to a more acceptable level.

"Cernusen ap Gwyddno, I hear your call." The Lord of Fire's voice crackled and popped, like a bonfire fed with sap-filled pine, and made Cassidy jump.

Stillman bowed and drew the last image. A perfect triangle, pointed down. Water. His voice faltered. The word of summoning didn't carry through the room as the others did, but dripped from his suddenly slack lips to fall flat on the shimmering lake surface. The old alchemist succumbed to the loss of his friend and daughter and toppled forward off the ledge.

Dev rushed forward, but their fallen leader was lifted by the very lord of that summoned element. The being held the Order's commander in his arms, much like Dev had held Wren earlier, and set him gently upon his feet on solid ground.

The Lord of Water regarded the remaining Knights as they stood in various poses in their haste to help their leader. He bowed to them before slipping under the surface and flowing up the last pillar to reform in the shape of a translucent man.

"Cernusen ap Gwyddno, I hear your call." The Lord of Water's voice fell on the Knights like a warm spring rain. It buoyed Dev's spirit and eased a fraction of his pain.

Stillman, recovered enough to bow to the water lord, leaned heavily on the golden staff. "Lords and Knights. We have come to send our Brother, Dronor, the eighth Knight of Water, on his final journey. Lord," Stillman addressed the Lord of Water, "Dronor has fought through the years with strength and valor. In battle this morning, he sacrificed himself to save a fellow Knight from the forces of Shadow. In honor, please take him home."

At the mention of their ancient foe, the Elemental Lords bristled. The quicksilver around their pedestals boiled.

The Lord of Water raised an open hand toward his Knight and called his champion home. The surface of the water bubbled around Dronor's remains. Churning slowly at first, it quickly gained momentum until it boiled and frothed, completely covering the Knight in its liquid turbulence. As the essence of water lowered his hand, the surface resumed its smooth-as-glass calm. The Knight had vanished.

After Dronor's acceptance, a brief rumble shook the back wall, accompanied by a plume of blue dust. When the dust cleared, the newly carved image of the Knight of Water appeared on the wall.

Rain fell in a light drizzle on the Knights and dotted the surface of the lake. "Another champion will be chosen." With that, the power holding the liquid man-shape together fled the chamber, sending the water crashing to the top of the pillar.

"My lords, another of our number has fallen this day." Stillman's form slumped further down the staff. Dev took a step toward him, but Stillman waved him off. "Wren Peterlin, my daughter of the heart, sacrificed herself in the battle against Shadow to save one of her own. While not a chosen elemental champion, her valor, honor and sense of duty was equal to any in this room."

Dev nodded, as did Magnus and Cyndralla, and sent a flurry of thoughts to the fire lord to support Stillman's claims.

"My Lords, I beseech you. Not as the Precept of the Knights Elementalis, but as a father. Will one of you accept her into your embrace?"

The Lord of Fire flared—a bright column of bluish flame towering toward the unseen ceiling. The heat from the display rushed over the chamber in a wave. The quicksilver in the lake hissed and bubbled, but the fire lord's intensity declined as it reached the Knights, arriving hot, but bearable.

"My champion," the Fire Lord began, "has recommended her unto mine realm. Upon his word, I accept her." The elemental changed color, dimming to a soft yellow.

"Thank you." Stillman's voice shook with relief as he fell to his knees. "In honor," his voice broke, "please take her home."

A pale glow surrounded Wren's body, highlighting her peaceful slumber. The light intensified, growing brighter until it was painful to look upon. Then, with a tremendous flash, Wren winked out and journeyed to the realm of fire. The back wall trembled and, in a puff of red smoke, the carved image of Wren appeared.

With a nod to Dev, its champion on Earth, the Lord of Fire shone crimson then vanished, leaving spots in the vision of those looking on.

Cassidy rubbed her eyes.

Stillman bowed. "Thank you, Elemental Lords, for attending this ceremony."

The Lord of Earth and the Lord of Air nodded to their respective champions and left with a rumble and a breeze.

With the departure of the Elemental Lords, the Chamber of Reflection seemed reduced, empty. Dev looked into the distance, over the quicksilver pool to the edge of the chasm and beyond to the far wall. He could barely make out the newest addition to the family etched in stone for all time.

I'll visit you often.

Stillman's unsteady gait made navigating the bridge difficult. Dev stayed close, offering the distraught Precept his support when he drifted too close to the edge. Despite the added challenge, they crossed safely.

Regal clomped over to the Precept and offered his metal shoulder. Stillman leaned heavily on the muncle captain as he made his way to the silver portal.

Dev had questions, but given Stillman's obvious distress, they could wait until the next day. Nothing he did or said would bring Wren back and, despite his desire for the truth, he believed a father had the right to grieve.

Over his shoulder, Stillman voiced one last command before beginning the solitary journey to his quarters.

"Get some rest. This battle has just begun."

৪৩

Jester stood upon the anvil and glared at Dev as he walked into the Forge. A patchwork of different colored stone—tan, brown, gold, and white—the forge's muncle posed with his big stone fists resting on non-existent hips and a wavy line across his face. A spark glimmered in its emerald eyes.

"I see you've been hanging with Wren. She used to stand like that when she was mad at me too."

At the mention of their absent friend, Jester lost his fierceness and his mouth curved down.

"I know, buddy, I miss her too." Dev slumped on the stool in front of the anvil. "I can't believe she's gone." He picked up a long metal file and spun it slowly between his fingers. "Huh. She used to take my files all the time, drove me nuts. Silly girl. But now..." Reaching to the counter, he reverently placed the tool in its proper slot.

Jester clopped to the edge of the anvil and bonked Dev on the head with a hard motley fist.

"Hey." The Knight's anger bristled. "Stop that."

The muncle straddled the anvil's horn, kicked his stick thin legs, large block feet swinging like mallets, and watched Dev expectantly.

Dev wasn't sure what to say. They'd been close for a long, long time, done many projects together, but he hadn't been around much since the Tampa assignment and he felt like he'd abandoned the little guy. "Thank you for all the metal."

Jester handed him a gold nugget and pointed to the trough.

"What? You want to make something now?"

The muncle nodded vigorously, nearly shook himself off his seat.

"Sorry, bud. I'm not up for it. Maybe a little later, alright?" The Knight of Flame got to his feet and glanced around his room.

Forge. Cot. Tools. Ore. Weapons. Nothing has changed. And yet...it feels so empty. Lifeless.

I let her down.

Jester stomped to get Dev's attention.

"What?" Dev asked, his tone sad and tired.

The little stone man insistently pointed at the trough then at the anvil then at Dev.

"Look, Jester, I—"

The little guy crossed his arms and realigned his mouth in a wavy line.

"Determined little bugger, aren't you." Dev sighed. "Alright, what do you want to make?"

Jester eyes sparkled as he shrugged.

Keep it simple and quick. Maybe this will make up for some of the time I spent away.

Dev checked the items on his wall—swords, axes, knives, and other items of destruction.

"How 'bout a golden knife?"

The muncle's mouth angled down.

"I'll take that as a 'no'."

Why do I always gravitate to something that can kill? Stillman said that Lancelot focused on love and beauty. Maybe I can try the beauty thing for a change. But, what the hell do I know about that?

"Tell you what, let's start working and see what happens. Okay?"

Jester hopped to his feet and stomped to the other end of the anvil.

Leaning over the empty trough, Dev called his element and focused the energy into his hands. They glowed red and whooshed into flame. Eyes closed, he felt the metal, gauged the heat. He didn't want to liquefy it, only change it enough to shape and sculpt. The nugget softened in his hand as he cranked up the heat. Applying pressure, he played around and shoved one thumb into the clay-like mass. Like a small child, he shaped it into a ball, flattened out a pancake, rolled it into a thin strand of spaghetti, and for the first time in what seemed like forever, found that spark of insight and fun that he'd been missing.

Wren always said I was too serious when I worked. What would she think of me now?

The golden pasta disappeared into a wadded up mass. Twisting and turning the golden mush, he pondered his next feat of artistry. Slowly a shape formed as Dev's fingers coaxed it from the lump of gold. He smoothed his thumb between its floppy ears to round the little dome if its head.

Voila! A dog. Wren always wanted a dog.

A lopsided golden dog, with one ear longer than the other and a tail long enough to make a monkey proud, stood on the anvil. *Maybe it's half monkey and half dog.* Its shoulders were too thick and it's haunches too thin.

Dev eyed the silly looking beast. It was the first he'd ever tried to make and, while it wasn't a masterpiece, zoologists should be able to identify it as some distant relative of the canine family.

"What do you think?" Dev looked at Jester.

The little guy walked around the dog, patted its backside. When he looked up, a huge smile stretched the line cross his block.

"We need to give him a name." With Jester's approval, he leached the statue's heat and completed the cool down in seconds. "How about…Rex?"

Jester shook his head.

"Spot?"

Thumbs down.

"I know, Mikey."

Jester mulled that one over then nodded.

"Good. Mikey it is. I want you to take good care of him, okay?"

The muncle nodded, slow and serious, and clutched the little golden dog to his breast.

"Sorry I was gone so long." Dev patted Jester on the head and moved to the stone cot as the events caught up to him. He lay back and stared at the ceiling, reliving the events and the losses.

Wren…

In the solitude of his Forge, the Knight of Flame swung his arm over his eyes and wept.

Chapter 42

THE SHADOW DRAGON GLIDED THROUGH HOT NIGHT AIR REDOLENT WITH STAG-
nant water and sulfur as Alexander searched the ground for a recognizable
landmark. Nothing but blurry patches of browns and grays, with an occasional
scrub oak cluster adding a touch of dimension, filled his sight. There had been
no sign of house, building or road for thirty minutes and he wondered what
Gothrodul had in mind.

I'm taking you to my lair, the dragon responded.

Alexander cursed his carelessness at leaving himself open to the curious
mental predations of the dragon.

Whatever for? The last thing he wanted was to wallow in the dragon's den.
It was a place for his brother, Thargen, not him.

A change of scenery, perhaps, the dragon offered.

The three-quarter moon hung bright in the sky. Atop the dragon, Alexander
felt he could reach out and touch it. Not out of any romantic sense, of course,
but to take it down, bury it and leave the night in darkness as it should be.

The bloody thing is almost as bright as the blasted sun.

The dragon banked left and angled for the formation of squat buildings
huddled beside the first hill Alexander had seen since his exile to this cursed
place.

Welcome to one of your outlying facilities. The dragon touched down in
the central square of the complex. Abandoned pick-up trucks with "Seagren
Chemical" emblazoned on their doors lined the outer wall of a long, half-
circle shaped metal shed, the largest of the four buildings.

Gothrodul loped toward the end of the building. Its ungainly movement
forced Alexander to hug the dragon's neck or get thrown from his perch
between its furled wings. Another smell intruded, this one as familiar and
welcome as Shadow itself...Death.

This had better be worth it.

The segmented metal door had been ripped from its track and discarded.
Even so, the dragon had to duck and crawl through the opening designed for
industrial-sized vehicles to get into its makeshift lair.

More than death assailed Alexander's nostrils within the confines of the
metal structure. Overpowered, he nearly gagged. But that clear sign of weakness would be unacceptable, so he covered his nose with his sleeve against
the intense rot and decay fouling the air. He slid to the ground and nearly
tripped over the severed head that had distanced itself from the rest piled in
the corner.

That would explain the smell.

"So this is where you go when you are not serving me. Again I ask, why are we here?" Alexander studied the slaughterhouse decor. A hand here, a foot there, if he gathered the disjointed parts, he might find enough scraps to stitch together a single malformed entity. No time for puzzles or sewing, he moved on to the ancient world map stuck to the floor with a mixture of old blood and dirt.

There is something I wish to show you. Gothrodul indicated the map on the floor that stretched across the entire width of the shed, some seventy-five feet. Big splotches of fresh blood and bone fragments decorated various regions, but the dragon did not make for those. Instead, he angled for the Americas.

We all have our secrets, Shadow Lord. I am about to confess one of mine.

Secrets? Curious, Alexander pinched the strange material upon which eight great land masses had been inked with painstaking care, and found it thick and supple, like the hide of some great beast. Within each region, an unfamiliar symbol glowed.

"What is it?"

Human flesh. The effort cost me a hundred years, but was worth every minute. Have you heard of the Last Clan?

Alexander rubbed his temple. *It is going to be a long night.* "No."

Do you see those symbols? Gothrodul waved a clawed foot over the map.

"Of course. How could I miss them?"

Each one represents a dragon clan. One clan per region. Within our own lands, dragons are, for the most part, social and willing to work together for the strength of the clan. However, if two different clans meet, they will fight until one or both are destroyed. There is no middle ground. That, Alexander, is what dropped Atlantis into the sea. Gothrodul pointed to a landmass in the southern Indian Ocean that Alexander could not remember seeing upon any other map.

"As fascinating as this lecture on dragon wars may be, why fly me out here to tell me now?"

I will get to my point soon, but to understand the magnitude of what I am going to tell you, you must understand the big picture.

"Hurry it up then."

Nine clan symbols for nine clans, the dragon continued.

"There are only eight land masses. You said one per land mass."

The ninth symbol represents the Last Clan or the Secret Clan. Dragon legends speak of a clutch of eggs hidden away against the day when the last of us roam the planet. Consider it a safeguard to ensure the survival of dragon kind.

"And your point?"

Have you found my services of value, Shadow Lord?

"Yes. You have been most effective."

What if you had access to more? Ten or twenty or even fifty loyal dragons fighting for you?

What indeed? The concept sent a thrill to Alexander's dark soul.

This story of the Last Clan was passed down from sire to younglings for eons. Most believed it only a myth, but some knew different, knew it to be the truth.

"Why have you not come forward with this before?"

I was unsure of the location, but now I'm close to finding the Last Clan. I believe they are here, in North America.

"Where?" *An army of dragons...*

I cannot enter the lair of the Last Clan without my...sister.

"Sister?"

Yes. We are the last. Only a mixture of our blood will unseal the gate. The time has come for the birth of the Last Clan.

With an army of dragons, I could subjugate my brothers and destroy my enemies. Not even my father could stand against that kind of force for long.

Alexander's shadow stretched over the Americas. "And where is this sister?"

Therein lies the problem.

"Oh?" Alexander turned to the dragon.

"She is of the Knights Elementalis."

Chapter 43

*I*T *SHOULD HAVE BEEN ME.* CASSIDY LEANED BACK IN HER CHAIR, ARMS CROSSED OVER her breasts, and watched the world spin. She rested her feet on the unopened medical kit. *Wren gave her life for me.*

The mood in the Womb was somber. Hunched over the shadow orb, Cyndralla plumbed its depths as she teased her long unkempt braid. Red and black stains marred her usually pristine white raiment. Magnus slouched in his chair, chin on his chest, eyes closed, hands clasped in his lap. His axe leaned against the table. Dev hunched over, elbows braced on knees, and flipped Cinder from one hand to the other.

Stillman sat in his customary spot, deep grooves lined his milk-white face. Half-lidded eyes, distant and haunted, stared more into the past than the here and now. Back iron-rod straight, he sat on the edge of his seat, fingers laced on the table, stare unfocused.

"The Mavens were an abomination," Stillman broke the silence, "constructed of the vilest shadow magic. Twins, Triessa and Agridda, beautiful little girls brimming with energy. They had messy brown hair and a penchant for mischief." He smiled to himself, lost in the memories. "When they were three, their father presented them to his father as a gift. It was that monster, the Gray Lord, who twisted those lovely young girls, transformed them into powerful creatures of Shadow."

And I thought Alexander Gray was bad.

"Triessa got the body, but less power. Agridda, though, became a being of pure Shadow. Extremely powerful. Nearly impossible to hurt."

"So how do we fight something like that?" Magnus asked. "My axe did no good. Everything I cut off found its way back to her."

"I thought my flame did some damage at first," Dev commented. "At least she seemed to retreat into the darkness, but that might have been a tactical move on her part to make us think she had left."

"Probably," Stillman agreed. "Cyndralla, what do you see in that ball of yours?"

"Nothing yet." The Knight of Air looked up. "I need to open it, see what makes it tick, but I will not do that until I have it under a shield in my lab."

"I'll work with you. Between your magic and my alchemy, we should be able to crack that egg," Stillman said.

"What about that shadow bitch?" Magnus rumbled to his feet. "We need to destroy her, and Alexander, and whomever else stands with them. Hit them now." He grabbed his elemental weapon. "They wouldn't be expecting us to attack. We know Gray is behind this. We can take out his headquarters and be done with him."

"I'm in." Dev lent his support, but his voice lacked his usual enthusiasm. If the shadow maven took out two of their number, how could the rest of them hope to stand against her and her father on their home turf? The plan was crazy, ridiculous, but it was better than sitting back doing nothing.

"No," Stillman spoke up. "While I support the idea in spirit, we cannot lose sight of our greater purpose." Voice calm, collected, and so very cold. "We must develop a counter to the orb's deadly magic as quickly as possible. Gray and his minions will escalate their plans, thinking us too weak to stop them. We don't have much time."

The commander paused, covered his face with a shaky hand, and took several deep breaths. Cassidy had used the same technique numerous times on the job when she didn't want to let her emotions out in front of a mangled patient or concerned parent. It did the trick for her, bought her enough time to mask her feelings. But when Stillman dropped his hand, the calm Precept's façade fell away, revealing the anger and agony of a grieving father.

"Make no mistake. I want this bastard and his vile spawn as much as you do. And we will get him." His shoulders trembled. "But not until we know more, until we're ready. I will lose no more to this darkness." Strength gone, he sat back down.

"So now what? Wait until you and Cyndy break this thing open? Gray could be doing all sorts of things out there while we sit around with our thumbs up our asses. This is absurd." Magnus strode from the room, big axe over his shoulder. "Call me when you're ready to fight. I'll be sitting around being useless somewhere else." Disgust hung thick in his voice.

Dev followed quickly after his friend. "Let me know how I can help with the orb," he threw over his shoulder.

"Strange," offered the Knight of Air, "I would have expected that outburst from Develor, not Magnus." Cyndralla scooped up the orb and left without another word, leaving Cassidy alone with Wren's father for the first time.

She placed a hand on his shoulder. "I'm sorry, sir. It was my fault. If I—"

"You may stop there, Ms. Sinclair." Stillman's tone was soft and sad. "Do not wear the mantle of blame. That creature of Shadow is at fault. It was she who took my daughter's life. Not you."

"But—"

"Not you. Do I make myself clear?"

"Yes, sir."

His words made sense. Agridda killed Wren. Still, she couldn't shake the feeling that if she hadn't been there in the first place, Wren would still be alive.

"Good. Spend your thoughts and energy in a useful way and figure out how we can defeat her."

"I will."

I promise.

ঞ৪

Blue, green, and yellow liquids bubbled and frothed in separate vials on the counter next to a pile of yellow powder. The shadow orb lay half-buried in a mound of salt beneath the soft pink light of Cyndralla's protective shield. Stillman stood to one side, swirling the smoking contents of yet another potion, this one purple.

The Knight of Air pierced the shield with an ash wood rod and tapped the hard outer shell of the orb as Cassidy approached the counter.

"Is there anything I can do?" she asked. She played with a few leftover grains on the table that had come from the barge. "What did you call this stuff?"

"Magnus called it perlite, said it was some kind of insulating agent," Cyndralla said.

Hearing that word again struck a chord with Cassidy. It rang that familiarity bell, but the specifics eluded her.

"The sulfide solution is ready, as are the other acids," Stillman said.

"Good." Cyndralla took the proffered vial with the purple liquid and breathed over the opening. The potion glowed for a second before changing to a light, bubblegum pink. With a nod at the result, she upended it over the orb. It splashed over the surface and ran down the sides to puddle in the surrounding salt.

Cassidy noticed both Cyndralla and Stillman watching intently so she struck a similarly intent pose. Nothing happened. The orb remained closed and unharmed.

"One down, three to go." Stillman sighed.

Perlite...perlite. Why is that familiar?

"Let's try yellow." Once again, Cyndralla breathed over the top. When the potion turned an awful puke-green, she poured it over the orb. The smell matched the color, made Cassidy step back lest she coat the orb with her own potion.

Don't try that one again. Bleh. Aside from the intense smell, nothing happened.

Stillman handed the pretty blue one to Cyndralla next. This turned brown and smelled like shit. Even Cyndralla balked.

"Oh, Stillman, that one's atrocious," Cyndralla complained and waved her hand in front of her face. Before dousing the orb, she held her nose. If the liquid didn't penetrate the shell, maybe the smell would.

Stillman laughed. It was good to hear him find a moment of humor.

"Heh, when I was a boy, we used that to fertilize the olive trees."

Fertilizer? That's it.

"Hey, I remembered why 'perlite' rings a bell." She filled them in on seeing the chemical company reps in the lobby of Gray's office building and found that they had been bought out by Gray's company. "There has to be some connection."

"It might be worth a look. Talk to Magnus. He's looking for something to do." Since they didn't get any kind of internet or cable in the Cradle, she would have to travel back to the world.

"I'm on it." Cassidy left with a little more spring in her step.

A research mission. Finally, something I can handle. Now...where did they put Magnus? Wait. That won't work. The big guy probably doesn't have any gateways for Tampa. His were probably tied to his band's tour bus or a recording studio. Need Dev. Where is—

"Oh."

Dev rounded the corner. "Any word from Stillman? Did they figure it out?"

"No, but we have a mission in the city."

Chapter 44

STEPPING INTO THE SWIRLING FLAMES OF DEV'S ELEMENTAL PORTAL WAS UNSET-tling. Cassidy hadn't thought about what choosing him would mean in terms of transportation until she stood before the hot door and he took her hand. He said it would take them to the center of the living room in his condo and from there they could get anywhere else.

"Ready?" Dev asked and squeezed her hand.

"Suuuurrrre." She eyed the portal nervously. *No way*, she thought, but closed her eyes and followed the tug on her hand into the heat anyway. It was over in an instant and wasn't nearly as bad she thought it would be. She expected to feel like a baked potato, and she did, but only for a second, then it was the normal moist heat of a Tampa night.

Something crackled under Cassidy's foot as she stepped down in the condo.

"Careful there." He rescued the DVD boxed set of *Red Dwarf.* Other DVDs and video games lay strewn about—on the floor, over the couch and loveseat, across the ottoman and coffee table. Clothes, Cassidy didn't know if they were clean or dirty, littered the floor alongside empty pizza boxes. She picked up one of the boxes and scattered a nest of roaches. The potent aroma of cheap cigar and urine clung to everything.

He's a pig. How could Wren live like this?

"Was it the cleaning lady's day off?" Cassidy asked as she pinched her nose.

Dev frowned. "No. Wren kept it spotless." Eyes roving, he motioned for her to stay put and stalked down the hall toward three other doors. Quietly and carefully, he twisted the knob on the closest door and pushed it open, then did the same for the other two. "They're gone," he called from the other room. "Whoever they were, they had bad aim."

Cassidy followed his voice into what she presumed was his bedroom. The sharp scent of urine smacked her in the face when she stepped through the doorway past what was left of a full-sized bed. It jutted out from the sidewall covered in dark stains. Springs and bits of soggy yellow foam poked through ragged gashes.

Across from the bed, next to a smashed combo TV/DVD player, sat a small dresser. The drawers had been torn out and splintered against the floor, their contents slashed and tossed in the corner.

"They didn't miss a trick, did they?" Cassidy looked around at the mess. "Is anything missing?"

"Nothing a quick trip to Wal-Mart won't fix." He eyed the door across the hall. The fingers on his right hand flicked against his thumb.

"Wren's room?" Cassidy asked.

"Yeah."

"Come on. We'll go in together."

"No. I got this." Dev strode across the hall with Cassidy right behind. A similar mess greeted them in Wren's room, only the smell wasn't as bad.

"Looks like they only whizzed in your room."

He grunted and surveyed the minimal damage. Pink frilly pillows and comforter covered the twin bed as if it had been made that morning, though the open dresser drawers left her wares on display. She guessed the perfume bottles and lip-gloss on the floor by the window had been on the top of the dresser.

Assholes.

She'd reported on crime scenes before, gleaned facts and procedure from the detectives, but nothing this close to home, this personal. While she tucked Wren's workaday cotton panties and bras back in the drawer and shut it—*No sense leaving them out on display*—she sneaked a few covert glances at Dev. Since the barge, he seemed quiet, reserved. Understandably so, but still...

Dev drew his finger along the dresser and ran his hand through the pink fringe around one of the pillows.

"Anything missing in here?" Cassidy asked.

He stood still as a gravestone at the foot of the bed and stared at its emptiness.

"Dev," she placed her hand on his arm, "Is anything missing?"

"Huh? Oh. Just Wren. But in terms of stuff, no. We didn't keep anything valuable, in case something went wrong."

This is really tough for him. "Good call."

In the kitchen, a second colony of roaches feasted on the dried milk, baby gherkins and clumps of rancid cottage cheese spilled across the linoleum.

Yuck. The reports of all these bugs must be true. Dev has only been gone a few days and already the creepy crawlies have moved in.

Cassidy picked up an ID badge on the counter. She cringed at an awful picture of Dev sneering for the camera. The name read "Stanley Rock."

Dev crunched his way across the bugs like Godzilla and grabbed a Cream of Mushroom soup can from the top shelf.

"Stanley. Seriously?"

"Nothing wrong with Stanley." He twisted the false top and shook out two sets of keys. "We got wheels. Where we going?"

"Didn't say there was." *Stan. Stan the Man. The Stan-meister.*

"Stanley's a good American name."

"Do you have a computer...Stan?" she teased lightly, hoping to evoke a smile

Dev raised one eyebrow. "Over there."

How could I miss that beast?

On the desk in the corner perched one of those sleek super-gamer models with the neon bulbs plugged into the motherboard that glowed through the clear plastic tower. The flat-screen monitors were cracked, their cut cables dangled like dried eels off the edge of the table. The keyboard had been snapped in half and a piece of pizza jammed into the DVD drive.

"You a gamer?" Cassidy asked as she examined several resin statues of fantasy creatures.

"Sometimes. I run a guild in one of those online fantasy games, but you probably never heard of it. While Wren watched TV, I fought in the virtual world." He twirled the key ring on his finger. "Funny. In the game, I always keep it together. Never lose control. Focus on duty and honor, make sure my guild members do the same. We are the leading guild on the server. Shame I didn't bring that over into real life."

Cassidy checked the CPU. "This is toast. Got a phone book?"

Dev tossed her the phone book that sat on top of the fridge. Cassidy found the address for the former Seagren Chemical Company and ripped out the page with several locations listed.

"We are going to Apollo Beach." She waved the page at Dev and shivered as a giant palmetto bug crawled up the fridge. "Ugh, I'm outta here."

"Hold on." He grabbed the boxed set of *Hogan's Heroes* and two *Benny Hill* DVDs. "These belong to Magnus."

Sure they do.

හ෴෴

Aside from an elderly woman shuffling along the sidewalk next to a decrepit poodle, and a few cars parked in the lot, the condo complex appeared deserted. Shimmering waves of heat rose from the blacktop, pasting Cassidy's shirt to her skin within her first few steps while Dev remained impervious.

Some things just don't seem fair.

The Knight of Flame led her down the steps in the front of his building and out into the parking lot.

What does an elemental warrior drive? Ooh, there's a nice Escalade near the back, or maybe the Explorer. I picture a big vehicle with lots of power. Past the big trucks and cars, he led her toward the back corner and a classic pink Chevy Caprice alongside something covered in a tarp.

No way. Cassidy fought a smile as she rounded the car to the passenger door, but Dev heaved the tarp to uncover a new Harley.

Oh hell no. "You're not really thinking about the bike, are you?" *I've scraped too many bikers off the street.*

"Why not?" Dev straddled the hog and winked.

She jiggled the door handle. "I'm not much of a cycle girl."

"The car was Wren's."

"So? It runs doesn't it?" *Please. Not the bike.*

Dev cranked it up. The beefy engine growled and spit before it settled into a solid throaty roar. He waved her over, patted the seat behind him, and offered her a matte black helmet.

I don't do bikes. She clung to the princess car, afraid to get close to Dev and his testosterone.

"You're burning daylight, Caz."

So now it's Caz, is it? Caz...I like it, sounds cool and hip. Listen to me...cool and hip. What the hell? I sound like my mother. If I say groovy I'll shoot myself.

He revved the engine. The sound thrummed against the car door.

After all the stuff I've been through with him, I'm scared of a little motorcycle ride?

Uh, yeah. The normal voice in her head sounded worthless and weak, but she hopped onto the back of the bike and wrapped her arms around the Knight of Flame.

Her thighs rattled and her ass vibrated as Dev threw it into gear and launched them across the lot. Not ready for the quick acceleration, Cassidy slipped back in the seat. She hauled herself forward and grabbed on tighter, feeling the hard contours of Dev's back pressed against her chest.

Maybe motorcycles don't suck.

"Huh?" Lost in the moment, Cassidy didn't hear Dev's first words, but she saw him look back.

"I said, where in Apollo Beach?"

"Near the power plant."

"Hold on."

Count on it.

೮ು౧౪

Traffic inched along, too slow for Dev. He wove in and out and between the barely moving cars. Cassidy should have been all over him, telling him to slow down or to be careful. But that's not how *Caz* rolled. She closed her eyes and enjoyed the wind in her face. Even contemplated yanking the helmet off and letting the wind whip through her hair, but a shade of her old self popped up just in time to keep it firmly strapped.

The exhilarating ride, unlike any she'd been on before, ended too soon and when Dev roared into the parking lot, she felt disappointed. Dev held her hand as her rubbery legs adjusted to being on firm ground again. And not just her legs, but her whole body tingled.

Never got that feeling from a car.

The big sign at the entrance still read Seagren Chemical, but an added placard announced the Daegon Gray buy-out. The building had been stamped from the usual mid-size Florida company mold—four stories, tinted blue glass and steel façade, small man-made pond out front with a spitting fountain in the center.

Cassidy eyed the fine-dressed folks coming and going. *Damn, forgot to dress for success.* Jeans and a t-shirt were fine in most places, but the business world still liked its button downs and pressed khakis.

"What's your plan?" Dev asked, ignoring the wary looks from the suits in the parking lot. She couldn't blame them. Bald head, stern, chiseled face, leather vest that bared his well-developed bi's and tri's, leather pants, black boots. Add a couple of screaming eagle tattoos and Dev embodied the biker from hell who had just rumbled into their lives.

Plan? Uh... "Get the information."

He gave her a look that said, "No, really?"

"I'll work the girl at the front desk." Cassidy brushed the road dust off her jeans. "Follow my lead and keep quiet." She sauntered through the main door like she paid the rent and smacked her hands down on the reception counter.

"I'm here to see the office manager." Cassidy glared at the receptionist hunkered down behind a black marble desk.

"I'm sorry, Ms....?" Black hair with streaks of blue, tight white blouse, phone jacked into her ear along with several studs and dangling earrings, the receptionist cocked an eyebrow.

"Drymold."

"Ms. Drymold, who are you here to see?"

Affronted, Cassidy leaned forward. "Who is in charge here?"

"Mr. Greenway. He's Senior Vice President and Int—"

"I'm here to see Mr. Greenway."

"Do you have an appointment?"

"I'm here on the order of Mr. Gray. Shall I tell your new owner that his personal assistant had to wait in the lobby?"

The receptionist's eyes flashed. Cassidy thought she pushed her luck too far, that the girl would see through the ruse and kick her out, but Cassidy held her ground and the receptionist blinked first.

"I'll call him now, Ms. Drymold. One moment please."

Cassidy turned to Dev who had come in during the exchange and rolled her eyes. He crossed his arms.

The man could turn looming menace into an art form.

The receptionist turned back and did a double take at the hired muscle over Cassidy's left shoulder. She couldn't take her eyes from Dev as she relayed that Mr. Greenway would be down in a moment.

"Good. Thank you."

Flushed and puffing hard, Mr. Greenway hustled into the foyer. The open panels of his navy blue suit jacket flapped against his ample belly in time with the jiggle of his second chin. His smile seemed genuine, though, as he swooped down on Cassidy and extended his hand.

"I'm so sorry to keep you waiting." Mr. Greenway pumped her hand eagerly then did the same with Dev's. "Let's talk in my office. Would you like something to drink?"

"No. Thank you. We only have a few minutes," Cassidy said.

Greenway's office turned out to be right around the corner from the lobby. Evidently word had spread of the visitors because the halls were deserted.

"Please, have a seat." Greenway sat behind his desk and rolled in until his belly bumped the edge. "What can I do for you?"

Cassidy sat demurely, while Dev guarded the door—a silent, menacing presence at her back.

"I'm here about the perlite shipping manifests. Mr. Gray was expecting them yesterday, but they never arrived. He sent me to pick them up."

Greenway looked puzzled as he tapped a few keys on his computer keyboard.

"I'm sorry, Ms. Drymold, but there must be some misunderstanding. I don't have any perlite shipping manifests."

Crap.

"What about other big shipments? Perhaps someone in your organization mislabeled them."

"Ms. Drymold," his voice rose an octave with his condescension, "We have one of the largest shipping infrastructures in the world. We ship by truck, train, plane, and boat every single day. We do not make mistakes when it comes to freight."

Cassidy felt her window of opportunity shrinking.

"Your boss knew this when he bought our company." A greasy smile spread across his chubby cheeks and he lowered his brow. He tapped away at his keyboard. "Who do you really work for, Ms. Drymold? One of Daegon Gray's competitors?"

Dev strode across the office, rolled Greenway into the corner and pushed him down the few times he tried to stand up.

"I will not be manhandled like this," Greenway huffed until Dev ignited one fingertip and placed it in front of the self-important man's right eye.

"Shut it," Dev said.

Greenway shrank away from the glowing finger.

"Caz."

Oh yeah. I like the new name.

"How are you with computers?" Dev asked without taking his eyes from the nervous executive.

"Pretty good."

"Saddle up and get the info we need."

Cassidy jumped out of her seat and examined the screen. Rows of data listed hundreds of shipments, but nothing showed in plain English.

I thought computers were supposed to make things easier.

"It's all in code. The products and destinations are all numbered and I don't have the translation matrix."

"Yeah, but we know someone who does." Dev waved his lit finger.

"I'm not telling you anything and I texted my receptionist to call the authorities." Greenway tried to act smug, but the tremor in his voice and the fact that he couldn't take his eyes from Dev's finger ruined the image. "I'm sure they are already on their way."

"Can you make any sense of it?" Dev asked.

"Well," Cassidy scrolled down. "It looks like about a hundred shipments of the same thing, number eighty six, were sent out yesterday from code zero one."

"Translate," Dev nudged Greenway.

"Bite me."

"*Ehhh.* Thanks for playing." Dev swiped the end of Greenway's bulbous nose with his fiery fingertip. The sweating man screamed as the tip of his nose sizzled and the sickly sweet scent of burning flesh filled the room.

Cassidy's stomach heaved. She understood why Dev did it, but she didn't have to like it.

"Next time I'll shove it up your left nostril. Now, spill. What do the numbers mean?"

Greenway's hands cupped his smoking nose. He whimpered and rocked in place.

"Zero one...stands for...Port of Tampa," he blurted through his clenched hands. "I, I don't know what the eighty six is."

"Bullshit." Dev brandished his finger, made the flame shoot out two inches like one of those tricked out Zippo lighters.

"Dev." Cassidy stopped him with a word. "Mr. Greenway...eighty six?"

His eyes darted from Cassidy to Dev and back. He licked his lips. "Eighty six is the code for insulation."

Sirens blared in the distance. They were out of time.

"Insulation...like perlite?" Cassidy asked.

Greenway's glance shifted to Dev's glowing brand. "Yes, I suppose it could be."

"Got it. Let's go."

Trailing his finger across the man's range of vision, Dev ordered him to be quiet before he followed Cassidy out the door. They were on the bike and burning rubber before the front door closed completely. Two police cars with full on noise and cherries whipped by in the opposite direction. Cassidy held her breath, glanced over her shoulder and hoped neither car turned around.

We got the info, but what does it really mean?

Three miles onto the interstate, Dev took the exit and pulled into the Mucho Taco parking lot.

"Why are we stopping? Shouldn't we keep moving?" She'd always thought that if you were trying to escape Johnny Law, you kept moving, put as much distance between you and the cops as you could. Stopping for a taco was not part of the plan.

"Where are we going now?" Dev asked. "We never talked about that and I'm really hungry." Dev patted his belly to emphasize his point. "Do you like Mexican?"

Cassidy pursed her lips and nodded slowly.

"Want a taco or burrito or quesadilla?" Dev asked as he calmly walked to the entrance of the fast food joint.

"Shouldn't we, like, go? Hit the road?"

"I'll just be a minute." Dev paused with his hand on the door. "So, no, on the taco?"

"No, thank you."

When Dev disappeared inside, Cassidy scanned the road for the cops, expecting to hear sirens closing in on them. She tapped her foot, shifted her weight and glanced back to the restaurant door.

"Come on. Come on."

Still no sign of pursuit, but her heart continued racing as she watched the road.

Is this what everyday life with Dev and the Knights is like? Living in fear, constant danger, always on the run? I don't know if I can take this.

She jumped at the slurp behind her, but it was only Dev. He held out his drink.

"Soda?"

She shook her head, short rapid movements that mirrored her frayed nerves. She couldn't understand why he wasn't in a hurry.

Dev leaned against the bike, crossed his legs at the ankle and took a long pull on his straw. "So, where we headin'?"

She wanted to scream, then throttle him. No, throttle him first and then scream.

"This is dangerous. We should be across town by now, shouldn't we?" She spoke through clenched teeth. His nonchalance stomped on every nerve in her already tense body.

"No, why?"

"Why?" Her question exploded from her incredulous face. A couple looked in her direction so she lowered her voice. "Does it mean anything to you that we might get caught?"

"We won't get caught. We're the good guys. The good guys always get away with this kind of stuff."

Does he think this is some kind of movie?

"So what do you think of the bike?" Dev asked.

"Huh? Oh. I like it—wish I had tried it years ago." *I bet it wouldn't have been the same without him.*

"What's your favorite type of food?" Dev smiled. "Mine is American. Give me a steak and potatoes or a hamburger any day. I don't go for that gourmet, fancy stuff. Keep it simple."

"I guess mine is Italian, love pasta."

"Pasta's good, but makes me sleepy," Dev said.

"Me too," Cassidy said.

"How do you feel now?"

"What?" Cassidy shook her head at the abrupt change in topic.

"You were going a bit schizo there. Better now?"

As conversations go, this one topped her chart as one of the strangest. But she had to admit, she did feel better. The panic was gone and her heart no longer tried to beat through her chest.

"Pretty slick." She nodded in appreciation.

"Stillman taught me that trick a long time ago, not long after we first met. He said I kept blabbering on about being some kind of monster, but I don't remember any of it. He told me he used it to calm me down so I could eat, drink and stay alive. You good now?"

"Yeah, I'm good." *Oh my god, I really am.* "Can we stop at the paper for a minute? I need to check in. My editor probably thinks I'm dead."

"Sure. Point me in the right direction."

A local branch of her bank next to the restaurant reminded her that she didn't have any money and her father always told her to have something secreted away just in case. He was right. That twenty she used to carry in her shoe had saved her ass on more than one occasion.

"Hey, before we go, let me pop into the bank."

"You don't need money. Stanley Rock has access to many accounts."

"Thanks, *Stan*, but I'd feel better with something in my pocket."

Dev waved her on, leaned back and sucked down his soda.

What I wouldn't give to be half that confident.

As soon as Cassidy walked into the bank, the lone teller behind the counter jumped to assist her. After five minutes of not being able to track down Cassidy's accounts or any record that Cassidy Sinclair ever banked with them, the stymied teller called the manager over. He went through the same routine, even offered to call her home branch to check for a signature card.

Frustrated, Cassidy waved him off and left empty handed.

How does something like this happen? My family has held accounts here for my whole life. They can't just disappear.

"Is something wrong?" Dev asked as Cassidy made her way back to the bike.

"My accounts don't exist." Cassidy climbed up behind Dev. "They didn't even have my name on record. Why do you think that is?"

Dev had no idea and kicked the motorized beast to life. The trip across town didn't compare to her first ride, with her mind all knotted up over the lost accounts, and before she knew it, Dev turned into the lot.

The Tampa Weekly office was located on the outskirts of the city in a former cigar factory. The paper's owner wanted to be close to the action without having to pay downtown rent. At three in the afternoon, there wasn't a parking spot to be had, so Dev made his own on the sidewalk near the front door.

"Wait for me. I'll be out in a minute," Cassidy said.

"Again?" Dev protested, but Cassidy stalled him with a hand on his arm. From the contact, she felt his concern and something else.

What? Affection, maybe?

"I'll be back." She smiled and filed away her secret knowledge.

As the door swung inward, Cassidy expected chirpy Rose to greet her like she did every morning with a bright, "Heya, Cassidy." But there was no Rose. The lobby was empty. An unstaffed reception area was a cardinal sin in her business. People came and went all the time. Their editor's policy was always to have a smiling face up front.

The receptionist also acted as the front line of defense and held her finger on the buzzer that allowed visitors through the security door. With no one up front, no one could get back.

I'm sure Rose'll be back in a minute.

The minute came and went. With a last glance out to Dev, she found the button under the desk and buzzed herself back.

The newsroom was always crazy in the afternoon. People screamed across the cube walls, conducted phone interviews, and checked last minute facts at the top of their lungs. Today, all was silent. Rows of people-less cubes clustered in orderly quad formations. The place should be humming, a giant beehive of activity focused on delivering for the King, Eric Rancor, Editor-in-Chief.

"Hello? Jim? Nancy?" There should be over a hundred people.

Cassidy had never been in the facility alone before. Even on the major holidays, someone always worked on the next big story. This eerie emptiness unsettled her.

I'm sure there's a reason. Maybe there's a big staff meeting or it's someone's birthday.

The editor had called all-employee meetings before, pulled everyone away from their pressing assignments to talk about the status of the paper. They'd cluster around the tables, munch on cake, and wonder if he would notice if they slipped out early.

Her steps faltered. *Yeah. I'm sure it's something like that.* But her gut told her different. Her gut said something was very wrong. Her gut told her to run.

The door to the editor's office looked to be shut up tight. Her cube sat right outside his door. She'd get her few personal items—pictures of Amy and the Montblanc pen she'd bought herself when she got the job at the paper—and get the hell out. It all felt too freaky. She'd call Eric from a pay phone down the street.

Palms sweaty, she slinked down the row to her cube. Only, it wasn't her cube any longer. Sally Crosstock's nameplate had been velcroed to the fabric wall.

Who the hell is Sally Crosstock? And where is all my stuff?

The cube she'd lived in was gone, replaced by the accumulated crap of this Sally person. And it didn't look like this woman had just moved in, but had been settled there for a while. It had that lived-in feel, like a worn, comfy shoe, only fit for someone else's foot.

Cassidy prairie-dogged to verify her bearings. *Yep. This is my cube.*

A low moan escaped from Eric's office. Her creep factor jumped up a few notches. It wasn't a sexy kind of moan. She'd walked in on Ed and Violet in the copy room a couple of months ago. Now that had been some sexy moaning. But this...this was anguish.

She tried to open the door, but after only six inches hit an obstruction on the other side. Though not wide enough to enter through, she could stick her head in and take a peek.

Am I really going to do this?

With the door partially open, the moaning sounded louder. *Definitely someone in pain. And what is that odd smell?* Warning bells gonged in her head like at a Greek wedding, but she couldn't ignore the person inside.

Cassidy pressed her forehead to the frosted window of her Editor's door, gathering her strength, but the cool glass did little to soothe the fear-induced pounding. *Right. Let's do this.* Holding her breath, she slid her head through the opening, pushing harder when her ears stopped her progress.

Oh my god. Cassidy yanked her head out, tearing skin off her ears, staggered back and puked all over Sally Crosstock's chair.

"Dev." Her voice lacked strength so she mustered her wind and threw it into her next shout, "Dev!" *He's outside. There's no way he can hear me.*

A loud crunch echoed through the room followed by Dev's strong voice.

"Caz?" he yelled.

"Back here."

Fast, heavy footfalls echoed through the cube labyrinth. Dev passed her aisle once, then doubled back and jogged to her, Cinder held tight in his murderous grip. He crouched by her side, concern obvious in the tight lines of his face and his pinched eyes.

"Are you hurt?"

"No. No. I'm fine." Cassidy looked back at the office door. "They're all dead. In there. I heard moaning, looked inside."

Dev helped her to her feet and pushed on the door. It didn't give the first time, but he put more muscle into it and forced it open. Gray-skinned corpses had been piled in the office. From the number of bodies, most of the staff had been killed. Atop the heap Eric Rancor presided in the chair he used to call his throne.

Eyelids pinned open, streaks of blood wept from his red, raw sockets into which black orbs had been inserted. Something blinked across their glossy surface. He moaned again.

"He's still alive." Cassidy covered her mouth with her hands.

Dev nodded. "Wait. What is that blinking?" Dev picked his way among Cassidy's dead co-workers. Her stomach heaved as he started to climb.

Scanning gray faces locked in horror and surprise, she found her friends—Rita, Carl, Jasmine, Hecter, and little Bob over there under sleazy Ron, all gone.

Dev called down from the top of the heap. "Flashing numbers. Seven. Six. Five." He bounded down the pile, threw her over his shoulder and bolted through the doorway. Halfway down the aisle, he shifted her position, crushed her face against his chest and dropped to his knees. His body shielded her as a blinding white flash slammed her eyes closed and an ear-drum bursting concussion blew out the windows, leaving her deaf and dazed.

Dev rocked, holding her tight, while the explosion raped the office space. A wave of searing heat flashed around her before disappearing in a whoosh. Cassidy opened her eyes. Flames whipped around them, incinerating everything in their path. When Dev lifted his face and opened his eyes, the flames caressed his bald head and licked his shoulders before flowing into his body.

Cassidy gasped at the beauty and raw power behind those crimson streaked orbs of the Knight of Flame. He looked like a god of fire in the center of a maelstrom. Her gift painted his emotional landscape as calm with an over-powering need to keep her safe. Again, she sensed a hint of something more, stronger than the last time.

The blast ended in seconds, redecorating the office in post-apocalyptic warzone. Dust, debris, and gray-skinned body parts lay everywhere. The cube walls had either been blown out the window or disintegrated on the spot. The entire outer wall was gone, exposing jagged hunks of cement and rusted rebar. Ragged ends of live electrical wires cavorted in their sudden freedom. Ominous creeks sounded from the ceiling.

"We need to get out of here," Dev said.

The sirens bayed in the distance like a pack of wolves. With the cube farm gone, it was a straight walk to the door. Dev shielded Cassidy from the worst of the carnage, but he couldn't block it all. A large number of blackened skulls, some intact, others cracked or missing large sections of bone, massed before the dented outer wall. The explosion had torn through the softer tissue of all those bodies, but turned the heads into projectiles.

Cassidy should have been horrified, but the absurdity of the situation made her feel like she toured a set from one of those cheesy slasher flicks. The lobby remained relatively untouched except for a few heads that made it through the door Dev kicked down earlier. She recognized the hank of red hair on the skull in the corner. The irony unleashed what the terror and disgust could not. Fat round tears rolled down her cheeks. She bid farewell to Rose as Dev led her out the door, onto the bike, and away from the approaching authorities.

I really need a swim.

Chapter 45

MOST DAYS, A NICE RIDE ON THE HARLEY CLEARED HIS HEAD, ALLOWED HIS MIND to breathe, but the explosion at Cassidy's paper put a crimp in that plan. Still, something useful came of the trip. Dev mulled over the shipping information and potential ramifications on his way to report in.

Cassidy wanted to come along, but the bleak look in her eyes spoke volumes. So, when he offered to take care of the debrief with Stillman, she didn't put up much of a fuss. With a tired wave, she moseyed off in the direction of Dronor's old room and, he suspected, the pool.

Voices drifted out of Stillman's office. Out of respect, Dev waited in the hall. The Precept's voice was obvious, but he'd never heard the second one. Male. Older. Worn out. A lot like Stillman's. Curiosity overrode his sense of decorum and he strained to make out the words.

"I lost another one, Brother."

Stillman. His words spoken in pain, but from grief or a sense of failure, Dev didn't know. "I did not see this coming."

Brother?

"You cannot be expected to see everything, Cernusen. No man has that power, not even one of us." The other voice was eerily similar to Stillman's.

Stillman brushed off the other's comment. "I know, but I'm blind to their games. Shadow has been a step ahead the entire time."

"Perhaps living underground and out of touch with the modern world has hurt you, Cernusen. At least you saw enough to put a Knight on the ground where Shadow would surface."

"There is that."

A light exhale tickled Dev's ear, as if someone at his side whispered an intimate secret, accompanied by the aroma of a coal-fueled fire and roasting almonds. The feather-light touch sent a chill across his shoulders and his skin prickled, but a quick scan of the hall showed no one about.

"Ears in the hall, my brother. Farewell."

Dev took that as his cue and strode in like he'd just pounded down the hall and snapped to attention. Stillman was alone.

"Sir."

"How much did you hear, Knight of Flame?"

"Sir? I came to report on Cassidy and my findings this afternoon."

Dev bore Stillman's suspicion stoically. His mind was a tempest of unanswered question, but he held his tongue until given leave to speak.

Stillman settled back. "What did you find?"

"At least a hundred shipments were scheduled from the Port yesterday containing a large quantity of insulation."

Fingers steepled, Stillman tapped his chin as he absorbed the data.

"No direct reference to perlite or the orbs," Dev finished his thought.

"I highly doubt Gray would list the orbs on his shipping manifests." Stillman stood, clasped his hands behind his back, and walked to the other side of the desk. "Where were the shipments bound?"

"From what we can tell, Sir, all over the country."

"That could mean millions will die."

"Unless we stop him," Dev said.

"Unless we…of course, of course, unless we stop him." Stillman echoed Dev's thought. With an abrupt turn, he changed topic. "We have unfinished business, do we not?"

"Sir?"

"Drop the pretense, Knight of Flame." The old man faced Dev. "You have questions about my daughter's death. I saw it when you came back with her in your arms."

Unprepared for this topic, Dev paused to gather his thoughts. Yes, he did have questions, but the rage that first accompanied them had diminished upon seeing Stillman's devastation.

"My power is both gift and curse." Stillman filled the silence. "The visions I see tell of a possible future, not an absolute. From each one I separate the grains of import from the chaff of the improbable to formulate our strategies. Not everything is known to me. In fact, very little is made clear."

Old news, old man.

Remembering the recognition and acceptance on Stillman's face when he walked through the gateway with Wren's body in his arms rekindled Dev's anger. Not in the mood for a long philosophical discussion, Dev jumped to the point.

"Did you know Wren would die on that mission?"

Stillman sighed. "Yes and no. I saw the possibility of her death. I also saw the possibility of Cyndralla's and Magnus's deaths as well. Nothing is ever certain. Events twist in the wake of a decision made."

"But you could have stopped her, could have kept her here and safe." Dev sensed the truth in Stillman's explanation, but he didn't want to let him off the hook.

Stillman laughed, a rich sound tinged with equal parts amusement and sadness. "Come now, Develor Quinteele. She was one of us, accepted the risks as we all do. My forcing her to stay would have destroyed her spirit as effectively as that creature of Shadow."

"Heh. I guess you're right." Dev tried to picture Stillman giving Wren that order and couldn't keep a small, sad smile from crossing his face. "She wouldn't have taken it well."

"That's putting it mildly, my boy. She was always a willful child. I will miss her terribly." The old man turned away, but not before Dev saw the tears form in his tired eyes.

"So will I." Dev reached out to put his hand on Stillman's shoulder, but hesitated. He'd never touched the Precept in anything other than an official capacity, and didn't know how his gesture would be received.

Screw it. Dev grasped Stillman's shoulder and almost jumped when the Precept laid his hand on top of Dev's and squeezed—a simple gesture of shared grief that brought tears to the Knight of Flame's eyes.

"Oh, I have additional news." His voice husky, Stillman strode to his desk and unrolled a long sheet of parchment. "A message came a little while ago. Evidently in a press conference this morning, Gray announced that his company has deployed a new vermin control system across the Tampa Bay area to combat the insect infestation."

Dev frowned. "He deployed the orbs."

"So it would seem. He also said that the people should expect to see a dramatic difference within twenty four hours."

"That doesn't give us much time." Dev ground his teeth in frustration.

"There's more." Stillman grinned, a nasty, sly piece of work that piqued Dev's curiosity. "The last part of the press conference was an invitation of sorts. Gray mentioned that if his competitors had a better way to deal with the vermin, they should meet him in his office tonight."

"The bastard called us out." Dev's imagined his own grin a mirror to that of Stillman's.

"That's the way I see it."

"Of course, it would be rude for us to turn him down." Dev's fire woke at the prospect of avenging his little sister.

"Indeed." Stillman spun about, the color returned to his face and the spark to his brown eyes. "Get Magnus and meet me in the Womb. I'll be there after I check on Cyndralla's progress."

Dev wondered if he should grab Cassidy on the way, but settled on Magnus reasoning that if Stillman wanted her involved, he would have mentioned her by name.

Excitement buzzing inside, he jogged to his brother's room.

It's about time.

Chapter 46

CASSIDY HAD BEEN OUT OF THE WATER TOO LONG. ASIDE FROM A FEW HOURS OF sleep when she first got there, she hadn't been able to rest. First the hospital and that dick, Alexander Gray, then her house, the barge, Wren...she needed time to decompress, to find some small level of sanity. When she asked Dev about a pool or underground lake, or even a bathtub at this point, he gave her directions to Dronor's room on the opposite side of the Cradle from his forge.

The thought of swimming in the Knight of Water's personal pool grossed her out. It wasn't that he just died, but her gift told her he was a pig, and she didn't know what else would be swimming around in his water. It would probably take a tanker full of chlorine to scour his yuck away. Expectations low and dropping further she imagined a small pit, half-full of brackish slop waiting at the end of her journey.

She smelled the fresh water long before she got to Dronor's room—a clean scent reminiscent of the stream in the backwoods of her Grandpa's farm where she swam as a child. Her steps quickened.

Barren, Dronor's room held no furniture, no mementos of his long life, nothing to prove he ever existed.

Wow. Where's his stuff? Not even twenty four hours and his life is gone.

All the negative thoughts and feelings that had been piling up vanished with her first glimpse of the gorgeous pool. Wide and deep, it took up most of the cavernous room. Like the other rooms in the cradle, crystals on the walls provided the ambient light, but she noticed a few under the water that gave the pool an inner glow.

Beautiful. I know it's going to be the perfect temperature.

She stripped down to her skin and dove in. Her lithe form knifed through the warm water, until she reached the wavy bottom of soft sand and pushed off to find the surface once again. Sparkling bubbles made into bright little gems by the underwater lights trailed her every movement.

As she dunked her head under, she heard that strange voice again, the one from her own pool, the one that had swam with her all her life. More than a voice, it felt like a physical presence in the water with her. She should have been frightened, but instead a sense of peace washed over her. In this magical Cradle, anything could happen. A sentient pool wouldn't even crack her top ten weird and wonderful list.

Breaststroke in one direction. Flip. Backstroke on the return lap. As hoped, the water caressed her immediate cares away, transporting her back to happier times of whiling away the hot summer days with her parents and Amy.

My little girl. The memory rushed back, but not the pain. It was a happy time, one that she could prop up on her mantle and live with. She slipped under and suspended her hold on the world of air. Sounds faded. Sights dimmed. Cares retreated. Her heartbeat thumped in her ear as she hung suspended between elements—earth below, air above.

Images of Wren came to her there, in that limbo. While Cassidy had only known her for a few days, the impact on her life was profound. Salty tears, shed for the girl who had saved her life in so many ways, merged with the crystal clear element around her.

Welcome, daughter of the waves. The words permeated her skin and spoke to her soul in a language she was at last ready to understand.

I...I can understand you.

Excitement bubbled up inside her as beads of water tickled her skin.

"It is well, Cassidy Sinclair. I am the lord of this element." The Lord of Water spoke through the natural sounds of the water all around Cassidy.

How do you know my name?

"I have known you for as long as you have been you."

Why now? Why make your language known to me?

"I have chosen."

Chosen? Cassidy had an idea where this was going. A deep feeling of honor suffused her spirit. It all started to make sense.

"I need a champion." The water bubbled around Cassidy, holding her in place.

Unable to move her body, she felt her lungs tighten and realized she'd been under a long time. She wanted to breathe.

"Let go, Cassidy Sinclair."

She kicked, waved her arms, reached for the surface, but remained locked in place. She stretched her toes toward the bottom, but it was too far down. Fear gripped her, added strength to her fight against the force holding her in place.

Let me go. I need to breathe.

"Breathe of me, Cassidy Sinclair, be my Knight."

What if I don't want to be your champion?

The bubbles propelled her to the surface where she breached and filled her lungs, but the conversation wasn't over, the choice not made. *Do I want to be a Knight? What does that really mean?*

Gathering her nerve, she took a long, deep breath, one that would sustain her for many minutes out of the air, and dove to the bottom. Bubbles surged and held her in place while the communion continued.

"The elemental knights are a force of good, with Water equally partnered with Earth, Air and Fire, to defend mankind. Though we are small in number, together we have great strength."

I am no fighter like Dev or Magnus.

"Nor should you be. As in all things, a balance must be struck."

As above, so below.

"I see you are not totally unschooled."

Cassidy felt a wash of satisfaction flow through the water.

My father was an avid collector of old books and his interests dipped a little into the occult.

"Balance. Fire, he is the strongest fighter. Earth, the protector. Air, the intellect. The role of water, therefore, deals in matters of the spirit or emotion."

Forgive my question—

"There is no need for formality between us. Ask and I shall answer."

From what I saw, the previous Knight of Water was more intent on fighting than on tending to the emotional stability of the Knights.

"Dronor was once a powerful Knight, strong in his conviction and resolve. Vigilant. Over the course of time he lost his way, grew envious of the others and their apparent power. Toward the end he realized his error and tried to atone, but it was too late."

Cassidy felt an overwhelming sadness embrace her.

"The dark powers stirring in the world are vast, far larger than it appears at the moment. The Order needs your power if there is any chance to stop Shadow."

Power? I don't have any power.

"Your gift is your power, Cassidy Sinclair. Wielded by the Knight of Water, it could turn the tide of battle."

She didn't see how sensing emotion through touch could be that powerful, but she wouldn't discount it. *Can you tell me more of the enemy we face?*

"If it were in my power to know, I would tell you; but, alas, I can only feel the stirring of the waters."

Cassidy felt the Lord of Water's frustration.

"I offer you a new life, Cassidy Sinclair, an opportunity to protect the helpless and defend the weak against the forces of Shadow in all its guises. What say you? Breathe now, child, and return to me with your answer."

Fractured thoughts and scraps of emotion swam through her mind as she rose to the surface. Amy, her parents, her job, her home, her life. All gone. Another round of images flew by. Wren, Magnus, Dev, Alexander Gray, the dead reporters at the hospital, the anguished, gray-hued face of the head nurse as she lay in a puddle of blood, the little girl who, without her help, would have been another of Shadow's small victories. All those loose bits of time, though poignant and at times gruesome, screamed to her of a greater purpose. The forces of Shadow, be they Alexander Gray or someone else, had to be stopped.

With the ghosts of her past put in perspective, the immortal words of Spock floated through her head, "The needs of the many...."

Cassidy sank below the water and filled her lungs with her chosen element. Bubbles surged around her, blocking her vision. Confused, she couldn't tell up from down. Her lungs burned.

Is it supposed to be like this?

Her heart thumped deep in her chest then stopped.

A bright light infused the water all around her as the Lord of Water empowered his champion.

Chapter 47

Dev and Magnus argued and jostled their way to the Womb. Dev bounced Magnus into the wall to make a point.

"So how do *you* propose we defeat her?" Magnus rebounded and sent Dev crashing to the wall on the other side. "Our weapons won't hurt Aggridda. Your fire seemed to do a little damage, but didn't keep her away."

Dev nodded. "She stayed out of Cyndralla's light, but we're not sure if that's because it hurt her or because she wanted to."

Magnus huffed. "So basically, we don't know shit."

"Right."

Stillman met them in the hall. Gone was the shambling gate of the defeated old man, he moved with the power and grace of the Precept of the Knights Elementalis. "Come."

The Knights fell into step behind their commander.

"Where are we going?" Magnus asked.

"To the Chamber. A new Knight has been chosen."

"Cool. What's the word from Cyndy?" Dev asked.

"Not good. She's exhausted and frustrated. She's used every spell she could think of. Even reverted back into her natural state and tried with muscle and claw, but to no avail."

Magnus squirmed. "I bet she hated that. I think it's been a while."

"Centuries," Stillman admitted, "But she's pulling out all the stops."

"What's next?" Dev asked.

"We'll figure something out," Stillman said.

The silver door to the Chamber stood open, expectant. The trio filed in. As before, the golden muncle, Regal, stood in front of an honor guard and held out a royal blue satin robe lined in silver filigree. Stillman grabbed it and headed for the landing.

The Lord of Water stood alone atop his pillar over the churning quicksilver pool. The transparent being raised his arms and a block of the reflective liquid rose up in a solid mass roughly the height of a man. The crash of breaking surf and the roar of a waterfall careened off the stone walls of the chamber and broke over the viewers in an exuberant wave of sound.

Dev didn't have to understand the primal language to feel the intensity of the emotion unleashed in the room. The Lord of Water welcomed a new champion.

Cassidy should be here to see this.

Layers of liquid silver dripped down the suspended form, eroding the dross, until details emerged—shiny face, thin, round shoulders, long legs, narrow waist, round hips, full breasts. She clutched a short, curved sword with a swooping edge in front of her.

A woman. Beautiful. If Dev were to sculpt the perfect woman out of silver, it would look exactly like her.

Lightning flashed. Thunder boomed. Creation complete, a storm opened up above the figure and washed the last of the quicksilver away. Streams of liquid silver washed down flawless, tan skin and out of long, auburn hair. Then she opened her eyes—glacial blue.

Dev's heart stopped. Cassidy was the new Knight of Water. The pieces fit together—her love of water, dedication, selflessness. It all made sense and Dev whole-heartedly agreed with the Lord of Water's choice.

Aided by the elemental lord's power, unabashed and unhurried, Cassidy walked across the quicksilver surface to the outstretched cloak offered by Stillman, who looked away from her nakedness out of respect. After adjusting the garment, she smiled at the stupefied men.

"Come on, boys. Was it really that much of a stretch?"

80C3

Cassidy was exhausted by her ordeal. Dev put her to bed, hoping to grab some down time himself before the attack on Daegon Gray later that night. Stillman set the time and laid out a simple plan. At ten o'clock, Dev, Magnus, Stillman and the new Knight of Water would storm the Daegon Gray building, take out all of the Shadow minions, kill Alexander and his daughter, stop the opening of the orbs and get away before the police arrived. Cyndralla would continue her work with the orb.

Simple. In and out. No sweat. Dev walked into his room, plopped himself down on his stone bench and slapped his hands over his eyes. *Gray is flesh and blood. If we can get close enough, we can take him. But the other one…*

Quick, light steps approached his room and Cyndralla flitted inside. "Help me." She placed the orb, safely shielded behind her magical pink ward, in a circular hollow on the anvil. "I've tried everything. I've hit it with heat, but I want to try something hotter. I need your fire."

"You got it." Dev leaned in close to the orb. "Can I hold it?"

"Yes, of course. Your hands will not penetrate the shield."

"Then how will my heat get…" *Magic is so not my thing. I'll take fire and metal for the win.*

"Develor," Cyndralla slowed down as if talking to a child, "your flesh cannot breach the ward, but your heat will."

"No worries then." Dev picked up the orb and tossed it from hand to hand like a basketball.

"Stop that." Flat. Out of patience. Exhausted. Dark circles marred her usually pristine countenance.

"Sorry." He placed it back on the anvil. "I'm going to call the fire so you might want to protect yourself from the heat."

"Do not worry about me." Cyndralla sat on the stone bench as if it were a throne. "Commence your cooking."

"Yes, ma'am." Lava responded to his call and filled the trough. The temperature of the room quickly surpassed human tolerance. Cyndralla showed only minor distress.

Blessed fire filled his being as he cradled the deadly orb between his hands. He drew more strength from the lava, opening the conduit as wide as he could, and channeled the flow to the item between his hands. All the heat, all the fiery power flowing through him, rushed to his hands and they exploded in bright orange flames that licked and rolled over his hands and the item they held.

Having conjured a magical barrier between her and the building heat, Cyndralla watched eagerly from the edge of the bench. "Hotter," she said.

He willed the flame hotter. Orange deepened to blue and the shadow vessel baked, but there was still no change.

"Come on, Knight of Flame. Is that all you can do?" she said. "Where is that legendary rage? All I see is a tiny human with hot hands. Come on! Push it!"

Intent. Desire. Emotion. Dev fed the fire with bits of himself—the anger of being defeated, the embarrassment at his loss of control, and the grief over the loss of Wren. The temperature rose, the flame darkened to deep purple.

His hands shook under the strain. He pulled more through the connection with the lava, drawing until he thought he would burst with the sheer volume of power coursing through him.

Cyndralla's dress smoked, the hem at her sleeve scorched. "Keep going, Dev." Desperate, she pleaded with him to hold on. "It has to work."

Smooth and cool, the orb felt exactly like it did when he first picked it up. He wanted to hurl it at the wall, watch it shatter into a million dark pieces, but he knew the impact would have no effect and the action paint him, once again, as a petulant, out of control child.

No, the answer to the riddle of the orb existed, he just hadn't found it yet. As he maintained his volcanic attack, the usual range of rage-inducing thoughts sparked in his mind with no increase in flow or heat. He'd reached his max and still the damn thing remained unblemished.

Balance. Unbidden, Stillman's voice rose above the cacophony of destruction playing in Dev's head.

The Knight calmed the rage in his soul, stopped the whirlwind of chaos spinning in his head. The color of his flame changed, backing down from purple through the range to flicker a merry yellow as his draw on the elemental force slowed.

"What are you doing?" Cyndralla cried out. "You cannot give up now."

Dev ignored her. *Beauty.* He pictured the majesty of Cinder and the elegance of Cassidy encased in liquid silver. With the flash of each image, his power grew. Increasing the pull on his element, he once again channeled the flow to his hands and into the orb. Orange flames flowed into red.

Another image came to mind, this one of the excitement on Wren's face as they drove up to Club Mastodon before this whole whirlwind started. It brought along a spike of righteous rage that added fuel to Dev's building fire. The flames changed again, red deepening into the light purple range.

"Yes, Develor," Cyndralla urged. "The heat is building once again. Keep it up."

And what of love? Dev thought of the love he bore for his brother-in-arms, Magnus, and for his little sister. His elemental power soared, reaching the same maximum intensity as before, but this felt different. In the past, holding this much fire in his system brought with it the overwhelming desire to rend and break and destroy, but not this time. This time he felt in command, the master of the flame.

"We need more, Knight of Flame." Cyndralla's voice cracked under the strain.

More? Where am I going to find… His body already hummed with the force surging through his veins. *More?*

He thought of Cassidy and the world of possibilities blossoming between them.

An avalanche of raw elemental fire tore through the link, dwarfing anything he'd ever experienced before, and filled his entire being. It pulsed against his flesh as it raced down his arms to the focal point of his concentration.

In a massive release of elemental power, his hands exploded into pure white flame.

I did it. Dev gaped at the spectacle.

The orb in his hands rocked and a tremendous crack echoed through the room.

Shocked, the Knight of Flame dropped the orb, which skipped across the floor and came to rest against the bench next to Cyndralla's white slipper.

The shock also terminated his connection. The flow ceased and his hands winked out. After the wide-open communion, the abrupt emptiness left him hollow and weak.

I did it. I found the white flame.

He stared at his hands in wonder, turning them in front of his face as if seeing them for the first time.

"What was that?" Cyndralla's question tinged with awe. "I've never seen you branch into that color spectrum."

He shook his head as he tried to remember how to speak. Eventually the words came to him.

"I listened to Stillman."

Cyndralla picked up the orb. "You did it."

"I know, did you see that?"

"No, I mean the orb. You broke it."

A large crack had fissured across its surface and released black smoke that fouled the air under the shield.

Cyndralla winced. "By the gods…they twisted the essence of life itself." She rushed out, but had the presence of mind to shout, "Thank you," from down the hall.

"Glad I could help." Dev murmured and went back to studying the new things at the end of his arms that for an instant glowed a beautiful, pure white.

I have got to try that again. He thought back to what he was thinking right before it happened, took a deep breath, and called the flame. Slow and steady he drew the heat from the lava and pushed it down to his hands. A small feed at first to get back into the rhythm. He focused on the fire, on the feel of the power in each of his fingertips. With a thought, they burst into flame.

Here goes nothing. He cranked the level from trickle to fire hose. Power screamed through him to the outlet in his hands, searing orange to light blue to deep indigo in a matter of seconds, but no white. He ran through the thoughts like before, sifting them into the fire-stream racing through his system. Rage, vengeance, love, beauty.

This has to be right. His hands burned hotter, but they didn't change, didn't turn white. *Why not? What's missing?*

Cassidy.

As soon as he thought of her, his hands blazed even hotter…but not white.

What am I missing? Somehow she is the key.

Dev gradually cut the pull until it was little more than a dribble, no longer enough to sustain the flame, and his hands went out.

He fixed the image of that pure flame in his mind.

It was perfect. Beautiful.

On impulse, he grabbed a gold nugget from the bin and dismissed the lava. Drawing from the remaining heat in the room, he channeled the energy into his hands and they flared up. Dev closed his eyes and focused on the image in his head.

Flawless. In his charged grasp, the gold softened to the consistency of yellow clay. Calloused fingers dug shallow grooves across the metal's surface to rough out the overall shape. Large sweeping arcs met in a round, tilted swoop; his hands traced the image in his head.

Someone walked into the room. Their movement summoned a cool breeze that kissed his bare shoulders and smelled of fresh, spring water.

Cassidy.

"It's cooler in here than usual." The sound of her light footfalls approached him, but he didn't turn or stop his work. "I wanted to—oh, sorry. I didn't know you were busy…" Her voice trailed off. She stood behind him.

Substance, character, depth, Dev merged them into his work. Cassidy rested her soft, slim hand on his shoulder.

Not until the image under his scrupulous touch matched the image in his mind precisely, did he open his eyes and set the finished work on the anvil. He leached the heat from the sculpture to harden the flame and killed the fire on his hands.

"Dev, it's…amazing." Cassidy spoke with a hushed awe. "Gorgeous."

"Thank you." She was right. It was gorgeous. A golden flame, its tip reaching toward the heavens, its base rounded into a bowl. In between, the individual licks and whorls of the fire seemed to dance before his eyes. It was the picture in his mind made solid. Flawless. Beautiful. He stared at his hands. The same hands that had made countless swords, axes and other weapons of destruction had just made this fragile depiction of his soul. Dev lifted the essence of his element and turned to Cassidy.

"There is a beauty behind the heat if one but looks for it," Dev said quietly.

Mesmerized, Cassidy turned the sculpture in her hand, examining all the subtle nuances of the artistry.

"It's…almost…alive."

"Pure. And, I would like you to have it."

She pushed the statue towards him. "Dev, I can't. This is too much."

"Please, Cassidy." Dev closed his hand around hers. "Please."

Chapter 48

So delicate. So beautiful. Cassidy cupped the newborn flame in her palm like a baby bird. As she made her way back to her new digs, she imagined the right place to display it. It had to be somewhere prominent, a place of honor.

On the desk? The dresser? No, too mundane. A creation of such beauty deserves something special. I'll talk to Magnus. Maybe he can use his power to create a small alcove or a shelf in one of the walls.

From inside her room, emotions not her own brushed against her awareness—eagerness, excitement, fear.

First Dev and now this?

In the Forge a few moments ago, she'd sensed the Knight's intensity and his reverence for the element that chose him *before* she laid her hand upon his shoulder.

That doesn't make any sense. My gift requires physical contact.

It happened again. She sensed the emotions of someone in her quarters and it was someone she didn't know.

"Hello?" she called from the doorway.

A shuffling clop sounded from the other side of the room and moved closer to the door, but remained just out of sight.

"Hel—what the?" Forgetting the stray emotions, Cassidy's mouth dropped open and she wandered into a room lost in an explosion of blue. When she left a little while ago, the room was bare except for the basic bed, dresser, desk and pool. Now, though, blue and silver pennants hung on the cerulean-colored walls. An ornate armoire had taken up residence against the far side next to the pool. Even the bed had changed, was bigger and higher with sumptuous sea-green sheets and comforter. A driftwood stand on the desk next to her bed displayed her elemental cutlass.

"This is so beautiful and...blue. Wow, so much blue."

The tight ball of emotions radiated pride.

Oh crap, forgot about that. It was on the other side of the bed, out of sight.

"Hello? Please come out."

Stone hands grabbed the comforter and pulled up the small head and body of a muncle she had never seen before. Made of rose-colored stone zigzagged with veins of silver ore, the little man set his hands where his hips should be and checked her out with brilliant ruby eyes. The line across his block head angled up.

Great. Mine has an attitude.

"Um, hi. My name is Cassidy."

The muncle bowed.

"Do you have a name?"

After a few short hops, he crunched to the floor and dipped a pudgy stone finger into the stone as if it were wet cement and drew the name "Brella" in neat, blocky print.

"Brella. That's a pretty name." The little *girl* muncle shuffled closer, stone feet grinding against the floor, with a big curved line across her block. Brella waved her arm around the room and swelled with pride.

"This room is gorgeous."

Brella nodded, a whole body affair that looked more like a bow than a nod. She took Cassidy's hand, led her to the armoire and opened the door. It wasn't a simple cabinet, but a doorway into a large walk-in closet cut into the bedrock.

Cassidy whistled. *Brella, my dear, you have been busy.*

Shooting a quick smile to Brella, Cassidy disappeared into the hidden room, which, in addition to a small table and chairs, contained full racks and shelves of clothes in every shade of blue Cassidy could imagine, and even some she didn't know existed. Jeans and t-shirts and gowns and sweaters and socks and underwear all stacked or hung by hue and style.

I love blue, but this is a little over the top.

In the far corner, a new suit of leather armor had been fitted to a Cassidy-sized dummy. She ran her finger over the chest, tracing the embossed cloud and lightning emblem of her element.

Leather, huh? I've never been much of a leather girl, but I'll try it. Hell, the motorcycle deal turned out pretty cool.

Brella took her hand again, led her to the desk—*she's a cute one*—and pointed to a scrap of parchment pinned under the cutlass stand.

Yo,

Bring your new blade to the gym. I'll grab the fireball and we'll meet you there. Let's see what you got.

Mag—

My new blade. Never in her life did she think she would handle, let alone own, a sword of any kind and now she had this work of art. A blue diamond blade etched with white-crested waves stuck out from a silver filigreed basket hilt. She hefted the weapon, admired its light weight, smooth lines and lethal grace. It felt like it had been made just for her.

On her way to her first battle, she patted Brella on the head and thanked her for the amazing room. She'd grown used to the halls and passageways of the Cradle in the short time she'd been there and soon heard the grunts and insults coming from the open doorway of the gym. They'd been at it for a few minutes and the testosterone hung so thick she could almost taste it. There was no anger or posturing here, just brotherly affection and camaraderie.

The boys stalked each other at opposite ends of the sparring circle with wooden replicas of their elemental weapons. Stripped to the waist, their wide shoulders, broad chests and sculpted abs rippled with their graceful movements. Magnus had grown big again to fight, his size half-again that of Dev.

Oh my...Dev looks yummy.

"Are you going to hit me this time, block head?" Dev taunted. He feigned a lunge that tricked Magnus into jumping back.

"Stop hopping around like a giant rabbit and I will." Magnus charged across the ring, but Dev ducked under and took up position on the opposite side. "Stand still and fight like a man."

"I could have gutted you on that pass."

"Yeah. Yeah. If I had seen your blade in motion, I would have taken action. Instead, you hopped away with your fluffy tail between your legs."

Dev grinned and dropped lower in his stance. In a blur, he flung himself across the ring, blade held at mid-level. Magnus blocked the slice, but not the follow-up roundhouse kick Dev scored to his left side.

Cassidy cringed at the solid *thunk* of foot and shin on ribs, but the big man didn't even blink. Dev retreated to his side of the circle before Magnus could launch a counter.

"Well aren't you Johnny Badass, with your fancy kicks."

"You ready for this one, big man?"

"Come on."

Dev dashed across the ring, movements so quick Cassidy had a hard time following. High. Low. Slash. Kick. Dodge. Reverse. Chop.

Her brain couldn't keep up. By the time she acknowledged one move, Dev had already executed three more. Magnus blocked the blade attacks, but allowed Dev the kicks and punches. As she watched, the words of the Lord of Water echoed in her head. Fire is the best fighter. Earth the best defender.

You got that right. Look at them go. Both warriors lived up to their roles perfectly. The speed and aggression of Dev fought the strength and fortitude of the giant, Magnus. Dev enjoyed the fight, but Magnus grew frustrated. She saw it play out on his face. If Dev wasn't careful, he would find himself on the wrong side of the giant's fist.

Before it got out of hand, Cassidy stepped in. "Hey." She held the pointy end of the cutlass pinched between her fingers at arm's length and batted her eyelashes. "Would one of you big, burly, men show me how to use this pointy thing?"

Magnus pushed Dev aside. "I'll handle this."

"Hold on there, tiger." Dev slid around him and got to Cassidy first.

"Seriously, though, you guys are amazing. Do you think I'll be able to fight like that in time?"

"Nope," Dev jumped in.

"Absolutely not," Magnus seconded.

"But, I..." Cassidy said.

Dev pushed her playfully and Magnus broke into a broad smile.

"We've been doing this for a long, long time, Cassidy. Perhaps you will get to this level, and we'd be more than happy to teach you everything we can." Magnus looked to Dev for corroboration, who nodded. "But I don't think that's your destiny."

"Still, it wouldn't hurt to learn the basics," Dev said. "Let's see you swing it."

As she did in the Forge with Cinder, Cassidy adopted the only stance she knew—body turned, right foot forward, left arm back for balance—and slashed a big 'x' in the air.

"She looks like a blue pirate," Magnus offered.

"Arr, matey." Dev played along.

"Guys, a little focus, please."

"Aye aye, Captain," Dev said. "Neither of us is much of a fencer, but we can show you the basics."

Dev walked her through the standard thrust, parry and slash maneuvers. Cassidy tried her best, but the motions didn't come easy and she found herself constantly off balance. After thirty minutes of pathetic attempts, Cassidy called it quits.

"I've had enough of this for one day. Can we do it again tomorrow?" The question popped out before she could stop it, dropping a shroud of uncertainty over them about what the next twenty-four hours would bring.

೮ාೞ

Stillman snored in the purple recliner, and Cyndralla slouched at the table amidst the empty vials, powders, broken wands and the cracked orb barely visible through the contaminated air under the pink shield. Anger and frustration radiated off the Knight of Air like steam from a boiler as Cassidy tiptoed in.

"I'm lost." Cyndralla lifted her head and peered at Cassidy through bloodshot, slitted purple eyes.

Those eyes.

Stillman coughed and Cyndralla turned, but the old man simply changed position and resumed his symphony.

"Stillman and I have tried everything," Cyndralla said. "I don't know what else to do."

Cassidy wanted to say something inspiring, like her coach did before a big swim meet, but everything that came to mind seemed inappropriate given that Cyndralla was trying to save thousands of lives. Instead of saying nothing, Cassidy settled for the heartfelt classic, "I believe in you," and placed her hand on Cyndralla's arm. If she could, she'd transfer all her good feelings and well wishes into the Knight of Air to help her out.

No sooner had the words left her mouth than a tingle started in her gut and raced across her breast, down her arm and out through her fingertips across to Cyndralla.

The Knight of Air shuddered then blinked her eyes several times while her expression brightened. Gone was the defeat and despair, replaced with the spark of hope.

"What did you—?" Cyndralla turned back to the table and grabbed the vial with the glimmering blue liquid. She held it before her lips and muttered a word below Cassidy's range of hearing. The liquid hissed and bubbled as Cyndralla poured it over the murky swirls within the magic shield.

Shiny blue met inky black with a crackling flash. Cyndralla's elixir washed the shadow in flares of miniature lightning strikes. At first the shadow seemed to falter, beaten back by the light, but that soon dimmed and the darkness prevailed.

"We're close…so close." Cyndralla bent to her task and Cassidy left the room.

She crept along the corridor and turned at the first intersection. Out of sight of the lab, she leaned against the wall and scratched her arms and legs. The itch had stopped once she had left the lab, but the vigorous action made her feel better.

What the hell was that?

Chapter 49

THE LAST TIME THE KNIGHTS STOOD PROUD AND CONFIDENT UPON THE SEAL OF THE Order, Wren and Dronor still lived and Dev, amped up and envious, had patted his friends on the back and sent them off in high spirits. This time, though, no one sat on the sideline.

Magnus, dressed for battle in a loose-fitting Quinsteele mail shirt over battle-worn leathers, spun the head of his axe behind his head as it rode his shoulder. The tightly woven links of his armor obscured the mountain-scape symbol of his element upon his breast. With his long blonde hair and beard, Dev thought he looked every part the Viking chieftain.

Cassidy squirmed on his right, decked out in leather so new and tight it squeaked when she moved. Her fingers absently traced the grooves and openings in the basket hilt of the elemental cutlass that hung from the navy blue sash at her hip. She could have been a warrior goddess fresh from the storybooks if it weren't for the neon white Nike's on her feet.

"Do I have to wear this?" Cassidy griped, and pulled at the waistband of her leather pants. "I can hardly breathe in this getup."

"It could save your life." Dev held out a fistful of Quinsteele chain. "Here. Cyndralla said you could borrow this." He shook out the mail shirt. The tight weave of metal links whispered as it settled into form. "But she wants it back."

Cassidy rolled her eyes. "Great. More uncomfortable crap."

"Oh, stop complaining and slide your arms through." Dev helped her wiggle into it and admired the fit. "Was that so bad?"

Cassidy looked surprised as she shrugged her shoulders. "It doesn't feel any different. I expected the chain to add a bunch of weight and be all noisy and stuff."

"That's the beauty of Quinsteele," Magnus said. "Stronger than Kevlar, lighter than aluminum and exceptionally quiet."

"It comes to this, my friends." Stillman's voice rumbled low and grave. "Gray must be stopped. I will continue to work with Cyndralla until you make it inside the building. At that point, use the scrying mirror to capture an image of the lobby so Cyndralla can open a gateway for me to join you." Stillman turned to Dev. "You still have the mirror, do you not?"

"Yes, sir. It's in the condo."

Stillman pulled a small pink item from his pocket and handed it to Dev. "Use this one. Cyndralla made it especially for Wren."

Roughly the size of small cell phone, Dev turned the plastic case in his hand then flipped the catch. One side sprang open, revealing a compact mirror.

"I assume it works like the big one, right?" Dev asked.

"Yes. Point and tap the glass. The image will be transported to the big mirror in Cyndralla's room. She'll create the gateway as soon as the image comes through." Stillman looked to each Knight in turn and raised his arm in farewell. "I must get back. May the elements shield us."

"And guide our way," the Knights responded in unison. Even Cassidy, having not been aware of the ritual, spoke the ancient words.

Stillman bowed and turned. "Oh," he spun back to the Knights, "Develor Quinteele, you are reinstated and free to, what is that term I've heard you use...kick ass." Pronouncement made, the Precept hurried from the room.

"Straight down Gray's gullet, right?" Magnus asked.

"Yep. Let's kick his teeth in." Dev summoned a gateway to his condo and led the group through.

8003

As a tribute to Wren, Dev wanted to drive her pink Chevy into battle. Magnus balked, but when Cassidy conceded shotgun and climbed into the back seat, he caved. He hugged his knees and fiddled with the radio until some suitable ass-kicking tunes rattled out of the tinny sound system.

Dev had ridden to war on a horse, in a tank, even standing in the back of a chariot, but never in a pretty princess mobile. He wouldn't have it any other way. Being in that car made him feel like Wren was there.

They rolled into Tampa with the windows down and Rob Zombie's "Dragula" cranked all the way up. Magnus shook the whole car with his head banging, but that didn't explain the vibration Dev felt through the wheel. Though he stayed in the middle of the lane, the wheel rattled as if he was running over the safety reflectors paved into the median. At first he thought his eyes were playing tricks on him, that the road broiled and seethed, but the headlights showed the real story. Bugs, millions of them, repaved the road with their shiny carapaces.

"Now that's gross," Dev said.

"What?" Cassidy asked.

"The ocean of bugs we're driving over," Magnus answered.

"What'choo talkin' 'bout Willis?" Cassidy looked out the car window.

In the rearview mirror, Dev watched the color drain from her face as she caught sight of the broiling black tide in a passing streetlight.

"You okay, Caz?" Dev asked.

"Sure."

Magnus grinned at her. "You don't look okay."

"I'm fine. Turn around. Mind your own business."

After he turned onto Kennedy, Dev cut the lights and the music. In the post-Rob Zombie quiet, the insect invasion performed their night time concert of chirps and buzzes. It was loud enough to drown out any noise their car would make.

In this racket, I could have brought the bike.

In addition to the noise, the creepy crawlies drove all the people off the streets after sundown, which would work in the Knights' favor. With no one around, they could focus on Gray and his minions.

"I'm going to park a few blocks away. We'll walk it from there. Hit the main doors."

"We're not going to have to stomp through the bugs, are we?" Cassidy asked, her voice quivering. "I…I don't know if I can do that." She shuddered.

Dev chuckled. "No worries. I can do something about that. They won't come near us."

"Are you sure?"

"Absolutely."

The Fire Knight parked next to a few cars in an otherwise empty lot two streets down from the Daegon Gray building. Dev got out first. Heat radiating out from his ankles, he cleared the area of insects before Cassidy got out of the car.

"There. See?" Dev pointed to the cleared ring of asphalt around the car. "They'll stay out of my heat."

Cassidy nodded and molded herself against his shoulder, her gaze darting from side to side to check the borders of their safety zone. She seemed to breathe deeper when the line didn't waver.

"Satisfied?" Dev asked.

She nodded.

While they checked each other's gear and Magnus got big behind the SUV, Dev scanned the rooftops of the surrounding buildings.

We're too exposed.

He never liked guerrilla warfare, preferring the simplicity of open fields and straightforward battles. There was something honorable about two forces standing toe-to-toe and duking it out until only the strongest and toughest remained. But tonight…he had a bad feeling that churned in his gut.

"I'll take point," Dev said. "Magnus, you've got the rear."

"Figures." Magnus's coping mechanism was to bitch, but he knew the drill.

"Caz, you're in the middle."

"Goody. I'm the creamy filling in this sandwich. A girl should be so lucky."

Magnus snorted. "You're going to fit in just fine."

"You goin' stone, big boy?" Cassidy asked when Magnus didn't finish his transition as she expected.

"If I need to. Slows me down."

"Gotcha."

Dev enjoyed the chatter. After all Cassidy'd been through, she'd held up amazingly well. Pride welled, but a sudden blast of bone grinding fear chased it away. Not for himself, but for her.

What if something happens to her? What if I lose her?

The questions turned his mood black, inviting the welcome sense of rage into his heart and soul. The familiar emotion uncoiled and pushed the heat of his element through his veins.

A low growl rattled in the back of his throat.

They will not get her.

Chapter 50

PALE MOONLIGHT SHONE THROUGH THE PENTHOUSE WINDOWS, BATHING HALF THE room in sickly white. The other half remained sheathed in gloom. Alexander sensed Agridda's eager presence veiled within the darkness.

He studied the roof across the street and looked for a sign that his snipers were in position. They would shoot anything that approached the front doors. That the Knights would come tonight, he had no doubt. They would not allow his challenge to go unanswered.

They come. Three of them. Gothrodul's thoughts penetrated Alexander's dark musings. *Fire and Earth I recognize, but not the third. A woman.*

Air.

No. The dragon's thought fired back, sharp and bitter. *I would know her. This one smells...fresh. Perhaps a new Water Knight.*

It matters not. They will soon be dead. How far?

Five minutes. No more. The dragon answered.

Good. I'll open the doors. Be ready.

As you wish.

Where are they...ah. The moonlight reflected off a high-powered rifle barrel. One of his hirelings hunched next to the ledge, rifle trained over the side. *Where there is one, the others will be as well.*

Soon.

"Father," Agridda's hiss sounded from inside the gloom. "The sacrifices are ready."

"Good. Stake them in the waiting room. I will be out presently."

"Yesss, Father."

The darkness shifted and a shade of malice peeled away.

Alexander pressed the panel and walked to his desk as the door in the roof opened. The pictures on the wall, where once his brothers' nasty faces leered, showed empty, solid canvas.

They closed their windows. Father must have told them about the plan. He studied the grim portrait of the Gray Lord. *Then why is that old bastard's spotted countenance still there?*

"No matter." A muffled gunshot popped across the street followed by another and another until a steady barrage of suppressed gunfire popcorned through the night. The sound made Alexander smile.

We have company.

Chapter 51

CASSIDY TOUCHED DEV'S BACK TO GET HIS ATTENTION. "I FEEL SOMETHING." THEY stopped under a blue awning four doors from the Daegon Gray entrance. "Confidence. Boredom. Over there." She pointed across the street from the main entrance. "More than one."

"It could be anything." He scanned the other side of the street—the coffee shop, a lawyer's office, a marketing firm. The buildings were no more than ten stories high. Nothing moved.

Magnus looked up at the same buildings with similar results. "I got nothing. Heat signatures?"

"Nothing in range. We'll keep moving. Caz, let me know if anything changes."

Back flat against the wall, Dev stepped into the clear.

She sensed a flash of anticipation a split second before Dev slammed into the wall and grabbed his left shoulder. The shock knocked him to his knees. Before he could scramble back under cover, two more hits plowed into his chest. Magnus jumped out, grabbed him by the collar and hauled him back.

Dev winced. "Did you see anything?"

"You've been shot." Cassidy stared at the flattened bullets embedded in Dev's armor.

"Flash from the roof across from Daegon Gray," Magnus replied and risked another peek from under the awning.

"You've been shot." Cassidy reached out to the lumps of metal.

Dev flicked the bullets off his vest. They had torn through the leather and exposed the thin layer of Quinsteele underneath.

"Caz, I'm okay."

Ensuring that the bullet didn't go through, she tapped the metal through the tear. No blood. No hole. The armor itself was unblemished and Dev showed no sign of pain.

Or fear or concern or anything other than curiosity. I'd be freaking out if I got shot and he's so...so matter of fact. What if the bullet had been higher? What if it hit him in the head? The unbidden thoughts raced through her head. *What if I lost him?*

Focus. He's fine. No blood, no foul, like Dad used to say. But her heart wouldn't give it up. Its pounding beat tried to convey a message that Cassidy wasn't sure she was ready to hear.

Magnus picked up one of the crushed bullets.

"One hundred sixty-eight grain hollow point. These guys are pros."

"Suggestions?" Dev asked and crouched.

"Make a run for it. I'll shield."

"Are you crazy?" Fear blossomed in her belly and spread to her limbs, turning them to lime Jello. "We'll never make it."

"Sure we will." Magnus reassured her. "No problem."

Dev nodded like they did this sort of thing every day. If Magnus had stood up and announced he liked pizza, Dev would have nodded the exact same way...for freaking pizza.

"Let me get ready." Magnus kicked off his boots and mumbled, "I don't know why I wear these darn things anyway." Barefoot, he closed his eyes. "Maybe I will try flip-flops."

Cassidy watched his body change, sensed his joy when he pulled his element. It came on quickly this time, skin going from tan to white to fissured gray in seconds. When he opened his eyes, they too were the same granite of his body.

Emboldened by their closer relationship, Cassidy rapped on his granite arm. *Solid.* Now she understood why his armor and clothes hung so baggy. In stone form, he was bigger and needed the room to grow.

Now that's cool.

"If both of you stay against the wall, I can shield you." Magnus's speech came out in a dry rasp, the grinding of stone on stone. "Whatever you do, don't stop. Walk at my pace." Magnus eyed them each in turn. "Dev, when we get there, get us in as fast as you can."

Magnus arranged them against the wall—Cassidy first, then Dev, with Magnus on the outside.

"Now we have a Dev sandwich." Cassidy covered her fear with a lame attempt at humor, but it seemed to work.

I hope Dev doesn't notice my trembling.

Magnus responded with a heartfelt, "Bleh. No thank you."

Dev just grunted.

"Let's go."

Magnus set a steady pace, taking one large step for every two of Dev and Cassidy's. His stone body completely engulfed theirs and kept them safe, but Cassidy felt the vibration as he took hit after hit. Stone chips flipped against the wall ahead or landed on the ground. One slipped past Dev and grazed her ear.

She sensed Magnus's pain. He may be made of solid granite, but the bullets hurt as they gouged out pieces of his broad back.

Hang in there, big guy. Just a few more feet.

"Stop here." Dev switched positions with Cassidy outside the first Daegon Gray window. "The doors are probably wired so we'll go in here." He drew Cinder and placed the tip of the diamond blade against the hurricane-proof glass.

Cassidy felt his body tense, his shoulders and arms bunch as he jabbed a hole through the shatter-proof glass. Twisting the blade, he enlarged it until it was the size of a quarter, and slipped in his finger.

Magnus grunted as the devastation rained down, the level of his pain grew with the pile of stone chips on the pavement.

Satisfaction flowed into Cassidy as Dev called his inner fire. His finger ignited, melting the film coating on the glass in a high-energy flash of green and blue. He reversed Cinder and shattered the window with a single blow.

"Let's go." Dev charged into the Daegon Gray lobby, knife ready, hungry for a fight. When none presented itself, he rushed over to the main desk. "Alarm," he responded to her questioning glance.

Breathing heavy, Magnus stumbled in and, out of sight of the opposing roof, collapsed to all fours. Cassidy rushed to check his back. Deep pits and craters, like the surface of the moon, marred his smooth surface.

"Oh, Magnus." Cassidy didn't know how to help the stone giant. "What can I do?"

"I'll be fine once I merge with the earth again. Just give me a moment."

Dev ripped the alarm's control panel out of the wall and smashed it against the marble tile. "I don't know if that will do the trick, but I feel better."

"I'm happy for you," Magnus panted.

Dev eyed the door and windows as he came back and knelt next to Magnus. "You going to make it?"

Magnus bobbed his head and Dev took up position by the hall that led to the stairway and elevators, taking the compact scrying mirror out of his pocket.

"We ready to bring in the boss?"

Magnus shook his head. "Let me get over this first."

The Earth Knight's pain assaulted Cassidy's heightened senses. While she didn't feel his physical distress, she understood how much it hurt him. *How can he stand it?*

While she watched, his body transitioned from granite to flesh, revealing the severity of the damage to his back. She could see how much the change hurt. He gasped, his body shook, and his fingers curled into the marble tile.

Cassidy assessed his injuries. The Quinsteele links had been shattered and in places ground into deep wounds. The leather underneath was shredded. Not even Dev's amazing armor could withstand a steady assault of that magnitude. Ragged flaps of skin peeled back on torn muscle and in some places bare bone. Blood slicked his back, ran down his arms and legs and spread out in a crimson blanket around his hands and knees.

"Maybe granite…wasn't the best…choice." Magnus hissed through clenched teeth.

"Shhh." Cassidy placed her hand on his trembling arm and sent cool thoughts of health and wellbeing.

The deep crease in his brow lessened and he breathed a little easier.

"Let me see if I can find some bandages." She cursed herself for not bringing any medical supplies. What did she think, that they were going to waltz in, kill Gray and walk out all suave and cool?

Rookie.

"It's okay. I'll be fine." Magnus reassured her. "The granite usually works, but that was too much." He tapped on the tiles below his hands. "Marble? No, too soft." He closed his eyes. "Hmm…iron it is."

Relief and a strong sense of wellbeing flowed from the injured Knight as his body changed again. The garish wounds closed. The skin on his back bubbled and flowed like water, rippling across the surface and smoothing the once ravaged flesh until not a mark remained.

Amazing. She couldn't help herself and touched the remade flesh. *Perfect.*

"Pretty neat, huh?" Magnus's strength returned. The transformation wiped away all signs of his agony along with his injuries. Continuing the change, his body hardened beneath her fingertips. His overall coloring darkened to a silvery-gray.

"Is the show over?" Dev asked from the low lit entrance to the hallway. "We've got work to do."

"Don't mind him." The iron giant pronounced each word slowly; his voice deep and hollow as though coming from the bottom of a well. "He's just jealous." He rose ponderously to his feet.

Magnus may have been joking, but his comment struck a nerve. Dev *was* jealous. Cassidy felt his emotion spike, raw and fast, then bury itself quickly under concern and taut aggression.

"I'm ready. Call the man."

Dev opened the mirror, aimed it at the elevator, and tapped the glass.

The air shimmered as the gateway took shape across the elevator's threshold. The gold glowing edges expanded quickly until it filled the dimensions of the doorframe. Cassidy glimpsed Cyndralla's tired face before Stillman stepped through and the gateway disappeared.

The Precept looked…different. Black tactical shirt tucked into black tactical pants stuffed into shiny new combat boots. If not for the saber at his hip and the crossed bandoliers of multi-colored vials filled with powders and liquids, he could have stepped off the cover of SWAT Quarterly.

The Precept took in his surroundings with quick efficiency. "Status."

"Snipers on the roof across the street," Dev reported. "No other encounters as of yet."

Stillman eyed the Knight of Earth, pulled a small, glittering object from one of a hundred small pouches lining his uniform, and placed it in the big man's hand. "Try this."

"A diamond?" Magnus frowned. "I don't do gems. You can see all my," he circled his hands in front of his stomach, "You know, innards and stuff."

"Go opaque. And trust me. You'll move faster and still be nigh invulnerable."

Magnus rolled his eyes, but began the transformation despite his modesty concern. Stillman gave a sharp nod of approval and turned to Dev. "Plan?"

"Upward and onward. Sir, what of Cyndralla and the counter magic for the orbs?"

The Precept's face fell and he sighed. "She is close. I thought we had it before you called, but it failed the final test. Let us hope she can find the right formula in time."

"This feels weird." His transformation complete, Magnus lifted first one arm then the other. Tiny facets covered every inch of his glass-like body and his internal core remained clouded. "Too light." His voice sounded higher, ranging closer to contralto than his normal he-man bass.

"Let's go pretty boy." Dev teased.

"Hey handsome," Cassidy chimed in, "Remember, diamonds are a girl's best friend."

Magnus blew out a deep breath. "I'll never live this down."

Belatedly, Dev remembered Stillman's presence. "Sorry, sir, I didn't mean to—"

"Nonsense, Knight of Flame. This is your op. I'm here to lend a hand. It has been too long since I sallied forth."

'Sallied?' You can dress them up...

The stainless steel elevator doors reflected the dim, after-hours lighting. On their left, the building's register, crammed tight with neat little rows of names and suite numbers, filled the wall.

"Are we taking the elevator?" Cassidy asked, finger poised over the arrow.

"No," Magnus barked and lunged for her hand. His fear filled the hallway. "I mean, that wouldn't be a good idea. Gray probably has them rigged."

"Yeah. We don't want to risk getting trapped. We'll take the stairs." Dev stalked to the other end of the hallway.

"Won't the stairs be guarded?" Cassidy asked.

"Most definitely," Dev said. "But we'll be in control, not at the mercy of electronics or some shadow bitch at the top of the shaft with a big pair of hedge clippers."

"And not stuck in a tiny metal room," Magnus mumbled to himself, but Cassidy overheard.

Dev led them around the corner to the door leading to the stairs. "Reverse order. Magnus, you first in case they open fire."

"I'm on it." The Earth Knight moved to the front.

"Cassidy next, then Stillman. I've got the rear." Dev looked at Cassidy. "Caz, do you feel anything?"

Cassidy opened herself up to the sensations around her. Beyond Dev, Magnus, and Stillman, higher in the building, she discovered a viscous soup of twisted emotions. Fear. Hate. Anger. Anticipation.

"I sense a lot of people up there."

"Gray?" Dev asked.

"I think so, but not close."

"Right. Up we go." Magnus grabbed the knob and glanced over his shoulder for a final check.

Cassidy swallowed the fear that would have buckled her knees before today and took her place behind the broad diamond back of Magnus, heartbeat hammering in her chest.

What the hell am I doing here? Panic leaked between her lips in a low, unconscious moan.

"Do you hear that?" Dev asked.

She clamped her lips shut and stifled the noise. Not to be denied, her panic found another avenue of escape as tears formed and began to fall.

"It's gone. Weird."

"Yeah. Haha. Weird." Cassidy wiped the tears away and took a deep breath.

Magnus shrugged and rolled his shoulders a few times. "Do you feel that?"

"What?" Dev asked.

"I feel...nervous." Magnus patted his belly. "I've got butterflies."

Dev raised one eyebrow and deadpanned, "Butterflies."

"Yeah. I haven't felt like this since, well, I can't remember when." Magnus squinted, mouth crooked into a scowl. "I don't like it."

"Now that you mention it," Dev cocked his head to one side, "I feel it too. Kind of anxious, jumpy." He held out his trembling hand. "What the hell is this?"

"Maybe we should rethink this. Come back at another time." Stillman rubbed the back of his neck and eyed the door to the stairs.

Oh no. This can't be happening.

"It came on all of a sudden." Magnus rubbed his eye with a finger. It came away wet and he held it out for Dev to see. "Look, I'm leaking."

"Put that thing away." Dev slapped Magnus's hand away.

I'm affecting them. Cassidy's breath came in short, quick gasps and her pulse jumped through the roof. She knew if she kept this up, she'd pass out. Already her vision changed, the edges of her sight closing in.

Dev grabbed his chest, his breathing labored. Magnus's color yellowed and he grabbed his stomach as if to ward off a bout of nausea.

Get a grip, Sinclair. Take a deep breath. This is just like competition. Breathe. Release. Breathe. Release.

Cassidy's panic receded. The pre-competition routine took the edge off. Her tears stopped and sanity returned.

Stay calm.

She could see the others regaining their composure. Dev shook his head to clear the alien sensations. Magnus rubbed his eyes, mining for more tears, but his fingers came up dry. Stillman shot Cassidy a thoughtful look.

"I'm not sure what happened," Magnus said, "But let's never talk about this again. Ever."

"Amen to that, brother," Dev said.

Cassidy gave a thumbs-up, not ready to trust her voice. She'd almost killed the entire mission. This emotional control thing was going to be harder than she thought. For now, she'd do her best Tinker Bell impression and think happy thoughts.

"When you're ready." Dev nodded toward the door. "Stick close to the wall."

Magnus opened the door and glided in slow, head twisted at an angle to peer up the chimney between the switchback flights of wide steps. Broad landings broke the steep climb midway between floors. The lights continued for three floors. Beyond that, darkness reigned.

Chapter 52

THE PENTHOUSE WAITING ROOM WAS PACKED. TWENTY FIVE ELITE MEMBERS OF Rangu Copa, Alexander's private army, trained their XM8 assault rifles on the doors to the elevators and the stairs. Hand-picked killers, the troops were force-fed Shadow dogma and trained since they were toddlers. Best of all, they were completely loyal to Alexander Gray.

"Commander." Alexander spoke to the burly soldier in the center of the line. Cold blue eyes stared out of deep sockets, locked in a face of sharp, deadly angles. Oily black hair hung in loose curls about his shoulders, a sign of his rank.

"Sir. As ordered, twenty five up top, fifty below."

"Fine."

Redundancy. The snipers failed and the Knights got into the building. Alexander had dispatched Gothrodul to address their failure. Fifty Rangu Copa on the stairs would be more than a match for three simple Knights. If not, the best of the best waited for them here.

And if that is not enough, I might have to get my hands dirty. In a perverse way, he hoped it came to that. He wanted to be the one to take the lives of these upstart Knights. Fighting three of them as opposed to only one may actually pose a challenge.

Agridda's work in the barge made them reckless, as expected.

For now, though, more pressing matters required his attention. Against the far wall of the lobby behind the row of soldiers, three sacrifices whimpered and moaned around their gags. Spread-eagle, affixed to crossed wooden beams with spikes driven through their wrists and ankles, the soon-to-be victims stared in helpless terror as Alexander approached. Blood trickled down their arms and filled their shoes. The one in the center lost control of his bladder and filled the room with the pungent tang of his fear.

Animals. Alexander sneered as he inspected each one. Chubby is what he asked for and all three fit the bill. Two women, and the coward in the center. He had seen them around the building, working in unimportant departments performing mundane duties, but that was about to change.

"Today," he preached, "your contributions to the company are finally going to be worthwhile."

A tingle began at the back of Alexander's neck, but he pushed it aside.

Agridda hovered above the captives, bright yellow eyes dancing through the thick miasma of fear in the air.

The tingle intensified to a sharp pinprick, but Alexander had felt much worse from his father. Excitement overrode the pain in his neck. The moment he had been working for since his banishment to this Shadow-cursed land had arrived.

Cupping his hands in front of his mouth, Alexander closed his eyes and drew on the dark power deep in his soul. The lights flickered as the threat of Shadow chased away the illumination. He coughed the word of power three times into his closed hands then shook them. The resultant angry buzz curled his lips into a malicious grin as eighteen hair-thin legs caressed his skin.

Yes.

Within his hands, three black flies with green wings zigzagged across his palms. He pursed his lips and blew them toward the guests of honor. With non-insect like precision, they landed on the foreheads of their respective hosts. Eyes wide and desperate, the victims watched the flies' progress as they navigated facial hills and valleys. Quick steps, pause, quick steps, the pattern continued until each fly sat upon a pair of quivering lips.

Will it be through the nose or the mouth? Fascinated, Alexander watched each fly choose its own course. Two crawled up their host's nose while the other worked around the gag and entered through the mouth.

No matter, in is in.

The pain in Alexander's neck intensified, as though his father stabbed a dagger and slowly twisted it from side to side. Annoyed, he left instructions for Agridda to watch for the changes while he took the call.

Rubbing the back of his neck, Alexander strode into his office, to the malevolent stare of his father. He'd come through the portrait and sat in wait like a hungry spider.

"Father." Calm. Emotionless.

"I see your brothers have already left." The Gray Lord glanced at the empty portraits to either side of his. "Good. This will be our last call."

Last call? An icy tongue of dread licked at Alexander's black core.

"I must admit, Alexander, I didn't expect you to get this far." Bestok Molan folded his hands in front of him and his expression softened.

What is he up to? I have not seen this tactic from him before.

"Knights dead. Orbs deployed." His father shook his head. "If I hadn't seen it myself, I would never have believed it. You actually pulled it off."

"Father, I—"

The Gray Lord held up his hand. "You bought us more time than I expected."

"What do you mean?"

"This was all a ruse, Alexander, a means to draw the Knights away from our other, more important endeavors."

Alexander let his confusion play out across his face and his father scowled.

"You were always dense," Bestok Molan said.

"I do not understand."

"Of course you don't, idiot boy. I'll slow it down for you. You. Were. Bait. A convenient way to locate the Knights and keep them busy at no cost to my organization. The Knights are coming, yes?"

Alexander nodded slowly as the meaning of his father's words began to sink in.

"You've been lucky. This time, you and yours have no chance. Your opponents will not make the same mistake twice. Goodbye, Alexander."

I have done everything you have ever asked of me. Rage bloomed, surging through his bloodstream. *And now you kick me aside like some leprous cur.*

"You bastard." Alexander whispered to the disappearing image of the Gray Lord.

His father's mocking laughter rang out as the portrait faded to black.

Alexander growled. It started deep in his chest and vibrated his ribcage until it worked its way to the surface and emerged as a roar. He bolted from the room, incinerating everything in sight with a sizzling bolt of shadow.

Kill. The mantra cycled over and over in his head. *Kill.*

In the waiting room, the disciplined soldiers eyed his crazed look. Alexander wiped the spittle from the corner of his mouth before turning his bale-filled gaze on the humans. The Rangu Copa uniform meant nothing.

Alexander saw only sheep ready for slaughter.

Alexander, stop. Gothrodul's thought banged uselessly against the solid mass of hate that was once Alexander's rational mind.

The elite soldiers turned in reaction to the new threat. Pinpoint lasers of indigo shadow beamed from Alexander's extended fingertips and cut the Rangu Copa down. Like a fistful of scalpels, the channeled darkness sliced through flesh and bone and the metal of the assault rifles. Bodies slid apart. Juicy gobbets of meat splashed down into spreading puddles of blood on the hardwood floor.

Alexander! The dragon screamed through the mental link.

What do you want? Alexander snarled back. *I am in no mood for your banter.*

Get a grip, Gray Lord. Gothrodul tried to calm Alexander down.

Do not speak of my father ever again.

I do not speak of your father, Alexander. I speak of you. There is another path.

Explain quickly, beast, or I will kill you along with the rest. Alexander knew Gothrodul hated the beast reference. He sensed the dragon's angry growl as prelude to his response.

Bursts of automatic gunfire erupted from the floors below.

Blast these interruptions. "Agridda, go."

An excited hiss escaped the dark patch with yellow eyes that zoomed through the closed stairwell door.

As for you, Dragon, Alexander pushed his irritation through the mental link. *We will discuss this* other *path at a later date.*

Regaining control, Alexander yanked on his jacket cuffs and turned to the sacrifices. Bloated stomachs. Blackened, distorted faces. Unblinking stares.

It is time.

Raising his arms above his head, Alexander called upon his darkest magic.

Chapter 53

THE STAIRWELL WAS AN OVEN. IT'S AIR HOT, MOIST AND STILL.

Perfect. Dev tapped into that heat, pulled it in, let it trickle through his bloodstream. His arms and legs tingled with borrowed energy. Though Magnus had point, Dev strained all his senses upward into the darkness, searching for the forces that Gray had undoubtedly set in place.

Can you feel us coming, Gray?

The fluorescent lights quit after the third floor. The other thirty-nine climbed in relative darkness, brightened only by the wan emergency bulbs set at ankle height along the outer walls. Dev embraced that absence of light, hungry for another chance at Shadow. Doubts about finding a way to kill the Maven fled in the face of battle. He would figure it out. He always did

"They're close," Cassidy whispered. "Only a few more floors."

Dev knew too. Their heat signatures gave them away. He whistled, barely audible, but loud enough to get the Earth Knight's attention. As the big man turned, Dev put out ten fingers. He pointed up and flashed a couple more fingers, indicating they'd find ten soldiers in two floors. Magnus acknowledged with a single nod.

Dev leaned his head close to Cassidy's. "What do you feel?"

"Anticipation. Annoyance. Boredom."

"No fear?"

"Far above. Not close."

"Time to change that." Dev pushed her gently against the wall. "Stay here. It'll be safer."

She started to protest, but stopped before any words came out. Instead, she nodded and squeezed his arm. He caught a flash of something more in her look, but it was too quick.

Concern, maybe. Fear?

He couldn't blame her. The last few minutes of anticipation before battle were ten times worse than the real thing. For her it must be doubly so, having never deliberately set out for a fight.

"What are your intentions?" Stillman asked.

"Take out the first group of defenders as quickly as possible. Sir, I would appreciate it if you would stay with Cassidy, keep her safe and guard the rear."

Stillman's eyes narrowed as if he saw through Dev's polite but obvious attempt to keep him out of the way.

"Are they human?" The Precept fished a small jar from another one of his pockets, unscrewed the lid, and dipped in one finger. "I want each of you to smear a little of this salve under your eyes, nose and mouth. It will counter any of the tools I use in combat." While the Knights passed the jar and followed his order, he thumbed a vial containing a blue powder through the loop of his vest.

This would be so much easier without the old man here. He's going to slow us down.

"Let's try something to make our ascent a tad simpler, shall we? Here, hold this." Stillman handed the vial to Dev and rummaged through a few pockets until he came out with what looked like an inverted salt shaker with two small tubes mounted to its side.

"Sir, are you sure we have time for this?" Dev asked as Magnus and Cassidy watched the strange procedure.

The Precept plugged the holes of the shaker with two fingers and took back the vial. "You should know that, being alchemically inclined, I am a strong proponent of non-lethal chemical warfare." He emptied the vial's contents into the shaker and looked at Dev. "How many floors?"

"From where we are, about thirty five."

"Hmmm, might not reach the top. Still..." Stillman capped the vial and slipped it back into place. He plugged the shaker, and, leaning over the rail, peered toward the floors above. Arm outstretched, he held the shaker in his palm aimed toward the top of the building.

"Sir." Dev marched forward. "We really need to—"

"Fire in the hole." Stillman reached over and twisted the cap until it clicked. "Three. Two. One." Like a miniature missile, the shaker zoomed up between the floors. A cloud of fine blue powder permeated the air.

"I smell blueberries." Cassidy inhaled deeply and smiled.

"Nice, isn't it?" Stillman sniffed the air. "Without that salve I had you apply, you would be sound asleep right now."

"So the guards upstairs should be asleep right now and we won't have to fight our way to the top?" Cassidy closed her eyes and her expression blossomed in wonder. "I think it worked. I don't feel anything but peace until near the top. Beyond that, all bets are off."

Magnus leaned over to Dev. "Kinda takes the fun out of it, doesn't he?"

Dev rolled his eyes and nodded. "Let's see what happens. Magnus, you're on point. I'll follow next in case we encounter any resistance. The stairs below are clear."

The Knight of Earth crept up the stairs to the point where Dev detected the first group of heat signatures. All ten guards had fallen where they stood. Magnus waved the rest of the team up.

Cassidy smiled at Stillman, who executed a little bow.

"How long will they be out?" Dev asked as he and Magnus collected the weapons and tossed them over the rail.

"At least twelve hours, maybe more."

"Well." Hands on hips, the Knight of Flame took a deep breath and nodded appreciatively. "Alright then. Let's move on."

℘℧

While the others disarmed a third group of sleeping soldiers, Dev scouted a few floors ahead. He hated to admit it, but Stillman's approach, though decidedly lacking in excitement, saved time and dramatically reduced the danger to Cassidy.

The shuffle of heavy boots and the muttered talk of bored soldiers drifted down to Dev from the floor above and his element stirred in response.

Well, old man, looks like your magic dust didn't get them all.

He wanted to charge, to take them out himself, but that wouldn't be fair to Magnus and would most likely land him back in Cradle jail. No. He'd be a good Knight, slink back to the team and bring them up to speed.

Dev bounded down the steps and met Magnus and crew on the way up. Putting a finger to his lips, he crouched on the stairs and the others followed suit.

"From what I can tell, there are two more groups of soldiers," Dev whispered. "The first group of ten is two floors up. The rest are a few floors above that. I count twenty in total. Magnus and I will take out this first group. I'll blaze up and run in first with Diamond Jim here right behind." He looked at Stillman and Cassidy.

"I know. I know. Rear guard. Got it," Cassidy said.

The Precept nodded. "Try to minimize the loss of life."

"But, Sir, the soldiers work for Gray." Dev remained calm, but inside his element flared.

"Most of them probably don't realize they are on the wrong side." Stillman clapped the Knight of Flame on the shoulder. "Take it easy on them. They are not in our class."

"Yes, sir."

Before Dev bounded up the steps with Magnus, he let loose a reassuring smile and brushed a fingertip across Cassidy's chin. The move surprised them both, but he leaped away before either of them could dwell on it.

Soldiers muttered on the landing above. Dev validated ten heat signatures. Opening the conduit to the fuel all around him, he turned up his heat and drew Cinder. The amber jewel pulsed a dull orange.

Dev touched his knuckles to Magnus's chest. "Fire and stone."

Magnus did the same, his crystalline fist covering nearly a third of the Fire Knight's broad chest. "Stone and fire."

Element focused into a solid wall of power just beneath his skin, fist wrapped tight around Cinder, Dev leaped up the steps and invoked his flame with an exultant roar. The blaze engulfed him and lit up the stairwell and the curious soldiers above. Deafening bursts of assault weapon fire reverberated off the walls of the vertical chamber, making it seem like the gunshots came from everywhere at once. But Dev knew different, knew the enemy fire originated from directly ahead. Without slowing, he charged.

Orange and yellow waves built, peaked and crested along his entire body. Drawing more power from the source around him, he formed a shimmering shield wall of blistering heat in front of him. The jewel at the base of Cinder's blade radiated thin beams of brilliant amber in all directions like a laser-beam disco ball.

The soldiers balked at the light show. Their hesitation gave Dev a momentary advantage. He streaked through the group, slashing and punching everything within reach. Soldiers fell. Some grasped gaping wounds while others frantically stamped out the flames that spread across their smart black uniforms.

When he reached the last in line, he spun and whirled back through their ranks. Slash. Spin. Kick. Thrust. Chop. Dev tore through those left standing like a fiery Cuisinart. In his wake, he left a bloody trail of gashes, stumps and moaning men.

The stairs trembled as Magnus caught up to the action, but only the cleanup remained.

"You suck." The big man surveyed the gory scene.

"What?" Dev asked innocently, breathing fire with each word.

Magnus pointed down the stairs as a reminder to collect the rear guard. Dev doused his flame and jogged the few flights to their level. Excited, he rounded the corner and found Cassidy huddled in the corner. She'd wedged herself into the smallest possible shape and covered her head and ears with her arms. Stillman knelt next to her and rubbed her back.

The sight nearly broke his heart and stomped all over his good mood.

Sorry, Caz. Tonight will not be pretty.

"I'll see if there is something I can do for the Knight of Earth." Stillman jogged up the stairs.

Cautious and slow, Dev knelt next to Cassidy.

"Caz. It's okay. You're safe." His voice was soft and tender. He stroked her hair.

Unwrapping from her protective bundle, Cassidy glanced up, eyes brimming with unshed tears.

"We need to move," Dev said.

"Are you hurt?" Iron supplanted the fear in her eyes as she inspected Dev. "Let me see." Before he could answer, Cassidy grabbed his chin and jerked it first left and then right.

"I'm fine." Dev squirmed out of her grasp.

"Then what's this?" She poked a finger in the tear across his bicep.

"Oww." Dev checked the wound. "Would you look at that, one got through. No big deal. Let's go." He took her hand and led her up the stairs.

At the scene of the battle, Cassidy gasped at the sight of so much mayhem and hurried to the nearest injured man who tried to stretch the edges of his torn flesh over the bloody meat and bone shard that terminated his right arm.

"We need to help these men." Cassidy looked on the floor for scraps of material to bind their wounds. "We can make a tourniquet to stop the bleeding."

"We don't have time." Dev sensed the movement of the other soldiers and eyed the next flight of stairs.

Stillman stomped over, brows knit, eyes flaring. "Do you consider this taking it easy on the soldiers?"

Expecting the accusation, Dev stood his ground, met Stillman's piercing stare with calm assurance. "I killed no one, Sir, as you commanded. I simply made sure they would not rejoin the fight. I thought it a sound military tactic. Do you have a problem with that?" Dev couldn't keep the fire from his tone. He had bigger fish to fry and didn't have the time or the patience to deal with a squeamish Stillman.

"No, I do not." Stillman searched the Knight of Flame's expression. "But I wanted to understand your reasoning. Well done."

The exchange rendered Dev speechless and he stared at the Precept as he moved a few feet away and drew his long, curved blade.

"Sinclair. Siggurdson." Stillman called the other Knights to him and pulled a tiny vial from yet another pocket. As soon as he removed the small dropper from the top, a beam of bright yellow light shot out.

"Present your weapons." The Precept carefully squeezed two drops onto his blade. The liquid hissed as it touched the metal and spread across the length of the saber. Once fully coated, the blade glowed a pale shade of yellow. "This exceptionally rare oil contains the essence of sunshine. It will empower your weapons against Shadow." Stillman applied the drops to each weapon and put the vial away.

A sad smile crossed Dev's lips as he watched Cassidy ogle her faintly glowing cutlass.

I hope she doesn't have to use that.

"This is amazing." She twisted the handle, examining each side of the blade. "Where did you get it?" She touched the metal with her finger, jerked it away with a yelp, and jammed it into her mouth. "Oww, it's hot."

"Don't do that," Stillman said.

Boots thumped on the stairs above.

"Here they come," Magnus said.

Side by side, the Knights of Earth and Flame waited at the foot of the stairs.

"Oooh." The color fled from Cassidy's face and she doubled over.

Dev turned. "What?"

"Something's changed," Cassidy mumbled, arms wrapped tight around her midsection, "Hatred. Bloodlust. Rage. It's bad." Her head shot up and she focused terrified eyes on Dev.

"She's coming."

∞∞

Knuckles white around the hilt of her cutlass, Cassidy fought to control the fear that set her bones to trembling. Stillman stood by her side. Rock solid, saber raised and ready, he scanned the darkness between the stairs. Dev and Magnus waited for the first sight of the incoming soldiers.

I can feel her. Cassidy bit back a whimper. *She's close. God, the hatred. It consumes everything in her path.*

The soldiers opened fire at the top of the stairs. Dev flamed up and struck hard, driving through the first pair like a hot Knight through butter. Magnus backed him up, a diamond wall of defense in case one of them slipped through the fire.

Where is Agridda?

Screams erupted below them. Cassidy jumped and looked to Stillman for direction. The Precept lowered his head and closed his eyes.

"She's feeding."

Feeding on what? Cassidy felt her now, only a few floors down among the wounded who appeared to Cassidy's senses as pinpricks of pain and horror.

"No...she's devouring them." Cassidy clapped her hands over her ears to block out the sound, but it did nothing to block out her gift. Agridda's shadowy wave of anger steamrolled over the other emotional blips, consuming them in a single pass.

"Perhaps keeping them alive was no kindness." Stillman pursed his lips. "She will be stronger now."

Anger, arrogance, and excitement swirled together and flowed toward them.

"Here she comes!" Cassidy yelled.

"Where?" Stillman's head jerked from side to side. "Where?"

Cassidy pushed Stillman out of the way and dove to the side as a cloud of boiling darkness burst from the landing beneath their feet. Eyes, bright yellow from the recent feast, fixed on Cassidy. Twin ropes of shadow reached out, tried to grab her, but she slashed with her cutlass, severing one of the ropes. The severed end sizzled as it fell and curled into a little charred ball on the floor.

Agridda hissed and recoiled.

Yes!

The tip of Stillman's sword emerged from the center of Agridda's dark cloud. Crackles of light played across her skin. She screamed in agony, and whipped around to face her attacker. The sudden move ripped the sword from the wound.

Stillman lowered his weapon and calmly faced the billowing evil.

He's not afraid.

Cassidy detected a sad confidence and regret, but no fear or concern.

The man is a rock.

The yellow eyes grew wide at the sight of Stillman. "You," she hissed.

"Hello, child," he replied. "It has been a long, long time. We do not have to do this."

Cassidy picked up on the isolation and doubt that flitted through the Maven before she squelched it under a veil of all-consuming hatred.

That can't be it…can it? Stillman said she was given to Shadow as a child.

The brief glimpse into Agridda's emotional turmoil sparked an idea. Cassidy allowed herself to feel. Not the terror, anger, and hate the shadow creature thrived on. No. This required something different.

Cassidy thought of Amy—the joy of holding her squirming daughter for the first time, the silken feel of her baby's hair between her fingers as she washed out the shampoo, the wonder twinkling in her daughter's eyes on Christmas morning, the pride when she took her first step. The parade of intimate moments flashed by in a second, each one a treasured keepsake of motherhood.

Tears trickled down. Cassidy reached out until her fingers brushed the stinging cold edge of Agridda's darkness and willed all of her motherly love out through the contact.

Agridda's form changed, solidifying into the shape of a young girl with long ringlets of hair the color of soot. She tilted her head and stared at Cassidy with curious yellow eyes.

After the change, Cassidy's fingers rested below the girl's slim throat.

"What ssort of creature are you, Casssidy Ssinclair?" Agridda's hiss sounded less pronounced in this form.

For the moment, Agridda's curiosity eclipsed her hatred, but Cassidy knew the distraction wouldn't last long.

"I am a mother."

"Mother? I…had one of those once." Agridda's body shuddered.

Cassidy felt the stronger emotions regaining control.

Come on guys. I can't keep her busy forever.

"What was she like?" Cassidy asked.

"I do not remember. Father took her away." Her eyes narrowed and her head jerked to the side. She snarled, the action more sinister on the face of a child.

A giant axe slashed across Cassidy's field of vision. Agridda's form split and reformed around the blade, careful not to let it touch her. Dev charged in from the opposite side, Cinder already in motion.

Agridda's body shattered. The pieces separated, flowed around the Knight, and reformed in the air above Stillman. She swung at his head with a mallet-shaped fist. He ducked, but not quickly enough, and caught a glancing blow that smashed his head into the wall.

Dev and Magnus closed in as Agridda retreated up through the free space between the stairs.

Cassidy rushed forward in time to ease Stillman's slumping form to the floor. Trained fingers probed the unconscious man's skull.

No broken skin. Ooh, there's the lump. It swelled and throbbed beneath her fingertips.

Dev extinguished his flame and knelt by her side.

Damn, he's hot. Sweat beaded across her brow.

"How is he?" Dev asked.

Cassidy felt the rest of the Precept's skull, traced the lines of his neck. "I can't be sure. Head wounds are tough. I have no idea what's going on inside."

"What can you do for him?" Dev sounded worried.

"Here? Nothing. He needs a medical facility, or at least to get back to the Cradle."

Dev got to his feet, face twisted with indecision. He looked at Stillman then followed Agridda's trail with his eyes.

"We go on. Now. Before Agridda has a chance to get set."

"What about Stillman?" Magnus asked.

"Leave him. We'll come back after we kick Gray's ass."

Cassidy settled Stillman to the ground, brushed a few strands of white hair out of his face, and kissed his forehead.

We'll be back. I promise.

Chapter 54

THE KNIGHTS RACED UP THE LAST FEW FLIGHTS OF STAIRS AND STOPPED OUTSIDE the door to the Penthouse. Cassidy splashed in a puddle, stirring up the familiar smell of blood. A wide range of crazed emotions boiled on the other side of the door.

What happened up here? There's blood all over the floor and even down the first few steps. She clamped her fear down tight and took a deep breath.

"We go in strong, take them out quick," Dev said. "Caz, do you think that Jedi emotion trick will work on Agridda again?"

"Yeah. These are not the Knights you're looking for." Magnus smiled. "That was awesome."

"I doubt it. She knows what to expect."

"That's what I figured. Okay. I'll take Agridda. Magnus, you've got Gray. Caz..." Dev looked at Cassidy, concern evident in his gaze.

"I'll figure out some way to help," she said.

"We need to move now." Magnus spat on the floor. "He's casting, I can taste it. Ready? I'll knock." Magnus kicked the door in and charged through first. Dev and Cassidy jumped through after.

In the far corner of the waiting room, Gray stood with his back to the door and his arms upraised. Bolts of black energy burst from his clenched hands, one for each of the bloated corpses propped up against the wall. The air was thick and sticky and clung to Cassidy like syrup.

Gray reared up on his toes. The lights dimmed as he reached a quiet crescendo.

"Stop him!" Cassidy cried.

Dev charged, engulfed in fire before his second step. Magnus pounded right behind, axe at the ready.

Undeterred, Gray spoke a word in the dark language of shadows, "Graelosch." A blast of dry air exploded out from the Shadow Lord and threw Magnus and Dev across the room toward the elevator doors. The ends of the dark beams detached from his hands and snapped into the three corpses.

Head bowed, arms hanging limp, Gray dropped to one knee.

The swollen bellies of the corpses split. First one, then a second, then a hundred black flies with bright green wings crawled from the ghastly wombs and took wing. Three amorphous clouds of shadow seethed, buzzed and flew through the doorway into Gray's office and out of sight.

I've seen a fly like that before, at the hospital, just before...

"Stop the flies!" She ran after the swarms. "They trigger the orbs. Burn them!"

The Knight of Flame ran for the door, but Agridda swooped in and knocked him off his feet. Her momentum carried her beyond the doorway. Cassidy slipped through to see the last erratic stragglers fly up and out of the open roof hatch.

"No!" she screamed.

We failed. She couldn't believe it and stared up at the moon through the roof. *After all the shit we've—I've—been through, we failed?* Anger bubbled inside her, blowing the lid off her cool containment.

Magnus and Dev charged into Gray's office ready to defend her from some new enemy.

"This ends now." The intensity of her emotion bled from her pours in beads of salty rage. She drew her cutlass and swung at the imagined image of Gray she conjured before her. Brows lowered, she eyed her friends, watched their demeanor change as her intent smashed into their psyches like a club.

A murderous glint flickered in Magnus's eyes. He bared his teeth.

Dev's flame changed from yellow-orange to a deep, intense purple.

As Magnus turned, a heavy weight struck him from the waiting room and knocked him off his feet. He crashed to the floor and lay still. Cassidy would have been worried if she hadn't caught the wink he directed at Dev.

Twin yellow eyes floated through the door within a net of silky black shadow. Agridda's hissing laugh filled the room when she saw the Knight of Earth down.

Dev growled and launched himself at the Maven who hissed and shrank back as his indigo flame kissed her essence in defense of the downed giant.

The Maven gave up ground, backing away to keep out of the reach of Dev's dagger. He pressed forward, drove her around the room. With each contact of the Knight's anointed blade, charred bits of shadow drifted to the floor.

Thank goodness for Stillman's oil. Cassidy's hopes flared. *We've got her.*

Out of the corner of her eye, she caught Magnus rise and raise his axe over his shoulder.

Cassidy wanted to help, wanted to slice off a hunk of Shadow, but to get that close would risk getting in Dev's way. Again, she felt more of a hindrance than a help. Emotions ran high, but they weren't right. She sensed the confidence and hope from her guys, but the only thing she got from the Maven was amusement and her ever present hatred. No fear. No concern.

Why not?

Magnus licked his lips and tightened his grip as Dev steered Agridda towards him, hacking to her left or right depending on which way she drifted. When she was in his sweet spot, he swung for the fence, put all his formidable weight behind the blow. It sliced her across the middle and parted her darkness like smoke. The force of his swing twisted him around so he didn't see her bottom half wither and slide to the ground.

"Pathetic." Arms crossed, Gray stood in the office doorway. "Thank you, my daughter, for entertaining our guests while I recover. Pull yourself together."

"Yessss, Father." Agridda floated into a pool of darkness in the corner and emerged whole.

"And you, Sinclair. You are harder to kill than one of my brother's little pets." A cruel smile crept over Gray's face. "I will see you dead tonight."

Cassidy's hopes fell. All the progress they had made, gone. And now they had Gray to contend with as well.

Dev redoubled his attack and threw himself into Agridda's shadowed center. Her essence sizzled, but that was all. She didn't scream or hiss like she did before.

Dev noticed and broke off his attack, but the Maven countered, took the fight to him. Dark tendrils speared out at him at varying heights and frequencies. Large, black shadow spikes, like the ones that killed Wren, tried to pierce his defenses, but Dev sheared through anything that got close. For each piece he cut off, another flowed in to take its place.

Magnus turned on Gray and brandished his axe.

That other feeling stirred, the faint one Cassidy felt before the gunshots outside hit Dev, only this time it was much closer. She looked up through the roof, half expected to see a face looking down, but saw only the night sky splattered with stars.

I'm useless. I brought emotion to a knife fight.

Dev backed up, Cinder a crystal streak in front of him. As he passed Gray's desk, he set it on fire. The ancient, dry wood blazed in seconds and banished the shadows within reach.

Gray drew a slim knife from his pocket and flicked it at Magnus. Razor thin slivers of midnight showered the approaching Knight. Most bounced off his faceted surface, but a few found their mark and stuck into his diamond surface. Before long, he looked like an enormous porcupine, but the shadow quills seemed to have no effect, didn't hamper his sweeping movements as he swung his axe at the Shadow Lord.

Gray backed away and sent more shadow quills across the room.

Magnus leaped forward and thrust the cap spike at his opponent's exposed chest, but Gray easily dodged the big man's attacks.

Cassidy hunkered in the corner and waited for her chance to strike.

Don't mind me. Focus on the big man. That's right. A little closer.

Though huge by office standards, the penthouse was a miniscule battlefield. While Dev and the shadow bitch fought near the back corner, Magnus and Gray battled near the doorway. As Gray evaded, he worked his way deeper into the room and closer to her.

Come on. She wiped her sweaty palms on tight leather pants and adjusted her grip on the cutlass.

Magnus backed Gray into the corner, but Gray only smiled. His eyes continually reassessed his position in the room. Magnus knew one direction, straight ahead, and kept his eyes buried in Gray's midsection.

Gray glanced up.

Something is very wrong here.

Gray escaped from the corner and turned Magnus around under the open sky.

Cassidy caught another quick glance up and twitch of Alexander's lips. The other sense she'd been feeling was close, right on top of them, and hungry.

"Magnus, look out!" Cassidy screamed.

A large black reptilian head snaked through the roof, bit down on the Knight of Earth, and lifted him out. The last image she had of Magnus was his huge legs kicking like mad as they stuck out from between giant white teeth.

"NO!" Dev screamed and slashed harder, but it made no difference.

Gray watched the fiery movements of the Knight of Flame and conjured a black ropy tendril that hovered over his shoulder while he contemplated the Knight.

No. Dammit. No.

Cassidy screamed, charged and swung her cutlass. Gray frowned and sent the tendril at her instead. It caught her in the stomach and drove the wind from her body. She dropped to her knees and gasped for breath.

The next tendril wrapped around her waist and pulled her in close.

"Agridda, Gothrodul, I grow tired of this charade." Gray marched Cassidy, lashed in shadow, to the center of the room, just below the opening in the ceiling. He willed another shadow rope into existence and snatched Dev out of mid-leap, who flared and thrashed against the pull, but had to douse his flame as Gray snugged him in with Cassidy.

She expected more rage or at least anger from the Knight of Flame, but what she sensed was determination, concern, and that other feeling, the one she'd noticed before but refused to explore. She could see it in the way he looked at her.

Her heart soared. After Amy, she thought herself dead. But the Knights brought her back to life. And Dev...he was at the center of it.

"How nice." Alexander bound them together, face to face, with a single inky tentacle. "As I said, Sinclair—"

"Don't say her name," Dev growled.

"Tonight is your last."

Gothrodul lowered his snout through the roof and sniffed Cassidy's hair.

She cringed from the dragon's maw, burying her face into Dev's shoulder.

Dev struggled as much as he could without hurting Cassidy, but all it did was brush his strong body against hers. When he met her eyes, they were pure crimson.

Agridda moved in close for the kill.

"I shall give Sinclair to my dragon. Would you like to watch, Knight of Flame? No? I can see your feelings for her."

Dev looked at Gray then back at Cassidy. She wriggled one hand free and caressed his cheek, his skin hot and smooth. His body trembled with the force of keeping his flame in check. Her own feelings crystallized in this place, under these dire circumstances. She named it.

Love.

It filled the emptiness in her soul. She let it spread throughout her being, and delivered it to Dev through a look, her radiant smile, and her new power as the Knight of Water. She'd say the words, but the presence of Gray and his minions would stain the moment.

His face opened in wonder, eyes as wide as his mouth. With the revelation, he lost control. His flame burst unbidden.

Cassidy hoped for that, wanted to be lost to his passion instead of the dragon's teeth. Heat washed over her, but his flame sizzled against the watery protection of her element.

"How touching." Gray's lips curled in disgust. "Time to die."

Cassidy cupped Dev's flaming cheeks and pressed her lips softly to his. She pushed all of herself into that contact, wanting him to understand how she felt.

The Knight of Flame jerked. His skin thrummed under her touch. His eyes turned white. His flame burned a pure, brilliant white.

The shadow bands holding them disintegrated. Dev pulled Cassidy in tight, out of the way of the dragon's descending jaws, which snapped on empty air.

Gray shielded his eyes while he threw everything he had at the glowing Knight, but no sooner had the shadow magic manifested than the Knight of Flame's righteous light burned it away.

Cassidy circled around to the other side of the desperate Shadow Lord, cutlass primed for a killing blow.

We've got him.

The dragon's head slammed down again, but the Knights weren't the target. It sunk saber-like teeth onto Gray's left arm below the shoulder and yanked him into the air. He squirmed like a juicy worm on a hook, features locked in a rictus of shock and agony. Blood and saliva sprinkled the floor as the black snout pulled the struggling Shadow Lord out and, with a beat of its tremendous, bat-like wings, disappeared into the night.

The snatch and grab happened too quickly for Dev or Cassidy to do anything about it. One minute they had Gray at their mercy. The next, he was dragon chow.

A small pocket of Shadow cowered in the farthest corner of the room, just outside the boundary of Dev's radiance. For the first time, Cassidy sensed fear from Agridda. Her insight into the shadow creature's emotional baggage might have earned her a little pity, maybe even a shot at mercy, but this bitch killed Wren...and enjoyed it.

So let the sunshine in.

Cassidy nudged Dev, pointed to the last remnant of Shadow in the room. The Knight's flame intensified, a star going supernova, and bathed the room in its glory.

Nowhere to run, Agridda reared from the corner and slinked across the room. She squirmed under the harsh light of Dev's retribution, looking for some bolt hole to escape as her body frayed and melted away.

Cassidy sensed Agridda's hope rise the closer she got to the doorway and the promise of cool shadows in the waiting room. Mere feet away from dark salvation, the Maven's body had been reduced to little more than a dark patch around her sickly yellow eyes.

Stillman, a resigned look on his face and a deep sadness in his eyes, stepped inside the office and slammed the door.

All hope gone, the Maven screeched, a piercing howl that sputtered and died as the light destroyed her.

Thunder rumbled and a light rain began to fall. The first few cool drops splashed onto Cassidy's upturned face.

I'm alive.

With the immediate danger gone, Dev dropped his glow. Sirens sounded in the distance, getting closer.

"We need to get out of here," Dev said. The weight of his arm settled comfortably over Cassidy's shoulders as he pulled her close.

"We can't go down."

"No."

"Any other options?"

On the roof, heavy steps crunched from the edge of the building to the lip of the opening. As they progressed, the tread changed from heavy to medium to light, until the footfalls barely registered at all. Cassidy peered at the ceiling as if she could see through it to the walker above.

Small rocks and debris rained down as fingers appeared over the edge. Dev stepped in front of Cassidy to face the unknown. Scraggly strings of long blond hair slid over the side before a familiar, yellow-bearded face entered the picture.

Magnus.

The Knight of Earth pulled himself over the edge and belly-flopped onto the hardwood like a dead carp. Scrapes and bruises marred his tan skin, but otherwise he appeared intact.

Dev eased him over onto his back. "I thought you were dead."

"Me too," Magnus rasped.

"How did you get away from the dragon?"

"When he couldn't bite through me, he threw me over the edge, but not far enough. I slid off the roof and managed to grab a ledge one floor down."

"We need to be gone from this place," Stillman said. "I had hoped Cyndralla would have been here."

I am here. The words sounded in Cassidy's head. Startled, she looked for their source. Dev must have heard them too for his gaze raked the room.

Cassidy felt exasperation above her and looked up into iridescent, purple-scaled nostrils perched over a giant snout full of sword-like teeth.

Another dragon? This one is...good? Maybe? At least it doesn't seem to want to eat me.

The dragon sniffed the air, like a bloodhound on a scent. *What is that smell, Cassidy Sinclair?*

"Wh-what smell?"

You do not detect that scent. The dragon inhaled deeply, drawing strands of Cassidy's hair toward its waiting maw. *It... cannot be. So long.*

Cassidy felt the pang of sadness directly above her.

The dragon shifted position and focused the point of her snout on the Water Knight.

I forget myself. Do not fear me, Knight of Water. The thoughts echoed in Cassidy's head. The tone was oddly familiar.

Are they coming from the dragon?

Yes. In this, my true aspect, I cannot form your human words. The dragon's maw shifted away and a brilliant, purple eye peered down at them. *It is I, Cyndralla, Knight of Air.*

Cyndralla is a...dragon?

Dev smiled. "She comes in handy sometimes."

You will be safe on my back, Knight of Water.

It all clicked into place—the odd comments, unusual, ignorant behavior, and strange physical anomalies.

With the dots connected and the knowledge that this dragon wasn't going to eat her, Cassidy admired the beauty and majesty of the Knight of Air.

Thank you, Cassidy.

Hey, that's not fair. Cassidy thought at Cyndralla. *You shouldn't be in my head.*

Is it not? The big purple orb narrowed. *You sense my heart. Why should I not be able to sense your thoughts?*

Cassidy hadn't considered that point. She did see into the hearts of those around her, eavesdropping on those most intimate things kept closest to the vest—emotion.

Do not worry. You will learn to control it in time. You are but a babe to the element. Give yourself the chance to learn. Cyndralla winked and reached a scale-covered arm down into the room. The few remaining fluorescent lights shimmered across her natural armor, challenging Cassidy to name the shade of purple.

We must hurry. The human authorities have entered the building.

Dev helped Magnus rise and straddle Cyndralla's arm. She raised him up and set him carefully between her wings. Stillman climbed up after, and steadied the injured Earth Knight.

Once we are airborne, my magic will hide us from the sight of the humans.

Dev followed next, and then Cassidy, who, as soon as she settled behind her Knight, wrapped her arms tight around his waist.

"What of the elixir?" Stillman asked.

It is done. Cyndralla informed them. *We should have enough to negate the orbs in this region, but we'll have to make more for the rest of the country.*

The orbs. In the excitement, Cassidy forgot about their failure.

Dev spoke up so everyone could follow the conversation. "We failed, Cyndy. Gray triggered the orbs."

That is unfortunate. In what manner did this happen?

"Flies. Swarms of flies," Cassidy answered.

Then we are safe for I found and destroyed them. In my journey to find your location, I sensed the evil on the wind. I tracked the source to two swarms and incinerated them before they touched the ground.

"Wait. Did you say two?" Dev asked.

Yes.

"But there were three." Cassidy said.

Chapter 55

LEFT ARM HANGING BY A THREAD OF MUSCLE AND SHATTERED BONE, ALEXANDER dangled from the teeth of Gothrodul. Wind whipped him about as the landscape rushed by under his feet. Soon after take-off he'd blacked out from the pain, but his rage woke him.

"Land, you stupid beast, before my arm comes off," Alexander commanded. "There, on top of that building."

The shadow dragon banked right, tucked its wings against is scaled side, and dropped like a boulder. At the last possible moment, mere feet above the tar and stone roof, he unfurled his wings and skidded to a rough landing. Alexander tumbled from his mouth and rolled across the rocky surface minus his left arm, which resided behind a wall of sharp teeth.

Gothrodul spat it out. *Whoops.* His long forked tongue slid out and licked the fresh blood from his snout. *Sorry for the abrupt landing. Misjudged the distance.*

Alexander stared, transfixed by the ragged flesh that jutted from below his shoulder. Blood spurted from the raw stump in time with the beating of his heart. He screamed and covered the flow with his other hand.

Use the Shadow, Alexander. Seal the wound before you run out of life.

Would that be so great a tragedy? Alexander shuffled to the ledge of the seven-story building. Dizzy from blood loss and his stunning reversal of fortune, he teetered. Drops of blood floated down on the breeze. He thought of the trail of blood he must have left across town in their desperate flight from the penthouse—an irregular line of crimson starbursts splattered on office and automobile windows, roadways and sidewalks. Some few may wonder how it got there. Most others, though, would simply wipe it away without a second thought.

Those that do not succumb to the orbs, that is. At least he managed to get that part right. By morning, this town would be dead.

He inched forward, the toes of his black Gucci loafers over nothing but air. A gust of wind ripped droplets of blood from his wound. He swayed and his head felt light.

We are not done. Gothrodul addressed the Shadow Lord.

"According to my father, we are dead." Alexander stared at the small cars parked on the street below him.

Your father is old and weak.

Nobody dares talk about the Gray Lord like that. The dragon's candor struck a chord.

Your plan for this place executed at your pace would have succeeded.

"You forget. We were not meant to succeed." Alexander turned to face Gothrodul, arm and stump wind-milling to regain the balance the move cost him. "We were a decoy. Expendable. A way to keep his enemies busy while he played with my brothers."

Brothers. Traitors, more like. Not a one of them clued me in.

Alexander, the wound.

Alexander sent a trickle of shadow down his arm. His musings had driven the agony from his mind, but it returned as the magic took hold. The mangled wound tingled and burned as if he had plunged it into a bucket of icy water. The bleeding stopped; however, the intense pain remained.

Lovely.

Perhaps a change is needed. The dragon suggested. *Mayhap the Gray Lord needs be replaced.*

Alexander snorted. "That could never happen."

Gothrodul turned his beguiling stare on the Shadow Lord. *And why not?*

"Because," Alexander responded, half-arm raised to make his point, "he's too powerful."

Are you not powerful?

"I'm no match for him."

Not today. But who's to say what transpires tomorrow?

"I grow weary of your circles."

You have it within you to lead, Alexander. Recruit. Train. Dominate.

"Dominate." He liked the sound of that word as it echoed inside his skull.

You could be a new Gray Lord, set to rule the world.

"Rule the world." Alexander dreamed of someday inheriting the mantle from his father and ruling a vast shadow empire. But that dream had been shattered back in the penthouse along with the other naïve cravings for paternal acceptance and respect.

Do you think you are the only one who feels this way? Feels that the Gray Lord has abandoned them?

Alexander had never ventured down that road before, too absorbed in his own dark machinations to think about the motivations of his peers.

Could there be some truth here? His mind chewed on the possibilities. Would it be possible to wrest the leadership from Bestok Molan and set himself up as the leader of shadow?

With the might of the Last Clan, you would be unstoppable.

The dragon's statement hung in Alexander's mind like a shimmering vortex. Either he gave up and threw himself off the roof to end this charade of an existence. Or, and he quickly warmed to this new concept, he realigned his goals and moved forward.

I see your thoughts, Alexander, perhaps clearer than you do yourself. Gothrodul placed his huge head on the same level as Alexander's. *If you give up now, the Knights and, more importantly, your father, win.*

Talk of the Knights kindled his anger. His journey to ruination began at the feet of the Knight of Flame. An image of the bald-headed knight and that whore of his, Sinclair, formed in his mind.

Develor Quinteele. That bastard killed his daughters, murdered his Rangu Copa, and destroyed his relationship with the Gray Lord. Rage bloomed in the cold wasteland of his soul, a jagged block of frigid intensity capable of inflaming the dark hearts of thousands. A strategy took shape, a two-pronged assault that would see Alexander perched atop the world.

As his mind cleared, and he cast off the limiting shackles of his previous life under Bestok Molan, Alexander watched the dragon from out of the corners of his eyes. An evil intelligence sparked behind those cold, black orbs. Gothrodul's comments were too directed, too convenient to be spontaneous.

No. This was a well thought out campaign to get me to turn. He needs my help to find those dragons.

Alexander sensed the smile on the dragon's thoughts. *I do have need of you, Alexander.* Gothrodul inclined his massive head. *Our destinies lie along similar paths.*

He accepted the dragon's words. An eleven hundred year association had some benefits. A fresh determination gripped him, focused his thoughts on the future. A sharp, debilitating pain from his missing arm drew his attention away from the new direction.

We cannot have that.

Calm and determined, he concentrated on the wound. A dark vine, thin and wiry, popped out of the bone fragment, flailed and lengthened until it matched its predecessor. At the wrist, it broadened into a hand that sprouted fingers and a thumb. Satisfied with the black and glossy look, he flexed his new arm and tested his grip.

Strong.

Before mounting the great beast, he turned and surveyed the Tampa skyline. "When I first set foot among these worthless hovels, I was naïve. Eager to please my master, I ignored my own instincts. But no more." He climbed aboard the dragon. "After being fired and tempered by the Knights, I leave this place reforged."

Where to, Alexander?

"North and west, my friend. Time to leave this training ground behind and find my brother."

Which one?

Alexander thought for a moment before responding. "Thargen, I think. Relegated to even worse places than I, he is our best chance."

North and west it is.

Chapter 56

CYNDRALLA FLEW SOUTHEAST AWAY FROM THE BUILDING SURROUNDED BY WHAT must have been every police car and fire truck in the city of Tampa. Cassidy watched the first responders surround the building and charge through the front doors.

She put the events of the past few hours out of her mind and reveled in the peacefulness of this lone minute. A cool breeze brushed her face. It felt nice after the oven of the stairwell and the craziness of the encounter with Gray. She pressed her cheek into Dev's back.

As a girl, she dreamed about a fairy tale moment like this. Usually, though, her prince picked her up on a magic carpet, but a purple dragon worked just as well.

Passed out, Stillman's head rested against the back of the Knight of Earth.

Cyndralla banked left, beat her tremendous wings, and accelerated away from the water.

"Where are we heading, Cyndy?" Dev asked.

After Gray.

"What about the orbs? We need to spread the elixir, protect the people," Cassidy said.

No. The Knight of Air's response brooked no argument. *We follow after Gray and...*

"And?" Cassidy prompted. Cyndralla was scared and on edge. Something had really upset her and she didn't want it to show.

And nothing, fledgling Knight of Water, stay out of my emotions.

"We need to protect the people, else why are we even here?" Cassidy asked.

Cyndralla sped up and ignored the comment.

"Cyndralla, how many dragons are there?" Cassidy asked.

Only m—I thought I was the last until I came here tonight. There is another. I smelled him when I picked you up and I must find him.

"Another dragon?" Dev asked. "After all this time, how could you not know?"

I...I do not know. Cyndralla's frustrated growl rumbled across the mental link. *But I need to find out.*

"I understand, but we must save as many of these people as we can," Cassidy said.

"It's what we do," Dev backed her up.

Gray is weakened. We can stop him now. Cyndralla sent.

"Right on, sister." Magnus chimed in. "We can stop that shadowy bugger before he escapes."

"You would doom the people of Tampa?" Cassidy asked, anger fueling her words. "Maybe Gray is weak, but the dragon was not injured. They are probably miles away by now in who knows what direction."

"I know," Cyndralla said.

"We need to save the people. Here. Now." Cassidy felt the dragon's emotions shift.

Cyndralla roared—a monstrous din filled with anger and frustration that rattled Cassidy's teeth.

The Knight of Air banked again. *We go to Hillsborough Bay to distribute the elixir.* Cyndralla beat her wings and increased speed.

"Thank you." Cassidy clasped her knees around the dragon's back and squeezed her Knight tight.

Are you ready, Knight of Water? Cyndralla asked.

"Ready for...?"

You need to feed the elixir through the water treatment pipes and into the sewer streams to counter the shadow magic in the orbs.

Is this chick crazy? How the hell am I supposed to do that?

No, I am not crazy.

Crap, she heard me.

You have the ability to manipulate the flow of water, Cyndralla thought. *Use it.*

"Is there some other way?" Dev asked and squeezed Cassidy's knee.

Not and be sure the area is covered sufficiently. Cyndralla replied.

"But—" Cassidy said.

Cyndralla snapped her mighty jaws. *The more we argue, the less time we have. There is no other way. You must do it now.* Over the bay, the Knight of Air dipped her wings and dropped close to the surface. *Dive in and get attuned to the water. Find the entranceway and let us know when you are ready to command the counter magic.*

Cassidy lifted her right leg over, slid off Cyndralla's scaled back, and splashed down. The warm water soothed her tired muscles and eased her stress. She wanted to close her eyes, luxuriate in the caress and gentle rocking of the small swells, but she had a job to do.

"You can do this, Caz," Dev shouted.

Yeah, right. I don't even know what I'm supposed to be doing. Get attuned to the water. What the hell does that mean?

In the middle of Hillsborough Bay, Cassidy Sinclair, the newly anointed Knight of Water, took a deep breath and sank below the surface. The world closed in until only she remained. Sound vanished, replaced by the all-encompassing drumbeat of her heart. Like she did in her pool back home, she reached out with her senses to feel the walls around her. Instead of marcite-covered concrete, her consciousness raced over the sandy bottom of the bay until it ran ashore or touched a man-made obstruction. A low murmur, similar to the one she encountered in the Cradle, whooshed between the pounding in her temples. It took her a moment to recognize the language of the sea and the waves; but, once she did, that primal knowledge flooded her mind. Local tides, depths, landmasses, temperature changes, sea life and the human intrusions of pipes, roads and filth flooded her awareness.

Attunement. This must be what Cyndralla meant. It's beautiful.

She rose to the surface and peered into a collection of anxious faces. "I can hear it." Her voice filled with awe. "The water. It spoke to me."

"Good," Magnus said. "Now ask it for directions."

Dev punched his arm. "We don't have much time."

Cyndralla sent her thoughts to the team. *I sense the buildup of Shadow. We are out of time.*

I'm too late.

"Caz, you need to command the water. Make it move." Encouragement sparkled in Dev's eyes.

Cassidy felt his confidence in her shining like a beacon. She took a deep breath and sank home.

A voice in the water told her to breathe, to relinquish her hold on the air and drink deep of her element. She hesitated. Thirty-three years of air breathing wasn't something to be kicked to the curb on a whim.

Trust. The watery command sounded familiar, but different from the tone of the bay. *You are safe, Knight of Water. Your element will sustain you.*

The Lord of Water himself.

With his encouragement, she discarded her last reservation along with her tightly held breath. Oxygen-rich water rushed in to fill the void. The water hurt, burned her lungs.

Something's wrong.

She flailed her arms and legs, tried to cough it up, but it refused to budge. Gradually, as her body got used to the change, the pain lessened and finally disappeared. Soon it felt like she'd been living underwater her entire life. Normal. Natural.

Water swirled around her waving arms. *Move the water. How do I do that?* She brought her hands together in an underwater clap and felt the surge around her fingers and over her forearms. The water didn't so much move forward as part and reform around her.

Brute force isn't the answer.

Cyndralla's thought burst through. *Hurry, Cassidy. The orbs are breaking. Magnus can taste it.*

Mind racing, she thought of all the mechanical ways to move water—rudders, propellers, even the big paddle wheels. None of those would help. The light hairs on her arms waved in the current. She sensed millions of little droplets dancing across her skin as they went about their water-borne lives.

Little droplets filled with emotion and purpose, filled with life.

Hurry, Cyndralla's thought intruded.

Focus on one drop.

Cassidy imagined a single mote in the untold gallons around her and concentrated on getting that single drop to circle her fingertip. In a bay full of millions of gallons of water, she couldn't see the result, but she felt it. The drop caressed the tender skin at the base of her nail in its journey.

Excited, she tried again with similar results.

That's it.

Thinking bigger, she grouped the drops together into a wave and instructed it to flow around her. This time, she felt the flow of the water push against her, opposite the outgoing current.

Yes. Bigger. Faster.

Still in control, she drove the wave around her. Faster and faster it spun until the pressure pushed her to the surface in the mouth of a water spout.

"Any time now, Caz," Dev called down and upended one of two lambskin bladders. A glittering silver waterfall arced into the bay next to Cassidy.

"Cyndy," Magnus asked, "How long will it take to flow thr—"

Cassidy responded before Magnus could finish his question. "Minutes." The elixir felt different, an alien liquid in her water. Its density greater than that of the salt water, the magic quickly settled near the bottom in a glittering pool. Its texture was oily and it slipped through Cassidy's growing control on her first few attempts. Another cascade splashed into the water nearly in the same place. The two doses attracted each other, merged into a single blob.

Millions of tiny creatures died as the shadow magic began its devastating work. The taint of their extinguished lives a greasy smear in the water that leaked into the bay. It fouled her concentration.

She tried again, collecting the elixir into a large reflective globe that she pushed towards the pipe. As her grip held, her confidence grew. The silver ball increased speed, raising a lump on the surface of the water.

When it got closer to the treatment plant's entrance, she squished it down and rammed it into the pipe. Reversing the water trail from the bay to the sewers, she navigated the silvery liquid through a complex series of sluices and pumps. In the sewers, pipes descended from all angles, feeding noisome waste to the main line. At these junctures, she fractured the magic and sent a portion spidering down the lines until it fizzled against the first traces of the orb's deadly magic.

Within minutes, Cassidy deployed the elixir across the region.

Exhausted. Disgusted. Cassidy ascended to her waiting brethren. When she broke the surface, Cyndralla swooped in low for Dev to lower a hand. He lifted Cassidy up and sat her between himself and Stillman. Back in the world of air, she needed to expel the water from her lungs to breathe and hoped it wouldn't be gross like in the movies. She hated when the divers ended up puking that breathing gel all over the platform. As the air came in to claim its territory, the water gently receded through her pores.

Aw, that was nice.

You've done well, Knight of Water. Approval and satisfaction infused Cyndralla's thought.

Cassidy had never felt this tired. Sleep pulled at her eyelids. Warm arms wrapped around her like a down comforter and she leaned back into her Knight of Flame.

"Welcome back, Caz."

Chapter 57

Without the towering presence of the Elemental Lords and the company of his fellow Knights, the Chamber of Reflection seemed little more than a tomb. Dev passed the silent muncle sentinel and his guard, who solemnly nodded their golden heads. He'd been dreading this visit and found myriad reasons to avoid this section of the complex.

After four days of recovery and shirking what he felt was his responsibility, the time had come. He couldn't explain his apprehension, didn't know why visiting Wren's memorial set his nerves alight. Under the judging stone eyes of those who had gone before, the weight of his actions bowed his broad shoulders and slowed his steps.

He followed the ledge. Wren waited for him on the other side. Her stone likeness, etched into the curve of the back wall, watched his approach. Beneath her delicate chin, forever blazed the firebrand symbol of his element.

"Hello, Wren." The carved face stared back. "Gray got away, but I got the Shadow who killed you." His bottom lip quivered. "We almost lost Magnus, but he's a tough stone to crack. Your father took a nasty whack to the head, but he's okay. And Cassidy..."

"And Cassidy what?" The soft voice of the Knight of Water washed over him.

Lost in the moment, Dev hadn't heard her approach. She eased up behind him and laid a cool hand on the back of his neck. His element spiked, rushed to the point of contact. A flame erupted across his neck, but her water protected her. It negated his reaction with a sizzle and a little cloud of steam. Like fresh aloe, her touch cooled his burning skin and conscience.

"I believe that's progress." Her laugh brought some life to the room. "Only your neck caught fire this time."

If I hadn't lost control, lost myself, would Wren still be here?

"Caz, what if I—"

"Stop. What if's are evil little things that serve no purpose. They do nothing but eat away at you. They won't bring her back." She turned his face to hers. "Trust me, I know. I lived with those little bastards after Amy died and they almost killed me."

"I guess you're right." *But she's gone and I miss her.* "What brings you here?"

"You. Stillman has news and sent me to fetch you."

"Cyndy?"

"Not a peep. It's been four days now."

That's not like her. She hasn't been out of the Cradle in over a hundred years and now she disappears for days.

"Come on." Cassidy tugged on his arm. After a quick glance at Wren and a vow to return soon, he let Cassidy lead him away.

ಎೲಅ

Stillman paced across the Womb, slapping a rolled-up newspaper in the palm of his left hand. The globe spun as it always did. Three lights showed in the Cradle, as they had since Cyndralla went off-grid.

Dev took his seat and put his feet up on the table while Cassidy sat next to him. When she had first done it, the day after the battle, Stillman freaked out. It changed the traditional order of things, he argued. Water was the opposite of Fire and should sit opposed at the table.

This Knight of Water saw things a bit differently. Instead of being opposite fire, water sat beside it. When she kissed Dev, Stillman smiled and took his seat without further argument.

Magnus jogged in, toweling sweat from his massive chest and shoulders. Dev crinkled his nose.

"What died in here?"

Magnus smacked Dev's legs from the table on his way to his accustomed place. "You will in a second, Sparky."

"The report from Tampa is around three thousand dead from a supposed gas leak," Stillman said.

"Three thousand." Dev slapped the table. "Damn."

Cassidy hung her head and Dev rubbed her arm, knowing she blamed herself for not being quicker. They'd had this conversation before, and no matter how much he argued against, she still held herself to blame.

Hell, they all were.

Magnus cleared his throat. "What of the other orbs? Any word?"

Stillman cocked his head as he studied the grubby Knight of Earth. "That's the odd thing. Our associates have searched for the orbs, but there is no trace. It's like the earth just swallowed them up."

"I would have known if that happened," Magnus said.

"What about the shipping manifests?" Cassidy asked. "Did they follow those leads?"

"Every one. The train cars specifically mentioned in the records are gone. Vanished."

Dev whistled.

"There's more. Alexander's eldest brother, Magdon, has released security video from the attack on the Tampa building to the press."

"What? There are more Gray's out there?" Cassidy asked.

Stillman sighed. "Unfortunately, yes. Magdon, or Michael, as he's known to the rest of the world, is the CEO of Daegon Gray. He's pressured the authorities to label you three as terrorists. They positively identified Stanley Rock,

Cassidy is considered a person unknown, and the images of Magnus are still being analyzed. Evidently a giant diamond man does not compute. Your pictures are being circulated globally."

"Figures," Dev said. "That's why we get the big bucks."

"We'll work around it," Stillman said.

"There's a storm coming." Cassidy turned toward the door as the Knight of Air charged into the Womb.

"You." Cyndralla, dress in tatters, hair tangled and twisted and sticking out in multiple directions, greasy black smudges on her face and arms, dug a talon into the chest of the Knight of Flame. "You knew about him all along."

Taken aback, Dev could only stare at the enraged Knight.

"What?"

Cyndralla pressed her face into his, reptilian eyes showing the barest slit of purple. "The other dragon. The one with the Shadow Lord. You saw him that first night, didn't you?" She pressed her claw in deeper. "Didn't you?"

Dev slapped her hand away as he stood up, face hardening at the accusation. "I saw something that first night. It was a big black head, but beyond that, I couldn't see a thing." His tone took on a hard, dangerous edge. Crimson flecks sparkled in his eyes.

"Why didn't you tell me?" Cyndralla lost some of her steam, dropped back on her heels and retracted her claw. "Why?" She swayed on her feet, the last of her energy used up in her outburst.

Dev grabbed her before she fell over and carried her to the closest seat. "I was too busy trying not to die."

"The only one," Cyndralla murmured, skin burning with fever. "Last."

Stillman rushed over, took her hand and felt her forehead. "Exhaustion. And maybe something…." He squinted in concentration. "…more. Garison," he bellowed. "Get my case."

While Stillman fussed over the incoherent Knight of Air, Cassidy motioned Dev away from the action.

"Question," Cassidy began. "Stillman mentioned associates. Who are they?"

"You didn't think we were in the battle against Shadow alone did you?"

"Well…"

"We are a very small group and can't be everywhere at once." Dev looked at Stillman to see if the old man's ears had perked up. "Our leader has contacts and allies all over the world, both human and other."

"Other?"

Dev smiled. "If you think we're weird, wait until you meet some of our friends."

A battered leather case covered in pouches and flaps emerged from the floor ahead of Garison, who hopped out behind it. The bag rattled and clinked as the muncle dragged it across the floor and left it at Stillman's knee.

"Thank you," Stillman said absently as he rummaged through the pockets and trolled its depths. "Where did I put tha—ah, here it is." Pinched between his fingers he drew forth a small glass vial no bigger than his pinky, topped by a cork stopper. A milky white liquid filled the bottom quarter of the vessel.

"Still good?" Swishing it around left a film along the walls and, when he removed the top, a citrusy orange scent permeated the room. "Magnus?"

"Sir?"

"Hold her shoulders. She's not going to like this."

Magnus clamped down while Dev and Cassidy moved closer. The Precept held the potion to her lips.

"Drink this. It will make you feel better."

The Knight of Air parted her lips just enough for Stillman to pour it in and stiffened like a board as it took hold. Her eyes opened wide and she thrashed in the chair. Magnus held her as best he could, but Cyndralla had the strength of a dragon under that human façade. She escaped his grasp, wriggled off the chair and convulsed on the ground.

Cassidy went to assist, but Stillman waved her off. "The worst is over. See?" Her struggles weakened. "It will be over in a moment."

With a last scissor kick, Cyndralla rolled on her belly and lay still. Breathing heavy, she slid her hands beneath her chest and pushed up to her knees. She eyed Stillman, promising payback in that cold stare.

Stillman grinned and shrugged. "What would you have me do? Let the spell drain the rest of your life force?"

Dev looked to Cassidy who looked to Magnus who looked to Dev.

"Wait a minute. What spell are we talking about here?" Dev asked, as he helped Cyndralla into a chair.

"Maybe spell is not the right word, although that's how it got inside." Stillman eased gingerly into his own chair, as if hurt. At the blank look from the mob, he continued. "She was infected with a magical parasite that, had I not fed it a hefty dose of my special brew, would have killed her within another couple of days."

"How did that happen?" Cassidy asked. "Did you run into Gray?"

Garison clacked to the table bearing a tray laden with wine and cheese. Cyndralla grabbed the bottle and drank deep, raising more than one eyebrow in the room.

"I was careless," the Knight of Air began. "Thought they'd be long gone. I was right, but they left me a gift."

Magnus shook his head. "Who are we talking about?"

"Gray and..." Upending the bottle, she took another swig and wiped her lips with a soiled forearm. Her face gentled, took on a distant, far-away look.

"My brother, Blackscale. Although before his supposed death, he took a new name, Gothrodul. I thought him killed by a Varangian prince from Novgorod."

Silence reigned in the Womb.

Cyndralla sat up straight and placed the bottle on the table. "You see, for the past twelve hundred years or so, I thought I was the last of my kind. And when I picked up the scent of another dragon at the penthouse, I had to know."

"Which is why you argued so strongly for chasing down Gray," Cassidy said.

Cyndralla nodded. "Thank you, Water Knight, for reminding me of who we are."

Cassidy blushed.

"Once you were safely back here, I left to pursue the trail."

Magnus shook his head. "Crazy dragon."

"Yes. I was." Cyndralla's flat tone betrayed her disappointment in her own choice. "The thought that after all these years another of my kind was alive overrode my reason, and I acted recklessly."

"So long as you know." The Knight of Earth rolled his eyes.

Magnus, always trying to lighten the mood.

A slim smile crossed her face and she cupped the big man's cheek with a slender palm. "I picked up the scent at the building where you fought and followed it to a remote location to the east. There, I found where Blackscale made his lair."

"What did you find there?" Stillman asked.

"The missing people, or, I should say, what was left of them, and many references to the Last Clan."

"The Last Clan," Stillman said. "I haven't heard that name in centuries."

"I remember my *mormor* telling me and my brothers about hidden dragon eggs nested in piles of gold and jewels," Magnus said.

"The eggs are right," Cyndralla said. "No gold though."

"I'm not surprised. Some old jarl probably added it in to make it more interesting," mumbled Magnus.

"What is the Last Clan?" Dev asked.

"The Last Clan is a myth told to dragonlings about a secret clutch of dragon eggs hidden away until the last days of our kind. The stories were told to quiet the young when the human hunters were about. Knowing that the race would continue no matter what, provided a sense of peace." Cyndralla yawned. "Forgive me. My strength is spent."

Cassidy rubbed her arm in support.

"I thought it a simple story," Cyndralla continued. "But now...I'm not so sure."

"What do you mean?" Stillman slid to the edge of his seat.

"Blackscale believes he found them."

"How can you be sure?" Stillman asked.

"He told me. You see, he was always a cunning one, and left a gift he knew I could not resist—something he gave to me long ago on my one hundredth name-day. A carving, made from the bole of the lightning shattered elm outside our home in the Caucasus, inscribed with the symbol of the Last Clan and a single word, "Remember.""

"It sounds beautiful," Cassidy said.

"It was, and as I traced the sharp lines of the rune inlaid with gold in the center of the world, the spell struck, rooted me to the spot until I finally broke free and returned to the Cradle. Embedded in that dark magic, though, my brother left a message. It started out with his usual hatred of human-kind and how he could not believe I defended them, but then went on to say that he had discovered the hiding place of the Last Clan."

"If he finds those eggs and discovers a way to hatch those dragons," Stillman said, "Gray would have more than enough power to tip the balance in Shadow's favor."

The room fell silent. This was all new to Dev. He'd never heard of dragon clans, or myths about long hidden dragon eggs in a big pile of gold. Alexander Gray escaped. Nothing else mattered.

"There's more." Cyndralla stood and limped over to the globe. "He wants to meet with me. Alone."

"Absolutely not," Stillman said.

"This is about more than Knights against the Shadow, Cernusen. This is about saving dragonkind from extinction. According to the legend, it takes both a male and a female to open the brood doors. When I thought I was alone, I did not consider the future. I hid down here, safe, and thought that while I yet lived, dragonkind survived. But this changes things."

"You cannot trust him." Stillman stood and approached the Knight of Air. "He is with Gray now. What he does, he does for Shadow."

"What if he's changed? What if he is a slave to the power of Alexander Gray and is forced to act against us?"

Stillman shook his head. "You can't be naïve enough to think that."

Cyndralla turned on Stillman. "It's a chance I cannot ignore. I'm going."

"Cyndy, wait." Dev clasped her arm. "You can't do this. We need you."

"Knight of Fl—Dev, Magnus, Cassidy." Cyndralla smiled to each. "You have earned my respect and affection. Let us part now as friends. I am the Knight of Air and sworn to the Order, but matters of my race take precedence. Do not try to stop me and mar this civil parting." The Knight of Air strode from the room.

"Let her go," Stillman said. "She has made her choice and we must not lose focus. Though she does not see it, our paths lie in the same direction." He clasped his hands behind his back and headed for the doorway. "Take your rest while you can, for I fear the war has only begun."

Develor Quinteele, sixth Knight of Flame, pressed his fist against the chest of the Earth Knight. "Stone and fire."

Magnus Siggurdson, fourth Knight of Earth, responded with his own fist to the chest of the Fire Knight. "Fire and stone."

Cassidy Sinclair, ninth Knight of Water, grasped their arms. "And water."

"And water." Dev and Magnus nodded.

The End

About the author

Since he was a kid, Scott wanted to be an author and explored many genres through high school and college. Fantasy, though, captivated his soul. Tales of knights and magic, dragons and elves filled his dreams. After greasing the gears of the corporate machine for many years, he escaped the Information Technology vortex to focus full-time on writing. The stories he'd envisioned years ago—of nobility and strife, honor and chaos—demanded they be brought to life.

Student of David Farland and apprentice to James A. Owen, Scott lives with his wife, two children, and a giant Chihuahua on the west coast of Florida.

http://www.scotteder.net/

If you enjoyed this book, please post a review
at your favorite online bookstore.

Twilight Times Books
P O Box 3340
Kingsport, TN 37664
Phone/Fax: 423-323-0183
www.twilighttimesbooks.com/